"I have loved the stars too fondly to be fearful of the night."
Sarah Williams

Aligning the Signs

Rebecca Rossi

MMH PRESS

Published by MMH Press 2021

National Library of Australia
:Cataloguing-in-Publication data

Aligning the Signs/Rebecca Rossi

ISBN 978-0-6452641-9-7

To Abigail, my brightest star in the entire universe…

Prologue

The dark, desolate wasteland before them was an empire in the making, the surface cracked, dry, and gritty. Visually, the landscape did not strike fear in the hearts of men, but Milo was determined to change all of that. He had come too far and deceived too many on his home planet, Cassius, as well as on Bastion to turn back now. He even had a love-struck minion from Earth to assist him in his ascension to ultimate power. Granted, the adoration from Graham was pure manipulation injected via the venom of his scorpion tail, but nevertheless, he had found somebody vulnerable enough to do his bidding. Provided his army had prevailed in their massacre, Milo would have an abundance of time to transform the decaying surroundings into a kingdom worthy of Scorpios and Scorpios alone. Those who survived the infiltration would be unable to locate their position.

His enemies were at a complete disadvantage. Furthermore, his flamboyant lackey would assist in travelling to neighbouring planets, recruiting those born under his constellation and returning them home, where a new civilization could bloom. A world that would house only the elite and discard the unworthy. A universe that dared not speak of nor acknowledge the disgusting Unsigned. Milo would be their king, their ruler. His authority would be recognised and feared. The counterparts who were not killed by his poisonous terrors would crumble without order. After all, without their united presence, who would provide starlight? Bastion would disintegrate without its life-source, and with it its inhabitants. If the scorpions didn't get them first…

Milo rubbed his hands together. The plan had worked effortlessly. His endless bribing and conniving to be voted in as representative by the Council on Cassius had succeeded. He had gained the privilege and right to visit Bastion and meet with the 'almighty' counterparts. He had always planned to leave Serket till last. It gave him the opportunity to plant seeds of discontent within their feeble minds. The plan had worked like a charm. The counterparts, minus the stony old crone, had agreed that they each should rule the stars. As they fought and rebelled amongst one another, Milo had slipped unnoticed into the Cavern of Maroon and ambushed the unsuspecting Serket. He couldn't resist a smirk in remembrance of that fateful day. After all, what is one big sacrifice for the greater good?

The real Serket in creature form had been burrowing in the sand dunes, completely unaware that his murderer was upon him. Scorpions in general had poor eyesight, relying purely on light and motion to take in their surroundings. In a flash, Milo had injected Serket with a formula fatal to all scorpions, counterpart or no. It was a loophole to their immortality he had discovered whilst in the Great Library on Cassius. By the light of his lamp, he had lost himself in a dusty tome documenting all species of flora and fauna in the surrounding galaxies.

A concoction consisting of a rare poisonous plant found only on a particularly treacherous planet combined with the paralytic venom of a serpent that slumbered in the craters of Mt Fosso could melt immortal blood. The journey to obtain both ingredients had been risky at best, but Milo had been driven by greed and a hunger for power. By mixing the two, he had formed a deadly liquid that had the ability not only to dissolve one's insides like acid but also to leave the victim an empty husk.

As Serket's venom oozed out into a pool, Milo had immediately stored it in a vial. Milo had then pretended to leave Bastion under the critical eyes of Asterion and Garth before returning to the Cavern of Maroon, burying Serket's body under the sand, and injecting himself with the venom, thus absorbing the counterpart's powers. The vial of venom had become irrelevant, as the powers had left Milo in possession of a scorpion tail filled with poison. Thrilled, Milo was able to concoct his plan to overthrow Bastion and rid the universe of those he deemed unworthy. He slipped out when he could and travelled to the planet they were now on to chart the territory.

The first time he stepped onto the land, scorpions from all over, intoxicated by the venom, had scurried towards him with eager red eyes. A willing army had formed and mourned every time he left to return to his Coloured Cavern. There was a reason he had chosen this place to build his empire. The time to strike had been approaching when Milo overheard that a group of teenagers were arriving from Earth to unite the counterparts. He had been expecting a beautiful young woman, but when Graham arrived, he knew he had to put on his most convincing performance yet. Luckily for him, Graham had already been eager for a relationship and was smitten with Milo before he was stung the first time. It hadn't taken much convincing at all.

His scorpion army had been secretly flown in that morning by a Cassius private aircraft carrier to lie in wait amidst the valley where the giant observatory named Constellar could be seen in the distance. Milo hadn't realised that his power of flight was a secret perk Serket had possessed. It had allowed him to fly the pair to his aircraft and whisk them back home to his undisclosed planet. He also had the ability to disguise himself, as a lot of the counterparts who wished to frequent Constellar did, and could bend anybody to his will with the sting of his tail, hence Graham's allegiance. He even had the gift to portal to his planet, but only within the Cavern of Maroon. It appeared the Scorpio counterpart had many talents that had never been disclosed to the others.

That evening, he had awaited Graham's arrival on the roof, and although he hadn't anticipated the Libran girl trying to interfere, the look on everybody's faces when they had learned his true identity was priceless. Flying through the air whilst his scorpion army attacked his enemies had been the best part of all. Now, with Graham in tow, Milo could build a new civilisation, and nobody but he would rule the galaxy ever again…

PART I
THE AFTERMATH

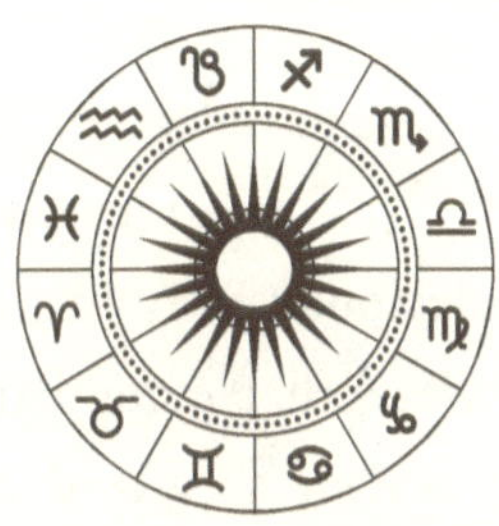

Chapter 1

Transformations

Parry awoke with a start to find herself completely alone in a bed that wasn't hers. From across the dark room, she could hear the sound of water running. It took her a second to realise she was in the Mission Base and the bed belonged to Hunter. With a shriek, Parry leaned over the side and realised why she was so cold. The clothes she had worn the night before were strewn across the stone floor. Slowly, she peeled the covers back and stared at her naked body.

Oh my... What have I done?

She went to smooth out her tangled red locks and jumped in surprise as her fingers brushed against the coarse hair and shaved sides.

Seriously, what have I done?

Sitting up, Parry took a deep breath and tried to recall the events from the night before. She had been lying on a bench on Bastion when she decided the only thing that would free her was a new look. Hunter would be the guy she would give herself to in order to prove that she wouldn't end up alone and ugly. Those things should not have mattered to her, but the Maiden had really gotten under her skin. Marching into the barber shop full of impulse and recklessness, Parry had essentially demanded the surprised hairdresser give her 'the Ambrite' as she waved the razor in his face.

After laughing maniacally at her reflection, she had thanked the barber and gone in search of an edgy but attention-grabbing outfit. A dingy store hidden down a cobblestoned alley in the fashion district sold revealing lingerie and 'nightwear' that made Parry wonder if Bastion had sex workers. She found an acid-wash grey denim dress that hugged her figure tightly and a pair of matching fishnet stockings. At the counter, a box selling chokers caught her eye. After fastening it around her neck and grunting Asterion's name at the store assistant, she walked out with her things.

Grateful that the Mission Base was empty, she had applied smoky eyes to her face and bright red to her lips. Pulling on a pair of grey combat boots, Parry had been ready to leave, albeit a little nervous. Was she really prepared to lose her virginity that night? Her counterpart would have laughed and called her impure. Such backward thinking. It had been obvious ever since the Astro A Team had arrived that Hunter was hopelessly in love with Ambrite. It had also been clear that she would never feel the same way no matter how long he stuck around. Parry had spent time with him during their 'least compatible pair' challenge and had found him to be quite uncharacteristically cute after his haircut. She remembered his concern whilst she had cried in the shower after visiting her counterpart. He was the perfect mixture of sweet and bad-boy.

She had been confident he would not deny her new look. Not only did she resemble Ambrite's sexier twin, but she could offer him things the Taurean couldn't. Parry had stalled for so long, until well after Muktu, Bastion's moon, had gone down. She talked herself out of it, then convinced herself all over again. The cycle continued until she finally forced herself into the lonely chairlift, which resembled more of a cable-car. As she ascended slowly to the top, where the beautiful observatory awaited, she pictured striding into Constellar with Britney playing in the background and seducing Hunter without a care in the world. They would sneak outside and, under the moonlight, or rather the 'Muktu-light', surrender themselves to the night.

When she arrived, however, to her surprise, Hunter had staggered over to her with a look of pale-faced shock. She had emerged from her transportation, feeling the energy pulse between them as he took her in. Her mother had once imparted some memorable words of wisdom to her from the inside of a tanning bed. "Parry," she had said, staring at the ceiling with ridiculous goggles on, "people say magic doesn't exist, but a woman can cast a spell on a cis-het man with just a flick of her hair. You don't even know what a regular woman can do,

let alone a Mason woman. Swish those hips as you walk and watch them fall to their knees. Pout and get out of a parking ticket. Flutter your eyelashes and watch the jewels flow. Do not be afraid to use that power, my darling. How do you think I got your father?"

Despite her mother's cringe-worthy 'advice', she could immediately tell that Hunter was under her spell, and his next word, "Wow," had cemented it. Parry told him what she wanted, and before she knew it, they were back at the Mission Base, kissing in his bed. She could not tell if his passion had been directed more towards Ambrite or herself, but in that moment she hadn't cared. It was the physical connection she had been waiting for. They worked through their insecurities together, and Parry remembered falling asleep very satisfied.

Now it was the next morning and they both had to face the awkwardness…plus everybody else.

Parry sprang out of bed and hurriedly put on her clothes. Surely her friends would have noticed when they came home the night before? She couldn't recall hearing anybody enter the Mission Base, although she had passed out quickly in Hunter's arms after they were intimate. Now, fully clothed, Parry turned in a full circle to scan all the beds. To her horror, they were completely empty. She let out a high-pitched scream which caused the shower water to stop running, and a moment later, Hunter emerged wearing only a towel and a concerned look.

"What's wrong?"

Parry was suddenly distracted by his chiselled body and wet locks. She had to steer herself away from thinking about the other parts of him.

"Uh, sorry, I just realised we're the only two people here. Where is everybody? Did you even hear them come home last night?"

Hunter's face went pale. He surveyed the cave as well and swivelled back to face her. "Ambrite," was all he could utter.

Parry felt a sharp pang in her chest. She knew the night before hadn't meant as much to him as it had to her, but knowing that was all he cared about made her recoil slightly.

"Where do you think they are?" Parry muttered. "Maybe they all partied so hard they stayed at the club?"

Hunter undid his towel and let it drop to the floor. Parry flushed at the sight and quickly averted her gaze as he slipped into some fresh clothes.

"I doubt it," he replied, pulling up a pair of red cargos and buttoning them. "I have a really bad feeling about this."

Parry suddenly felt it too. A deep sense of dread began to sink in. She had been concerned about Graham's odd behaviour over the last day but had been too caught up in her own wallowing to reach out. Now, she began to fear that he was in trouble.

The Coloured Caverns remained dormant, the buffet trays were devoid of food, and it was so eerily quiet within the Mission Base that Parry could hear the tap still dripping from the showers. Without another word, she ran towards the gigantic purple doors and attempted to open them, but they wouldn't budge.

Hunter ran over to help her and together, they spent several minutes gasping with red faces as they used all their might to open their only means of escape. It did not matter the amount of force, the doors refused to move.

Letting out a sob, Parry slid to the floor and buried her head in her hands. She felt Hunter sit next to her and place his hand on her back.

"What are we going to do Hunter?" She looked up at him with bleary eyes. "I'm sure there is a logical explanation, but my intuition is going nuts. How do we get out of here and make sure they're okay?"

"I have no idea," he sighed deeply. "Asterion and Garth can't be here either otherwise they would've shown up by now."

Parry stared up at the ceiling feeling hopeless. They didn't say anything for several minutes. After a prolonged period of silence, she heard a faint clicking sound.

"Do you hear that?" she whispered, grabbing Hunter's arm.

He went to shake his head when the sound suddenly reached his ears, causing him to freeze.

They both stood and stared at the direction it was coming from: The Cavern of White.

Suddenly, a pair of gigantic white legs appeared in the entrance that was now glowing. Parry let out another scream and clutched at Hunter. An enormous ivory crab emerged sideways out of the cavern and began clicking along the stone floor towards them. Hunter chivalrously positioned himself in front of Parry which pleased her immensely, but it didn't stop her from trembling like a leaf. The crab stopped short several metres away and stared at them with beady, red eyes. It appeared just as terrified as they were. In an instant, Parry knew this was Hannah's counterpart. The Cancerian girl had professed her adoration for the crab when they had all swapped stories. Surely the massive creature before them wasn't a threat?

"Please don't hurt us," Parry pleaded. "We are friends of Hannah's'. She loves you, she told us!"

The crab froze. When it spoke, the tone was soft and feminine.

"Hannah? Is she okay? I went to communicate with my friends Sirena and Calypsee this morning and noticed they were gone. The goat is gone too and the lion and the scorpion and the centaur. I am worried…"

"All of our friends are gone too, including Asterion and Garth," Hunter stepped forward. "Something must be really wrong. Can you help us open this door?"

The crab nodded and waved a pincer at them to stand aside.

Parry dragged Hunter over to the buffet table. She watched as the crab sidled back towards the Cavern of White, preparing to make a run up.

With a deafening sound, the crustacean before them click clacked along the stone floor at a rapid rate and threw its big white husk against the purple doors with full force. To their surprise, the door cracked open slightly and light streamed through. The crab repeated the process two more times and finally, the door broke enough for them to squeeze through.

Parry ran over to the crab and rubbed its claw in happiness. The creature shivered in delight.

"Great work…er?"

"You may call me Karki," the crab responded. "You are a friend of Hannah's and therefore a friend of mine."

"Thanks, Karki." Hunter smiled. "Are you coming with us?"

Karki shook its head. "I cannot leave looking like this. The townspeople have never actually seen a counterpart. They would lose their minds."

Parry remembered the banners and posters all over Bastion worshipping the unidentified counterparts. They were the unseen celebrities of the planet.

"Can you disguise yourself?" Parry asked. "I know some counterparts do it so they can go to the club and mingle with the citizens."

Karki looked incredibly hesitant. "I never use my human form… It displeases me."

"Please, Karki." Hunter moved to stand next to Parry, and, like her, he stroked the crab's pincer. It shivered again. "We need you to help us… Hannah could be in serious danger."

The crab paused for several moments, then began to shake violently. Parry and Hunter stepped back in alarm and watched it vibrate as a powerful glow formed around its body. They stared in awe as the crustacean began to shrink and morph into the body of a young girl wearing a white nightdress. Her face was as pale as a ghost and her hair was dead straight and white and hung down to her lower back. She was the epitome of a creepy-looking kid in a horror movie but kind of cute at the same time.

"I look awful," Karki moped.

Parry was now significantly taller than her. She strode over and laid a hand on the girl's bony shoulder. "You are perfect just as you are. Let's go and find our friends."

She noticed Hunter smiling at her, and for the first time, Parry had meant her words. Karki laced her fingers through Parry's and Hunter's hands, cementing her stance in the middle of them. Together, they marched outside, ready to face whatever lay beyond…

Chapter 2

The Collapse of Constellar

Everything had happened so quickly that the events of the night were a series of blurry flashing images. Danni remembered people screaming. She remembered the bodies lifeless on the floor, their expressionless eyes staring up at the sky. She remembered the scorpions emerging from every direction and cornering her group on the roof of Constellar. She recalled being pushed out of the way and hitting the stones hard as a scorpion's poisonous tail just missed stinging her by a centimetre. But the worst memory, burned in her brain, was Graham's dreamy, drugged face as he rose into the air, clutching tightly to his beloved Milo, a deadly and dangerous traitor.

Milo had started everything. He had manipulated her friend and taken him to an unknown location. It had been the perfect evening. Ronan had not only kissed her but professed his love, which Danni had reciprocated. She had finally found a stable relationship; the Astro A Team had been 'successful', or so they had thought, and were due to leave for Earth the next day. Next minute, Bastion had been overrun by Milo's venomous minions focused on wiping out the entire planet. The group's first strategic move had been to arrange themselves around Brodie, who had been knocked unconscious by Milo earlier. Slade was kneeling by her side, his face ashen. Brodie and Slade could've been twins, despite having two different zodiac signs, because they looked so similar. They were even referred to as 'the twins', but Danni could see the vulnerability and youth in Slade's face as he did everything in his power to protect his older sister.

Their second strategy had simply been to stay alive. The group had obviously not been prepared for combat. They had been dressed up and unable to locate a single object lying around to use as a weapon. Asterion and Garth had jumped in immediately, wielding powers that allowed them to repel the approaching forces, but the group had been too out-numbered. Not only that, the club itself had become infested with scor-pions, and Danni remembered hearing the horrified screams from down below. No matter how many scorpions were knocked back, five more would spring forward.

Danni's heart had stopped when Ronan and Crawford ran forward to tackle an advancing scorpion and push it off the edge. Her Capri-corn had turned to give her a reassuring smile and taken off to ambush another one – this time with Drew in tow. Seeing their success, Danni had formed a pair with Reilly. She had watched Ambrite and her new tattooed friend point to their target. Hannah had bravely grabbed the hand of Charlotte, who surprisingly hadn't pushed her away, and the boys had taken it in turns ducking and weaving between the spiky tails, taking the scorpions unaware. Some of the creatures had died on impact; others were able to land in the crevices around the high hill and crawl back up again.

Danni had known their luck would run out soon and somebody would get stung. Sure enough, as Reilly pulled her towards a scorpion that was facing the other way, it had spun suddenly and jabbed her best friend's arm. Reilly let out a wail and the skin around her wound began to instantly blacken. Danni roared and slammed into the scorpion from the right, watching in satisfaction as it teetered against the edge and finally lost its balance, succumbing to the depths below. She had grabbed Reilly's other arm and dragged her to the inner circle, where Slade was still trying to revive Brodie.

"Slade, she's been stung," Danni said, panicking. Reilly howled in pain as the sore began to spread up her forearm.

Slade stared in horror at the festering wound, clearly unsure how to proceed. Just then, Garth had stepped forward and picked up Reilly in his arms. She was whimpering and shaking from fright. It had broken Danni's heart to see her best friend so terrified.

"Am I going to die?" Reilly trembled.

"Not if we get you an antidote fast." Garth frowned.

"How do we get an antidote in this chaos?" Danni yelled over the commotion.

Garth was clearly concerned, which made tears well up in Danni's eyes. She couldn't lose her best friend. Not now. Not this way.

"The only person who can heal her is her counterpart…"

Slade looked up in surprise. "Her counterpart is here! Brodie and I saw him before she came up here, looking for Graham. He's in love with Reilly!"

At this point, Reilly had passed out from fear. Her arm had turned a sickly dark green.

"What?" Danni shouted. She noticed Garth looking amused and a little bit more relaxed.

He turned and stood at the entrance of the opening where the stairs ran down into the club. Danni's stomach lurched at all the bodies lying on the dancefloor.

"Chiron!" Garth bellowed.

In an instant, a handsome unshaven man in a purple suit with glittering amethyst-coloured eyes had appeared next to the Chief Advisor.

"What? I was helping the situation down there. Leonis, Agape, and the Mermaids are assisting the live civilians in the club."

Suddenly, he registered that the limp body in Garth's arms belonged to Reilly. Chiron's gorgeous face paled.

Wow, maybe he does love her...

He reached out and snatched her aggressively from Garth, who glared back at him. Lying Reilly on the floor, he took hold of her wrist and closed his eyes, muttering under his breath. Danni and Slade watched in wonder as Reilly's arm slowly transformed back to normal. Her eyes began to flutter open, and she flushed in recognition of her saviour.

"You," she whispered.

Danni ran over and squeezed her best friend's hand. Chiron looked up, focusing his rage on Garth.

"She would've died in a few minutes had I not been here."

"Well, you *were* here, and you might as well help us finish this fight now." Garth bristled defensively. "Summon the rest and join us. We are clearly outnumbered here!"

Chiron looked at Reilly for several seconds before nodding and disappearing back downstairs into the club.

Danni helped the still dazed Reilly to her feet. "I thought Chiron had treated you horribly, but Slade said he's in love with you."

"What?" Reilly laughed. "That can't be true. He was disgusted by me. But he did save me, which he didn't have to do."

The girls didn't have time to ponder it any further. A loud bang bought them back to the present moment as Asterion fired a ball of white light at a scorpion towering over Hannah, who had fallen.

Drew let out a rather high-pitched shriek and raced to his girlfriend's side. The scorpion had exploded, its guts covering her beautiful white outfit.

Danni had watched in despair at the number of scorpions still left on the vast roof. They just kept coming, and she could see Asterion and Garth were getting tired. Where were the other counterparts?

As if answering her prayers, a mob of interesting characters stepped out from the club below. Chiron led the way in his dapper suit. To his left stood an odd-looking old man with spectacles and a forest-green suit with patches on the elbows. To his right, a teenager with a shock of orange hair and a tight red bodysuit looked ready to fight. Two stunning females walked in front of Chiron, holding hands. They were both wearing sea-foam strapless dresses with bright purple lipstick. One was Asian, with flowing black locks, and the other had golden blond hair and blue eyes.

Danni immediately identified them by their colours. The women were Drew's lusty mermaid counterparts, the old man was Ronan's goat counterpart in human form, and the teenage boy was either Hunter's ram or Crawford's lion. She couldn't tell, because he was wearing red, but his hair resembled a true Leo. Her speculations had been put to rest when the teenage boy morphed into a lion, let out a terrifying roar, and pounced onto a pair of scorpions advancing at Crawford. The old man remained human but rubbed his temples as though he were experiencing a severe migraine.

Seconds later, the army of scorpions appeared dazed, looking around in confusion. The mermaids blew bubbles that popped on impact and disintegrated their targets to fine dust. Chiron transformed into a centaur and took out his bow and arrows to fire at the now stunned creatures. Asterion and Garth slumped next to Brodie, allowing the counterparts to finish the battle. The rest of the Astro A Team had watched in awe. Danni noticed Chiron looking at Reilly every time his arrow hit a scorpion, hoping to impress her. She saw her best friend flush, trying to avoid his gaze.

Ronan ran over to Danni and took her face in his hands. "Are you okay?"

She nodded wearily. "Your goat has some serious mind-melding magic." She pointed.

The goat – or Aegipan, as Ronan corrected – was remarkable in battle.

He didn't need to move at all. He could warp their brains with a simple touch to the sides of his head.

"I know," Ronan breathed, releasing Danni's face. "I think his power is related to logic. He must remove it so the scorpions have no idea what they're doing."

Danni was impressed. She was also annoyed that her counterparts, who had professed themselves to be superior warriors, were nowhere to be seen. Garth gestured for her and Ronan to come over. She was surprised to see Asterion looking so sickly, his face white and wan.

"He's exhausted," Garth explained. "It's not often that we are forced into battle. Using our powers is incredibly draining. I need you guys to round up the other members of the Astro A Team and try to help any civilians you can inside the club. Hopefully, we can save some more people. By the way, where are Hunter and Parry? I hope they're okay."

Danni and Ronan blanched. The pair dispersed, grabbed their able-bodied friends, and tore downstairs to survey the situation within Constellar. Slade carried Brodie. It was a lot worse than Danni had anticipated. The entire stage was covered in blood, grime, and scorpion guts. The green viscous fluid was sticky, making it difficult for Danni to traverse the grand observatory. Bodies littered the floor, some human, some beast. The lights against the bar were smashed, as were all of the bottles. Millions of tiny glass fragments glinted dangerously wherever they trod. Danni searched wildly for Hunter and Parry.

"I don't think Parry ever ended up coming, Dan." Drew sidled over, breathing heavily. His dark hair was matted with slime.

"I hope so," Danni sighed. "With any luck, she stayed in the Mission Base. But Hunter...he was here, drinking with Slade. Where did he go? If anything happens to him, I swear..."

"It will be okay, Dan." Drew hugged her. "We will find him."

"Dan!" Ambrite ran over to her, breathless and crying. Behind her trailed the cute punky DJ with wide eyes. It was the most unfortunate timing to be meeting Ambrite's potential new girlfriend.

"Hunter," she sobbed. "Where is he? This is all my fault! If I hadn't pushed him away, he might still be here. What have I done?"

Danni grabbed the Taurean's shoulders, forcing her to make eye contact. "Ambrite, we don't know where he is. Try not to panic until you need to. We are looking for him right now, and so far, I haven't found a single body resembling his. This is not your fault."

Ambrite continued to sob. Danni met eyes with the DJ, who extended her tattooed hand in greeting.

"Wasabi. Don't worry, I will take care of her."

Danni shook her hand gratefully. "Danni. Thank you. I will find him, I promise. We just need to help whoever we can right now until the situation is contained."

Confident that Ambrite was in good hands, Danni spun around to see a woman wailing near the ladies' bathrooms. Her leg had a gigantic splotch on it similar to Reilly's arm, and the poison was spreading upwards. Danni's heart sank when she realised the woman was clad in a yellow strapless dress. She was a Gemini, and her counterparts were selfishly holed away in their Coloured Cavern.

"Garth!" Danni screamed.

The Chief Advisor appeared a moment later, looking exhausted and pale despite his brown complexion. Danni motioned to the woman on the floor.

"What do we do? Castor and Pollux aren't here."

Garth frowned. "Danni, not all of the counterparts are good, and we can't save everybody. There's nothing we can do for her. Even if the Gemini twins were here, I doubt they'd help her."

The woman, who was slowly drifting in and out, clutched her chunky yellow necklace and rasped, "Charlie."

Who was Charlie? Her husband?

"No!" Danni yelled. "We can't just let her die! Summon them, please!"

Garth sighed deeply. Clasping his dragon necklace, he closed his eyes and muttered an ancient language under his breath. His face contorted, his forehead creasing under stress. In an instant, he opened his eyes and shook his head sorrowfully.

"They aren't interested, Danni. I'm so sorry. Let's move her into one of the private rooms so she can die with dignity."

"They are evil," Danni whispered. Garth nodded sadly and made his way to the woman. The black mark had now disappeared up her dress, making its way to her heart. In a few minutes, she would be dead. Garth picked up the now unconscious woman and carried her into the curtained-off room to lay her down on the dirty couch. Danni stood behind him, weeping silently. Garth placed his hand on her shoulder.

"I wish the twins had as big a heart as you, Danni, but alas, they don't seem to have one between them."

They walked out of the room together, not wanting to witness the woman's final breath. Danni had no concept of time. The night had seemed to drag on forever, and nothing felt like it would ever be good again. She didn't know how many more friends she could lose before she threw herself off of the observatory.

"How did this happen, Garth?" She turned to him tearfully. "We were ready to leave. Everybody was happy. Now, in just one night, I have lost Graham, Brodie is unconscious, Hunter and Parry might be dead, hundreds of Bastion citizens are dead, and I nearly watched my best friend die. We need to find Milo – and fast."

"I completely agree."

Garth led her over to the dancefloor, where Drew, Hannah, Ronan, Ambrite, Wasabi, Reilly, Charlotte, and Slade were bent over Brodie, who was beginning to wake up.

The Libran's beautiful blue eyes began to blink open. The group crowded around her.

"Graham," she whispered.

"Shh." Slade stroked her hair. "Milo took him, Brodes, but you need to take it easy. You were knocked unconscious."

"Milo?" Brodie sat up rapidly. Slade laid her back down, gently fussing over her like a child.

"Yes," her brother groaned. "Serket, Graham's counterpart, turned out to be Milo in disguise, and he took him. We're not sure where, but he's gone, and we somehow managed to survive his army of scorpions."

Brodie widened her eyes in disbelief, turned a sickly shade of green, and heaved all over his shoes. The Astro A Team took one giant step back. Garth clucked his tongue in sympathy. The Libran whimpered in apology. Hannah moved in to cradle Brodie so Slade could clean his shoes in the bathroom.

"Garth," Ambrite pleaded, "we have to go back to the Mission Base and see if Hunter or Parry is there. They could be seriously hurt."

"Nobody is going anywhere." A croaky voice emerged from the staircase. Danni looked up to see Asterion limping towards them, looking significantly older and more decrepit. She was certain a strong wind would blow him into dust. Garth power-walked over to the Keeper of the Stars and offered his right shoulder as a post. Asterion leaned on his Chief Advisor gratefully and hobbled over to join the remaining members in the centre of the dancefloor.

"We may have neutralised the situation at Constellar, but we have no line of sight regarding the rest of Bastion," Asterion wheezed. The battle and use of power had completely drained his energy. "I know you're all exhausted, scared, and worried about Graham, but right now we need to clean up all of this scorpion slime and assist any injured civilians. Once we have done our part and regained some strength, we can all move together to the Mission Base and exterminate what may be waiting for us along the way. Garth and I could teleport you all, but we want to make sure the town is safe. I am sure Hunter and Parry will be fine. Let's not worry unless there is something to worry about."

Danni and her friends worked tirelessly into the early hours of the morning, clearing Constellar, dragging unidentified bodies, and mopping up slime with supplies they found in one of the bathrooms. A Capricorn victim was fortunately revived just in time by Aegipan. Danni desperately wanted to talk to the other counterparts but reminded herself this was not the time or place. The rest of the Bastion residents were either dead or severely injured by falling debris. Hannah patched them up in whatever way she could, even ripping small parts off of her long skirt to act as bandages. It would be a long time before Constellar was back in action. Danni's friends were exhausted and moved very slowly in the process. Brodie was still traumatised, and Slade kept glancing over at his sister with worry. Charlotte avoided Crawford at all costs, leading the civilians to the portal Garth had created to transport them back to the town. They were advised to stay inside their homes and keep all doors closed and lights off.

Danni noticed something different about her 'evil twin'. She didn't seem quite as hostile or self-absorbed. The mermaids, along with the Leo, had disappeared, and Chiron was doing some sort of magic that dissolved any Scorpion residue. It wasn't until she felt a firm hand on her shoulder that Danni realised she had been shaking violently. She looked up to see Ronan assessing her with concern.

"Danni, we are all going to be okay, I promise," he stated confidently.

"How can you be so sure?" Danni felt a tear splash onto her arm. "This is all my fault…"

"It's not." Ronan shook his head. "You brought us all together, and we would've saved this planet if it weren't for Milo. You can't blame yourself."

"Oh, yeah?" Danni's face began to burn. "What about Hunter and Parry? I am trying to keep it cool for Ambrite, but my gut is telling me something is seriously wrong. If they are dead, I will never be able to forgive myself."

Ronan used his thumb to wipe at Danni's crumpled face. "I can't take away how you feel, but please don't assume all the responsibility. Let's put our heads together and find our friends, including Graham."

Danni nodded appreciatively. She kissed her boyfriend's cheek and turned to face the others. "Guys, I think we've done as much as we can do here. Let's move back to the Mission Base, call on all the counterparts, and figure out a plan to get Graham back. Hopefully, we can find Hunter and Parry along the way."

She saw Asterion rise from a bar stool, looking slightly more refreshed. He gave her a weak smile and gestured for all of them to follow him. Reilly and Drew sidled up on either side of Danni and linked arms. Ronan fell back to talk to Slade and Brodie.

"Danni," Reilly whispered, "you truly are a natural born leader."

The morning rays of Muktu were shining down upon them as they left the ruined nightclub behind.

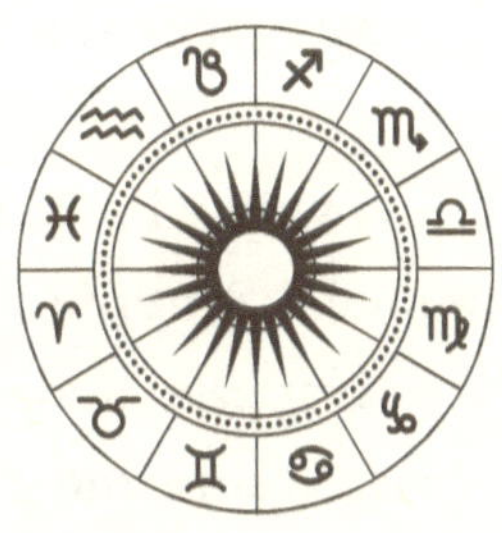

Chapter 3

The Journey Back

Amidst all of the chaos, Ambrite hadn't forgotten one important thing: she was cursed. Her awful counterpart had tricked her into immortality, and now she had to decide whether she would spend eternity back on Earth or there on Bastion. Selfishly, she was glad for the extra time to make her decision. Initially, the answer had been very clear. She would go home with all her friends and somehow make it work. They would know of her 'condition' and support her. Except now, she wasn't so sure.

Ambrite realised she didn't want to go back home to her negligent parents. As painful as it was to admit, her friendship with Hunter had been altered permanently due to his romantic feelings, and how could she possibly remain in Juggler's Corner whilst everybody around her aged and she didn't? Ambrite would have to spend the rest of her life moving and changing identities. That was no way to live. At least on Bastion, she would be able to live peacefully as an immortal. Garth had mentioned that it wasn't entirely uncommon there. She could start a whole new life, and the company wouldn't be so bad either…

Ambrite gazed at the beautiful girl standing next to her. They hadn't even known each other for a full day, and yet there was something there.

Wasabi was confident, caring, and, if Ambrite wasn't mistaken, into her. She had not left her side all evening, occasionally squeezing her hand or rubbing her back.

The group, unable to stop yawning, broke into two groups and took the chairlifts down the mountain. Ambrite wasn't sure about the other half, but her friends Drew, Hannah, Ronan, Danni, and Wasabi remained silent. Pressing her face against the glass, Ambrite scanned the tiny town below, seeking out familiar faces and potential threats.

Even this early in the morning, Bastion appeared eerily empty.

"Most of the townspeople were at Constellar last night," Wasabi murmured behind her.

Ambrite turned to see Wasabi's eyes awash with tears. She hadn't even considered all of the friends her new companion had lost.

"I'm so sorry," Ambrite whispered, taking Wasabi's hand.

The girl nodded gratefully. "I have to say, I'm really surprised that the counterparts actually turned out to be real!"

Ambrite laughed weakly. "When things finally…*if* things finally calm down, I'll tell you everything."

Including my deep, dark secret…

The chairlift touched down and everybody filed out, forming a circle by the station. Ambrite noticed Wasabi looking longingly at her tattoo parlour. She was probably worried it had been invaded.

"Okay, friends." Garth cleared his throat. "We need to get across town and back to the Mission Base but with our magic completely depleted, we're going to have to rely on good old-fashioned brute strength."

"How the hell are we supposed to do that without a single weapon?" Crawford demanded. "I'm still amazed we somehow survived the scorpions."

"Reilly nearly died!" Drew shouted.

"We are basically screwed," Charlotte huffed.

The group began talking over one another, not considering the nearby enemies that could be alerted to their presence.

Ambrite spun to face Wasabi. "Didn't you say your father used to own a hardware store that is now your tattoo parlour? Did you keep any of his old tools?"

Wasabi looked relieved. She was clearly itching to check on her store. "Yes, I have a room in the back with all of his stuff. I didn't have it in me to get rid of it. You're welcome to use whatever you like as possible weapons."

"QUIET!" Asterion roared. The group stopped chattering at once, including Garth, who was bright red. The Keeper of the Stars put his head in his hands. Any slight exertion weakened him.

"Guys!" Ambrite grabbed Wasabi's hand. "Wasabi's late father used to own a hardware store. She still has all of his old tools in her shop. She's going to let us use them as weapons!"

It was at this point Garth noticed Wasabi for the very first time. "Um, who is this, and has she been here this whole time?"

"This is Wasabi. She owns the tattoo parlour and was the DJ at Constellar," Ambrite growled. "What's your point?"

The Chief Advisor frowned. "Well, how to put this delicately… She's seen and knows too much. We will have to kill her."

The entire group, including Asterion, gaped at him in complete silence.

In true Garth fashion, he erupted into peals of laughter. "It's too easy sometimes." He wiped away a tear.

Asterion groaned, shaking his head. He turned to Wasabi. "Thank you for your kind offer. Let's get moving before anything else finds us."

Ambrite followed as Wasabi led them from the chairlift station to her outrageously funky tattoo parlour. A sigh of relief escaped her lips as she opened the door. The store was still intact and undamaged. Ambrite marvelled at the glow-in-the-dark stickers of zodiac symbols smattered along the walls, which paled once the lights were switched on. The parlour was an experience in itself. Black vinyl beds lined the walls, with rack upon rack of tattoo guns and a plethora of coloured inks.

Posters of imitation counterparts were tacked all over the room. Ambrite chuckled at the supposed Capricorn, who was a gorgeous young man with rippling pectorals. More like an old, crazy-looking professor. Towards the back of the parlour, a dirty white door stood apart from the rest of the edgy space. Wasabi made for the door, gesturing for everybody to follow. Inside the dark room, Ambrite could make out shelves and drawers filled with various sharp instruments. It smelled like sawdust and copper.

"Go nuts." Wasabi waved at the deadly treasures before them.

Her friends took turns picking out tools they understood how to use and were practical against enemies. Drew cackled as he snatched an abnormally large hammer.

"Oof," he groaned a second later as his right arm sagged from the weight. Reilly rolled her eyes and handed him a hammer no bigger than his palm.

Waiting till last, Ambrite discovered a medium-sized nail gun hidden by a box of nails on the bottom shelf. With help from Wasabi, she loaded the gun with as many rusted sharp nails as possible. It made her feel remotely better that her weapon was a ranged one. She wouldn't have to get too close to her enemies to strike them down. When all were armed and comfortable with their choices, they huddled by the entrance, where a giant book filled with colourful tattoo designs sat on the front desk.

"Listen up," Asterion declared. He was holding a bright red fire axe. "We have no idea what lies between here and the Mission Base. There might be nothing, but there is a good chance we could be ambushed. I have no doubt Milo has more in store for us. Let's go over some quick ground rules. One, do not by any means sacrifice yourself to save a civilian. We keep moving no matter what. I need all of you safe and alive. Hopefully, the ones at the club followed our instructions and are holed up indoors. Two, if by any chance you are stung by a scorpion, we run to the Mission Base regardless of who is left behind so the proper cure can be administered by the counterpart. Three, don't be a hero. Defend yourselves, but don't seek out victory if it means your life. Any questions?"

Hannah raised her hand. Ambrite mused at the Cancerian's development. When they had first met, the pretty young girl had been scared of her own shadow. Now, here she stood with a ripped skirt, power tool in hand, and a look of determination. She was a warrior woman.

"What is our planned route? Are there any shortcuts we can take from here to the Mission Base?"

Garth nodded. "Once we leave, I think we should turn right down the side of the medical clinic which leads into the fashion district. It's one of the entrances to where you would've gotten your clothes. Follow that path all the way to the end, turn left, and make your way through the alley. This will take us to the main square near the fountain. We just have to run down those stairs, cross the bridge, and go through the field to the Mission Base entrance."

"What could go wrong?" Drew sighed rhetorically.

"I'm going to be a little slower," Slade said, his arm around his sister. "I need to help Brodie."

"I'm fine." She shrugged his arm away. "It's just a minor concussion. Don't you dare risk your life for me. I can keep up just fine."

Slade opened his mouth to protest but thought better of it.

Ambrite stayed silent. Despite Asterion's rules, if she found Hunter and Parry along the way, she would risk life and limb for them.

Danni's voice broke her out of her worst-case-scenario thinking.

"Guys, I know this is kind of lame, but in case something happens, can we have a group hug?"

Nobody protested, not even Charlotte. In complete silence, the group, along with the higher powers, embraced tightly. Ambrite had a feeling what was waiting for them would make the battle at Constellar seem like a tea party.

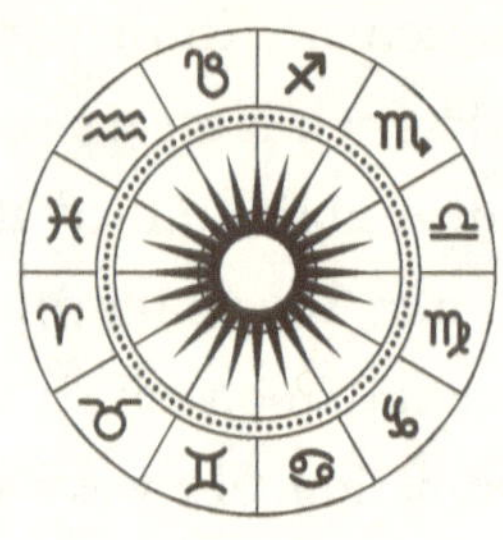

Chapter 4

The Fallen

Graham woke with a start in the most comfortable bed he had ever been in. The silken sheets and pillows enticed him to slip back into a deep sleep full of romantic dreams. Resisting the urge, he sat up and let his eyes feast on a beautifully decorated chamber cloaked in shades of deep purple and maroon. The four-poster bed, seemingly made of rich mahogany, enveloped him in sheer nets of burgundy. It faced what appeared to be the door to the exit. To his left, Graham could see a whitewashed bathroom with a clawfoot tub and bronze faucets. In the available corners of the room, large vividly green ferns sagged majestically, giving the space an exotic feel.

Marble candleholders on the desk to his right sprouted thick yellow wax candles that were lit with bright flames. They illuminated a crisp piece of parchment with a tiny scrawled message next to an oval inkpot and quill. Graham arose from the bed to find himself in satin maroon pyjamas that slid deliciously against his skin with every movement. Stretching out a hand, he picked up the note and read it aloud: *My love, I trust you slept well? Whenever you're ready, do come down to breakfast so we can discuss next steps. Milo.*

Milo. His saving grace. He had revealed his true nature, but none of it mattered. He was still the same man he adored. Graham recalled soaring high above the world of Bastion in the arms of his companion. They had travelled via a hidden aircraft nestled in the valley. It was hard to believe that had been only a bit over a day ago. It had looked completely barren. It had been pitch black. Surely this place did not exist on the same craggy, gloomy world where Milo wanted to build their empire?

His hand along with his head began to ache. He gazed in confusion at the red mark on his palm. It hurt to touch. What did it mean? Flashes of his friends passed through his mind. A part of him wanted to explore these trains of thought further, but much like opposing magnets, they kept bouncing away from an invisible force whenever he got too close. After setting the letter down, Graham blew out the candles and opened the wardrobe lined perpendicular to the desk. The smell of fresh wood was heavenly. The quality garments within were even more angelic. Graham pulled out a burgundy vest, soft black shirt, and matching fitted pants. Having laid them on the bed, he strode over to the bathroom and turned the bronze faucets of the bathtub. It was time to scrub up nicely for Milo.

*

Her beautiful white skirt was in tatters. Her arms and legs were bruised from running into the sides of scorpions, bumping them off of the roof. Her feet ached from hours of walking around in heels, attending to the injured. But despite it all, she felt strong. Stronger than ever. Last night had been both terrifying and exhilarating. She was no longer afraid. She had even caught her friends staring at her in awe. *No backbone, hey?* Hannah was 'spine-full', not spineless. Drew couldn't stop glancing at her milky white thighs, bare from the battle. She gave him a flirtatious grin and wiggled the electric blue power tool in her hand. His mouth opened in wonder. Drew already lapped after her like a love-sick puppy; now he would worship the goddess she was becoming.

The group were ready to leave Wasabi's shop. Garth had provided the most efficient route for them to get back to the Mission Base, where hopefully Hunter and Parry were waiting. Hannah wished Karki had shown up the night before to help them but understood her 'crabby' counterpart would've been too frightened. Bravery emerges only from the big moments. Quickly and quietly, Hannah's friends dashed towards the medical clinic and waited for Wasabi to lock up and follow. The deathly silence surrounding the town suggested Constellar wasn't the only place to have been attacked. In fact, every single store in their eyesight radius was unopened and empty. There was no sign of entry. No evidence of damage. No life whatsoever. A ghost town.

"Wasabi says most of the people of Bastion were at Constellar," Ambrite whispered to nobody in particular.

"Yeah, and what of the children and the elderly?" Ronan mumbled.

Garth and Asterion had their eyes closed, attempting to sense what lay beyond. Hannah watched Garth's eyes flicker open after a moment, followed by Asterion. They looked at one another and shook their heads simultaneously.

"We are still too weak," the Chief Advisor explained. "With any hope, any children or elderly are hiding inside their homes and will be reunited with the few survivors we portalled back to town shortly."

"Does this mean the town is safe? I mean, there is no damage here or sound of more scorpions," Drew suggested.

Hannah hoped her boyfriend was correct.

"We won't know until we reach our Mission Base," Asterion warned. "Even if the attack was focused only on Constellar, we have still lost. Our population is nearly devoid of adults. Our doctors, our workers, and our community have been wiped out. We cannot attempt to rebuild unless we wait until the children grow and repopulate with one another. Now more than ever, we need as many people as we can get."

Hannah noticed Ambrite shifting from foot to foot and fidgeting with her hands. She felt her eyes fill with tears. So many children were about to learn their parents and siblings were dead. So many elderly people would learn their sons and daughters were no longer alive.

"Could we bring in people from other planets to settle here?" Brodie piped up.

"What about the Unsigned?" Wasabi added. "I live in the valley beyond. There's not many of us, but most of the people there don't bother going to Constellar because it's too far and they cannot use the bathrooms."

"Oh, sure," Garth snorted. "Hey, everyone, our people were wiped out by an army of scorpions, so…wanna come live here and adopt some kids? We could offer the abandoned houses in town to the Unsigned if they like. They could get them at a discounted…"

"Garth," Asterion hissed, "you of all people should be sympathetic to the Unsigned. Let's get to the Mission Base first. We need to hold counsel with the counterparts and discuss our next movements. Don't forget that we have to do everything in our power to get Graham back and annihilate the biggest threat of all…Milo."

Garth flushed. He had no issue being sassy until reprimanded by the Keeper of the Stars. Hannah couldn't believe how close they had been to going home. There was no way they could leave now until their friend was safely back, the counterparts were truly united, and Milo was punished for what he had done. Hopefully, there was a chance for a decent night's sleep somewhere in between saving the universe.

They had to stop talking and keep moving. Hannah took Drew's hand and followed him closely as they turned right into the fashion district, where she had confronted Sirena and Calypsee. The lights and flashing signs that had blinded her just the day before were now off. The entire line of shops were dark, the displays motionless. They had to pass through a long alley before they reached the brick wall at the end. The group refused to speak, scared that they would awaken some dormant beast lying in wait.

Charlotte leaned in close to Hannah and whispered, "If only we could break in and steal all the clothes." Hannah stared back in surprise and didn't answer. Charlotte shrugged at her reaction and walked beside Brodie. She had appeared genuine last night, but Hannah had a feeling Charlotte had a long way to go before becoming a decent human being.

They trudged carefully down the path, scanning each window for any signs of life and jumping at the occasional crunch of stones underfoot. They had almost reached the end when the sound of muffled whimpering reached Hannah's ears. She thought it was just her imagination, desperate for signs of life, but the rest of her group screwed up their faces and began looking around. Asterion made a gesture for them to stand completely still and silent. After a minute, Reilly moved towards the last store on the left, which sold astrological jewellery, and opened the door. Sure enough, the whimpering became slightly louder. The team moved towards the shop and watched from the entryway as Reilly walked behind the counter and crouched down, disappearing. A small scream sounded from behind the register, followed by Reilly repeating, "It's okay, it's okay, it's okay."

Drew took a step forward, but Hannah pulled him back. Too many unfamiliar faces could unsettle the unidentified person further. There was the sound of shuffling, further whimpering, and Reilly's inaudible soothing voice. Shortly, the Sagittarian emerged from behind the counter holding the hand of a dusty blond-haired little boy who was about five years old. He had black cargo shorts and a t-shirt with the Capricorn symbol emblazoned on the front in forest green. His green eyes were red from crying, which he continued to aggravate by rubbing them with balled-up fists. Hannah's heart melted at the poor distressed child in front of her. Was this his mother's store? Was he waiting for her to return?

"Quickly, everybody," Asterion urged. "Let's get in and close the door so as to remain undetected."

The child kept darting from face to face, his nose dripping like a tap. He refused to let go of Reilly's hand. Hannah pulled off yet another piece from her skirt and handed it to him with a warm smile. Soon, she would have nothing left! He gingerly accepted it with his free hand and blew his nose, staring at her warily.

"What's your name, sweetheart?" Danni strode forward and crouched to meet his level.

"Ch—Charlie," he blubbered.

Hannah witnessed Danni's face turn white, and she stood quickly and took a step back. The child threw the tissue on the floor and buried his face against Reilly's stomach. She patted his thin hair.

"What's wrong?" Hannah whispered, catching her shoulder.

Danni clutched at her chest. "I hope I'm wrong, but there was a woman in the club wearing Gemini jewellery, and she D-I-E-D from the scorpion venom. Before she lost consciousness, she said the name Charlie."

The group crowded around Charlie and fussed over him. After five minutes or so, he stopped crying and sat on the floor, cross-legged.

"Do you know where your parents are, Charlie?" Ronan tousled the boy's hair.

Charlie shook his head. "Mama went to Constellar last night to sell her necklaces. She left me in the shop and said she wouldn't be long. My papa is working on Liria."

Hannah turned to Garth, an unspoken question on her lips.

"Liria," Garth answered. "It is not too far from Bastion via spacecraft. The planet isn't inhabited by people but rather is a goldmine of resources. A lot of workers visit its vast landscape to forage for food, materials, and rare stones. They will sometime stay weeks at a time just to gather valuables."

The little boy nodded excitedly. "Papa goes there to get jewels for Mama's store."

Hannah looked at the display cases and racks inside the store. The necklaces, rings, earrings, bracelets, and tiaras glinted and gleamed in the morning light. Whorls of patterns and colours shone vividly from various corners of the room. She was entranced by the quality of the gems and their hues. There was a romance to a man collecting jewels on another planet for his wife to sell. How terribly sad he could no longer gather them for her. How were they going to break the news to Charlie?

As if reading her thoughts, Asterion stepped beside Charlie and mimicked his seated position on the floor. It was amusing to see an old man with golden sandals and a white robe sitting like a child. He fastened his kind gaze on Charlie and wiggled his eyebrows. The boy let out an adorable laugh.

In an instant, his look turned serious.

"Where is my mama?" His bottom lip quivered.

Asterion inhaled deeply. Hannah hovered nearby, ready to comfort the poor boy.

"Charlie, your mother…she was injured at Constellar and fell into a deep sleep. Unfortunately, we cannot wake her up, but your father will be back from Liria soon to take you home. In the meantime, would you like to come with us?"

Hannah sucked in a breath, awaiting the inevitable outburst of sobs. Instead, Charlie nodded bravely and stood up. He hadn't really understood the 'never waking up again' part, which was a blessing. He held out a hand to Asterion. The old man smiled warmly and took it. They made for the door.

"Let's get going," he announced to the group. "We are bringing Charlie with us to the Mission Base. Who knows when his father will return, and I don't want to waste any more time putting you all in danger."

With that, the oldest and the youngest member of the pack walked outside, hand in hand.

*

The smell of delicious, stomach-pleasing food enticed Graham to follow his nose down the stairs. His bare feet sank comfortably into the plush carpeting that covered the wooden steps, and his soft hand ran along the length of the glossy dark banister. For the hundredth time that morning, Graham struggled to place where he was, exactly. So far, he had been exposed to a life of luxury that did not match the planet he had been formally introduced to. Reaching the ground level, Graham wandered into a brightly lit room that resembled a small hipster warehouse. A large wooden table that could seat forty was filled with hot continental-style breakfast items. Pitchers of brightly coloured juices were placed on a separate station behind the table.

More exotic plants hung from the rafters of the high ceiling, nestled in woven baskets of straw. A kitchen of white ceramic and stainless steel was situated on the right and sparkling clean. The warehouse walls were tinted glass. He could not see out of them or determine the weather outside. A large door with a brass doorknob lay beyond the table. Who was all this food for? Surely not for just him and Milo? Before he could pick off a fresh blueberry from the colourful fruit platter, a gaggle of voices and thunderous footsteps trudged in from the northern entrance.

Graham threw himself behind the kitchen countertop and peered out at the funny little men who marched towards the feast. Strangely, they all looked slightly similar to one another. They were clad in black armour that resembled thick leathery skin rather than metal. Their hair was scruffy, dark, and wild. Their eyes were blood red. In the most unrefined manner, they grabbed at their food with dirty hands and scarfed it down. Their loud chewing noises made Graham lose his appetite. He was about to sneak upstairs again when a familiar honeyed voice echoed throughout the room.

"Greetings, minions," Milo boomed. "I trust you're enjoying the feast?"

Graham scrambled to the left and gazed up in awe at the beautiful man standing before him. Milo was wearing a black and burgundy cape with tailored black skinny jeans and a burgundy fitted shirt. His hair was slicked back, and his lips were turned up in a sexy smirk. Graham shivered at the memory of kissing that mouth.

The men had barely acknowledged him, continuing to shovel their breakfast in. Graham had no desire to eat ever again. He watched Milo's foot begin to tap dangerously, his rhythm mounting to rage. The minions took no notice as their master's blood pressure began to reach boiling point. Suddenly and without warning, a long black pointed tail lashed out and swept their plates off the table. They crashed to the floor with a deafening sound. Miraculously, nothing had broken. The minions stared at the empty places where their breakfast had been a second earlier in complete silence. One smaller man at the back dared to pick up a piece of his pancake and was pinned against the wall by Milo's scorpion stinger. He dropped the pancake to the floor and whimpered supposed apologies, his words gibberish. Graham watched Milo unhook his victim as he slid to the floor in deep shame.

"I will be merciful today because we have company. Graham, darling, do come out from behind the kitchen, will you?"

Graham slowly stood to his feet and shakily walked next to his master. The minions looked up properly, fixing their stares on him. There was something very unnerving about forty or so beady red eyes being alerted to his presence. Milo placed a hand on his shoulder and caressed the hairs at the back of his neck. Graham immediately softened.

"I would like to introduce you all to my partner in crime, Graham Maltin, from planet Earth." Milo beamed. "He so kindly assisted in the takeover from Bastion yesterday evening and will be working with you all to recruit new Scorpios for our empire. Please treat him with the respect you should be showing me – and, stars above, save him some food, you loathsome beasts!"

Milo waved them off to begin eating again and turned to face Graham.

"I hope you eat before they finish it all. They disgust me," he sneered. "How are you, darling?"

Graham flushed. "I'm well, thank you. Um, where are we, and why do those *things* all look the same?"

Milo placed a hand on the small of Graham's back and led him towards the fruit platter. He plucked a juicy blueberry from the bunch and fed it to Graham. The burst of sweetness filled Graham's mouth, making him feel like the healthiest being alive. He wanted more. He wanted to be fed by Milo all day.

"I know what you're thinking," Milo murmured. "How is this the same place I took you? Do you remember the crumbling tower you saw the first night I took you here?"

Graham recalled a tumble-down structure in the distance that lay beyond the craters and the eerie skeleton he had discovered. It had looked so dilapidated. Surely that wasn't where they were now?

"That is not where we are now," Milo answered, seeming to read his mind. "My minions tore that ugly hazard down. Just to the west of it is the beginning of our empire. Our palace is currently being erected, but we need a larger army of soldiers and workers. This is the servants' quarters for the time being, with the mess hall here and our bedrooms upstairs. Our minions, plus a bit of magic, helped put this temporary lodging together."

Graham realised that what he had seen so far was it. There was only the warehouse and the room that he had slept in above. It had been decorated beautifully by Milo, no doubt, but it was hardly a palace or an empire. This was going to take a long time.

"Where do the servants sleep?" Graham began munching on a crunchy slice of melon. It tasted very similar to honeydew but was bright pink.

Milo laughed. "Who cares? The craters, I suppose. Graham, they are the scorpions you would've seen lurking in the dunes. They are welcome to eat in the mess hall in their hideous human forms, but after that, they are to go back outside and serve us. Right now they are building our throne room, but I need some materials I can get only from the planet Liria. I need you to go there and recruit some more workers. Only Scorpios, mind you… That's my one requirement, and bring them back here to help us."

Something did not feel right. That familiar nagging sensation tugged at Graham once again. The way Milo had said the word 'recruit' made it sound much more threatening than it needed to be.

"How do I recruit them? And how do I get to this planet? I don't want to hurt anybody."

Milo's hand cupped Graham's chin, and he pulled him in close so their noses were touching. "My love, don't you wish to make me happy?"

As Graham nodded, so did Milo.

"Good. Well, then don't ask too many questions, all right? I will arrange your travel once you are fed and ready. You are my representative and a fine-looking one, at that. They will have no choice but to meet your requests. You will know who the Scorpios are by their colours, of course. The only people on Liria are workers who travel from neighbouring planets. I will ask that you don't return until you have all of the ingredients on this list plus at least fifty workers in tow. We can always get more later."

Milo handed him a list on the same parchment paper from the bedroom. It was filled with items and complicated measurements that were scrawled in Milo's perfect calligraphy. Graham folded the paper neatly and placed it in his pocket. Boldly, he leant in to kiss his man on the lips but felt his heart sink as Milo recoiled.

"Ah, let's not in front of our servants," Milo hurriedly explained, patting Graham on the back. "Finish eating and meet me by the door when you're done."

As Milo walked away, Graham watched one of the minions sidle up to his master and whisper in his ear. He couldn't understand what the scorpion was saying, but Milo looked less than pleased.

"Really, all of them?" Milo snarled, his black eyes flashing. "What about Ichoris? Okay, make sure he doesn't let them get through. He's my top beast. The next time you report to me, you'd better tell me they are all dead, especially that fool in the top hat, or I'll grind you to a fine powder."

Graham scratched his head in confusion. Who was Ichoris, and who needed to die?

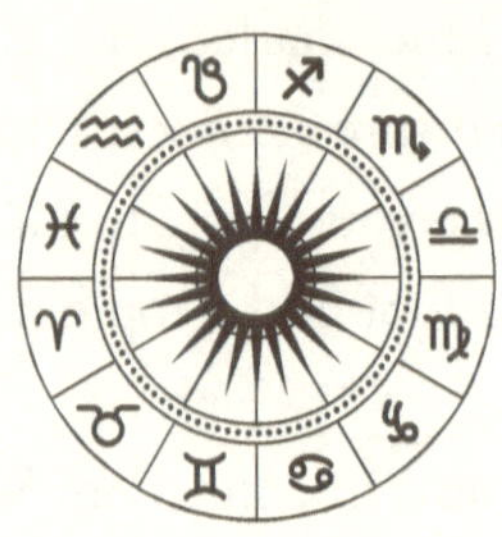

Chapter 5

Ichoris

Every so often, Hunter would gaze at Parry and see Ambrite. It was always the initial glance that made him confuse the two. Once his eyes adjusted, he saw the gorgeous Virgo who had shaved her precious hair off to prove a point. He knew she was interested in him. There had been a power and passion in the way she touched him the night before. He couldn't tell if he felt the same. It had all been so unexpected. It was like looking at a completely new member of their group. Whatever the case, it had been sorely needed, especially after seeing Ambrite holding hands with the DJ. That was when it had really hit him that she would never be interested romantically. He missed her deeply and prayed with every footstep he took that nothing had harmed her or his friends.

Karki skipped along, hand in hand with her new human pals. She was so innocent and fragile for a counterpart. They had just crossed the bridge past the field and into the empty town square. The fountain was not running, and the shops were all closed with the lights off. Hunter let go of Karki's hand and ran to the nearest red-bricked home to peer inside. Nothing. No signs of life. His stomach twisted in sheer terror. Something was seriously wrong.

"Karki," he croaked, "where is everybody? What has happened to this town?"

The little girl gazed up at Hunter with wide, fearful eyes. They had flecks of red around the irises. She resembled the sweetest demonic child ever.

"Something is definitely wrong," she whispered.

Parry stepped forward and placed a hand on her shoulder protectively. She felt like a babysitter to an incredibly powerful child. "Let's make our way to Constellar," Parry pushed. "We will surely find more answers there."

Or bodies…

Hunter didn't dare say that aloud or think about it for too long.

The trio moved through the empty square, not daring to speak lest they miss any important noises or voices. They were about to reach the entrance to the fashion district when they heard a group of people muttering. Karki snuggled into Parry, and Hunter squeezed her hand comfortingly. He pushed a finger against his lips and motioned for them to press themselves against the wall.

"Don't move a muscle," he whispered fiercely.

The incoherent sounds were becoming louder. He could now hear the soft tread of footsteps approaching. He gazed over at Parry, who had her eyes closed in fear.

"Hey," he urged. Her green eyes flickered open and fixed on his. "It's going to be okay. I promise nothing will happen to you both."

She nodded and resumed closing her eyes. Karki buried her face in Hunter's side. They had no weapons or ways to defend themselves.

Hunter saw a small foot emerge from the alley and blinked in surprise at the little boy who appeared. Karki jumped up from the wall.

"Oh!" she squealed. "Hello there! Who are you?"

The boy's eyes locked on to the strangers, and before they could introduce themselves, he began to howl.

"Run!" Hunter yelled, grabbing both of the girls and pulling them towards the fountain. The disembodied voices were now alerted to their presence and shouting. They threw themselves behind the stone platform and flattened their backs against it. Parry leaned into Hunter and spoke softly in his ear.

"In case this is the last moment we ever share, I just wanted you to know you were really good in bed. Not that I had anything to compare it to…"

He flushed and turned to answer her when Karki screamed. A boy with dark curly hair was hovering over them with a hammer the size of a mouse in his hand.

"Freeze, you varmints!" he screeched.

The three of them threw their hands over their faces and tensed all of their muscles in preparation for their death. When nothing happened, Hunter realised who their potential attacker was. He grinned at his open-mouthed assailant.

"Drew?"

The gaping Piscean was barely registering who was in front of him. It wasn't Hunter who confused him but Parry. He squinted at her like a grandparent being shown something on a mobile phone.

"Ambrite, do you have a twin we don't know about? Because your sister has been with us all this time…and, OMG, is this your love-child?" Drew pointed to Karki.

Hunter laughed and pulled the girls to their feet. Looking across the square, he registered that the group he had heard earlier were all his friends. He counted them without speaking, but his stomach churned when he saw Graham wasn't amongst them. A moment later, his heart shifted gear when he caught sight of Ambrite staring at him in disbelief, her eyes filled with tears. The DJ was gazing at him as well. Without a care, he ran over to his best friend and took her in his arms. She broke down sobbing against his shirt, repeating over and over how sorry she was. He cradled her closer as he felt his other friends, including Garth and Asterion, crowd around him. Their eyes were shining with relief. They were together again. Breaking free, Hunter gestured for Parry and Karki to come over. As if she were a mirage in the desert, he noticed the group struggling to comprehend who the gorgeous young girl was in front of them. As she neared closer, holding Karki's hand, they registered.

"Parry?" Crawford whistled.

"Oh, wow, your hair looks amazing!" Reilly gushed.

"You look so much like Ambrite." Brodie ran forward to examine her.

Hunter imagined that for the first time in her entire life, Parry did not want the spotlight focused on her. She blushed a red the shade of her cropped hair and looked down at her feet. Everybody was so overjoyed to be reunited, they had forgotten the two strange children from both parties.

"Who is this cutie?" Hannah knelt at Karki's level.

Karki's smiled filled her entire face. She threw her arms around the surprised Hannah's neck and nuzzled her.

Hunter grinned as it dawned on Hannah who the affectionate child was.

"Karki? Oh my gosh, what a beautiful little girl you are!"

The pair hugged one another and cried.

"Cancerians." Danni grinned. She clapped a hand on Hunter's back.

"I'm so glad you're both alive. We were so worried about you."

She went on to embrace Parry. Ambrite didn't appear to want to leave Hunter's side, which pleased him immensely. He caught sight of Wasabi watching them both carefully. It was petty, but he sidled up even closer to Ambrite to mark his territory.

In between everybody oohing and aahing over Parry's new look, she took several steps back and reminded Hunter of a question he'd had moments before.

"Where is Graham? Where is he?" Her voice was panicked. Hunter was torn between wanting to comfort her and not leaving Ambrite.

The group gathered around the fountain. Karki sat in Hannah's lap and allowed her hair to be played with. The pair looked like sisters. The little boy Hunter hadn't been introduced to yet followed suit and plopped by Reilly's feet. She feathered his hair lovingly. Garth and Asterion remained standing and relayed their account of events since Hunter had left Constellar until then.

When they revealed that Graham had been abducted by Milo, Parry broke down into sobs. Ambrite rubbed her back. With their heads bent over, they looked like twins. It was a very confusing and erotic moment for Hunter. He shook his head, ignoring his perverted thoughts.

"I know how you feel." Ambrite hushed the inconsolable Virgo. "When I couldn't find Hunter, I blamed myself, but it achieves nothing. We will get Graham back, I promise you."

As awful as it sounded, Hunter was secretly pleased that Ambrite had been so worried about him. He meant something to her. They were introduced to the adorable Charlie, who seem fixated on Karki, and then Hunter disclosed the details of their evening. Of course, there was one major part he didn't mention. In his version of events, Parry had taken him home from Constellar to care for him as he drunkenly vomited his guts up. No one could ever know they had slept together. Least of all Ambrite.

Parry gently pushed Ambrite aside and stood, smoothing the wrinkles out of her clothes. Her mascara had run, smudging her face and dotting the flawless skin underneath her eyes.

"Now that we're all caught up," she choked out, "what is our plan? We have to get Graham back and kill that bastard."

"Yes, exactly." Asterion nodded. "We must return to the base and figure out our next steps. Have you seen any civilians?"

Hunter shook his head. "The houses here are empty, but they could be hiding. I hope they are safe somewhere. There's hardly anyone left."

"No time to waste," Garth urged. "The base is just beyond the field. Let's go."

Feeling much braver than before, Hunter trailed after his friends carrying weapons over the bridge and into the field. The flowers waved lazily in the wind, unaware that tragedy had ever befallen their small planet.

He sidled up next to Parry, who appeared lost in her own worries.

"Hey…I just wanted to say, you were really good too."

She met his eyes, her face expressionless. Overhead, the sky seemed to darken.

As the cave entrance approached, the atmosphere began to change and thicken. Hunter felt his legs buckle as a sudden deafening rumble caused him to lose his balance. His friends froze in place, their eyes darting around for the impending threat. Before they knew what was happening, a gigantic black form moved into view, blocking their only way into the Mission Base. From what he had heard about the battle at Constellar, Hunter expected it to be another scorpion, but this creature didn't resemble anything he had ever read about before. It was enormous and entirely black save for two dagger-sharp white teeth in the middle of its face. Along the length of its body, tubular appendages dangled, some shorter than others. Its left arm was fashioned into a glittering onyx cleaver, and the right was a bulbous fleshy stump. It did not have visible eyes or a nose, but it could clearly see them and smell their fear. If that weren't enough, Charlie and Karki began screaming simultaneously.

"Children," warned Asterion, "do not try to fight this thing. It's a beast that guards the planet Talonis. Milo has clearly manipulated it to do his bidding."

"Well, what the hell do we do, then?" Charlotte yelled.

"You're still too weak, my lord," Garth pleaded.

Asterion turned to face the beast, who was seemingly amused by their display. It stood watching them as if it had all the time in the world and wanted to savour their complete annihilation.

"Ichoris!" Asterion boomed.

The creature leaned forward as if to say, *You called?*

"Be gone whence you came and do not return. You will not win this battle, and Talonis requires a keeper. Do not incur the wrath of our counterparts, because you will lose."

Ichoris had now lost its patience. It stepped forward, and with its right arm, it swung towards where Ambrite, Wasabi, Slade, and Brodie were standing.

"Move!" Hunter cried.

He watched in horror as everybody ducked except Ambrite, who was knocked so forcefully her skull had to have caved in. The impact sent her flying into a field of purple poppies.

"No!" Hunter ran straight past Ichoris into the section of plants where Ambrite lay dazed and confused. He threw himself onto the grass and stared in shock at her physical body. There was not a single thing wrong with her. Where there should've been blood, there was none. Where broken bones should've been protruding, there were none. Her skull was completely intact, and she wasn't even unconscious.

"How?" he whispered. "How is this possible? You should be dead."

"Don't sound so disappointed." She smirked. She stood up and moved to leave, but Hunter grabbed her hand.

"How?" He gritted his teeth. He needed answers – and now.

She turned back to him, looking slightly queasy. "Hunter, I will tell you everything, but right now just be thankful I was the one hit and nobody else."

He had no idea what that meant but followed her back to the clearing, where the battle continued.

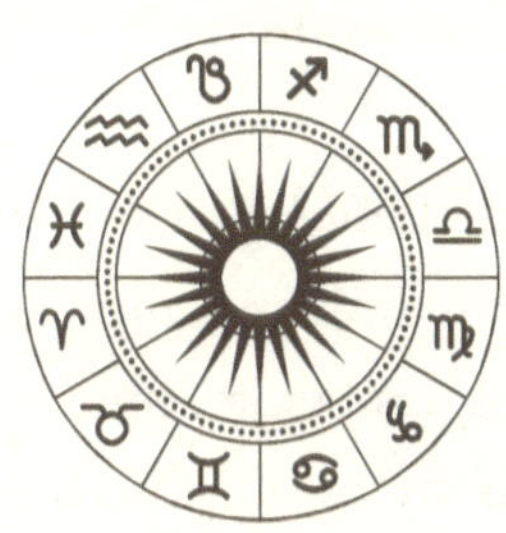

Chapter 6

A Moment of Clarity

The ship was ready for boarding. Graham kept glancing at the list in his hand: *fifteen vats of Glarafae sap, twelve sacks of iron ore, three sacks of silver ore, twenty-five full-length logs of Glarafae wood, forty to fifty Scorpio workers (alive!), a melting pot for our crowns, and two large bars of gold for melting.* There was also a lot of food Milo had requested. Species of bird and cattle he had never heard of before. He assumed the minions who were accompanying him would assist in hauling these materials and animals onto their vessel. He still wasn't sure how he was supposed to persuade fifty people to work for them. His boots felt heavy on his feet. The north entrance of the warehouse had led to a landing bay of sorts where aircraft could dock. Graham looked up to see Milo striding towards him in his trademark flowing black cape. His features were perfectly shaped to suit his face. His smile lit up something inside Graham. It all felt worth the trouble just to make this mysterious man happy.

"Are you all set, love?" Milo purred. He adjusted Graham's collar with nimble fingers.

Graham nodded nervously. Milo brushed his bottom lip with his own, only for a second. It wasn't enough and it never would be.

"Now listen, some of these workers may be reluctant, but as the list dictates, we want them alive, so do not let any of our minions do anything rash. Here is something that may persuade them to our cause."

Milo pulled out another longer piece of parchment from inside his cape. This one was full of unfamiliar names and faces. Graham raised his eyebrows at the sea of strangers before him.

Milo chuckled. "Everybody on this list is connected to families back on Bastion. Tell them I will have them killed if they do not comply. Little do they know, most of them are probably already dead."

An electric current raced through Graham's nervous system. It was like the inside of his body was flashing red in alarm. He must've been frowning, because Milo extended a hand and stroked the side of his stubble.

"You will do as I say, Graham Maltin. You will please me. Understood?"

Graham gasped as he felt a quick jab prick his palm. It happened so quickly he couldn't identify the source of the pain. Instantly, his body was relaxed. Life made perfect sense.

"I live to serve you, my honey," Graham drawled.

"Good. Now do not disappoint me. Our empire depends on you."

*

He was going to save the day and be the hero. Just let this Ichoris thing stop him. Drew looked down at his tiny hammer, all bravado gone. Who was he kidding? This tool couldn't hurt a caterpillar. Did they have caterpillars on this planet? Were chrysalises a thing?

"Drew!" Hannah screamed, snapping him out of his foolish daydreaming.

Ichoris had brute strength on its side, but its weakness lay in its lack of agility. The creature was not fast, and this allowed its enemies to dodge every attack it tried to make. There had been no time to question why Ambrite looked like she hadn't just been crushed by its gigantic baton of an arm earlier. There was no time to formulate a plan. All they could do was keep moving around and hope that Asterion would regain his powers shortly. The counterparts had not budged from the cave. From a distance, it looked like the big purple doors had been smashed open. Either they didn't know (which was unlikely) or they didn't care (which was more likely). The only counterpart who cared was frightened out of her life, squealing as she tore this way and that, her straight hair flying all over the place. Hannah's counterpart was adorable, but she was awful in a crisis.

His warrior woman, on the other hand, was a completely different girl to the one he'd first met years earlier as a kid. He knew the timing was terrible, but he wanted to throw her down in the field and experience a very primal Tarzan/Jane moment with her. Her torn skirt would be used for role-playing when they finally made it back to Earth. *If* they made it back.

Asterion had told them their weapons were useless, but that hadn't stopped them trying. Ambrite fired nails from her gun into its side. Brodie flung a hacksaw, and Charlotte seemed to think her stilettos would do the trick. Granted, those things hurt if you stepped on them or they stepped on you. Hannah turned on her power tool, which didn't seem to have much life left, and weaved in between its legs, digging the whirring needle into its thick flesh. It was an admirable effort, but Ichoris didn't even acknowledge their feeble attempts. It kept trying to stomp them underfoot and butcher them with its shiny blade in place of its hand.

Asterion was still spent from his magic use, and Garth was having no luck communicating with the other counterparts. This battle was going nowhere. Drew was about to try hitting one of its toes with his baby hammer when a high-pitched squeal rang out. Hannah's skirt had been pinned down by the sharp end of Ichoris's blade, and its right arm was ready to bludgeon her.

"Hannah!"

Drew raced towards her and pulled on her skirt, which just made Ichoris dig the blade in deeper. She was well and truly stuck.

"Drew," Hannah begged, "let go and move. He will kill us both."

"No!" Drew pulled harder. Ichoris shook as if it were laughing. It raised its right arm and pulled back into a swing.

He saw his friends standing in shock. There was nothing any of them could do. By the time they ran over, they would all be crushed. He shielded her body with his and clutched her tightly.

"I love you, Hannah May Chase. I will always love you."

As they braced for impact, a white glow surrounded the clearing and a strong vibration shook the earth beneath them. Ichoris bellowed as another gigantic creature threw all of its body weight against the beast. As the beast began to fall, Hannah's skirt broke free, and the pair raced to safety as it hit the ground with an epic thud. Drew and Hannah stared up at Karki in her true counterpart form, no longer frightened. Her red eyes glowed with menace.

"How dare you attack my Hannah!"

As Ichoris began to stand, Karki let out an almost tribal cry and scuttled over to the alarmed creature. With her jagged pincers, Karki began snipping at the beast's tubular appendages. It roared in pain as she began dismantling Ichoris piece by piece.

"Oh yes," Drew breathed to Hannah. "This is exactly how video game bosses work. They all have a weakness. Man, this is cooler than cool."

"Drew," Hannah growled, "it almost killed us!"

"Oh yeah… Come here, you." Drew pulled Hannah to him and peppered her with kisses all over her face.

When the last appendage had been cut, Ichoris lay still in a big black blobby heap. It would not be guarding Talonis anymore. Wherever that was.

Wearily, the group gathered together and cheered as the little Karki emerged once more. She looked so happy as she ran to Hannah and pushed Drew out of the way. He almost knocked Karki over but allowed the girls to hug. She had saved their lives, after all.

"Karki, you did it. You brave, special girl," Hannah whispered, her thumb rubbing her counterpart's cheek.

"Love fuels us forward." The child beamed.

Drew choked back a sob. He was getting soft in his age, and there were way too many feels happening in this place. Charlie had been hiding behind a rock during the whole battle. As he came out from behind it, he stepped towards Karki and handed her a purple poppy. She took it gracefully and kissed his cheek. Charlie flushed and ran giggling to Reilly. Drew laughed and then quickly remembered in the heat of battle that Ambrite had been attacked. He turned to find everybody crowding around her, examining her impossibly uninjured physique. She looked supremely uncomfortable. Hunter could not stop staring at her in awe, which really wasn't that different to normal. They kept throwing question after question at her, which she was about to answer until Asterion interrupted rather loudly.

"Thank you so much, Karkinos," he near shouted. "You served us well, despite breaking down our Mission Base doors. I think it is time we finally held counsel with the counterparts. Don't you?"

Everybody nodded and trudged towards the cave entrance. The large purple doors, still broken, opened automatically in the presence of Asterion, and one by one they filed in. Drew was about to gorge himself on buffet food when he noticed they weren't alone.

His mermaids, a goat with a fish tail, a lion, a centaur, a hunched woman made of stone, a sexy redheaded woman, two athletic dude twins, a man dressed in a toga holding an urn, a bull, and a ram were all standing around, staring at them.

One of the twins stepped forward, smirking. The other one hung back, his face furious.

"My brother is angry because he just lost a bet. He said Ichoris would kill you all, so now his jewelled dagger is mine…"

PART II
THE CHALLENGE

Chapter 7

Competition

One could've slept soundly in the silence that followed. Nobody spoke, just stared dumbly as though they were a whole new race of people missing a chromosome. Finally, Reilly not only broke the awkwardness, she shattered it with her yelling.

"You knew? You knew this whole time that we were under attack and you didn't bother to help us? We could've died! Ambrite could've died!"

The bull let out a bovine snort, its eyes glinting wickedly. "I highly doubt that would've happened."

Reilly noticed Ambrite flush a deep crimson. She stepped back behind Slade and Brodie as if hoping to disappear.

Her best friend strode angrily towards her counterparts in agreement. They regarded her with amused eyebrow raises.

"You let a woman die at Constellar." Danni jabbed at the air with a menacing finger. "A child is now without a mother! She needed her counterparts to cure her scorpion sting and you refused to answer Garth's call. You are both selfish. I've never hated anybody in my life as much as I hate both of you."

She spat the last part with such venom that Reilly felt slightly nau-

63

seous. She felt a tug on her dress and saw little Charlie staring up at her in fright. A sad smile passed her lips. She had never seen Danni this furious before. Asterion looked disgusted at his two sons. Amidst the tension, Reilly took the opportunity to glance at Chiron. Back at Constellar, Danni had told her that he was in love with her. It had to have been a mistake. Their first encounter had left her in tears after he unashamedly belittled her. He had saved her life, though.

Her eyes took in his centaur form. She refused to admire his strong legs and…carriage? His upper half, however, was perfect. She gazed at his strong chin, ungroomed face, and lilac irises. He met her stare and matched it with intent. Her entire body began to quicken. If she wasn't mistaken, he no longer seemed so repulsed by her as he had initially. His eyes trailed over her dress, eating up the sight before him. She had a sudden urge to splash cold water on her face.

"If you had been in mortal peril, we would've stepped in."

Reilly tore her attention back to the centre of the room, where one of the twins had huffed dramatically. He had darker hair and ivory skin.

"Oh yeah, and do you consider Ambrite being thrown halfway across the field mortal peril?" Hunter roared back.

"Calm yourself, boy." The ram trotted forward. He was completely blood red except for his gleaming white curved horns. Reilly took a moment to appreciate how cool it was to finally see all the counterparts in one place, apart from Serket.

"This gave our darling Karki here a chance to prove herself." The Aries counterpart grinned with alarmingly white teeth. Reilly saw Hannah place a protective arm around the cute little girl, who, moments before, had taken down a gigantic black beast.

"Plus," the man in the toga with the golden hair drawled, "Cerus said Ambrite would be fine."

Reilly assumed he was Slade's counterpart. He was clutching his urn rather tightly and stealing glances at the pristine woman with luscious red locks. She looked like the old Parry's posh older sister.

"Why?" Hunter demanded. "Why would Ambrite be fine? Why didn't Ichoris kill you?" He now spun to face Ambrite, who no longer had cover. The Drayman siblings had stepped aside. "Any one of us would've died from that attack."

Ambrite's friend Wasabi reached out, grabbing her hand in concern, but the Taurean shook her head and released it.

Asterion cleared his throat. "Dear, maybe it's time you told them?"

Garth muttered something, and their two thrones appeared. They seated themselves comfortably and gathered everybody to sit around them just as they had during their first mission briefing. Nobody took their eyes off of Ambrite as they sat zombie-like on the stone floor. Even the counterparts appeared intrigued. The twins feigned boredom but didn't move away.

Cerus, the bull, swished his tail in glee. He was enjoying Ambrite's discomfort without shame. Reilly and her friends had been warned that their counterparts wouldn't all be nice, but a lot of them were just downright jerks.

Wasabi and Hunter sat front and centre, both vying for the prime position to comfort their girl.

Ambrite stood in front of Asterion and Garth with a drooping mouth. She looked ready to burst into tears. Reilly wanted to hug her tightly. She remembered how they hadn't been able to stand one another in the beginning, but now she loved her edgy friend. Whatever she was about to tell them, they would get through it together.

"I'm sorry I've kept this from you," she stuttered. "I wanted to tell you all so many times, but it required me making a decision which I wasn't ready to make. I think I'm ready to make it now, though…"

She took a deep shuddering breath. Nobody dared move a muscle.

"Not many people know that back on Earth, I tried to commit suicide after my grandfather, who was like my best friend, passed away. I've never had loving parents. They have literally never cared about me at all, and with him gone, I didn't see the point in living. After taking a whole bunch of sleeping pills, I fell sick with a stomach bug and threw it all up. I took it as a sign from my grandfather that he didn't want me to throw my life away…"

Reilly felt her heart tighten. She looked over at her cousin's face, wet with tears. Drew was nodding earnestly. Hunter clearly already knew this part of the story, but Wasabi had her mouth open in shock. She clearly cared deeply for Ambrite despite their extremely short-lived relationship.

Ambrite exaggerated an inhale before continuing. "When I went to see my counterpart, he already knew about my 'attempt' and decided to punish me for it. For not valuing my own life, he tricked me into eating an apple from this world's Tree of Life, which made me…immortal."

Reilly was sure she had just heard the word *immortal*, but the definition hadn't sunk in properly.

"Wait, what?" Reilly echoed all her friends. "You mean you cannot die?"

Ambrite sniffed woefully. "It cannot be reversed, either."

Everybody kept looking from Ambrite, to Cerus, to Asterion, who all nodded in confirmation. It suddenly made sense why Ambrite hadn't been hurt in the attack. She couldn't die. Immortality on Bastion must have included invincibility, as well. There was not a scratch upon her.

"What happens now?" Hunter choked out in disbelief. "How do you live a normal life back home?"

Ambrite smiled sadly at him. "Well, that's just it… I'm not coming home."

"What?" Hunter jumped up defiantly. "What do you mean? Your whole life is back home. You can't stay here."

This felt like it should've been a private discussion between the two of them, but now that it was out in the open, Hunter couldn't hold back.

"What is left for me back home, Hunter? Aside from my friends, I have nothing," Ambrite tearfully declared. "Bastion needs more people, and it's not uncommon here to be immortal. If I go back home, I'll have to keep moving around and never forming relationships because everyone I know will age and I won't. At least here, I could help rebuild this planet."

She met eyes with Wasabi, who smiled. Reilly could see how happy the DJ was to know Ambrite wasn't going to leave her.

Hunter let out a frustrated growl and ran into the showers, slamming the door. The ram shook his horned head.

The rest of the group, having heard her story, seemed to understand and accept Ambrite's decision. It was the only logical move, and at the end of the day, they wanted their friend to feel valued and happy. She looked like a giant weight had been lifted off her chest. Her shoulders were no longer hunched up by her ears, and her lip didn't quiver when she spoke.

"I hated you at first." She turned to Cerus. "But now I realise that I probably belong here. I finally appreciate life, so I'll honour my gift by helping Bastion heal."

The bull nodded in response. He had wanted to teach her a valuable lesson. Life was precious and not something to waste. Reilly admired Ambrite's resilience to turn her situation from negative to positive.

"That's wonderful, sweetness, but can I just interrupt for one second?" Garth stood, taking his hat off to wipe his brow. He looked hot and bothered. Everyone turned to focus on him. "Are any of you – I'm just talking to counterparts here – upset that Serket is dead? I was expecting some emotion from you all."

Karki burst into tears in response. The woman made of stone let out a creepy guttural cry. The man in the toga shook his head, looking down, and the mermaids clutched each other as if in agonising pain. The rest appeared neutral. Reilly glanced at Chiron again. He appeared to be purposely not making eye contact. It was as if a teacher had asked for an answer to a maths problem in class. Nobody wanted to volunteer their thoughts.

"Leonis," Garth called. The lion lying dormant on the cave's cool floor looked up. Reilly instinctively took a step back. "Didn't you visit Serket often in the desert? I'm certain there was a friendship there."

In an instant, the lion was a boy with flaming orange hair. Reilly remembered his assistance at Constellar. He was quite cute, but the red bodysuit was a little too sprayed on.

"We were friends, but it's no secret that out of the twelve, he was the weakest one. None of us would've been caught out like that. You know I value courage above all else. I highly doubt Serket put up much of a fight…"

The Maiden nodded in response, as did the twins, ram, bull, goat, and centaur.

"Our order was already beginning to fail," Chiron said.

Reilly caught herself staring at his chin. She wanted to kiss the cleft she had just noticed.

"None of us could agree on who should rule, and now we are missing a spoke in the wheel. It was only a matter of time before something like this happened. Bastion has barely any citizens left. Why should we bother rescuing this boy and avenging Serket's death? We have nothing left, and we're never going to agree. Plus, who could possibly become the new Scorpio counterpart?"

"He's right," the Maiden purred. She was so regal and elegant. It was easy to get lost in her movements. "We are nothing if we are not twelve. Serket is gone, and so is Bastion. I say we stop producing starlight and go our separate ways. Maybe we can be of use somewhere else in the galaxy."

"No!" Parry yelled. Tears were cascading down her face. The Maiden narrowed her perfect eyebrows at the Virgo's new look. Her expression was more surprised than judgemental. "You guys can do whatever the hell you want afterwards, but we are not leaving Bastion until we get back Graham. You have to help us. It's the least you can do after putting most of us through so much crap."

Reilly knew without knowing all the details that Parry's counterpart had messed with her something bad. She would never have cut off her gorgeous mane for nothing.

"We need you guys," Crawford begged. "Milo and his army are unstoppable. What we faced last night was just round one. We barely made it out alive. Don't you want revenge against the guy who manipulated his way into power and killed one of your own? Tell me at least that is worth fighting for."

There was a lot of tension and resistance in the air. Reilly was reminded of their original mission: unite the counterparts and save the planet. But it ran deeper than that now. It was about giving them a purpose to continue being counterparts altogether. Serket's death had only driven them further apart. The longer they stood there arguing, the chances of Graham returning home with them were slim to none. Suddenly, she was hit with an idea. If they couldn't appeal to their sensitive side, what about their competitive side?

"Listen up, everybody," she shouted. "I wish to make a deal."

The counterparts plus her friends froze, waiting for her to continue. She smirked at Chiron, who raised his eyebrow in a maddeningly sexy way. Inside, her nerves raced. "So far, my friends and I have been less than impressed by all of you. In our opinion, none of you deserve to rule the stars…"

Danni and Drew were beginning to smile devilishly. They had caught on to her plan.

"I think it's only fair that we get to decide who best deserves that title. So on behalf of the Astro A Team, I am setting a competition. Whoever can retrieve Graham and annihilate Milo will become the rightful ruler of Bastion. You can rebuild the entire planet as you wish, and the rest of the counterparts have to forever serve you. You also get to pick the Scorpio replacement. It will be the highest honour…"

Asterion and Garth were shaking their heads at her with eyes wider than those of a possum caught in the light. They clearly thought this was a terrible idea. Her stomach dipped and dived. Drew looked close to bursting into laughter and fist-pumping the air. She was about to say, *Just kidding*, when the ram bellowed a response. Everybody, including the counterparts, jumped.

"I love it! I am in. The human is right. How can we possibly expect to be worthy of ruling this sad, lonely planet when he haven't proven ourselves? Let these children decide. I will get him back long before any of you have even left."

What happened next was exactly what Reilly was going for.

"Your horns are curled too tightly, sheep," the Maiden spat. "Not a single person can resist my charms. I'll have Milo worshipping my dainty feet. Just you watch."

The twins jumped up and tore off their shirts. Reilly caught sight of Charlotte leering at the blond one. She remembered hearing from Danni that Charlotte had fainted after touching his abs the first time they had met. Pollux, the darker brother, pulled out Castor's jewelled dagger he had won and brandished it in front of his twin, taunting him. Castor snarled and pulled out a slightly small dagger with a hexagonal ruby in the hilt. They began to slash and parry. One would swipe and the other would crouch. They moved so quickly Reilly couldn't keep track of who was who. Charlie whooped with excitement. Castor jumped over Garth's throne and thrust the point of his dagger at the hollow of his twin's throat. Garth let out a squeal, and Pollux dropped his weapon to the floor in defeat.

"Bigger isn't always better, brother." Castor grinned.

"We are a formidable team, but I will be victorious." Pollux laughed. "Perhaps we should compete not as a team but as individuals…brother?"

Reilly couldn't help but chuckle at their enthusiasm. The rest of the group joined in except Danni, Garth, and Asterion. They still held reservations about the twins' behaviour. However, the Keeper of the Stars and his Chief Advisor seemed much more relaxed by the plan. For the first time in months, the counterparts were all together and fighting for something, even if it was petty competition. Reilly nodded at Asterion, taking a step back. He moved forward to finish the rest.

"Ground rules, counterparts," Asterion boomed. "Firstly, you will not sabotage one another. Whoever reaches Graham and dispatches Milo must do so fairly. If you are caught trying to manipulate the competition or take out a competitor, you will be deemed a coward and not someone worthy of ruling the stars. Secondly, in order for you to be kept accountable, you will be accompanied by your human counterpart. You will work together to seek out Graham's location and get him home safely. Please protect your member of the Astro A Team at all costs. They do not have magical abilities like you all do…"

Reilly felt her face flush. She was going to work with Chiron. Would he confess his feelings? She wasn't entirely sure of her own. The Sagittarian refused to look in his direction, completely aware that he was transfixed by her.

Asterion walked towards Wasabi and took her hand. She smiled, her cheeks pink.

"Dear Wasabi, please do us a favour, will you?"

"Of course." She nodded. "Anything. I just want to help."

Reilly could tell Asterion was fond of the unique Unsigned girl. He was like a father to them all, approving of their love interests and giving silent blessings.

"As you so wisely mentioned earlier, please make your way to the valley and ask all of the Unsigned to move into town. It's time we stopped this ridiculous separation, and let's face it: we need Bastion to grow again. Can you do this?"

She stole a glance at Ambrite, who gave her a thumbs-up. Wasabi inhaled loudly. She looked nervous. Unsure.

"I will do this for you. I want my people to feel safe, loved, and accepted. But promise me that once Milo is eradicated, the Unsigned will no longer feel so segregated. If Constellar is rebuilt, there will be bathrooms for everybody to use. We shouldn't be made to feel like freaks anymore."

Asterion placed a hand on her shoulder. "Bastion will be reborn. Everything is about to change for the better. I can feel it. The Unsigned will be treated as the equals they are."

Garth let out a dramatic sob that he quickly turned into a cough.

"I'm pretty sure whoever is deemed ruler of the stars gets to make that decision?" Cerus snorted. His tail twitched in irritation.

Ambrite threw him a glare. Asterion merely chuckled. "Well, my dear Taurus, you'd better make sure you win, then."

Reilly saw Asterion make a face at Wasabi, who giggled.

"Sir," Garth croaked, dabbing at his moistened eyes, "what shall we do in the meantime? Just say the word and I'll make it happen."

Asterion clapped his hands together in satisfaction. "I'm so glad you asked, Garth. You and I are going straight to Cassius. I think it's time the Council knew they voted in the wrong man…"

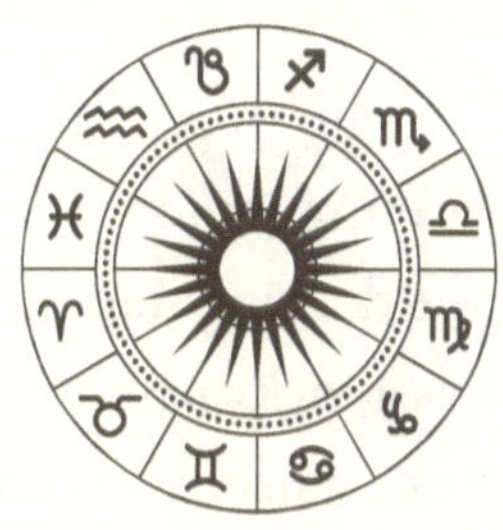

Chapter 8

Liria

Earth needed to take a leaf out of Liria's book. Whilst Graham's planet back home was dying, this one was positively thriving. It was lush, abundant, and full of life. It had to be the work of magic that the resources foraged there never seemed to run out. Graham glanced at his list for the hundredth time since the aircraft had left. Where would he even begin to collect everything Milo had requested?

A group of minions had joined him on the journey but had kept to themselves, muttering incoherently and sneaking looks at him when they thought he wouldn't notice. He had noticed. It had felt like a day's worth of travel when, in reality, it had taken only about two or three hours. Graham felt incredibly lonely without Milo by his side. Why couldn't they have done this together? What was more romantic than spending the day in paradise?

Liria's atmosphere was fresh. It smelt like pine needles, icicles, and wood shavings. Whenever he inhaled, he swore his lungs were sighing with happiness. Whenever he exhaled, they mourned. The minions appeared extremely bored. They had finally all shuffled off the aircraft, which was now flying to the docking station, and were staring at him with blatant irritation. Clearly, they were not impressed that Milo had left him in charge.

Graham turned around, trying to get his bearings. There was a vast, dark forest to his left and the entrance to a gigantic underground mine to his right. Behind him was the docking station, filled with dormant space vessels, and in front there was a rocky path that seemed to lead to a range of greyish mountains in the distance. Not too far from Liria was a tiny planet where the workers would stay if they were planning on gathering supplies longer than a day. It was against intergalactic law, according to the ferryman, to live on Liria. Visitors took what they needed during the day and let the land rest at night to renew its treasures.

"Please make sure all of your items are checked by myself or the other ferrymen before departing," the short, gruff man grunted at Graham.

Graham nodded and asked where he could get all of the supplies on Milo's list, omitting the section that asked for workers (alive). He swore one of the minions rolled its beady red eyes. It was going to be quite difficult getting fifty workers to board the aircraft willingly. Hopefully, Milo's idea would see them come quietly.

"Glarafae in the forest to the left, ore and melting pots to the right. If you want any beasts or plants, you have to go down the path in front of you and look around the base of the mountains. Some caves will have what you need, but be careful. The animals don't take kindly to people who want to eat them. We are not held responsible for what happens to you there."

Graham swallowed nervously. He was going to save that part till last.

He turned to face the minions, all disgusting and leathery.

"Let's start in the forest."

*

All she wanted was to sleep. Instead, Brodie found herself back in the Cavern of Blue, lounging on the chaise and admiring the sweet-smelling garden. Equas was more hunched over than ever. With Serket dead and no replacement, balance was clearly non-existent.

"I can't believe you knew all this time and nobody listened." Brodie sighed. "I wonder if Asterion will apologise to you."

Her counterpart let out what she assumed was a laugh, but it sounded gravelly. Brodie clenched her teeth at the sound. During their first encounter, Equas had been the only counterpart Milo had never visited. He knew he couldn't fool her and therefore hadn't bothered. She had been trying to tell Asterion for months that something sinister was on its way, but he'd refused to listen. Now the foreseen trouble had arrived.

"I take no pride in gloating," the woman rasped. "He knows I was right, and that is enough for me. What matters now is getting your friend back and reinstating a new counterpart for Scorpio."

The Libran tried to be sensitive, but she couldn't deny the obvious. "Uh, I want to help more than anything, but how do we get started?"

Equas used her left hand to propel herself forward. Slowly, she made her way to where Brodie was lying. The statue was blind, but her other senses were heightened. "I see what you are trying to say. How can we, as a team, find Graham Maltin when I can neither visually see nor move quickly?"

Brodie didn't confirm or deny her counterpart's statement. They remained in silence for several moments, the fountain trickling peacefully in the background. Couldn't she just stay there and let it all play out? In an instant, she dashed that thought away with guilt. She had found Graham on the rooftop before any of the others. She remembered Milo's menacing voice and emotionless expression. *If you do not get rid of her, you will not have my love.* She recalled Graham's torn looks of despair. He had tried to fight it but wasn't strong enough. Neither was she. In a matter of seconds, she had been knocked unconscious on a planet he was no longer a part of. A single tear rolled down her cheek and dropped onto the chaise lounge. Equas reached forward with her right hand and gently scraped the side of Brodie's face.

"You forget, my dear, that I do not need vision to see and feel. I saw what was happening long before it did. I saw what those with actual vision could not."

"So what do you propose? We aren't going to get very far like this." Brodie sat up.

Their team had such potential but unfortunate physical limitations.

"Who says we need to go anywhere?" Equas murmured. "It is a fool's errand to gallivant all over the galaxy without a precise destination. We need to discover exactly which planet holds Milo's new headquarters..."

"Agreed." Brodie nodded. "But how? We have absolutely no place of reference to start. It's not like Milo left any 'Evil Plan' manila folders lying around or emails we can hack into."

"Emails?" Equas grunted.

"It's an electronic letter you receive on a computer...? Never mind! What I'm saying is how can we possibly locate Milo when we have nothing to go on?"

The garden began to buzz in excitement. Brodie turned around and watched the colourful tulips sway in the artificial breeze. The fountain flowed gold, the trees rustled as though they were whispering secrets, and the air around her pulsed with energy. It reminded her of warm summer nights in California with Slade and their group of friends. Endless possibilities and time to be young. She looked to Equas for an answer but saw that she was completely alone. A portal similar to the one Garth had created in Bouquet Reserve rippled in the distance.

"Are you coming?" Equas's voice boomed from every corner of the Cavern of Blue.

Brodie leapt up from the lounge and ran to the portal. It looked like a fathomless black hole and not at all inviting.

"Where does this lead?" she yelled.

If Slade had been there right then, he would have forbidden her to enter. Despite being younger, he always felt the need to protect her.

"If you want to be noticed and earn your place amongst your friends, take a leap and meet me in the Place of Pages."

Equas's voice sounded nearby, but Brodie knew the Place of Pages, whatever that was, was not in the Mission Base. It might not even be on Bastion…

With eyes closed and hands clenched, she walked into the unknown.

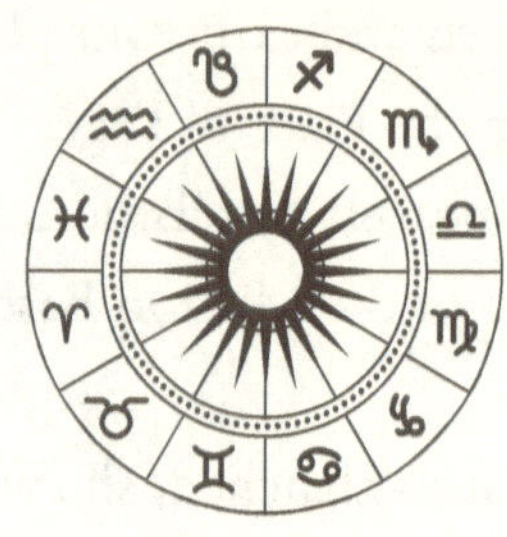

Chapter 9

Great Minds

The Mission Base was buzzing. The game was on and every second count-ed. Asterion had fixed the gaping purple door with a wave of his hand. Garth had given everybody access to all of the Coloured Caverns, not just their own. The archways, in their many colours, gleamed invitingly around the circumference of the cave. The Astro A Team had been given forty-five minutes to shower, change, and stuff their faces at the buf-fet. Luckily, Capricorns were known for their patience. Aegipan waited with amusement as Ronan said his farewell to Danni. Everybody else had gone into their respective Coloured Caverns with their counterparts. Charlotte hadn't even bothered to wait for Danni, following Castor and Pollux like a drooling servant.

"I feel so weird knowing the goat is watching us," his girlfriend mut-tered. She looked much more comfortable now in yellow skinny jeans, a cropped jumper, and considerably less makeup. Effortlessly beautiful. He couldn't wait to be back on their planet, doing normal couple things. Watching movies in bed, cooking dinner for his father again, going to the beach…

Aegipan cleared his throat rather dramatically.

"Maybe you shouldn't call him 'the goat' or anything of that nature." Ronan grinned.

He wasn't comfortable knowing Danni was about to spend quality time with awful people who had tried to hurt her before, but he had to let it go. If anybody could make them see sense, she could. After all, he was a completely different guy to the ignorant, negative one she had met at the library.

Danni ran her fingers through his sandy blond hair. He loved how she had to stand on tiptoe to do it. He leaned in and kissed her softly.

"When all this is over, promise me one thing?"

"Anything." She smiled. Her breath was minty fresh.

"Let's go on a date. A proper one. I feel weird that I've confessed my love for you but have never paid for any of your meals."

She pressed her cheek against his and laughed. It was a sound he could gladly get used to.

"Deal! Although you will be pleased to know I'm a very low-maintenance kinda gal. You don't have to pay for my meals or open car doors for me. My ideal date is stargazing in a field on the hood of your car."

Ronan would've laughed at the idea of stargazing in the past. He had never been a fan of 'woo' stuff, as he called it. Now, the idea of lying side by side in the middle of nowhere, looking up at the vast universe, sounded like his idea of heaven. He missed his little brother, Brandon, and his father. Thanks to Garth, they had no idea he had ever left, but he felt their absence strongly. "Find a woman who makes you a better man, Dad," he wanted to tell him. His selfish mother had abandoned them for a superficial life. She had left destruction and damage behind. Danni was clearing the rubble one rock at a time. They would have the kind of relationship he wished his parents had had from the beginning.

He kissed her nose in response.

"It's funny, we are light years away from home on a planet surrounded by astrological beings, and you cannot wait to stargaze?"

"Don't you see?" Danni exclaimed. "That's how I'll know this was real. Whenever I miss Bastion or feel like I must have been dreaming, the stars will remind me."

"Let's make this a place worth remembering and get Graham back," Ronan declared.

The pair kissed one last time and walked to opposite ends of the Mission Base. Aegipan was leaning against the wall next to the Cavern of Black.

"Aren't you glad you listened to me and professed your love for Danielle Hamilton?" the counterpart bleated obnoxiously.

"Oh, shut up, you old goat…"

*

The valley of the Unsigned seemed untouched. A pale river ran through the low hills beyond the decrepit observatory of Constellar. On both sides of the river, tiny ramshackle houses sat side by side. There really were only about fifty Unsigned in total, including Garth. They were the equivalent of orphans who didn't know their dates of birth. Wasabi had never known her parents. She had been adopted by a loving mother and father who were quite old and could no longer have children of their own. They had lived on Bastion. When they both passed away, Wasabi had been sent to the valley.

Children of Unsigned parents knew their zodiac signs but remained in the valley with their families. Wasabi had never given much thought to being different. A lot of the citizens around Bastion adored her. Sometimes they would hang out at the tattoo parlour just to talk and watch her work. Others would get up on stage with her and dance when she was playing a set. Now the majority of them were gone. Wasabi rarely stayed in the valley. She spent many nights sleeping inside her adoptive father's hardware store, which she had turned into her tattoo parlour after he passed. It made her feel closer to him. Her mother had been a retired librarian for a secret library that she had refused to speak about. Wasabi had convinced herself that her mother had been a spy or an assassin and just couldn't reveal what her true profession was.

She wasn't sure how she was supposed to convince her neighbours to move back to Bastion. They had made comfortable, peaceful lives here, and she figured most of them would be offended by the suggestion. What would the elders think? The elders…were they even still alive? The elders were on a board made up of three women and two men who had lived on Bastion all of their lives and had been very involved in the community throughout their time. They answered to Asterion, who answered to the counterparts. Wasabi had seen them getting absolutely sozzled at Constellar on many a night, drunk on their 'power' and occasionally leaving with a younger companion.

All five did not look kindly on the Unsigned, but they had allowed Wasabi to at least keep her father's store and work two jobs in town. They hated that Garth was the Chief Advisor to Asterion. It was a downright insult in their eyes. The elders lived in town along with the rest of the residents. There was no rich part of Bastion. The counterparts were the only 'royals' of the planet. Wasabi wondered what *they* thought about the Unsigned. They didn't seem to mind Garth. It had been so surreal hanging out with all of them earlier in the Mission Base. She would be sworn to secrecy once everything went back to normal. If it ever did.

Shivering in the wind, Wasabi pulled her rough grey coat tighter around her blue jeans and knit green jumper. Ambrite, Parry, and Brodie had been kind enough to lend her some clothes after she showered in the Mission Base. Leaving Ambrite had been difficult. She barely knew her, but they had connected almost instantly. Wasabi had never bothered finding love on Bastion. She didn't know any lesbians willing to date an Unsigned. Ambrite was a breath of fresh air. She didn't care about labels and possessed a gentle soul beneath her edgy demeanour. After hearing her tragic confessions in the Mission Base, Wasabi wanted to be her girlfriend more than ever.

They had both been neglected by their parents in different ways. They shared a similar style and hardened outer shell for protection. Ambrite stood up for what she believed in, and so did Wasabi. She had never been ashamed about being an Unsigned or liking girls. What was there to be embarrassed about? A lot of the Unsigned didn't venture near Bastion for fear of ridicule. Wasabi mingled with the townspeople on a regular basis. Ambrite had that same confidence. She was what people back on Earth called a 'vegan'. Wasabi had no idea what that was, but it didn't seem to be a very common thing. She liked that.

"People fear what they don't understand," the Taurus had stated matter-of-factly.

Ambrite had told her as they were getting dressed that she was the first in the Astro A Team to get a Taurus tattoo on her ankle. It had inspired her group to do the same. Wasabi had knelt down and traced the symbol with her finger, causing Ambrite to shiver.

"Maybe one day I'll show you all of mine." Wasabi winked. Her new friend had blushed adorably.

They hadn't had a chance to discuss Ambrite's biggest revelation: she was immortal. She was going to remain there on Bastion. Finally, someone Wasabi cared about wasn't going to leave her like everybody else had. There was just the small, or not so small, matter of Hunter. Wasabi was fascinated by him. From what she had deduced, he was madly in love with Ambrite (that much was obvious) but was furious that she didn't feel the same way. He was even more enraged by Ambrite's decision to remain on Bastion. Wasabi was torn between wanting to comfort him and wanting to tell him to suck it up. She did not appreciate the glares he threw in her direction as if she had somehow bewitched Ambrite. He was going to have to accept and respect her Taurean's choice. If she wasn't mistaken, Parry seemed quite into him and had a similar do to Ambrite's, although hers was bright red. Whatever happened, Wasabi was content that she had a potential new companion to start over with.

She made her way down the steep hill to the community of houses on the left side of the river. Her house was at the far back, right near the wooden bridge that ran over the water. It was a simple stone cottage with one bedroom, a kitchen, a bathroom, and a living area. A small supply of starlight heated and lit up the valley homes, but it was never enough. She was constantly freezing in her house, hence spending more time on Bastion. Her neighbours all had the same structure of home, with more or less space depending on the number of occupants. In the evenings, they would bring food out by the river, and anybody was welcome to join them for a chat.

"We never see you there, dear," Mrs. Borea had once said. She was a widowed mother with two Cancerian twins who loved marvelling at Wasabi's tattoos.

"One day, when I'm no longer so tired, I'll be there." Wasabi had laughed.

But she was always tired. She worked all day and night. She stole naps in between sets or clients at the parlour. Something had to give.

Wasabi opened her front door with the key. The cold stone walls suddenly felt very claustrophobic. She pulled a slice of slightly stale bread from the cupboard and nibbled at it, slumping onto her ratty, ugly brown couch. Her eyes began to glaze over as the exhaustion and excitement of the night before caught up. She pulled the musty couch throw over her aching body and curled up. Whatever the world needed right now, it could wait…

*

Ronan knew their plan would be all logic and no action. How could it not be? They were Capricorns! For some reason, Aegipan had decided to morph into his human form. He looked like a stereotypical odd professor, right down to the spectacles and patches on his green suit. They were leaning against the rocks where Ronan had first spotted his counterpart in the Cavern of Black. The grass was completely covered in random bits of trash. It was an environmental hazard.

"Let's put our great minds together, my boy, and show them how fit we are to rule." The goat clapped. Hands, not hooves.

Ronan rolled his eyes. This astrological pissing contest was starting to irritate him. None of them were fit to rule, in his opinion.

"Great minds do think alike, as they say," Ronan drawled sarcastically.

Aegipan looked down his nose at him, spectacles balancing on the bridge. "Do you not want to win fair Danielle's heart further with your victory?"

"I've already won her heart." Ronan snorted. "What would make me *keep* her heart is getting our friend back safely."

"Well, what are we waiting for? Tell me everything there is to know about your friend Graham Maltin."

Ronan didn't see the point, but he started from the very beginning. He told Aegipan about Graham's close friendship with Parry, how he had nearly left the group because he felt too different, how they all had convinced him to stay, and his strange behaviour after visiting his Coloured Cavern. He finished by detailing the events of the night before, finding a confused Graham on the rooftop and flying away with Milo.

Aegipan listened with an intense, scary expression on his face. It was very off-putting. When Ronan stopped speaking, his counterpart nodded slowly. "I see… So what I've deduced is that Graham has been manipulated by Milo somehow through his stinger. He must have been injected with the substance upon their first meeting and ordered to manipulate you all in order to further Milo's ambitions. What I want to know is how did Milo kill Serket to begin with? We counterparts are very much invincible. He must've absorbed Serket's powers through the process of murder and used them to coerce Graham to do his bidding."

Ronan opened his mouth to speak, but Aegipan cut him off before he could make a sound.

"Furthermore, from what I have gathered, your friend Graham has felt vulnerable all of his life. He is different because he prefers men, no? I don't find this to be a matter of importance. Ancient history saw men of all classes frolicking with one another, but perhaps in the modern day it is frowned upon?"

"It's not frowned upon unless you're a homophobic idiot," Ronan explained. "Graham just felt a bit like an outsider because he was more mature and 'flamboyant' than we were. Parry told us back on Earth that Graham wants love more than anything else. He is a hopeless romantic... if you know what that means?"

Aegipan shook his head. Ronan noticed he had tiny little horns peeking out of his messy hair. "I don't, but it doesn't matter. What matters is that Graham was seduced by substance, yes, but also because somewhere inside him, he wanted to be. Milo showed a fake romantic interest, and that was all it took. He preyed on Graham's vulnerabilities and desires. He could not have achieved the same outcome with any of you."

Ronan let out a laugh. "Well, that's true, but that's because we prefer women, not shady-looking men in capes."

Aegipan bleated in anger, which made Ronan jump. "Forget about the sexual interest and listen to what I am telling you. Graham was influenced because he was romantically lonely. If Milo wanted to get you on his side, Master Tate, he would have threatened your family or Danielle. The poison could do only so much, but the heart...well, that is the only organ that can blind the brain."

Ronan recalled the night Graham wanted to leave. It had felt like years ago, but it was the same evening they had all left Earth through the pond portal. He had seemed wise beyond his years. He knew exactly what he wanted and wasn't afraid to share it with the group. He wanted to feel accepted above everything else. They could shower him with friendship, but none of them could be his answer to true, everlasting love.

"Are you saying that Graham can fight this poison? That if he used enough willpower, he would see right through it?"

Aegipan straightened up. He had terrible posture as a human. "That is exactly what I am saying, Ronan. If we can discover how Milo absorbed Serket's powers, we may learn how to reverse it. That is the first step. Once we have that information, we need to find Milo and Graham. He will continue to inject his subject, but if you all work together, you may just be the antidote."

Arching backwards, Ronan let the rocks massage his lower spine. The Cavern of Black could've been a nice place to hang out if Aegipan hadn't treated it like a garbage dump.

"You're making it sound way too easy, but I'm not convinced. Where does one even begin to source that information?"

Aegipan wiggled his bushy eyebrows. "The Place of Pages, of course!"

Chapter 10

Team Up!

"Damn those temptresses," Garth growled as Sirena and Calypsee sashayed through the aquarium. He was standing in Asterion's private chamber, trying with all his might not to indulge the Piscean mermaids.

"They get you every single time." Asterion chuckled, emerging from his bedroom wearing a freshly pressed robe. His golden sandals glinted with every step. Garth noticed with amusement that his beard had been trimmed ever so slightly.

"My lord, you are the keeper of the flipping stars! You don't need to scrub up for those buffoons."

He caught a flash of sparkly scales and whirled around the room. Nothing. They were messing with him. Stinking merbabes with their sexy tails.

"This is not for them, Garth. It's for me. I don't venture out very often, and I'm about to deliver delicious news. I'm not going to pretend telling the Council they were wrong about Milo isn't going to be extremely satisfying."

"I'm sorry, but how stupid are they?" Garth huffed, feeling dizzy. "Surely they've noticed he's been gone awhile? How long can he claim to be on representative business?"

"You know the rules on Cassius. The representatives serve for two years. In that time, they can do whatever they please, provided they check in from time to time. He hasn't been gone that long, actually. Also, I am the stupid one, Garth. Equas warned me about Milo and I didn't listen."

A girlish giggle made Garth spin on his heel. Calypsee, the raven-haired one, was pressing her…'shells' against the aquarium glass. The Chief Advisor's jaw dropped open. It was no fair. He took a step towards the tank, but a strong arm pulled him back.

"Be gone, Calypsee," Asterion hissed.

Calypsee pouted, let out a deafening wail, and swam off.

"Thank you for saving me from myself, oh great one," Garth whimpered.

"Maybe it's best we get away from here." Asterion frowned. "You never seem to learn. If you don't pay them any attention, they won't try to seduce you so much."

Garth took off his top hat and wiped his sweaty dome. He needed a cold shower. "I don't know how Drew did it. How he fought them off. We don't all have Hannahs to keep us on the straight and narrow."

Garth felt Asterion's hand pat him on the back. They were pals, him and the kKeeper. Asterion had never treated him differently because he was an Unsigned. He had been born without parents. Well, apparently, he had a mother and father who had been murdered on a research mission, but he couldn't remember them. They had been intergalactic explorers searching for relics on uncharted planets. For some strange reason, they had thought it wise to bring a newborn with them on their dangerous expedition. Garth had been found howling inside their shuttle, wrapped only in brown linen, with a dragon necklace hidden in a labelled pouch. Their remains had been kept from him for obvious reasons. Asterion had been the one to discover him. He had cared for Garth inside the Mission Base until he was a teenager. When the boy was old enough, he had been given the choice of immortality. He'd refused.

"Why would I want to live forever with an old man? That is so boring!"

"I need you, Garth," Asterion had begged. "Please reconsider. Our jobs are vital to this planet's protection."

"I didn't ask for this job. Find someone else!"

Yes, Garth had been a bratty, hormonal adolescent.

When Garth had reached adulthood, he was approached again with the same life-changing offer.

"Garth, I've let you live your wild teenage life. You've partied at Constellar, woken up with random women, and done who knows what else. It's time to step up and take responsibility. By the way, I had to wipe all of their memories because you know we are the only ones allowed in the Mission Base."

"Thanks, man." Garth had laughed. "I was getting tired of them hanging around me all the time. You cannot tie this man down!"

"Garth," Asterion had pressed, "I found you on a random planet as a baby. Now, I don't believe in coincidences. Never have. I found you for a reason."

"Hmm," Garth had pondered. "Speaking of, you never told me why you were in such a place to begin with. Do you just spend your spare time looking for babies to raise?"

Asterion had paced impatiently throughout his private chamber. Garth had tried not to be distracted by the mermaid counterparts. They had just started noticing his interest.

"Believe it or not, I had a vision that somebody vital to my future was in danger. I borrowed the Aquarian Air from Ganymede, travelled seven gruelling weeks to a hostile planet, and found you. Unfortunately, I arrived just as your parents were killed by the guardian beast. Tell me that doesn't mean anything."

"It doesn't mean anything!"

Asterion had been about to give up when, suddenly, he ran into his bedroom and came back out a second later with a small brown pouch. The name Garth was embroidered in tiny letters under the drawstring. Asterion opened it up and let something silver fall into his palm. It took a while before Garth registered that it was a necklace with a dragon pendant. He had felt instantly drawn to it.

"This is the only thing your parents left in the cloth you were wrapped in. I have been studying it for years, trying to decipher its power. It was obvious your parents were relic hunters. They must've found this on a previous expedition and wanted you to have it."

Garth stretched out a hand to take it. Asterion had hesitated but passed it to him.

"So…what does it do?"

"It bestows the wearer with the ability to track important things. It can also reveal memories from the past and create portals. Your parents gave you the most wondrous gift. Don't waste it."

That night, as Garth got ready for bed, he'd fastened the necklace on and refused to take it off ever again. The next morning, he had asked for immortality. What he had never told Asterion, not even till this day, was that he had used the necklace to recall memories of his parents. He had seen only fragments, but it was enough. They had been born on Bastion but refused to wear specific colours. It didn't fit their 'free-spirited' lifestyle. When they weren't in the valley of the Unsigned, they were off on new adventures. His necklace revealed terrifying monsters, shimmering planets, and dazzling jewels. They had truly lived. They had died doing what they loved. The last fragment had shown a baby being held and sung to with deep love. Garth had sobbed when the vision faded.

Over the years, Garth had not changed appearance, but his attitude had undergone a complete makeover. He began to see Asterion as a friend and father figure. They bonded over their mutual annoyance for the counterparts, went on grand adventures, and worked brilliantly as a team. If anybody said a bad word about the Keeper of the Stars, Garth would sock them in the face. Eternal life wasn't so terrible when you got to spend it with a man like Asterion.

He gazed at the wise Keeper now with adoration. He owed him everything. Quite literally his entire life.

"Let's go before I propose to Calypsee…again."

*

The Maiden had decided to form a team with her two allied counterparts. From her cold expression, Slade figured she would probably use them both and claim the victory as her own once they found Graham. Ganymede was no longer a sane, functioning person. He kept bouncing on the balls of his feet with a sickly look of adoration at his unrequited love. Cerus, on the other hand, could not have looked more bored if he tried.

"We will increase our chances of victory if we band together," the beautiful counterpart declared.

"So, when we find him, who gets to rule?" Cerus grunted. It's not something you can divide three ways."

Why did Cerus even consider himself an ally of the Maiden, anyway? Slade wondered. He was so obnoxious and full of superior airs. His question was answered a second later when she turned to the bull and stroked his nose lovingly. A look of pure bliss crossed his face. He pushed his ringed nose against her palm for more affection.

"We are still in competition, my darling," she crooned, patting him further. "Whoever is the first to make contact with the boy is the rightful ruler. However, the counterpart in power can favour his or her two allies over all the rest. Is that not fair?"

Ambrite coughed loudly, causing the three counterparts to face her in annoyance. "Don't forget about the rules. If you want to work as a team, then you must invite myself, Parry, and Slade into the mix. We are to be informed of all plans and make decisions together."

The mission briefing was being held in the Cavern of Green. The sky was a clear blue, and the mock-sun threw radiant rays upon the group. Slade wanted to stretch out on the grass with a good book, listening to the rustle of the tall waving wheat in the wind. The field seemed to stretch on for miles. There were rolling green hills in the background that could probably never be reached, such was the illusion. A cute little barn with a thatched roof stood off to the side. It looked like part of a movie set. Slade was certain if he attempted to open the door, there would just be a wall of brick.

Ambrite was standing her ground, locked in an epic staring contest with the counterparts. The Aquarian imagined the moment she realised she had been tricked into immortality. She had been standing there, in that very place. How does one even begin to process that kind of information? Slade had never been more glad of his own mortality. To live forever meant loneliness. It meant a world where nothing was ever enough. Impending death forced him to live and create memories. It gave him a chance to write an epic story with a satisfying ending. Imagining a story without an ending made his head hurt.

Parry stood sullen and silent. She hadn't spoken much since the team reunion. He suspected a lot of it had to do with Graham's abduction.

"Very well." The Maiden broke the tense silence. "You may have input, but just remember that we are the carriers of special abilities. Therefore, this gives us a higher status."

If she weren't such an icy bitch, Slade would've joined her fan club with Ganymede. She had piercing blue eyes, deep crimson hair that tumbled down her back in waves, and a knockout figure. Her skin looked porcelain smooth in a grey gown fringed with tiny pearls. She wore a matching string of pearls around her neck, silk grey gloves, and silver stilettos. There was no practicality to her clothing, but damn, did she pull it off! Parry had been beautiful, but the Maiden was beyond flowery adjectives. She was perfection. Untouched. Shame the personality didn't match.

"How could I forget?" Ambrite sneered. "The gigantic pole up your ass is a constant reminder."

Ganymede gasped, Cerus bellowed, Parry produced a subtle grin, and Slade took a step back on instinct.

"How dare you, you preposterous child?" the Maiden spat viciously. "Just because you have immortality does not give you cause to speak such filth!"

Ambrite didn't flinch. "I want to work together as equals, not as side-kicks. This has nothing to do with my immortality. If you want respect, you have to earn it, lady."

Slade sighed. This was not a promising start.

The Maiden was speechless, clearly not accustomed to being spoken to with such sass.

"Guys, can we please stop arguing?" Slade interrupted. He was not going to be trampled by hooves or heels. "Graham needs us. This is so stupid."

Parry shot him a grateful smile. Ambrite nodded, her cheeks reddening.

The Maiden softened, pressing a thoughtful dainty finger to her ruby-red lips. "The boy speaks truth. We must focus on the task at hand or else we will be bested."

So close yet so far…

"Let's discuss strategy. As you all know, I have access to a magic mirror. Ganymede, you have your Aquarian Air, and, Cerus, your sense of smell could track a rotting rodent five galaxies away."

"What does your mirror do besides ruin people's lives?" Parry muttered.

The Maiden gazed at Parry with sympathy. Slade began to wonder if she was just a big softie underneath it all.

"My dear, my mirror showed whom you would become if you valued beauty over everything else. It appears you've made some major changes since our last meeting…"

Parry touched her cropped hair insecurely. Whatever that mirror had shown, it couldn't have been pretty.

"That is not all it can do," the counterpart continued. "My looking glass can reveal whomever I wish to see in the present moment."

"Well, if that's the case, what the hell are we waiting for?" Ambrite cried. "Let's go to your pad and find Graham, already!"

The Maiden sniffed at Ambrite as if she were a bad smell. "Yes, child, but the glass will reveal only where he is; it won't specify which planet he is on. If it shows him only sitting in a room, that is not sufficient information."

"Still, it's better than nothing," Slade said. "We might be able to identify where he is by his surrounding markers."

Ganymede nodded, clutching his urn tightly. "If we are able to locate Graham, we will use my Aquarian Air to reach him. It will be a wild ride, but it's the most accurate."

Despite the artificial setting, the sun began to set over the field. The warmth slowly dissipated, the wind stopped blowing, and creatures similar to cicadas started to chirp. It was a sign that they needed to get moving.

"What about you, Cerus?" Ganymede turned to the surly bull. "Shall you sniff him out once we arrive?"

The Maiden let out a tinkly laugh.

Cerus lowered his horns in warning. "You may find me useless, but I am the only counterpart with access to the Tree of Life. I have not seen you grant the gift of immortality before."

"Your 'gift' makes others miserable. Just look at the girl." Ganymede pointed to a fuming Ambrite.

"Yes, well at least I don't pine after the Maiden like some pathetic fool," Cerus sneered. "She will never be interested in a toga-wearing pretty boy like you."

"Enough!" the Maiden screeched.

Slade bit his tongue in fright. "Ow!"

Parry and Ambrite rushed over to him, patting their pockets for tissues. Blood was pouring from his mouth.

"Damn, I don't have any tissues," Ambrite huffed. "Do you?"

Parry shook her head. Cerus trotted up to Slade with a smarmy look on his face.

"This is what I can do," he announced. He swished his tail clockwise, then anti-clockwise. In an instant, the bleeding had vanished and the pain was gone. Slade touched his lip in astonishment.

"You healed me."

"Big deal," Ganymede scoffed. "We can all heal humans."

"Actually, you cannot," Cerus retorted. "You can heal Aquarians. The Maiden can heal Virgos. I can heal any sign, not just Taurus. If we find Graham badly injured, I can heal him in an instant, no matter the damage. Serket is no longer alive, so without me, the boy could potentially die."

Ganymede crossed his arms with a pout. The gesture made his urn stick out at a funny angle.

"If you can heal any of the signs, then where the hell were you during the scorpion attack?" Ambrite shouted. "We needed you. So many lost their lives because their counterparts weren't present. You were the wildcard that could've saved them all."

It was the bull's turn to look ashamed. "I am sorry. I did not realise the gravity of the situation until it was too late. I, unlike the Gemini twins, actually do care. Whether you choose to believe this or not is up to you, but I do. Let me make amends by making myself available to Graham should he require medical attention."

It seemed to be enough for Ambrite. She stepped back and shrugged.

"No more time to waste." The Maiden took charge once more. "First stop is my Coloured Cavern. We determine where Graham is by what we see. Ganymede will then so kindly allow us to use his Aquarian Air. We travel to said destination, recover the boy and heal him if necessary, and return to Bastion triumphant."

"My lady, I will follow your lead without question." Ganymede bowed.

Cerus snorted a little too loudly.

They were about to leave when Slade remembered something Ganymede had told him in the tower.

"Wait a minute. You said that Aquarian Air takes you the full distance of travel. What if Graham's location is weeks or months away?"

The group turned to Ganymede for a response. It was an almost comedic moment of silence broken by chirping in the field.

"I will be of no use to this team, then." Ganymede hung his head. "This is my only power. If it takes months of travel, we will need Garth to create a portal with his talisman. The other counterparts can create small portals to specific places, but they cannot jump to unknown planets. I'm hoping that I can be of service; otherwise, I am clearly not fit to rule…"

Slade touched his counterpart's shoulder. Ganymede produced a weak smile.

"It's funny," he began. "The counterparts are so similar to the Astro A Team. We all just want to feel accepted and special. We don't have one ruler. Danni may have started this whole thing, but she has never seen herself as superior to the rest of us. You guys could learn a thing or two from us mortals."

Parry and Ambrite smiled at him. He braced himself, ready for the counterparts to laugh in his face, but nothing happened. They merely looked thoughtful.

"Shall we?" Slade grinned.

He could've sworn the fake cicadas were cheering them on as they left the Cavern of Green.

Chapter 11

The Hunt

When the world begins to fall apart, make sure you are there to do your part, Leonis had told him at Constellar. He didn't like himself. And yet here they were, working together. When Crawford first met Leonis in the Cavern of Gold, he had been accused several times of being a coward and a disgrace to his zodiac sign. The counterpart had ordered him not to return until he had learnt self-respect. At the club, Leonis had apologised for calling him a coward, having known about his break-up with Charlotte. However, he still expected the boy to commit an act of great bravery. Now more than ever, Crawford had the opportunity to be a hero.

Both boys were shirtless, hiking through the lush jungle towards the cave beyond the waterfall where they had first met. The humidity hung above them like an oppressive heavy cloud. It reminded Crawford of his trip to Bali when he was fifteen, minus the bout of terrible diarrhoea…

When they reached the lake, they left their shirts, shoes, and pants on the soggy bank and dove in. The water was heavenly. Crystal clear and refreshing. Crawford's body came alive as though his entire being had been dying of thirst. The boys laughed and raced each other to the waterfall. It felt like a carefree friendship where neither person needed to speak in order to connect. In that moment, all of Crawford's troubles were non-existent. Leonis won, of course. He *was* a lion in disguise. With a cheeky grin, he hauled himself up onto the stone slab and waited for Crawford to reach the finish line.

"You know, this is kind of an unfair advantage," Crawford panted out. He pushed with both hands onto the slippery rocks, letting his knees land on the hard surface.

"Perhaps, but in this form I am a mere child just like you," Leonis declared with a sparkle in his eyes.

"I'm not a 'mere' child," Crawford growled. "I'm a man."

The pair padded into the cool dark cave. He shivered at the sudden drop in temperature. Leonis chuckled and turned to a pile of driftwood lumped in the centre. Crawford's eyes widened as his counterpart blew a bright ball of fire onto the pieces of wood. Orange flames devoured their target, rising high and burning strong. Crawford sat close, exposing his palms to the heat.

"A man does not simply declare himself a man," Leonis said softly, gazing into the fire. "Age does not matter, nor does appearance. If you want to be a man, act like one. Prove your worth."

Water dripped from the tendrils of Crawford's brown curls. He shuffled backwards so the blaze could continue. He had a feeling that fire born from the mouth of a counterpart could not be so easily doused.

"I will," he sighed. "I want to show you and myself that I'm worthy of being a Leo. I'll do what I can to find Graham. Just point me in the right direction."

The crackling of the flames echoed throughout the cave. There was nothing special about the space, but Crawford could see how happy it made his counterpart. Leonis stretched out his lanky legs and yawned, his teeth sharp even as a human.

"I'm glad you said that." He nodded thoughtfully. "I want you to be in charge of this mission. Whatever you suggest or wherever you go, I'll follow. It's time you stepped up."

Crawford literally stood up at those words. "But…but…" he sputtered. "I don't know where Graham is or even how to travel between planets. How the hell am I supposed to lead a mission? I'm so…ordinary!"

"Crawford, you are not ordinary." Leonis shook his head. "You need to start liking yourself and backing your own capabilities. You know your friend more than I do. Think. Where is a good place to start? Did he provide you with any clues? If you want to go somewhere, tell me and I'll take you there. Just start acting."

Crawford swallowed a dry lump of nervousness. He had absolutely no idea where to begin. Guilt took over as he realised he had never made much of an effort to get to know Graham back on Earth. He was completely and utterly useless. He was about to tell Leonis that he was a failure when he realised the boy had disappeared. The fire was still burning but much lower and less intensely than before. The waterfall rushed in the background, but the cave itself was silent.

"Leonis?" Crawford called. He stood and rubbed the goose-flesh on his arms.

Nothing.

Crawford inhaled deeply and turned to look outside. His counterpart was probably waiting for him in the lake. He edged closer to the mouth of the cave, gingerly stepping over sharp stones and slippery moss. Suddenly, a shadow darted past his field of vision. Crawford turned, feeling a strong sense of déjà-vu. Before he could scream, Leonis, in lion mode, leapt from the darkness and flattened Crawford to the ground, paws pressed on his chest. He knew it was a test, but he screamed anyway.

"Get off me, man! This is not funny!"

Leonis snarled and gnashed his teeth together, saliva dripping from his canines onto Crawford's face. His breath smelled rotten. Crawford tried to push him off, but the beast didn't budge. Leonis lunged forward and nipped at Crawford's ear. The boy let out a yell as blood trickled down his cheek. Instinctively, he stretched out a searching left hand. His palm fastened itself on a sharp stone, and he hurled it with all his might at the lion's head. Leonis yowled and jumped back. His claws curled into the floor in fury. Squatting low with a level gaze, his counterpart wiggled his trunk, ready to pounce.

Crawford took the opportunity to dash towards the fire and pick up a lone piece of driftwood to the side that hadn't been lit. With his left hand clutching his bleeding ear and his right on the stick, Crawford thrust the tip into the flames. It ignited instantly. Before it could burn through, Crawford flung it at Leonis, who was mid-leap. The wood connected with the beast, sending sparks flying. Leonis roared with pain, swatting the fire with frantic paws.

Crawford took the opportunity to race out of the cave and dive into the lake below. With heavy strokes, he propelled his body at rapid pace to the shore where his clothes awaited. His stomach lurched as the blood from his wound infused the water. He refused to look back in case Leonis or the crocodile from last time was following. Crawford took hold of the bank and launched himself up. He grabbed his damp clothes and threw them on quickly, not bothering to tie up the laces of his shoes. As he made for the entrance to the rainforest, a figure with a wicked grin blocked his path.

"Now that's what I'm talking about." Leonis crossed his arms. He looked to be in pristine condition, as though their fight had never taken place.

Crawford gaped at his counterpart for a second before rage took over. "You!" he yelled. Without thinking, he marched over to Leonis and pushed him. The gangly teenager barely flinched. He let his arms dangle by his sides, inviting Crawford to continue. "You could've killed me! What are you playing at? Only a coward strikes when his opponent isn't prepared."

Crawford swung a punch, which Leonis easily sidestepped to avoid. He was laughing hysterically.

"Stop laughing!" Crawford grabbed his shoulders and made to knee him in the unmentionables. The counterpart head-butted Crawford to the floor before he could make contact.

"Hey!" Leonis stopped laughing. "There is a code among men. You just don't go there."

Crawford lay on the dirty floor, head throbbing and ear pulsing. He refused to stand up. Leonis sighed and extended a hand to pull him up. Reluctantly, Crawford accepted. His counterpart placed his hands on the Leo's temples and closed his eyes, muttering softly. The pain lessened into a dull ache and then…nothing. His ear was no longer bleeding.

Crawford stepped back and rubbed his curls awkwardly. "So…what was this all about? Some sort of test?"

"Precisely." Leonis nodded. "You doubted your abilities and I proved you wrong. In the face of danger, you hit a lion with a rock and threw fire at his face. I would say you've got some courage and the ability to think on your feet. Just the perfect two ingredients needed to rescue a friend. Wouldn't you agree?"

A rather large mosquito landed on Crawford's leg, eager for a feast. He slapped his skin, crumpling the hungry insect. Leonis smiled.

"Okay, so maybe I can defend myself when the adrenaline starts flowing. Did you have to bite me?"

"Child, it was a mere nip. You're lucky I didn't do worse. Plus, I have the ability to heal other Leos, so I wouldn't have let it go too far."

A comfortable silence settled between them. Crawford was still on a high from all the action.

"Now, as we were saying before you began to feel like a failure, I would like you to lead this mission. Tell me where to go and what to do. It's entirely in your hands. You know you have what it takes, so no arguments."

Crawford rolled his eyes. He walked back towards the lake, where he slipped his shoes off once more. Leonis stared after him, confused.

"Well…what are you waiting for?" Crawford grinned. "I'm not done kicking your ass."

*

Glarafae sap was disgusting. It smelled like gasoline and medicine mixed together. The texture and consistency churned Graham's stomach. It oozed out of the brown bark in chunks. When it hit the barrels, some of it splashed back onto his hands, thick and sticky. All around him, minions were rolling steel barrels that were available for hire in the forest. They used their stringers to pierce sections of the Glarafae tree and collect as much sap as it could provide. Once the wood had been drained completely, they set to work sawing off full-length logs to cart back.

The thicket of Glarafae towered high above them, stretching on for miles. Tiny specks of light filtered through the branches, but the overall atmosphere was gloomy. Nobody spoke. Human workers all around went about their duties. They did not seem surprised by the ugly, leathery minions attacking the trees with their sharp tails. He met eyes with an unshaven middle-aged man holding an axe. They nodded at one another amicably. Graham wondered if he was a citizen of Bastion. Did he have a family back home? Were they on the list Milo had given him? Would he come back with them willingly?

He must have been staring, deep in thought, because the worker cleared his throat uncomfortably.

"Are you all right, buddy?" His gruff voice reached Graham in concern. The man had a thick, bushy eyebrow raised. His hair was sandy blond, wild and quite long. He was dressed in sturdy maroon cotton overalls and a thick woollen jumper underneath. Scorpio. Dark steel-capped boots protected his feet. Eyes, blue as the ocean, searched his in concern.

"Oh, yes, sorry." Graham shook his head.

"I've never seen you on Liria before." The man stepped forward. He rested his axe against the trunk of a nearby Glarafae and held out a gloved hand.

Graham shook the stranger's hand with a smile. "That's because I've never been here before. I'm working for M…" Graham stopped himself before he revealed too much. "I'm from another galaxy, gathering supplies to build a new home."

"Which planet would that be?" The man scratched his blond beard.

Even if Graham knew the name of Milo's planet, he wouldn't reveal it. That would disappoint his love greatly.

"Maltin," Graham lied. "Not many people know about it."

The worker narrowed his eyes. Graham felt his hands begin to moisten in anxiety. It was obvious the stranger didn't believe him. He was about to excuse himself when the man let out a deep chuckle.

"You meet all sorts of individuals working here. I'm Issac. My home planet is Bastion."

Bastion. Graham had come from there. His friends were still there. What were they up to? His head ached at the vague thought of them. A sudden surge rushed through his heart as a vivacious redhead with emerald eyes clouded his field of vision. Parry! She hadn't been there that night. She didn't know his good news. Graham smiled at different memories of him and Parry gabbing about cute boys at Maltin's Tanning Salon. They would paint each other's toenails and feed each other chocolates from boxes of assorted treats. If she had seen Milo, she would've swooned and encouraged their union with animated hand gestures. Why hadn't she been there? When would he get to see her again? A throbbing in his palm brought him back to the present moment. He looked down at the red mark and then to Issac, who, once again, was gazing at him with confusion.

"Graham," he replied. "I know people who live on Bastion. Friends."

Issac picked up his axe again and what resembled a closed metal pail.

Graham wrinkled up his nose at the smell. Glarafae sap. Issac caught the reaction and laughed.

"You get used to it. My wife makes jewellery back home on Bastion. She uses this stuff as glue. After this, I'm heading to the mine to grab her usual request of coloured stones. They sell really well. Even though we've got a little one, she spends many a night at Constellar making quite a pretty penny from drunk customers. The neighbours don't mind looking after little Charlie, though, when I'm here. Constellar is our nightclub, by the way. Do you want to join me? I sure could use the company."

Issac seemed nice enough, Graham thought. It couldn't hurt to have someone to talk to and show him around. The minions were not exactly the warmest 'colleagues'.

"Sure, why not? I need to go there anyway. Can you show me where to get iron ore, silver ore, and gold bars?"

"The iron and the silver are easy – that stuff is everywhere." Issac nodded. "The gold bars are deeper in the heart of the mine. We may need some assistance, but it can be done. What are you building that requires gold? You're not undercover royalty, are you?"

Issac grinned, but Graham laughed nervously. *Not yet.*

The pair began to walk towards the entrance of the Glarafae forest. The minions, who had finished gathering resources, eyed them suspiciously. Graham would never get used to their creepy red eyes following him.

It was at that moment Issac noticed them watching.

"Are they with you?" he said in a hushed tone.

"Ah…yeah," Graham muttered. "They are helping me with my big order."

Issac widened his eyes, then tapped his nose in excitement. "You are royalty, aren't you? That's why you haven't lifted a finger since you got here. Don't worry, I won't tell anyone. It will be a pleasure to serve you and your odd-looking army… No offense."

Graham decided to play along. It was much easier that way. Plus, it was far simpler to lie when the truth was mixed in.

"None taken! Yes, that's correct. We require supplies for the kingdom of Maltin, but please keep it to yourself."

Issac nodded eagerly, looking quite starstruck. Graham turned to the minions, excited to act the part.

"Please take all of the supplies to get checked before loading them onto the aircraft," he boomed. "I will meet you inside the mines."

Milo's army glared at him, their tails twitching. Graham let out a breath as they began to move a second later with the vats of sap and bundles of logs in tow.

"If only my son could see this," Issac marvelled. "He's obsessed with other galaxies and intergalactic creatures."

Graham let out a shaky laugh. "Shall we make our way to the mines? I have a lot of work to do back on Maltin."

Issac spun to face him, tearing his gaze from the grumbling minions marching out of the thicket. "Absolutely. As you wish, my liege. Come this way."

Graham listened to Issac as they walked through the moody forest. He was so grateful to have found a friend amongst the unfamiliar. As Issac nattered away about his family, Graham pulled out the long piece of parchment Milo had entrusted to him. He hoped against hope that he wouldn't see the worst. His heart sank at the very first name scrawled on the paper: *Issac Venturion – husband of Ella Venturion and father to Charlie Venturion.*

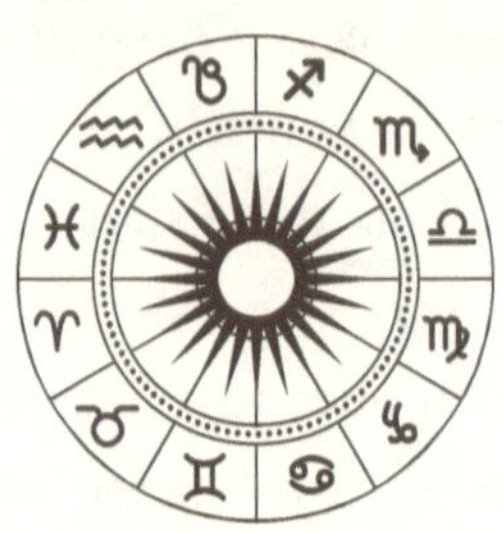

Chapter 12

Sibling Rivalry

It was official. The best way to get over somebody was to get under a counterpart. Especially when the rebound in question looked like *that.* Charlotte drooled as Castor wrestled with his brother sans shirt. He may have had the personality of driftwood, but his looks more than made up for that fact. The brother, Pollux, was also pleasant to look at, but Charlotte had always preferred blonds. Maybe that was why she and Crawford had never worked out. Or maybe it was because he was a douche who couldn't make up his mind.

She saw the way he had looked at Danni at Constellar. Now that her 'twin' was happy and in love with somebody else, he wanted her back. Typical! If he had wanted to break up, he could've done it in a much softer way. She recoiled at the memory of his anger. The way his nostrils had flared as he yelled, "The entire group hates you and you're nothing but a whinging brat!" Was he telling the truth? Did everybody really hate her? Charlotte had only really confessed her change of heart to Brodie before the poor girl was knocked out, so it would make sense that nobody else had warmed to her yet. Brodie had probably forgotten everything. Still, she was going to try to prove herself useful once and for all.

She turned to an exasperated Danni with an unnaturally genuine smile. "Hey, girl, you and Ronan are endgame, by the way. I ship you both hard-core."

The Gemini met her gaze with a furrowed brow. "I have no idea what you just said…"

The pair were sitting on the grass by the golden water in the Cavern of Yellow. The counterpart brothers were completely ignoring them. Their shouts and grunts rang across the room as they fought to prove who was physically stronger. It was irritatingly hot.

"I mean," Charlotte drawled, "you two are great together. I think it's an awesome match."

Danni's eyes widened first in confusion, then horror. "Oh my gosh, you drank from the water, didn't you? I have to call Garth somehow. Hopefully he can work some magic to get it out of your system."

Charlotte let out a heavy sigh. The hardest part of trying to turn over a new leaf was the lack of trust. It was going to take a hell of a lot of convincing to change the minds of twelve teenagers.

"Eww, I didn't drink river water. Who knows what makes it so yellow…?"

Danni rubbed her palms down the legs of her skinny jeans. "Okay, so you didn't drink it, but what is your game? Are you going to try to break us up too?"

The comment stung, but it was well deserved. Charlotte had been an undeniable bitch.

"I'm sorry for what I did. I was a horrible person, but since Crawford dumped me…"

"Crawford dumped you?" Danni jumped up. "Why? What happened? What did you do?"

"Excuse me." Charlotte bristled. "Why do you assume it was something I did?"

Danni threw her a deadpan look.

"Fine." Charlotte frowned. "I guess he was over my crappy behaviour, and I get it, but he didn't have to scream at me and say that everybody hates me."

Danni settled back down next to Charlotte, crossing her legs. "He said that? We don't hate you, Charlotte. I mean…you're not our favourite person, but can you blame us?"

A loud *oof* made the girls' heads whip up. Castor had one bare foot pressing down on Pollux's chest. His brother lay flat on his back with his hands up in surrender.

Charlotte caught Danni rolling her eyes and grinned. "Say what you want about me… I'm nowhere near as bad as they are."

"Ugh, nobody is," Danni groaned.

The girls cracked up and, in that moment, things felt normal. Charlotte was happy.

"So how do we get them to stop this macho madness and find Graham?"

The twins were up and sparring again, this time with blunt spears. Charlotte winced with every connecting *thwack*. This could go on all day.

"Hey!" Danni yelled.

Castor and Pollux continued to dance around one another with lightness in their feet and selective deafness in their ears.

"Hey," Danni shouted again. "When are you two going to take this competition seriously? The more time you waste here, the less chance you have of winning."

Charlotte smiled at the pricking of their ears. Now they were paying attention.

Castor threw his spear down and turned to glare at Danni. Once Asterion had revived Charlotte, she learned how close the light-haired twin had been to destroying Danni's face with his foot. At the time, she hadn't really cared, but now she felt a strong urge to protect her 'star sister'.

"Training is not a waste of time," he sneered, green eyes flashing. "We must be prepared; otherwise, how shall we be victorious?"

Danni jumped up again in rage. Charlotte grabbed at her hand, but she shook it off angrily.

"Are you freaking kidding me? All you ever do is 'prepare'. You're both as fit and strong as you're ever going to be, so what are you waiting for? Are you just scared of what's out there?"

Charlotte leapt to her feet, ready to shield Danni if need be. Castor clenched his fists in fury. Pollux had his hands on his hips in disgust. They were both so dramatic.

"Scared," Castor spat. "We are the bravest, fittest, and strongest, as you say, and most intelligent in the zodiac. What do we have to be scared of? You should watch your tongue that I don't rip it out. The old fool and his simpering pet aren't around to save you this time."

Charlotte stood behind Danni and hissed urgently in her ear, "Be careful! He's right. Asterion and Garth have left for Cassius. If we provoke them, they will mutilate our pretty faces. Yes, I'm admitting you are pretty. Not as much as me, but…"

"Shut up!" Danni hissed back. "I am not going to be bossed around anymore by these jerks. Graham is in danger and they are doing absolutely nothing. Let them try to hurt me. My dad taught me how to kick a man in his family jewels when I was little, and I never forgot it. Counterpart or no, that will make them cry."

"What the hell are family jewels? And don't tell me to shut up!"

"You know we can hear you." Pollux smirked. Both girls stopped whispering and looked up with flushed faces.

"Ah, children," he continued, "you may call us whatever you like, but we have something you two don't: sibling love. For centuries it has always been me and my brother. Our mother died giving birth to us. We were humans before Asterion made us counterparts out of pity. We vowed to isolate ourselves from everybody else. After all, there is nobody we trust more than each other. Why should we care about anyone else? All that leads to is bitter disappointment."

Charlotte stared at the dark-haired twin in surprise. Danni's eyes widened in agreeance.

Suddenly, she saw through their complete tough-guy façade. The pair were horrible *on purpose?* They had never planned to help Graham. They were just pretending to be alpha males. She could tell Danni had had the same realisation. Charlotte pictured two little boys left without a mother, forced to grow up faster than they knew how to. They had never asked to be counterparts. They felt safest when they were together, playing as two young brothers would.

"That must have been awful." Charlotte spoke softly, taking gentle steps towards them. "You are so lucky to have each other. I am an only child and get lonely sometimes."

Charlotte stopped in her tracks. She was supremely jealous of Danni's close friendship with Reilly and Drew. She resented her parents for leaving her alone all the time. And yet she had pushed them all away instead of bringing them closer. Charlotte had never thought she would be able to relate to Castor and Pollux, but now it all made sense.

She felt a soft hand take hers. Danni stood beside her, warm and comforting. She squeezed back in gratitude.

"I'm so sorry for your loss," Danni said. "I cannot imagine what you two have been through, but now you have a chance to do some good and make your mother proud. That little boy, Charlie? His mother died at Constellar because you wouldn't save her. His father is somewhere on Liria. Let's go find him and get Graham back, as well. Charlotte and I are willing to work together like proper sisters. Will you help us? We can't do this without you."

Charlotte's heart leapt. Had Danni just referred to her as a sister? Maybe once they returned home, they could try hanging out, just the two of them...

Pollux and Castor exchanged telepathic twin looks. The heat had definitely died down in the room. After several seconds of silence, Castor spoke.

"Do you really think…Mother would be proud if we helped a human?"

His voice wavered, and he couldn't meet their eyes. Pollux had a hand on his brother's shoulder. Who were these men? Charlotte eyed the water suspiciously. Was this all just a big hallucination?

"Yes," Danni soothed. "She will be so proud of both of you. It is far braver to open your heart than close it off. Show her that you aren't afraid."

This time, Castor didn't even defend himself. He looked up with fresh determination. "We will help you both. Let's reunite that child with his father on Liria. Then we can seek out your friend. If we lose the competition in the process, so be it."

Charlotte and Danni grinned at one another. Who knew kindness and empathy would be the key to unlocking the twins? Who knew that kind of behaviour would make Charlotte a much better person in general? Asterion would be impressed.

"But," Castor continued, "we make the rules. You listen to us and follow our lead. You are not trained for combat, nor do you possess the powers of counterparts."

"Deal." Danni smiled. "Thank you. Reilly is looking after Charlie right now. Let's go get him, and you can take us all to Liria."

The brothers nodded seriously. They still looked so unsure. Charlotte breathed a sigh of relief. They were all going to work together now. She looked down to see that Danni was still holding her hand. This was much better than fighting.

*

Charlie was keeping the situation G-rated without even realising it. If he hadn't been playing sweetly on the mass of multi-coloured cushions,

Reilly would've thrown herself at Chiron by now…and vice-versa. Strong currents of energy crackled between them. Lust and disgust seeped from her pores. She hated him for how he had treated her the first time she had set foot in this room, but, oh boy, how she wanted him now that the proverbial beans had been spilled. There were some serious Bella and Edward vibes happening. Did Chiron sparkle in the sunlight too? Wait – he wasn't a vampire.

Charlie whooped and cheered as he threw himself from pile to pile of plush pillows. The soft velvet rug softened the blows whenever he slipped.

Chiron grinned down at him in amusement. Did his torso have to be so shiny? Reilly stared hungrily at the wisps of chest hair poking through his open shirt. She thought only food could make her salivate this much.

They stood on either side of each other with Charlie deliriously happy in the centre. Now that Reilly took a proper look, the Cavern of Purple resembled the perfect bachelor/make-out pad. Sandalwood incense burned from the hand of a large stone centaur, intoxicating her nostrils. Chimes dangled and tinkled. Purple paper lanterns swung in the light breeze from the forest outside. A plethora of comfort awaited them on the floor…which a little boy currently occupied.

Damn, Charlie, you are ruining my game!

Reilly didn't really resent the kid. She had loved him instantly as if he were part of her own family. He was too young to understand what had actually happened to his mother. It broke her heart. She prayed that his father would come home soon and pick up the pieces. A small selfish part of her, however, didn't want to let go of him. They had instantly bonded. He felt safe with her. She would take care of him until it was time to say goodbye.

"Loves it rough," Chiron muttered.

"What?" Reilly squeaked, her cheeks flaming.

"The boy." The centaur smirked. "He isn't afraid to get hurt. Look at him throwing himself all over the place."

Reilly took a deep breath, willing her face to cool down. "Well, it does help that he's landing on soft cushions."

Chiron nodded thoughtfully. "Yes, but it's symbolic too, isn't it? Children are innocent. They don't worry about consequences or pain. Nothing bothers them until they fall over and scrape their knees. That's when the wailing begins."

Reilly felt a tug at her heart. He was so deep and intense. The crush she had had on Slade back home was nothing compared to this. This felt more...adult.

"If only we could retain that innocence," he continued wistfully. "Why does it leave us?"

Reilly let out a laugh. Charlie giggled in response.

"What do you or any of the counterparts have to worry about? You don't pay taxes or work jobs or care what others think of you. Try living in the real world – then you'll see."

His stare bored into her soul. Reilly was torn between looking away and losing herself in it. She opted for gazing at her purple sandals. She was wearing a purple high-waisted skirt with a lilac shirt tucked into it. Her raven waves rippled down her back. Yeah, she looked good.

"Counterparts have different worries," Chiron mused. "We produce starlight and fight amongst ourselves. Now one of our own is dead. How are we going to replace him?"

Reilly nodded. That was a lot of pressure. She wouldn't be a counterpart even if they paid her.

"Plus," he breathed, "how will I live once you go back home?"

The question hung between them like static electricity. Reilly could hear the trees rustling in the wind. She met Chiron's purple eyes with shyness. He gestured for her to move closer. Tentatively, she took slow steps towards him until she was close enough to smell his breath. He smelled of icy pine-needles. He closed the gap between them and tilted her chin up with his finger. His lips looked brand-new, like they had never been chapped before.

"I don't understand," Reilly whispered. She stole a glance at Charlie, who was building a fort out of the cushions, blissfully unaware of what was happening.

"What is it that you don't understand?"

"When I came here, you told me that I wasn't worthy of any man. I cried on this very floor, and you left me here. How can I trust you?"

He took a step back, his arms slumping to his sides. "Counterparts are forbidden to engage romantically with humans – although a lot of them don't care. I wanted you the moment I saw you, but I couldn't admit it to myself. I left because your crying hurt me. I'm a coward, I know. We shouldn't even be having this conversation, but with everything that has happened, I don't see why I can't have you."

Reilly knew for a fact that the counterparts didn't play by the rules. Sirena and Calypsee had tried to maul Drew during his first visit. This was about more than just a silly rule.

"What is this really about?" Reilly urged. Chiron met her gaze in surprise. "Sagittarians are meant to be the most honest signs in the zodiac, so spill it. As if counterparts care about what they can or can't do. Why did you really push me away and say those awful things?"

A glow began to emanate from Chiron's bottom half. Reilly shut her eyes in case this was his version of undressing. A sharp intentional cough forced them open. He stood in his true form with four legs and the carriage of a horse. He was breathtakingly beautiful.

"This is why." He gestured to his body. "I figured you wouldn't want to be with a man who is half-beast, so I pushed you away before you could reject me. What woman would find this attractive?"

Reilly let out a noise that sounded like a laugh mixed with a sneeze. "You were worried I would find you gross because you're a centaur? I thought I was the one who made you sick."

Chiron smiled sheepishly, running a hand through his lustrous hair. "You are the most beautiful being I have ever seen. I was head over hooves the minute I saw you. So my 'situation' doesn't bother you?"

Reilly moved towards him again. "It truly doesn't. Besides, you can just transform into a man when we do stuff, right?"

"Do…stuff?"

She wanted the ground to open beneath her and swallow her whole. Why had she said that?

"Ah, I meant dates and whatnot!"

Smooth, girl.

Chiron's face lit up. "So you'll stay here? You won't go back to Earth once this is over?" He pulled her closer once more, thumb grazing her lower lip.

Reilly closed her eyes, waiting for the kiss of her life, when a flood of people entered the room. Danni, Charlotte, Castor, and Pollux were panting but seemingly full of energy. Charlie squealed and hid inside his makeshift fort.

"Did we interrupt something?" Danni grinned. Reilly glared at her best friend's terrible timing.

Pollux tutted. "Chiron, surely you weren't doing anything unsavoury with a child present?"

The four of them cackled like old chums.

"Since when did you all become besties?" Reilly gaped at them.

"Yes, and since when did you visit me here?" Chiron asked the twins. "In all of the centuries, you both have never once set foot in my Coloured Cavern."

Reilly watched Danni kneel on the plush rug and coax Charlie out of hiding. He wriggled out commando-style on his stomach and sat himself in her lap. She ran her fingers through his sandy-blond hair lovingly.

"Calm yourself, pony," Castor growled. "We are here to take Charlie to Liria in hopes of finding his father."

"Daddy!" squealed Charlie, overhearing their conversation. He leapt out of Danni's lap and ran circles around the room.

"I never thought I'd say this, but I miss Colin right now." Danni chuckled sadly.

Colin was Danni's younger brother. They fought all the time but loved each other dearly. Reilly missed her own family too. It felt like they had been on Bastion for years.

"Pony!" Chiron bellowed, stamping his hooves in rage. "How dare you come here unannounced, insult me, and threaten to kidnap Reilly's boy?"

Castor and Pollux stood side by side, fists balled with whitened knuckles. Charlotte took a giant step back.

"He is not *her* boy," Pollux snarled. "He belongs to his father, who is a worker on Liria. Put aside your pride and let us deliver him safely."

"What makes you think he is any safer with you two?" Chiron sneered.

"Stop it!" Reilly shouted. The room instantly fell silent. Even Charlie had frozen mid-prance. "Nobody is going anywhere with Charlie unless I can come too. If we are taking him to Liria before finding Graham, that's fine by me, but we all go together. Understood?"

Chiron turned to face her, looking slightly shaken. "But, my love, if we go to Liria first, we won't stand a chance of winning the competition."

Reilly flushed. Charlotte and Danni mouthed *my love* at her in amusement. The twins looked like they were about to barf.

Wow, the counterparts moved fast. They hadn't even kissed yet and she was already his love? It felt nice and really weird. Now everybody in the room knew she was semi-dating a centaur. Her mother would be so proud…

"Screw the competition," she fired back, feeling empowered. "Graham is my friend, not a prize, and this boy deserves to be with his father as soon as possible. I am going. Come with me or get left behind."

Chiron blinked in surprise. For a moment, she worried he would opt to stay back, but a second later, he trotted to the mouth of the cave. He turned back with a flourish and a wink that sent his wavy hair floating in the wind. The chimes made beautiful music. It reminded her of those shampoo advertisements on television. She swooned like a lunatic, imagining his strong arms sweeping her off her feet like some Spanish telenovela star.

From behind her, Castor and Pollux let out an exaggerated groan. The moment was over.

"Wait!" Danni called. "We can't leave Bastion without Drew. He will kill us, and he doesn't go anywhere without Hannah, so it looks like we need to gather the troops."

Reilly sighed. She was right. Drew would never let them live it down if they visited a whole new planet without him. Plus, Hannah was her cousin. It was best they stuck together.

"Okay." She grinned. "But if any of you fight, we are turning this car around and you won't get any ice cream."

*

Wasabi woke with a start. How much time had passed? She jumped to her feet and ran to the window. It was still light outside. Good. Wrinkling her nose, she picked up the piece of half-nibbled bread that had fallen on the floor and threw it in the trash. She wondered how Ambrite was faring. She prayed to the stars above that her new friend would not get hurt. Then she remembered that Ambrite couldn't get hurt and her clenched muscles sagged in relief. Nevertheless, she had a duty to do. The quicker she achieved her objective, the faster she would be reunited with the Astro A Team.

Wasabi made her way to the bathroom to touch up her smudged makeup. She applied near-perfect winged eyeliner, a deep purple lipstick in the shade 'Bruise', and voluminous lashes with a mascara wand that looked more like a weapon. She kept the same clothes on because they were warm and new. When she looked halfway decent, she smacked her lips in the mirror and made for the front door. It was time to door-knock. Wasabi stepped outside into the frigid cold air of the open valley and began making the rounds on her side of the river before heading over the bridge to spread the word. At each door, the same message was delivered: "I have important news – meet me at our spot by the river in half an hour. Bring the whole family. This is not optional."

Making her way to the river, Wasabi rubbed her stomach, feeling queasy. It was something her adoptive mother used to do when she felt ill. The habit had stuck. What if her community laughed in her face? Worse, what if they shunned her or rioted in rage? She had to be confident or they would never take her seriously. With a deep breath, Wasabi stood up straight and squared her shoulders. One by one, different Unsigned civilians shuffled towards her warily. She waved to some, hugged others, and smiled at them all to keep the mood light. Mrs. Borea kissed Wasabi on both cheeks, happy to see her finally attending a river gathering. The Borea twins jumped into her arms, gently tugging on her many ear-piercings.

"I missed you guys," Wasabi crooned. The Unsigned were her family whether she spent much time with them or not. They all shared a common bond. They understood what it felt like to be born without a zodiac sign, aside from the children. She sighted a familiar sweet face and ran to Mr. Arthurton to help him over to the clearing where everybody else stood. He gave her a toothless grin that was always alarmingly charming. She took hold of his elbow and led him through the crowd. Mr. Arthurton was the biggest mystery of their small community. Nobody knew where he came from and what his story was. He always wore the same brown tweed jacket and tan slacks and never spoke a word. His cane was there to assist him, but Wasabi thought it slowed him down even more. He nodded in gratitude as Wasabi released him and stood at the front. One of the ladies on the other side of the river, Mrs. Nilmorn, kept a strong hold of him. The Unsigned stood in silence, waiting for her to begin.

"Thank you all for coming," Wasabi said, a slight waver in her voice. "I'm not sure if you are aware of what happened at Constellar last night, but basically…it was attacked by outside forces." She opened her mouth to continue but was suddenly drowned out by the high-pitched wails of the Borea twins. Mrs. Borea knelt down to console them as the other members of the valley began talking and shouting over one another. For a small group, they made a racket.

"Attacked? Are these attackers coming for the valley now?"

"What happened to the Bastion civilians?"

"Should we pack our bags and run?"

"Where would we go?"

Wasabi's head began to pound. She probably should've worded her intro better. The twins were gulping from all the tears shed.

"Listen!" Wasabi roared. Everybody stopped, even the children. "I will explain everything and answer any questions at the end."

When she was assured that she had their full attention, Wasabi launched into the events that had occurred only the night before. Asterion had not asked her to keep quiet about the counterparts, so she relayed every single detail. There were many gasps, hushed whispers, and nudging. It had been a lot for her to take in at the time. She completely understood all of their reactions.

"So you see," Wasabi concluded, "with the severe loss of civilians, a lot of the homes on Bastion are free. Asterion wants to put aside this divide, and I agree. Come rebuild our planet and live where it's warmer. We need you all. There is no reason for us to stay here anymore…"

Wasabi expected resistance. She had anticipated anger, confusion, and aggravation, but nobody reacted. They all stood perfectly still as if stuck in the ground. After several seconds that felt like hours, Mrs. Nilmorn stepped forward, still holding Mr. Arthurton, who moved with her.

"But…this is our home," she uttered, eyes filling with tears.

Everybody nodded sadly. Wasabi's heart broke just a little.

"Are you telling me that you would rather live here even though there are enough comfortable, already established, and free homes for you in town?"

Mrs. Borea picked up one of the twins, Janie. She could tell them apart by the smattering of freckles blanketing their noses and cheeks. One of them had just a little bit more. Priscilla pouted at being left to stand on her own two feet.

"Wasabi, dear, the valley is more than just our home; it's our community. I know you may not understand, because you lived there before your dear parents passed, rest their souls, but to us it's everything. To leave this place where we all truly feel connected would be devastating. We cannot just uproot our lives because Asterion wants us to fill some space. We have never felt welcome there. For stars' sake, they don't even have a bathroom for us at Constellar. I'm sorry, but they will have to think of something else. Maybe recruit civilians from other planets?"

Kiran, a bulky man with a shaved head, pumped his fist in the air. He owned a barbershop for men in town. Business typically boomed unless a smart-mouthed civilian said something rude about being an Unsigned hairdresser without any hair. It was at that point the civilian would usually receive a punch to the mouth! Wasabi wasn't sure how they would all work and earn a living now without a steady flow of customers.

"Yes," Kiran exclaimed. "If this tragedy had never occurred, we would've been segregated for the rest of our lives. Why do big things have to happen for change to take place?"

Wasabi couldn't help but agree. She was an Unsigned through and through. Nothing would ever change that. Nevertheless, this was a big opportunity for the Unsigned to be treated as equals. It was worth fighting for.

"I understand your feelings completely. I know I spend most of my time at Constellar and the tattoo parlour, but I am still an Unsigned. I know what it feels like to stand out for all the wrong reasons. Trust me. But don't you see that this is in our best interest? We can take down those walls of discrimination and start afresh. We already work and shop there. Why not make a home there? Asterion is of course going to be recruiting new civilians; we cannot possibly have a livelihood without them. But in the meantime, we have the power to make a real difference. Let's show the newcomers who choose to settle down here that we are all equals."

A new energy moved through the crowd. Wasabi smiled at the impact of her words.

"If we do this," Mrs. Nilmorn said, "Asterion has to ban this colour nonsense."

"Yes!" Kiran fist-pumped again. A cacophony of agreeance reverberated throughout the valley. Sounds were always amplified in the open air. Even Mr. Arthurton wiggled his cane.

Wasabi paused, her heart sinking. Would Asterion agree to ban the colour system? Would the counterparts? It was such a big part of Bastion life. It was how everybody identified themselves. So many stores had been established to sell clothing, trinkets, jewellery, accessories, and more for those who knew what signs they were born under. A lot of the customers at Constellar specifically made moves on those they deemed romantically compatible. The counterparts themselves, now that Wasabi had seen them, were coloured. Karki was a giant white crab, for stars' sake. Wasabi herself had spent hours tattooing hundreds of people with the correct shades of ink. It seemed too large a shift, but if those were their terms, surely the powers that be would concede?

"How about this?" She sighed heavily. "If Asterion and the counterparts agree to ban the colour system, will you all move into Bastion and help us rebuild?"

Mrs. Borea put down Janie and picked up Priscilla out of fairness. Janie stuck her tongue out at Priscilla. Her twin sister cried at the naughty gesture.

"Stop it, you two," Mrs. Borea said, fussing. She turned to Wasabi with a weak smile. "Dear, give us a couple of minutes to discuss as a group."

Wasabi held out her hands, giving them her blessing to take their time. The crowd shuffled down the river, whispering and muttering to one another. Wasabi picked at the material of her grey coat. She was slightly hurt that they had excluded her from the group discussion. They clearly viewed her as more of a town supporter than one of their own. As the wind whipped around her, she felt a sudden longing for her adoptive parents. They would have known just what to say. She quirked an eyebrow at the theatrical gestures Kiran was making to the rest of the group. He had once expressed interest in her, which had been super awkward. Wasabi cringed every time she thought about it.

She was considering going back home for another nap when her people scuffled back. They kept pace with Mr. Arthurton, who grinned the entire time. That didn't give Wasabi hope. Mr. Arthurton grinned at everything. They gathered around her in a semi-circle with bright eyes of determination.

"So." Wasabi tilted her head. "What did you all decide?"

Mrs. Nilmorn brushed a wispy strand of ash-blond hair out of her face. Wasabi didn't know her as well as the others, living on the right side of the river. No matter the outcome, she made a mental promise to attend any social events they organised in the future.

"We have decided we will all move to Bastion provided the following terms are met," Mrs. Nilmorn continued. Wasabi waited with bated breath. The ban of the colour system was already a huge ask.

"One, Asterion bans the colour system. If we want to wear all blue, for example, we are allowed. Nobody is to give us any grief for this or isolate us. If Constellar is rebuilt, we will have only one male and female bathroom for everybody to use. This includes those who don't believe in gender or have transitioned. Two, we get to choose which empty houses we want. Some of us have children and deserve to be comfortable. Mr. Arthurton will live with one of us so we can look after him. He will receive top medical care. Three, we are doing all of this on a trial basis. Our homes in the valley must remain as they are. If we feel this isn't working out, we have every right to move back home and resume our normal lives."

Wasabi swallowed. Bastion really was going to change completely. She just hoped that the counterparts and Asterion would allow it to.

"Finally," Mrs. Nilmorn finished, "the term 'Unsigned' is to be banished forever. We do not define ourselves by where the sun was placed when we were born. It is time we were all treated as equals."

The crowd erupted into applause. Kiran put two fingers in his mouth and created a piercing whistle. The twins jumped up and down, laughing hysterically. The atmosphere was electric. It felt like the beginning of a revolution.

"Thank you, everybody." Wasabi smiled. "I am going to return to Asterion and put these conditions to him right away. I will let you know as soon as he responds. I'm sure he will be reasonable."

At least, she hoped he would be...

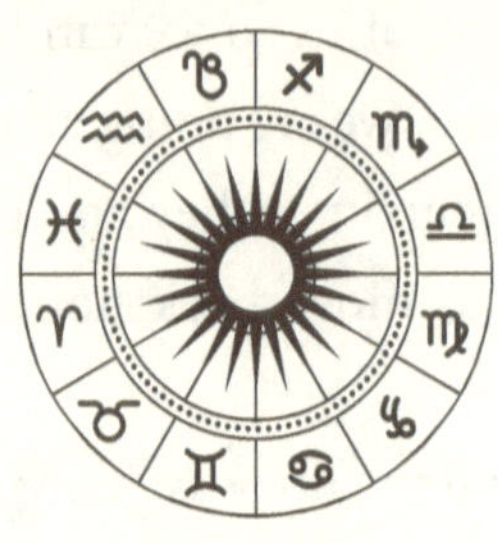

Chapter 13

Surrender

He had returned to hell, or so it resembled. The Cavern of Red was essentially a volcano with a long, rickety wooden bridge spanning both ends and a stone cot at the end for his counterpart to relax in. The sweltering heat made it difficult to breathe. Hunter removed his shirt and hiked up his skinny jeans. The last time he was there, he had nearly died traversing the bridge. Ares had played a dangerous game involving confrontational questions that were difficult to answer. As a result, Hunter had learned he was a lot like his father, angry and forceful – not physically but emotionally. He had wanted Ambrite to return his feelings, and when she hadn't, he had lost his temper. Now here he was again, furious at her decision to remain on Bastion as an immortal.

He couldn't accept it. He wouldn't accept it. What right did she have to live out the rest of her life on a completely different planet? What about the rest of them? More importantly, what about him? How would he cope without her? Ambrite was Hunter's crutch. She had created a safe space to be completely himself around her. They had held each other and cried, swapped stories of childhood trauma and laughed until their sides hurt. She was irreplaceable, and it was killing him. Sweat dripped from his forehead onto his nose. He made to wipe it away, but not before it splashed onto his salty upper lip. The slippery sheen on his exposed skin triggered a memory of the night before. Limbs entwined, heavy breathing, raw moaning, and perfectly manicured nails raking the length of his back.

Parry had been…*wildfire.* There had been such urgency in the way she had kissed him and tugged at his hair. It was as if her entire world had been ending. It felt like his had been too. The whole thing had surprised him on several levels. For one, he hadn't expected somebody as beautiful and popular as her to target him. He also hadn't anticipated reciprocating so intensely. Granted, alcohol and the fact that Parry resembled Ambrite had played a significant part, but still…he had wanted it to happen. What did it all mean now? Did she want a relationship?

"Penny for your thoughts, dear boy?"

A mischievous voice snapped him out of the vortex of overthinking. Hunter looked up to see Ares prancing around his cot with twinkling eyes. He was infuriatingly perceptive.

"Never mind," Hunter growled. "I want to know why you were acting so competitive before when you told me you weren't interested in ruling."

"Yes, well, I'm a wonderful actor, aren't I?" The counterpart grinned, revealing his frighteningly sharp white teeth. "Frankly, I saw through your friend Reilly's plan immediately, and I must say, she's a genius."

Hunter snorted a little too strongly. A dizzying wave of heat caused his vision to blur and his balance to waver. Ares didn't appear at all concerned.

Righting himself, he focused a glare on the ram.

"You're hoping they all end up uniting in the process, don't you?"

"We don't know what we are up against," Ares confirmed. "The truth of the matter is a counterpart was killed, and a counterpart has never been killed in the history of the universe. Milo may be able to take more of us down, and for that, we are better off standing together than alone.

With our powers combined, we are formidable, young Hunter."

The heavy heat of the room was stifling. Hunter wanted nothing more than to move the meeting elsewhere. Why did he have to be born an Aries? All fire and fury.

"So what do you suggest, then?" he croaked from dehydration. "What is our plan of attack?"

Ares rolled his eyes without any subtlety. He raised a bony leg, pointing his hoof down into the lava below. "Did you know that it is all an illusion?"

"What is?" Hunter shook his head, sweat flying in all directions.

"The lava. It looks like it would burn you alive, but really, it's just a pool of refreshing cold water."

Hunter peered over the edge, his breathing shallow. He recalled racing across the bridge, terrified that it would snap at any moment and force him to his death. He remembered the burst of hot liquid that hit him in the bellybutton.

"Bullshit," he growled. "I felt that stuff splash back on me when I was crossing the bridge. It was pure agony."

Ares tilted back his head and laughed. Hunter would've been amused at the sight had his counterpart not just tried to trick him into burning himself alive. Sadly, this hadn't been his first attempt.

"Oh, you earthlings are such good value." Ares guffawed. "Hunter McGowan, do you honestly think if you were hit by lava from an active volcano, you would be able to walk away as though nothing happened? Did your stomach have third-degree burns like it should have? No, it didn't. You were just caught up in the fear of the moment. Call them phantom pains if you will. Believe me, real lava would've left a scar."

Hunter gazed down at his hardened, flat stomach. It was slightly pink from the atmosphere but clear.

"That whole truth and lies game on the bridge." Hunter looked up. "That was just a big trick to get me to confess. I never would've died…"

As the Coloured Cavern rumbled around them, Hunter wondered just how many more surprises were in store for him that day.

"So," Ares dared, "are you going to dive right in? The water is real refreshing."

The temptation was strong. Hunter was so hot he wished he could rip off his own skin just to feel lighter. He hopped from one foot to the other in frustration.

"You don't trust me, do you?" Ares arched a single eyebrow, appearing slightly wounded.

"Do you blame me? You always seem to have some sort of messed-up agenda."

At that comment, the counterpart's face blackened. The tips of his horns seemed to grow sharper, and Hunter swore his entire body turned a darker shade of crimson.

"Messed-up agenda?" Ares growled, inching forward. Hunter took a step backwards, careful not to topple into the volcano below. "If by messed-up agenda you mean pulling you up on your terrible behaviour towards your supposed 'best friend', then you have a long way to go and a lot to learn."

Ares was now close enough for Hunter to smell the slightly sour tang of his breath.

"Do you remember what you said to me last time, boy?"

Hunter threw his hands up as a useless protective shield. Ares sniggered in response.

"No, I don't remember," Hunter shouted. "I'm going to fall! What did I say?"

The counterpart didn't answer. Instead, he stared into Hunter's eyes for an eerily long time. Hunter struggled to gulp in enough lungfuls of air, overwhelmed by fear and lack of oxygen.

Suddenly, Ares let out a piercing shriek that caused Hunter to jump so fiercely he fell backwards into the gurgling molten liquid below. Ambrite's beautiful face flashed through his mind right before his body made contact with the orange goo. The impact sent a wave of pain through his tense muscles and bones. Hunter gasped and choked as he surfaced, pawing at his eyes to improve his vision. It was at that moment he realised his entire body hadn't gone up in flames. There was no searing flesh and, more importantly, no instant death.

From above, Hunter heard haughty cackling. Peering up, still squinting, he saw Ares looking down at him with roguish eyes.

"I told you!" the ram shouted. "Did I not tell you the truth?"

Hunter spat into the water, furious and relieved at the same time. Ares had been right. The water was unbelievably refreshing as if it had come from a natural spring in an isolated forest. He swam from one length of the volcano to the other, marvelling at the fact that to foreign eyes, it would appear he was immune to liquid fire. It was heavenly. After several minutes of floating on his back, ears submerged, Hunter wondered how he was supposed to get out. He straightened and craned his neck upwards to see Ares had disappeared from the edge.

"Hey! How do I get out of this thing?"

Last time he had been there, a mist had transported his body out of the Coloured Cavern before he could hit the lava. He treaded water impatiently, waiting for that same mist to be summoned by his counterpart, but nothing happened.

Hunter was about to call for help again when a loud "*Yahoo!*" echoed around the room. He spun in time to witness a blurry muscly male fall through the air, knees hugged up to his waist. Moments later, a deafening splash drew him back underwater. He felt strong hands grip his shoulders and pull him up. Shaking the water out of his ears, Hunter blinked his eyes open to see a man grinning at him with perfect white teeth and skin so red he resembled a burn victim.

"Ares?"

His smile widened even further, making him look like a villain in a horror film. It was frightening. His skin was so smooth and red it could have been a leather bodysuit. Despite everything, he was built like a heavy-lifting champion.

"So this is your human form, hey?" Hunter gulped. He preferred his counterpart as a ram.

"Yes." Ares nodded, treading water. "As you can see, I cannot really frequent Constellar looking like this, so I never leave my domain."

Hunter stuck a finger in his ear to drain out the liquid. "Really? That sucks. What do you do all day?"

"I do what all the counterparts do. Produce starlight and radiate awesomeness."

"Does it really take up a lot of time to make starlight?" Hunter lifted an eyebrow.

"That is a secret that all counterparts are bound to keep," Ares said softly. "I cannot reveal to you the process, but it involves deep concentration. Without Serket, it is more intensive, and now, with all of us at war, I imagine the planet might suffer. I know that Equas, myself, and possibly Aegipan will remain here to assist whilst the rest go on the mission to save your friend."

"Wait," Hunter started. "You're not going? But that means I can't go. Graham is my friend. I need to go save him!"

"Hunter," Ares soothed, "we can't all go or the planet will be plunged into darkness. Some of us have to stay and carry the burden. You're welcome to join another team, but for now, I was hoping we could work through all of this anger."

"What anger?" Hunter cried. He could feel his own blood boiling.

Ares shook his head, emitting a dramatic groan. "Need I remind you of your reaction when Ambrite confessed her secret? You lost your mind."

Hunter's hands began to shake, and he knew with absolute certainty it had nothing to do with the temperature. Forcing one hand to quell the other, he met his counterpart's knowing gaze and sighed.

"Okay, I admit I didn't handle the news in the best possible way, but I can't help it. She's being so selfish!"

"I think *you* are the one being selfish." Ares bit his bright red bottom lip thoughtfully. "If she returns home, she will have to watch all of her friends and family die. She will never be able to settle in one place out of fear that her secret will be discovered. Not to mention she has a broken relationship with her parents, who do not seem to care about her at all. Face it, kid. You are angry because you feel rejected once again. Your father rejected you, your best friend rejected you, and she is now deciding to remain here on Bastion."

Silence followed the counterpart's psychoanalysis. All around them, the lava bubbled and popped without a care. Hunter refused to meet the ram's concerned gaze lest the truth in his eyes confirm what had just been said. This was the second time Ares had tried to address the destruction of his childhood. Hunter had, without wanting to, absorbed his father's fiery temper and carried it within like a burning orb of hate, ready to tear apart anybody who dared treat him unfairly.

He recalled his terrible behaviour towards Dr. Yates and Danni when they had first met. They hadn't deserved the tongue-lashings he had given them, and yet they still persisted kindly. Dr. Yates had never given up on him, and Danni had welcomed him into her life with an opportunity to make friends. The one thing that was keeping him from becoming just like his father was the strongest need not to. He would not drive everybody away. He expected Ares to be grinning in that smug fashion of his, but surprisingly, he found only kindness in his stare.

"I think," Hunter said, "I'm going to see Dr. Yates again when I get home. This time, I'm really going to listen and contribute. It's something I didn't do before.

Ares nodded. "Anything else?"

A searing pain tore through Hunter's chest. He winced but continued. "I'm going to apologise to Ambrite and let go of her once and for all. She deserves to be happy, and I can see that Wasabi is good for her…"

It had taken every particle of him to get the words out, but once he had, a lightness had followed. He realised that he actually meant the words. He would always care about Ambrite, but if he really loved her, he had to prove it by allowing her to live her happiest life. He had to learn, moreover, how to live without her.

"And what else?" Ares pushed.

Hunter shrugged. "Be nicer to people? Don't rage so hard? I don't know."

Ares clucked his tongue in irritation.

"What?" Hunter scowled.

"Do you think you could maybe give the red-headed beauty a chance?"

Hunter's cheeks flushed the same colour as his counterpart's skin. Ares barked a laugh in response.

"I know what you two did here last night…"

Stomach churning, Hunter placed a hand against the surprisingly cold rocky wall to his left. His face burned. "You didn't…watch, did you?"

The counterpart's eyes widened until they looked ready to burst from their sockets. "Are you insane? What kind of a sick beast would I have to be to watch such a disgusting display? I know what happened because I can sense all manner of things. Even a simpleton could deduce that the fiery Virgo has a fondness for you."

Hunter blinked in confusion. Did Parry really have feelings for him or was she just going through a 'bad boy' phase? He remembered how shyly she had confessed that he was good in bed. Her features had softened before leaning in to tickle his ear with her generous whisper. It had been a first time for her, which made Hunter feel slightly guilty. If he had known, he could've made it semi-more romantic. He had spent a lot of his 'angry years' attending parties, drinking copious amounts of alcohol, and going to bed with girls far more intoxicated than him.

It had been nothing new in his eyes, and yet with Parry…there had been a depth there that hadn't existed before. She was his friend, even if they hadn't been super close since the formation of the Astro A Team. They had even hung out together for a week back home, and in that time, he had witnessed her surprisingly gentle nature. Beyond her stunning exterior beat a vulnerable heart full of insecurity. He still didn't understand why she had cut her hair to look like Ambrite's. Did she really want him to notice her that badly? Whatever the case, it had worked. When they returned home, would there be anything still lingering between them? He didn't want to treat Parry as a rebound – she deserved better than that. They had to talk it out and determine what this was and what it was going to be.

"There is a lot of stuff I need to figure out." Hunter sighed.

Ares laughed heartily. "That's life, is it not, young Hunter? Humans spend years trying to work it all out, and in the end, they realise that time would better have been spent living outside of their heads and just following their hearts. Think less, do more."

The sides of Hunter's mouth quirked up into a smile. "Excellent advice. How about we stop all of this talking and start making ourselves useful?"

*

It had been a while since Garth had set foot on the planet Cassius. They could've portalled, but Asterion had wanted to appear official. He had forgotten just how extremely boring and lifeless it was. The entire realm was filled with scientific laboratories, research libraries, observatories for analysing the flow of meteoroids, and bland housing estates. There wasn't a single cute café, nightclub, or fashion district in sight. The artificial lights of the planet were blinding, giving Garth an instant headache. He glanced over at Asterion's screwed-up nose and knew he was thinking the same thing.

Their aircraft had flown them directly to the base of the CASCH building – Cassius Astral Security Council Headquarters. It, like all the rest of the land's structures, was constructed from steel and glass. The HQ was fifteen storeys high and flanked by two shorter flagpoles on either side bearing the planet's signature flag: a golden crest with a green star and an open tome representing knowledge and science. A concrete path from the stone slab landing space led to the entrance of the revolving glass doors.

Garth sniffed in disapproval. *Not even a garden to pretty up the place. The planet suited Milo's black heart perfectly.* As the aircraft ascended to find a more suitable place to land, Asterion and Garth were met by a bodyguard clad entirely in black. He nodded at them amicably, face devoid of any emotion, and gestured for them to follow. The building stank of sterile chemicals mixed with a strong dose of citrus. There was no life or warmth breathing from the whitewashed walls or hallways. The receptionist behind the stainless-steel desk did not look up as they approached. Her pointy nails clacked obnoxiously against the keys of her modern, extremely expensive computer.

If there was one thing Garth hated, it was minimalism. He loved decorating his chambers and Asterion's, much to the Keeper of the Stars' chagrin. The receptionist's desk didn't hold a single knick-knack or trinket – it was all business. The bodyguard cleared his throat loudly and left as the receptionist finally acknowledged their presence. She had mousy brown hair tied up into a perfect military bun and black glasses with small square frames. Her deep-plum shaded lips pursed at the eccentric figures before her.

"May I assist you?" Her voice was gruff and heavy.

"Ah, yes." Asterion drew himself up. "We have a meeting with the Council scheduled. Can you please alert them to our presence?"

The receptionist sniffed but pressed a shiny black button set into the desk's surface. A moment later, a crackling voice echoed throughout the room.

"Sir, the representatives from Bastion are here for the meeting."

"Stars and comets," a tired voice sighed. Garth grinned in amusement. "Send them up. Oh, and, Kresta, do send up the latest impact report, won't you, dear?"

"Right away, sir," Kresta replied. She waved a hand to the left, dismissing them.

Garth and Asterion made their way down the stark white corridor to the steel levitator at the end.

"Where to, gentlemen?" a tinny robotic voice inquired.

"The Council boardroom," Asterion answered.

In silence, they rose to the very top floor, which opened up into what resembled a five-star hotel lobby. Fake plants adorned every corner, snuggled into heavy stone pots. Black lounges and plush couches filled the centre space, with work-stations available nearby. To the right, a marble counter ran along the length of the wall, filled with steaming trays of baked goods and drinks of every colour. Men in charcoal suits milled about, eating and relaxing. One very tall businessman with snow-white hair and piercing green eyes flirted shamelessly with the waitress refilling the food platters. She giggled and pressed a fresh pastry to his lips. He took a bite and winked at her, sugar covering his mouth.

"You know…" Garth began.

"We are not hiring waitresses for the Mission Base," Asterion said, cutting him off sharply.

Garth glared at the long-limbed lothario before him and stalked towards the large boardroom doors at the back. He burst through the doors rather dramatically to find four elderly men examining a complicated chart on the wall. At his sharp entrance, they all looked up in surprise. Asterion walked in a second later, his face apologetic.

The Chief Advisor disliked every single stuffy individual in the room besides Asterion.

To the far left was Marlin Frost, a pudgy man with permanently blotchy red cheeks and a few wisps of grey hair on top. His gut bulged out from his white shirt, which was usually patchy with sweat. Marlin had been a huge advocate of Milo's. What a fool. Next to him stood Jimnian Yu, a recently appointed Council member who had been head-hunted from a distant planet. Garth had met him only once before, but it had been enough. Jimnian believed himself highly superior, having been specially recruited for important work on Cassius. His eyes swept over Garth's top hat with a haughty smirk. Garth narrowed his eyes in return.

To his right stood Council President Hammond Voran. Hammond enjoyed nothing more than competing with Asterion, despite being a full head shorter than him. It had always been enjoyable to watch. He had grey receding hair slicked back, with a bushy moustache and eyebrows to match. At the far right, Garth bit back a laugh as he met eyes with Nivil Jishi. Similar to Jimnian, Nivil had also been hired from a foreign land but had been a Council member for many years. He was the Council Vice-President, a title he bore bitterly. It was evident to everybody except Hammond that Nivil resented being second to a blithering windbag. It had been the four of them who had voted Milo in as their current representative. Garth rubbed his hands together, eager for the blowback to commence.

"Gentlemen." Asterion strode forward and sat down, steepling his fingers. Garth followed, draping one leg casually over the other. He watched Jimnian's eyes narrow in judgement at his poor etiquette.

"Asterion." Hammond nodded, the same sigh in his voice as heard on the loudspeaker earlier. He gestured to his colleagues, who sat around him at the head of the large wooden boardroom table.

"To what do we owe the pleasure?" Hammond continued wearily. He had the consistent appearance of somebody who never got enough sleep. Large, sagging bags hung underneath his eyes, both purplish and blue in colour.

Asterion leaned forward, all business. Garth sat up a little straighter.

"I am here to discuss your representative, Milo. Have you any idea of his whereabouts?"

The four men exchanged confused glances, shaking their heads simultaneously.

"Isn't he supposed to be on your planet?" Jimnian drawled.

Garth raised an eyebrow. "You do realise he's been gone for a really long time, right? He came to Bastion over a month ago. More, I think."

Marlin inhaled deeply. On the exhale, his protruding stomach stretched out a little further, resting on the edge of the table. "I don't see what this has to do with either of you," he wheezed, cheeks reddening even more than usual. "As a representative selected by the esteemed Council, he has the right to conduct business where he sees fit. We require updates only a few times a year. If he is no longer on Bastion, then he is probably off on another planet, gathering further intelligence."

Garth chuckled. "Oh, he's 'gathering intelligence', all right. Your beloved representative had much bigger plans after you pathetic cronies voted—"

"Garth!" Asterion warned.

Garth slunk back into his chair, but not before tipping his hat and flashing a mischievous grin.

"Forgive my ignorance," Nivil said, his crisp accent hugging the words. "What are you implying? Did Milo offend your counterparts?" The last word was tinged with condescension. Garth felt a strong urge to push him out the window.

"More than that." Asterion nodded gravely. "Milo came to Bastion and tried to turn all of our counterparts against each other. Amidst the feud, he killed our Scorpio, Serket, and absorbed his abilities. Just twenty-four hours ago, he unleashed an army of scorpion minions on the rooftop of our nightclub, Constellar, and killed the majority of our people. Not only that, he hypnotised and kidnapped one of our representatives from Earth. We have no idea where he is, and now our entire planet desperately needs to rebuild from the destruction."

The Council stared at Asterion blankly for several seconds before erupting into a harmony of laughter. Marlin wiped tears from his blossomed cheeks, and Jimnian kept shaking his head, his body shuddering from mirth. Asterion met Garth's scowl with a simple shrug. He had known they weren't likely to be taken seriously.

"So are you meaning to tell me," spluttered Hammond, "Milo is now a gigantic scorpion with an army of smaller scorpions fuelled by lust to annihilate the galaxy?"

His accurate assessment set the group off once more. Nivil clutched his abdomen in pain.

"Stop," he howled. "You're killing me!"

"If only that were true," Garth growled, rising from his chair.

Asterion placed a hand on his shoulder, gently pressing him back down. "We thought you might be cynical." His voice rose above the din. "That is why I keep my gifted Chief Advisor by my side."

Garth leapt up, pulling his dragon necklace out from his shirt. The room began to quieten as the men gathered around the table watched what would happen next. Holding the chain between his forefinger and thumb, Garth allowed the silver pendant to rock back and forth until its tiny metallic eyes began to glow. The boardroom hummed and throbbed with the weight of the increasing power. The Council members stared, no longer laughing, as white light burst forth, projecting a screen over the chart they had been analysing earlier. Garth sat back down to watch a familiar scene play out.

Milo was standing on the roof of Constellar, long maroon robe waving in the night air. His face wore an arrogant sneer as Asterion, Garth, and the Astro A Team, minus unconscious Brodie, Hunter, and Parry, surrounded them. Graham was pleading with them not to hurt him.

Garth watched in sadness the strong effect the scorpion's venom had on the young boy. He heard Marlin suck in a shuddering breath.

"Graham," Asterion warned, "that is not Serket."

"What are you talking about? You said you have never seen him in his human form, so how would you know what he looks like, anyway?"

"Because we know who the human is before you." Garth scowled.

Nothing could have ever prepared them for Milo's betrayal. Seeing him instead of the placid Scorpio counterpart on the roof had struck fear in their hearts. Not because of his power but because of his unpredictability and sheer ambition. A man like him had no issue doing whatever it took to get what he wanted.

"What happened to my real counterpart?" Graham had cried, his drug-addled state slowly wearing off.

"Dead!" Milo snarled. "I drained him of his power when I came to visit and took all his abilities. After I pretended to leave Bastion, I doubled back and resided in the Cavern of Maroon, where I plotted my uprising. I had already started a war amongst the other counterparts and was ready to make my move when I found out you brats were coming. It was then that I saw my window of opportunity. What better way to hide in plain sight than by seducing a vulnerable boy who needed to be loved and accepted? I stung him with my tail when we met, injecting him with a poison that would make him bend to my will, and convinced him to gather all of you here in Constellar. Now, if you don't mind, I will be taking Graham and beginning a new life on a faraway planet that is devoid of disgusting Unsigned and those not born under Scorpio."

Garth watched Milo abduct Graham for a second time, flying off into the sky, before unleashing an army of vicious scorpions to eviscerate them all. The glow in his dragon's eyes began to dim until the projection on the wall disappeared completely, leaving the chart in full view once again. The noise had stopped, the boardroom silent save for the titters coming outside the door.

Asterion's brow furrowed. It had clearly troubled him to watch that again.

"Well, gentlemen," he croaked, "you have now seen exactly what occurred not twenty-four hours ago. Do you concur that Milo is a direct threat not only to Bastion but to the entire galaxy should he deliver on his promises?"

The four men shuffled awkwardly, not meeting their eyes. Their discomfort was exactly why Garth had come. He patted his dragon pendant, making a mental note to watch re-runs of this delicious scene later.

Hammond finally looked up at Asterion, refusing to meet Garth's victorious grin.

"What is it you want, Asterion? Do you want us to find and arrest the guy? I'm not sure what this achieves, exactly."

Garth choked on his own saliva, earning a firm pat on the back from Asterion.

"You're not sure what this achieves?" Garth spluttered. "You hired the wrong man! For starters, you can take accountability and promise never to repeat this idiotic mistake. Maybe do some background checks first?"

He expected Asterion to interject, but the wise old man just nodded in agreeance.

"Excuse me, but how is this our fault?" Jimnian leered. "Yes, we may have voted him in, but it's not as if we knew of his master plans beforehand. He fooled us just as much as he fooled you."

The three other men murmured in agreement. Garth rolled his eyes.

"Maybe so, but what about having tighter security on your newest recruit? You let him onto our planet without so much as an escort. He has been gone for so long, which you barely noticed. You made this mess. Now you're going to fix it!"

Hammond threw his frustrated hands in the air. "I repeat, Asterion, what do you want us to do? Hire somebody new? We will have to do that anyway, but this time I will ensure tighter security checks. Other than that, I am at a loss. I cannot locate him and therefore cannot apprehend him."

Asterion scratched his chin thoughtfully. "I am not asking you to find him, gentlemen. We already have a team of children far more competent than yourselves on the case. I am here first and foremost to inform you that your representative is dangerous. It is in your best interest to be aware, as he could attack Cassius. Secondly, as Garth mentioned, we are here to ensure you never hire such a villain again, and, thirdly, we are here to collect from your grievous error."

"Collect how?" Marlin huffed impatiently.

Asterion and Garth exchanged knowing smiles. They both leaned forward, knotting their hands.

"Milo's scorpion army murdered half our population," Asterion said. "Bastion was already quite a small planet, but the citizens thrived there, earning a living and contributing to our humble society. Without them, our stores will close, and our community will die out altogether. He has caused unspeakable damage, and we want adequate retribution in order to re-build."

"Ah." Hammond barked a bitter laugh. "Now I get it. You want money. You know, Asterion, you may be Keeper of the Stars, but Cassius is a growing enterprise of…"

"I couldn't agree more," Asterion said, cutting him off coolly. "But we don't want money. I'm not about to indebt myself to power-hungry cretins such as yourselves."

His tone was biting and icy. Garth rarely saw Asterion so irritated. He loved it.

"Well, if money is not what you seek, what could you possibly want?" Nivil groaned in exasperation.

Asterion produced a smile that didn't quite meet his eyes. His lips puckered as he spoke. "Your people…"

PART III
THE RESCUE

Chapter 14

The Place of Pages

On the other side of the portal lay a room hushed and dim, lit only by several small oil lamps scattered around the area. Brodie sucked in a breath. Before her, stacks upon stacks of bookshelves lined the walls almost decoratively. Long wooden tables ran through the centre, with comfortable velvet chairs flanking both sides. Only a handful of people roamed the room, plucking books off shelves or sitting at the table, running fingers under scrawled writing. The musty, beloved smell of old parchment and ink hung in the air, confirming Brodie's suspicions that she had just set foot in a very sacred space few entered. Equas remained silent as the portal faded to black behind them.

"What is this place?" Brodie breathed, filled with the sudden desire to sniff every dusty tome in the library.

"The Place of Pages," Equas whispered, her hushed tone emitting a low vibration. "It is accessible solely to those born with the gift of magic. The reason for this is it does not exist on any particular plane. The only way to reach it is via portal. Only ten people or fewer are allowed in here at one time. This revered library is said to hold all of the knowledge in the universe."

As she spoke, a shadowy figure sitting at the table jerked its head up in irritation. The moment its steely gaze landed on Equas, it flinched, eyes wide, and returned to reading.

"Did Milo ever come here?" Brodie murmured. "Is this where he learned how to kill Serket?"

"No, I am absolutely certain he does not know the Place of Pages exists."

The bookshelves appeared to glint mysteriously, stretching onwards into the darkness. Brodie wondered how large the room actually was beyond what she was seeing.

"Why?"

"Because," Equas muttered in response, "a portal will not work if the answers you seek here stem from evil and wickedness. The Place of Pages knows what is in your heart. It understands what you desire. You cannot deceive these hallowed halls. I believe Milo discovered that information at the Great Library on Cassius. Only government officials and people in power are given access there. Nobody in history has ever thought to murder a counterpart before, so they didn't know where to look, but Milo did."

An elderly man cloaked in a hooded charcoal robe moved slowly down the aisle, pushing an ancient trolley filled with books so large they could have been used as weapons. Brodie guided Equas out of the way. The man paid them no notice.

"So people work here?" Brodie's eyes followed the hooded figure until he disappeared from view.

"Yes." Equas wobbled from the sudden movement. "Old mages who have served the galaxies for centuries. Wasabi's adoptive mother worked here before she passed away. She was not a particularly strong mage nor blessed with eternal life, but she was faithful and respected amongst her mentors."

"Wow. I wonder if Wasabi knew…"

"She did not," Equas confirmed, shifting slightly. "Wasabi knew her adoptive mother worked in a secret library but was unaware that the woman was a mage."

"Was Wasabi's adoptive father a mage?" Brodie felt a sharp sting nip at her heart. She couldn't imagine what it was like to grow up without parents and then have both adoptive ones die as well. It made her truly grateful for her mother and father waiting back home.

"No. He was a tradesman, but they loved one another fiercely. Now, let us begin our search for the truth."

Brodie grinned at her counterpart's no-nonsense approach. She wanted to tell Wasabi about her adoptive mother, but it would seem odd coming from a stranger. Would she take it well or be furious that Brodie, a mere girl from Earth, had found out before her? She tucked the information deep inside herself for later and faced the shelves.

"Right – what exactly are we looking for, again?"

"A book that lists every single identified planet in the universe relatively close to Bastion. You will not find such a tome in regular libraries, but here, in the Place of Pages, answers are limitless…"

*

"Where the hell are we?"

"Hush," hissed Aegipan in his quirky human form. "You stand in a place more sacred than every single church on Earth."

Ronan was about to argue, despite not being religious, but stopped as he took in the majestic surroundings. He was standing in a low-lit atrium with two sweeping circular staircases on either side leading to a landing filled with shelves of books. Gazing upwards, he was reminded of the library in *Beauty and the Beast*, the way the ladders ran high to the very tops of the sturdy wooden cases. The room was virtually empty save for a couple of dark figures passing through and ascending the steps. Directly in front, to his left and right, hung crushed velvet rose curtains masking hidden passages beyond. Ronan longed to explore all this realm had to offer. He felt slightly guilty for being there without Danni, knowing she would have been in heaven amongst the mystery.

"This place is huge, isn't it?" he wondered aloud.

Aegipan merely nodded, making his way to the left spiral staircase. The balusters were made from cast iron, weaving their way around and around, cool to the touch. Ronan felt slightly dizzy at the ascent, peering down at the ground floor he had been on just moments before. The landing was fitted with the same rose hue as the curtains downstairs, crinkly and springy underneath his shoes. Closer now, Ronan could see the large spines of red, blue, green, and brown tomes fitted neatly together in each row. The titles were difficult to make out, some in cryptic languages, some with strange symbols in bold print. It reminded him of a movie he'd once seen where a boy in a library opened a book that contained pages rippling and moving with magic.

"How do we know what we're looking for?" he whispered to Aegipan, who was sniffing the shelves.

"We are searching for a book that can provide us insight into how Milo drained Serket's venom. If we can obtain such a book, we might gain access to how to reverse the effects."

Ronan rolled his eyes in annoyance. "I repeat…how do we know what we're looking for? It's not like this place has any sort of order."

Aegipan swivelled around to face Ronan with a frown. "This is the second time you have disrespected the Place of Pages. Unless you have something useful to contribute, keep it hushed, boy! In answer to your question, the library senses your desires. The books know what you require. You just need to pause and pay attention."

The sceptical nature of a Capricorn resurfaced within Ronan. Only months ago had he been a bitter, sarcastic boy who thought astrology was a load of nonsense. Danni had taught him a balance between logic and faith, but his doubts generally won out in the end.

"So do we meditate or…"

"Shh!" Aegipan yell-whispered. Ronan's heart somersaulted in shock.

His counterpart closed his eyes behind his strange spectacles and hummed softly to himself. Ronan watched his human ears prick up and nostrils dance as he concentrated. After several minutes of this, Aegipan blinked rapidly and made his way quickly down the stairs. Ronan took them two at a time to keep up. On the ground floor, Aegipan made a sharp turn left and pushed through the heavy curtain into a darkened room full of dimly lit lamps. Ronan was about to chastise his counterpart's reckless behaviour and hypocrisy when he noticed a familiar figure with silvery blond hair standing next to an odd-looking stone woman in the stacks.

"Brodie?"

The girl stepped forward, suddenly illuminated by one of the glowing burners. Her face was beaming.

"Ronan! What are you doing here?"

Aegipan marched over to Equas with evident disdain. The woman barely acknowledged him, her face a mask of stone. Literally.

"I should've known you would be here," he huffed. "Tell me we are not searching for the exact same book?"

"And if we are, Aegipan?" Equas's voice rasped. Ronan cringed. He was not used to her gravelly tones. "I seem to recall a saying…something about multiple heads surpassing a singular one?"

Brodie giggled softly. Ronan grinned at her reaction. The counterparts had just as many personality clashes as the Astro A Team.

"Well," Aegipan spluttered, "be that as it may, we are in direct competition. Do you really advise that we work together?"

Equas merely stared at him blankly. She was blind but incredibly perceptive.

"Dude, does this competition really matter?" Ronan cut in. "Let's just figure out how to get Graham back. Equas is right – if we work together, we can reach him faster."

Aegipan looked ready to argue but instead sighed heavily, his shoulders dropping dramatically. "If we must… Are you also seeking answers regarding Milo's extraction of Serket's venom?"

Ronan noticed a flicker of surprise in Brodie's eyes. Equas shifted ever so slightly, inclining her heavy head towards them.

"That is very clever, Aegipan," she rasped. "It is no wonder you are marked as the most logical sign. Brodie and I are looking for a tome that contains every single identified planet relatively close to Bastion. We don't believe Milo would've built his empire too far away. I am quite familiar with many of the planets within this galaxy, but I never paid much attention to those desolate and devoid of any life or civilisation. I believe he is residing on one of them. Hiding in plain sight, as it were."

It was Aegipan's turn to look impressed, though Ronan knew he would never openly admit to it.

"Hopefully, both of our objectives lead to the same outcome. I say we do our research quietly and discuss our findings once we have discovered something worth discussing. What say you both?"

"Aye-aye, Cap'n." Brodie winked.

Ronan's counterpart raised his bushy eyebrows at her in confusion and irritation.

"She agrees with your plan of attack," Ronan whispered.

"Indeed," Aegipan drawled.

Brodie flashed him a *How do you put up with that pain in the ass?* glance. Ronan shrugged, stifling his laughter.

Coincidentally, both books were located only two shelves apart. The tome listing every single planet within the galaxy was enormous, black and leather-bound. It had no title, but Equas assured her present company that it was the one. Ronan prodded Aegipan sharply in the ribs when he didn't offer to carry it from the shelf to the table. Aegipan glared at him menacingly but conceded. It was far too difficult for Equas to transport a book that large in her position, and Ronan had been taught by his father that whilst women were capable of doing the same things as men, he should always offer as a sign of chivalry.

Their book was significantly smaller, pea-green and roughly worn. The pages were yellowing and brittle. Embossed on the cover was the fading brown title *Florae & Faunae of the Hyrin Galaxy*. Ronan and Aegipan sat farther down the table, away from the curtain they had entered through. Brodie and Equas sat opposite the shelf where they had located the tome.

"Not once has anyone mentioned that the name of this galaxy is Hyrin," Ronan muttered.

"Did any of you ever ask?" Aegipan chuckled, flipping to the very back of the book.

"I guess not…"

Ronan had been on Bastion for only a very short time, but a large part of him wanted to know more about the realm he had entered via a portal in a pond. He wanted Aegipan to teach him all the great histories and mysteries Hyrin had held for the last millennia.

"I would gladly lecture you any day at any time, boy," Aegipan responded, reading his thoughts without shame.

"Ugh, I forgot you could do that." Ronan shook his head as though that could keep his counterpart out.

Aegipan chuckled once more, scanning a gnarled finger down the index. Ronan leaned in closer, unable to decipher any of the strange terms listed alphabetically.

"How do you know what you're looking for? None of this makes any sense to me."

Aegipan rolled his eyes underneath his odd spectacles. "Why would it? You didn't even know Bastion existed a few days ago."

"Salty," Ronan muttered, sinking back into his chair.

They didn't speak for close to an hour. As they studied, shadows moved in and out of the darkness, selecting books or returning them.

Ronan watched them, making up stories in his head about their mysterious identities. Complete silence stretched across the table from where Brodie and Equas sat. Aegipan let out obnoxiously loud exclamations whenever he felt he had found something of value but always grunted a second later, pressing his face closer to the pages as if that would make the answers leap out at him. After the fourth time of this happening, Ronan was ready to slap the spectacles off his nose when Aegipan raised a single hand in the air.

"Young Ronan, tell me if this makes sense to you."

Ronan leaned forward, still unable to decipher the words in front of him. "What am I looking at?"

"There is a plant listed in this book," Aegipan whispered. "It is aptly named *Venominulae mortalis* – venomous death – and can be found only on a planet bordering on Hyrin's outer rim named Darkstrom. I have heard many legends tell that a single piece can stop a man's heart in just three seconds. It is the most delicate and subtle way to kill somebody. Once plucked, it will not grow again for several months."

Ronan gulped. He imagined it growing in a castle's keep surrounded by deadly thorns and dragons.

"So Milo took the plant for himself and, what, slipped it to Serket when he was eating grubs for dinner?"

Aegipan snorted. "Serket did not eat grubs. He was partial to the jade scarabs that scuttled around his desert. I believe that Milo did indeed harvest this plant, but if he fed it directly to Serket, it wouldn't have killed him. It would've taken the whole plant to make a counterpart suffer, and even then, death wasn't guaranteed. No, no, Milo combined the leaves of *Venominulae mortalis* with something just as poisonous. I cross-referenced every item of flora listed with the plant, and not a single one had any significant effects once combined. At best, the victim could die and develop a nosebleed, but what would be the point of that? Also, it doesn't tell us how Milo managed to kill a counterpart. Then I decided, on a whim, to look at the fauna. That's when I found Mamboa venom…"

"Mambo what?" Ronan sniffed.

"Mamboa are paralytic serpents. One bite and you will be paralysed for eternity. According to the text, they are found in craters on Mt Fosso, which is located on a planet named Ravine. They have been purposely isolated from all beings due to the nature of their venom. If you are stupid enough to journey to Mt Fosso, you deserve to never move again."

Ronan felt his stomach lurch. He had never liked snakes. There were plenty back home in the countryside that could do some serious damage if one ventured too far into the tall grass.

"How did Milo get venom from a Mamboa without any repercussions?"

"That I do not know," Aegipan replied. "But a man who has done extensive research like this would've educated himself before setting foot on Ravine. According to the book, 'Mamboa venom, if combined with a specific lethal substance, has the ability to melt blood both mundane and superior. If harvested, the vitals can be ingested, with supernatural results depending on the victim. The trace elements found in the victim's contaminated blood contain magical properties. The rest of the venom will dissolve the victim's insides, leaving an empty husk.'"

"Man," Ronan breathed. "Milo took a huge risk. That could've gone horribly wrong for him."

"Indeed." Aegipan nodded. "Serket's superior immortal blood infused with both plant and serpent venom allowed Milo to absorb all of his abilities without a single consequence. Once he became Serket, he no longer required the concoction. The scorpion venom resides in the tail, constantly refilling itself. He is a genius."

"*Was* a genius." Ronan bared his teeth. "He went to great lengths just for greed and power. I'm going to kill him."

"You cannot kill him," Aegipan sighed. "You would need to create the same concoction, and that is not an option. It is far too dangerous, and

I'm not sure the plant will have grown back yet. There is no time."

"What about the rest of you?" Ronan sat up straighter. "Don't eleven counterparts trump one?"

Aegipan appeared thoughtful, bouncing his knee up and down. "We may be able to overpower him, but to kill a counterpart is a grave act. Whether we like it or not, he is one of us now. We will also need somebody to take his place should he fall. A zodiac is incomplete without twelve."

Ronan felt a sharp pang in his chest. Without Graham, the Astro A Team was also incomplete. There seemed no happy ending to this story.

"So we can't kill him, which means nobody can take his place. This seems pretty hopeless to me."

"Not so." Aegipan frowned. "We can force Milo to rule with us and make sure he is watched day and night."

"That's a great plan." Ronan slow-clapped.

"I agree it is not ideal. No matter. We know now how Milo became Serket. Once Equas and Brodie discover the planet where he is building his empire, we can make our way there and put a stop to it."

At that very moment, as if conjured, Brodie let out a cheer of triumph from down the aisle.

*

"Gnarly waves, bro," Drew whooped as he stood on a lonely beach, watching the ocean roar in and out of the shore.

"Gnarly?" Karki repeated, staring at Hannah with wide eyes for confirmation.

Hannah giggled. Her boyfriend was such an adorable loser at times. The three of them were standing on soft sand in the Cavern of White. The last time she had been there, Hannah had nearly drowned as punishment for plucking and pocketing a pretty shell. The memory plus the biting wind made her shiver. Much to Drew's disappointment, she had thrown out her destroyed outfit from the night before. She was now wearing a cotton white turtleneck with fitted sleeves, a pair of white jeans, and comfortable sneakers. Drew was wearing a sea-foam hooded shirt and baggy cargo pants with sandals. Boys…

Karki had resumed her human form. Ever since her victory against Ichoris, she had not stopped beaming. There was an actual spring in her step. Hannah understood. Fear, once conquered, was a door that could no longer be closed. Both she and her counterpart had shown considerable amounts of courage in the past twenty-four hours. She felt powerful.

"I hope you don't mind," Karki chirped, twirling on the sand. "I invited Calypsee and Sirena over to join us. They are so beautiful and smart. I'm sure we can locate your friend if we work together."

Drew and Hannah froze simultaneously. The Piscean mermaids had tried several times to interfere in their relationship. They were flirtatious women with absolutely no shame. Hannah recalled their last encounter in a dress shop on Bastion. She may have called them 'sea-bitches'…

She had also threatened to sic Karki on them to snip their tails off. Uh-oh.

"Not a problem at all," she replied sweetly, her smile just a little too wide.

"Yeah, the more the merrier, they say," Drew half-laughed, half-groaned.

Right on cue, the ocean began to rumble and roil, spitting thick droplets at the three figures standing on the beach. Hannah felt her face burn in rage as two sultry women walked out of the water as if they were on a catwalk. Both were clad in ripped sea-foam dresses that showed off their flat stomachs and tanned thighs. Calypsee, the darker of the pair, blew Drew a kiss with blood-red lips. Sirena smirked at Hannah, clearly not over her outburst in the fashion district. Drew choked on his saliva and turned to his girlfriend with pleading eyes. Karki, completely oblivious to the tension, rushed over to her friends.

"Oh, it is so good to see you, sisters!" She hugged both of them, receiving only docile pats on the back in return.

It appeared, Hannah mused, that Karki's fondness for the mermaids was much more one-sided than she had made it out to be.

"Hello, little one," purred Calypsee, flicking her jet-black tendrils.

"How are you, Karki?" Sirena fluttered her long lashes.

Hannah resisted the urge to roll her eyes.

"Fantastic." Karki beamed. She began hopping on one foot and then the other. "I vanquished the evil Ichoris and saved my friends from danger. Hannah and Drew said I am super brave and…"

"Fascinating," Calypsee said with a yawn, cutting off the girl. "What do you require of us?"

Karki didn't seem to notice the rude interruption. It made Hannah even more fiercely protective of her than before. How dare these wenches act superior? Where had they been when Ichoris was bearing down on them all?

"Well, we are going to work together as a team to find Graham and thought it would be much more useful to all work together. Isn't that fun? What do you guys think?"

The counterparts grinned in a way that made Hannah's gut churn. She knew exactly what they were thinking. They took long, slender steps towards Drew, who looked like he was holding his breath.

"That is a great idea." Sirena licked her lips. "Nothing like a threesome to make some magic."

Hannah coughed rather loudly, interrupting their advances on her boyfriend. They swivelled to face her, eyes narrowed.

"Um, aren't you forgetting Karki and myself? That makes five, but I understand if drinking the sea-water has made it hard for you guys to count…"

Karki turned to face her, eyes wide. "Hannah, that's not very nice."

In an instant, the mermaids dropped their glares and began smirking.

It reminded her of a sibling's smug satisfaction when a parent scolded a brother or sister.

Hannah knelt in front of Karki so they were level. She took the pale girl's cold, clammy hands in hers and squeezed gently.

"Karki," she murmured so nobody else could hear them, "I know you consider these sea-b…women your friends, but they are truly awful. They are always trying to seduce Drew and take him from me. Do we really have to work with them?"

Karki appeared thoughtful, screwing up her nose and swaying from side to side with her hands still in Hannah's. From the corner of her eye, Hannah could see the mermaids still trying to flirt with Drew. They appeared positively pathetic with their chest thrusts and hair tosses.

"I will talk to them," Karki whispered, snapping Hannah back to attention. "They love me so much, I'm sure they'll listen."

Hannah highly doubted it. She let go of Karki and marched straight over to Drew, then kissed him full on the mouth. It was petty, but it felt good. Calypsee let out a growl, whilst Sirena pouted.

Drew winked at her. "I could totally get used to chicks fighting over me."

She smacked him hard in the arm but grinned.

"My friends," trilled Karki, "it has been brought to my attention that you are making my friend Hannah uncomfortable. Drew is her property, and to take him would be stealing. Please respect her wishes so we can all have lots of fun on this adventure together."

Hannah bit her tongue to stop herself from correcting the girl about the whole 'property' thing. She felt a hand slip around her waist and looked up to see Drew smiling at her.

"She's kind of right, you know," he murmured. "We belong to each other."

She nodded and kissed him on the cheek. Calypsee and Sirena were fuming. They kept casting furious glances from Drew, to Hannah, to the

Cancerian counterpart. Karki, once again, appeared not to notice.

"Thank you all for your cooperation. Shall we begin forming a plan?"

Hannah nodded gratefully at her friend. "So where do we begin searching for Graham? Does anybody have any idea where he might be?"

The mermaids drew themselves up rather haughtily. It was amazing how many emotions they could experience in one sitting.

"Well," Calypsee chortled, "we would of course scour the oceans, but as none of you possess the ability to breathe underwater, you are quite useless to us."

"Well," Hannah bit back, "Graham isn't in the ocean, so your search is rather useless too." She couldn't believe how sassy she had become. It was awesome.

Bracing herself for a torrential downpour of hissing and spitting, Hannah steadied the slight knocking of her knees but instead felt a rumble beneath her feet. A stirring in the sand.

The counterparts, including Karki, looked just as confused. Everybody began turning in place to decipher where the sound was coming from.

The rumbling grew louder, thrumming under their toes and shaking the cavern walls behind them.

From the mouth of the cave, Hannah heard the clacking of…hooves? Suddenly, Reilly burst forth on the back of a gorgeous centaur. She recognised him from Constellar and their meeting in the Mission Base. Chiron. He was altogether dreamy. Behind them, Danni, Charlotte, and the Gemini twins strutted out with some serious attitude.

Since when were those four chummy? Behind them trotted Charlie, who squealed when he saw Karki and raced towards her with open arms. She swung him around, laughing and crooning.

Reilly dismounted Chiron, smiling shyly at him. Drew noticed the exchange and let out a breath.

"No way… Girl has got some serious freak in her."

The new arrivals clambered down to the sand and removed their shoes.

The twins ripped their shirts off and jumped into the ocean, cackling. Hannah saw Charlotte's cheeks redden at the sight.

"Gnarly waves, bro," Danni breathed.

Drew let out a laugh. "Dude, that is exactly what I said!"

The pair high-fived, making Hannah smile and Reilly shake her head with a glint in her eye. Since she was a little girl, she had always envied her cousin's friendship with Danni and Drew. One could not find a trio more inseparable. She had never imagined that Drew would develop feelings for her. Wasn't it the tried and true stereotype that if there's a group of mixed friends, the guy will fall for one of the girls? That had never happened. The bond they shared would never be tainted by romantic feelings, jealousy, or heartbreak. It was so refreshing.

"What are you guys doing here?" Hannah walked forward and embraced Reilly. She loved her fiery cousin dearly.

"We are here to take you guys on an adventure." Danni wiggled her eyebrows. "Who's up for a trip to Liria?"

"Liria." Drew wrinkled his nose. "What the hell is there?"

"Charlie's father, for one." Reilly stood behind the boy, protective hands on his shoulders. "We need to get him to come back to Bastion and restore his home. That is the most important thing right now."

"What about Graham?" Drew tilted his head.

"We will ask around," Danni answered. "The workers may have seen or heard something. At least we aren't the only ones looking for him."

The mermaids were now leering with Charlotte at the twins splashing and play-fighting in the water. Hannah was hoping they wouldn't join them in their quest.

"So what are we waiting for?" She grinned nervously. "Let's get the hell out of here…right now. Who wants to make a portal?"

Sirena and Calypsee turned to her and snorted. Chiron chuckled haughtily, and Karki's mouth drooped.

"What?" Hannah frowned.

"We can portal only to special places like the Place of Pages, Hannah." Her counterpart sighed. "Garth's dragon pendant has the ability to create portals, but he and Asterion are on official business right now on Cassius."

"Okay, so we call him back," Drew said.

"No," Karki replied. "They are on very important business. We must not disturb them. There is another way, but it might be slightly…trying."

Hannah knew this was Karki's kind way of saying irritating.

"Tell us," Danni urged. "Who knows how long they will be there? We need to do this now."

Charlie jumped in the sand, marvelling at how his feet sank whenever he landed. The poor kid had probably never seen a beach in his life.

"Ganymede," Karki muttered. "His urn contains Aquarian Air. It can take us straight to Liria, which is only a three-hour flight."

"Great!" Drew exclaimed. "So what's the catch?"

"Ganymede is the catch," Chiron harrumphed. Hannah watched him watch Reilly dancing in the sand with Charlie. "He is a gigantic pest. Thinks he is so high and mighty because he is the keeper of the Aquarian Air. Fool."

"Wow, do any of you counterparts like each other?" Danni rolled her eyes. Hannah saw her produce a weak smile to Charlotte, who returned it. Was Charlotte finally becoming a decent human being?

Chiron threw a look of disgust at the mermaids and the twins. "I like some more than others. Equas has my respect, as does Ares. Most of us are quite fond of Karkinos."

Upon hearing her name, the pale child beamed up at the centaur with rosy cheeks. He nodded affectionately in her direction.

Hannah squeezed her counterpart, causing the girl to giggle. She was adorable.

"Enough of this sap," Drew groaned. "It's melting my heart. Shall we make our way to Ganymede's lair? He and Slade might have left already to go somewhere else. We don't want to miss our ride."

"I'm pretty sure Parry and Ambrite are with them too," Hannah added. "Also, what the hell is the Place of Pages?"

"All the more reason to get going," Danni agreed. "Come on, troops, let's march!"

*

The underground mines were much warmer than the air outside on Liria. Graham found himself repeatedly swiping at his sweaty brow with his sleeve, which was disgusting. Milo would have been repulsed by his boorish behaviour, and who could blame him? Issac, used to the change in conditions, nattered alongside him about being away from his family for periods at a time. Graham was happy the minions hadn't caught up to them yet. They were still loading the Glarafae sap and wood onto the aircraft. He was tired of their creepy company already.

"Charlie sure is growing up fast." Issac cut through Graham's wandering mind. He pointed left as they approached a muddy fork and continued talking. "One minute I'm holding the cutest Capricorn child you ever did see, and the next he's telling me that when I'm at work, he's the man of the house! It blows my mind how much can change in the blink of an eye. Makes me wish I didn't have to leave Bastion to earn my keep. I feel like the longer I'm away, the more I'm missing."

Issac ducked suddenly, causing Graham to bump into a strange-looking plant growing arrow-shaped leaves from the roof of the mine.

"Careful now," Issac called back. "You don't want to let those linger on your skin. You'll break out into nasty hives."

"Now you tell me," Graham grumbled as he hurried forward.

They hadn't come into contact with anybody since entering the mines on the opposite side of the forest. The valuable ore and melting pots were to be found deep within the narrow passages. The lower they went, the hotter it felt. Graham was convinced the humidity alone could dissolve any metal into liquid.

"How many bars did you say you needed?" Issac asked.

Graham pulled out the crumpled list, which was close to falling apart.

"Twelve sacks of iron ore, three sacks of silver ore, and two large gold bars as well as a melting pot."

Issac let out a whistle that made Graham wince. "It sure is lucky that you have all those workers. I saw how strong they were with the Glarafae. I don't envy them having to carry all of those heavy sacks plus a melting pot back to your ship. They have a long way to walk too."

Graham shrugged half-heartedly. He wasn't in the mood to pretend he cared for their wellbeing.

"This line of work will keep you strong," Issac continued. "I come down here and mine for rare jewels for my wife, which in turn keeps her business thriving. Lugging those beauties back and forth all day will give you some mighty muscles."

Graham couldn't help but appreciate what working on Liria had done to Issacs's physique. A moment later, he shook his head, worried that Milo could sense any disloyalty.

"Didn't you say the iron and silver ore was everywhere? I haven't seen a single thing yet," he groaned. If they didn't reach their destination soon, the claustrophobia would take over.

Issac let out a hearty laugh. "Just a couple more twists and turns, son. Then you'll see."

After a few minutes of silent trudging, Graham began to smell something akin to blood and coins. It was the familiar scent of metal.

"That smell always lets me know I'm close," Issac murmured, seemingly reading his mind.

As they rounded a particularly long stretch of path, the tunnel widened into a large circular cavern glinting with treasures. Bars upon bars of pure metal were sticking out of the earth-packed walls, with workers crowded around them, thrusting pickaxes into the crevices to loosen up the dirt. Graham remembered his old history lessons from school, when they had covered the Gold Rush in Australia for two weeks. It hadn't happened like this at all, but then again, they were on a completely different planet. It was best not to overthink it.

"Wow," he breathed. Issac looked at his expression and nodded.

"This is all renewed the very next day. Doesn't make it any easier to extract, though."

"Don't people just mine gold and get super rich, then? I don't really understand how the whole galaxy isn't swimming in wealth with a place like this."

Issac chuckled. "You really are from another planet, aren't you? Iron, silver, and gold don't have the same value in our galaxy as they do in yours. Here they are purely for practical purposes. You could build a house of silver, but it wouldn't make people think you were any better than them. You would sell it for a modest price, not an exorbitant one."

"Then why did you ask me earlier why I needed to build something with gold and if that meant I was royalty?"

"Because it's rare, that's all," Issac explained. "Gold is much harder to mine and transport. Those who seek it out are usually serving a higher power. You may need only two bars, but they are going to be a challenge to get."

For the hundredth time that day, Graham was glad he didn't have to do any manual labour. He did need to gather more than just inanimate objects, however. Scanning the area, Graham noticed there were at least close to a hundred workers. The problem was he didn't know which ones were the citizens from Bastion on Milo's list. He guessed the minions could make them talk, but how? Graham felt a sudden urge to protect Issac. The nice man had been so friendly and helpful. He adored his family. Was Milo really going to keep him on their planet forever? It didn't feel right. Suddenly, his heart began to beat at an alarming rate. Graham reached out a hand to steady himself against the wall, beads of sweat trickling down his chin.

"Hey, man, you okay?" Issac edged closer, his brow furrowed.

Graham nodded, willing his ticker to calm down. He waved off Issac with his other arm. "I think it's just a bit too stuffy in here. I'll be fine."

Issac ignored Graham's gesture and helped him slide down the wall gently so his back was supported. He pulled out a canteen of water from his baggy overall pocket and handed it to him.

"Drink," he urged.

Graham took the canteen gratefully and bought it to his lips. Icy fresh water slid down his throat and lowered his temperature.

He couldn't explain what had just happened, but it felt like Milo had been watching him or reading his thoughts. There had been a presence before that had now passed on. Had he witnessed Graham's doubts? Was this punishment?

Wiping his mouth with his sleeve, he handed the canteen back to Issac with a weak smile. He was being treated with a kindness he knew he didn't deserve.

"How about we get out of here?" Issac suggested, packing his canteen away. "We can get some fresh air, eat a snack, and let your minions do the rest. I don't need to get all of my jewels now."

Graham was about to protest when he heard a thundering from the tunnel behind them. Issac widened his eyes as he helped Graham to his feet. Minutes later, all of Milo's minions poured in with gigantic pickaxes and cold expressions. One of them shot a glare at Graham and shook his head as if to say, *Look at this useless piece of human.*

They fanned out and began striking at the glinting walls full of ore with force. A couple of the minions rudely pushed some of the workers out the way.

"Sheesh," Issac whistled. "Do you work for a merciful royal or a vengeful one?"

Graham held his breath, too terrified to think either way should Milo sense it. He resolved to make it up to him that evening. Perhaps a bath in the beautiful clawfoot tub? A massage? He would convince Milo to treat Issac with the best care and release him the moment the work was complete so he could return to his family. Did they have Skype there?

Issac clapped Graham on the back and went to speak to another worker with red floppy hair and freckles. They seemed like good friends. The other man was pointing at the minions with a strong frown. Issac shook his head, his hand firmly clasped on his friend's shoulder. He appeared to be placating him. Graham watched him lean in and whisper something. A look of surprise dawned on the man's face. He looked at Graham and clumsily bowed to him. It made Graham giggle. He nodded in return. He could get used to this 'regal' lifestyle. Issac grinned and gave Graham a thumbs-up.

Graham was about to join them when a cacophony of noise erupted in the mine. He let out a gasp as he watched the minions capturing each and every worker, tying them with thick rope and shoving them all against the wall. Issac yelped as he and his friend were dragged by their hair and bound back-to-back by three snarling minions. Many screams of protest were silenced by what appeared to be duct tape doled out by one of the scalier scorpions.

"Hey," Graham shouted. "Let them go!"

The minions stared at him with pure hatred. One of them marched forward, ripped the list from Graham's pocket, and shoved it in his face.

"Yes, I understand," Graham hissed, snatching it back. "But Milo specifically said not to do anything rash. You treat them well or you'll make the master very angry."

"Graham," Issac pleaded. He hadn't been taped yet. "Help us. What is happening?"

Graham felt his eyes well with tears. This would've been so much easier if Issac had been horrible, but he wasn't… He was kind. A sharp pain in his palm caused Graham to yell. He stared at the puncture mark. It was beginning to blacken and fester. Milo was angry. Graham looked up and met Issac with a sorrowful gaze. He shook his head and remained where he was.

The rest of the workers were taped and bound as tightly as possible. A few had managed to kick at the minions, but that had only made things worse. The minions retaliated with sharp stings that left the workers unconscious. Issac kept staring at Graham with so much confusion and hurt. His friend was wriggling around, trying his best to untie the knots enslaving them.

Graham looked down at the list of workers' names. Not all of them were Scorpios. Issac's friend was a Taurus, judging by his forest-green attire. He still wasn't sure why they had to be. Would the others be released? Would they alert the 'space authorities'? They still had to visit the mountains to gather food. The black hole on his palm began to bubble and ooze. He could sense his love's anger intensifying. It was time to step up and show his worth.

"Listen up, everybody," Graham boomed. He trudged forward, hoping the workers couldn't sense the jelly attacking his joints. Issac still looked hopeful, like it was all a big hoax.

"Our master, Milo, requires fifty working Scorpio citizens from Bastion to help him build his empire…our empire. If you are not a Scorpio or on this list" – Graham brandished the parchment – "you will be set free."

The minions hissed and spat in Graham's direction. Clearly, they wanted to leave no survivors or witnesses.

"*They will be set free*," Graham roared at the evil scorpions. "You have the ability to render them unconscious with your venom, so do that instead of killing them. Do not argue with me."

Graham sounded a lot braver than he felt. He expected his hand and throbbing head to explode, but nothing happened. Milo must've approved his wishes. Breathing a sigh of relief, he continued.

"Your families are currently being held hostage on Bastion…"

The workers who were still conscious began struggling and screaming with muffled voices. Issac let out a sob. Graham hated himself.

"If you wish to see them again, please come willingly and easily onto our aircraft. The faster you work, the faster you can go home. I will now read all the names from the list. Once you hear your name, you will know what is at stake for you and your family. Resistance is useless. They will not come to harm so long as you cooperate."

Graham wished and hoped the words he was saying were true. He had an awful sinking feeling that the workers would be killed once they were finished.

His voice trembled as he spoke the next words: "Issac Venturion, husband to Ella Venturion and father to Charlie Venturion…"

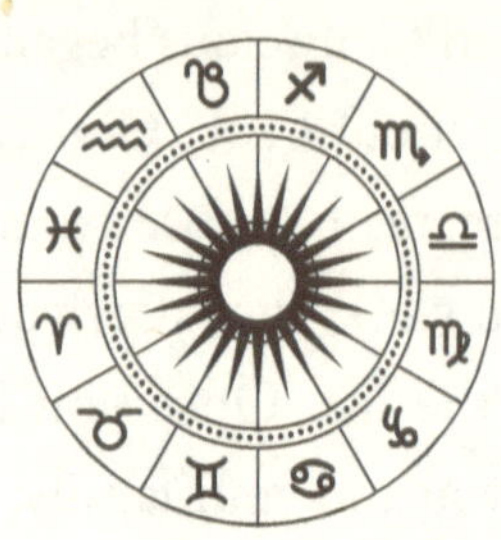

Chapter 15

The Lying Glass

Parry stiffened the moment she entered the Cavern of Grey. She felt her jaw clench and stomach roil at the sight of the beautiful yet evil mirror amidst the swirling mist. The image of the toothless, decaying old hag would haunt her forever. It had been enough to inspire a completely new look and make her sleep with Hunter out of fear of loneliness. She refused to go anywhere near it lest she come face to face with her nightmares again.

Ambrite and Slade were mesmerised by the transparent throne situated to the left of the mirror. To the newcomer, it appeared to be made of ice, such was its cool and glassy design, but to Parry, who had sat in it, it was an uncomfortable heap of junk. She watched her friends make for the mirror, curious about what it beheld for them, when they froze suddenly mid-step. Parry blinked in surprise. She turned to see the Maiden scowling, porcelain palm thrusted forward.

"Nobody else is to look in my glass except I." Her lip curled.

Cerus and Ganymede hung back, clearly acquainted with their idol's wishes. The Maiden snapped her fingers, and both Ambrite and Slade unfroze, looking slightly confused.

"Don't go near the mirror, guys," Parry muttered. "Trust me, you don't want to see what it has to show you."

Ambrite strode over to Parry and placed a hand on her shoulder. They could've been sisters with different-coloured hair.

"What happened to you, Parry? Why did you change to look like me? You look amazing, by the way, but I'm curious…what did the mirror show?"

Everybody in the room turned to look at Parry. She felt her cheeks redden. This was not the kind of spotlight she preferred.

"I saw…me…but old."

Ambrite let out a laugh and Slade joined in. Parry glared at the both of them.

"That's it?" Ambrite cackled. "News flash, Par, we are all going to get old one day."

The room went quiet, and this time it was Ambrite's turn to flush.

"Well…not all of us."

Cerus was the only one in the room who grinned.

"You don't get it," Parry shouted. She batted angrily at a cloud of mist that was getting too close to her nostrils. "I wasn't just old… I was hideous. A hag! I had no teeth, liver spots, disgusting hair, and blue lips like I was already dead. I looked like a villain in a horror movie! There was no life left in me at all. The Maiden told me that would be my future if I didn't stop caring so much about looks and pushing potential good guys away. So I decided to completely change my look and sleep…" She clapped a hand over her mouth before confessing her dirty little secret.

Ambrite glared at her with a force that could have shattered every mirror in the world. For a second, Parry was certain she had put the pieces together.

"So what you're saying is," Ambrite said between gritted teeth, "that looking like me means you don't care about your looks?"

Parry immediately regretted her choice of words, but how could she explain why she had asked for 'the Ambrite' at the barbershop without revealing her night with Hunter?

"No, that's not what I meant at all. It's actually a compliment…" Parry sputtered.

"Whatever." Ambrite shrugged. She turned to the Maiden. "So, let's get on with it so we can get the hell out of here. Where is Graham?"

The Maiden, seemingly amused by the verbal transaction between the two girls, smirked and sauntered over to her glass. She put up a misty force-field to prevent anybody else coming forward.

"Is this the part where she says, 'Mirror, Mirror on the wall'?" whispered Slade to Parry. She knew he was trying to make her feel better, but she felt lousy. Ambrite hated her and rightly so. She didn't even know the worst part. Even though they had never been an item, Parry strangely felt like the 'other woman'.

The Maiden stared into her glass and pressed her forehead against it. From where they were all standing, the haze was too thick to see anything that was projected back. She murmured something unintelligible and kissed the surface with her full red lips. When she turned around, not a smudge was to be seen. Ganymede let out a lustful sigh.

"Bitch," Parry heard Ambrite mutter. She agreed. It wasn't fair that one person could be so unbelievably flawless. It made the rest of the galaxy look like trolls.

"Well?" Slade quirked an eyebrow.

The Maiden brushed the misty force-field away with manicured fingernails. However, she remained standing firmly between her companions and the mirror.

"It was a strange vision to be sure," she mused. "The boy was sitting on a dirty floor, drinking from a bottle."

"Uh, are you saying he was drunk and drowning his sorrows with booze?" Slade snorted.

The Maiden wrinkled her nose in disgust. "No, silly boy. He was reviving himself with water. His face was sweaty and strained. Almost as if he had just fainted. The location was filthy, but I cannot place it."

"Describe it, dear," Cerus grunted. "I know the galaxy quite well. What else could you see?"

"The boy looked completely dishevelled. Honestly, I'm not sure he's worth saving in that condition." The Maiden pouted.

Ambrite let out a savage growl which bounced off the Coloured Cavern's walls, startling everyone in the room. "I have had it with you egotistical counterparts! Can you just let us see the mirror? Maybe we can figure out where he is. He is worth more than all your lives put together."

With that, she strode forward and grasped the edges of the glass before the Maiden could even squeak in protest. Parry watched Ambrite's facial expression turn from wildly angry, to confused, then back to wildly angry as she studied the mirror.

"Is this supposed to be a joke?"

"What? Is Graham okay?" Parry's heart thundered a mile a minute. She missed her best friend more than she could express. The guilt of not being there for him when he was abducted was ravenously eating away at her.

Ambrite looked ready to reply in a scathing manner but stopped when she saw Parry's stricken expression.

"Graham isn't here." She fixed a penetrating gaze on the Maiden, who wasn't meeting her eyes. "It's just that ugly old hag you described."

Parry felt her gut twist. She faced the Maiden, determined to get answers.

"How can that be? Ambrite is immortal, and even if she weren't, she wouldn't look the same as I will in the future."

Slade ran forward and gently pushed Ambrite to the side. He looked into the mirror, frowning at what was reflected back.

"That's strange. I see the same hag, and it's definitely not male."

"Hey!" Ganymede called. "Come back here, you impudent Aquarian.

If my Maiden does not want you touching her personal property, it's for a very good reason."

"Yeah," Ambrite sneered. "The reason being she's a dirty liar."

"How dare you!" the Maiden shrieked. The entire Cavern of Grey rumbled and shook with the force of her ire. Ambrite yawned. "I never lied," the Virgo continued. "I saw Graham sitting in a place resembling a mine. When I finished using it, the mirror returned to its usual projection…the hag, as you call it." She uttered those last words with a sombre moan. Parry had never seen her look so forlorn.

"Darling," Ganymede gushed, "come to me and let me wrap you in these loving arms."

Cerus hit the mooning counterpart in the face with a loud thwack of his tail. Ganymede pawed at his cheeks, snarling at the grinning bull. Parry had to stifle a laugh.

"Enough, you idiot," Cerus sighed. "You are the last person she would come to for comfort."

"Oh, and I suppose a smelly beast like yourself would win her affection?" Ganymede chortled, arms crossed.

"Silence!" the Maiden demanded. The room fell quiet once more. She turned to Parry with sad eyes. Her vulnerability was beautiful. "I owe you an explanation and an apology, Parry."

"Just tell me," Parry croaked, a lump forming in her throat. "Is that hag me when I'm old?"

The Maiden shook her head.

Parry didn't know whether to jump for joy or throw up. "Well, who is it, then?"

"Me," the Maiden whispered.

A hush filled the room as Parry tried to process what she had just heard and what that meant for her future. It took her only a second to realise she would never be able to cope with this revelation. Her friends and even the counterparts had enough sense to remain silent. They knew this was her fight and her fight alone. She wanted to scream until her throat was raw, but all she could manage was a choked whisper.

"How could you?"

The Maiden opened her mouth to respond, but it was too late.

"How could you?" Parry shrieked. "You have no idea what you did to me!" Tears began streaming down her cheeks faster than she could wipe them away. The pain poured out in reckless waves; the fury followed. "You made me believe that I would die alone and ugly. You forced me to do something I never would. I lost my virginity because of you!"

Parry grabbed at her coarse hair and moaned pitifully. Ambrite, no longer angry, tried to embrace her, but Parry stepped aside, her arms raised defensively.

"Just tell me why," Parry continued, sobbing. "Why are you so awful? Why did you make me feel like a miserable human being? Why do you pretend to be so perfect when you're clearly not?"

The Maiden drifted forward. "Parry, if you would just give me a chance to explain…please."

"No!" Parry cried hysterically. "Why should I? How do I know anything you say is real? Because of you I made stupid, irreversible decisions and wasn't with Graham when he needed me most. I could've saved him."

This sudden realisation made her all the angrier. She let out another scream and strode over to the mirror. With all her might, she attempted to push it over and watch the glass smash with satisfaction, but it didn't budge. She repeated the same actions three more times before bursting into a fresh wave of sobs and sinking to the floor next to the throne. Ambrite and Slade ran over to her. This time, she allowed them to show affection. They draped their arms around her shoulders and cuddled her closely. She wept miserably in the folds of their clothing.

The Maiden cautiously edged towards her throne and sat down, smoothing out her dress. She placed a hand on Parry's head and gently stroked her hair. It felt comforting. Much like her mother used to do when she was sick. Back before looks meant everything.

"Parry," the counterpart crooned, "I am deeply sorry for your heart-ache. I would not have told such a damaging lie had I known you would react so strongly. When you caught my 'other self' in the mirror, I panicked and used it to my advantage. You see, whilst I professed that you would look this way in the future, I was not being dishonest when I said that your pride and superficiality would be your downfall. If you had continued to view the physical as the most important thing, you would've ended up leading a very lonely life. You may not see it as I do, but my lesson had a positive effect on you. In a matter of hours, you chopped off your beloved hair and allowed somebody to get close to you…intimately."

Parry's face burned. She immediately regretted mentioning the loss of her virginity during her mental meltdown. Her friends stared at her with eager questions in their eyes.

"Without even properly realising it," the Maiden continued, "you took the first steps in changing the course of your destiny. Do you remember the promise I made you?"

Parry looked up, shaking her head and sniffing.

"I declared that if you could prove to me that beauty was not the most important thing the next time we met, I would surrender fighting and convince my allies to join me as well. Well, you have satisfied my requirements. I am very proud of you."

Ambrite released her hold on Parry and gazed up at the Maiden. "Does this mean the three of you will stop competing to rule the stars?"

The Maiden giggled. "Oh, we are still very much in competition, dear immortal, but the outcome no longer matters. Whoever is victorious will be rewarded with praises, not prizes."

Cerus let out a huff of discontent but didn't argue. Ganymede stood enraptured by the beautiful Virgo.

"So…obvious question," Slade said. "Why does your other half look like that? I mean, who is the real you?"

Parry shot Slade a grateful smile. She had been very curious about that herself.

"The real me," the Maiden said, "is both what you see before you and the mirror's reflection. Every single counterpart has two forms. The animals like Cerus have human forms. The rest of us have identities that resemble our limitations. My 'companion' is who I would've become had I never been transformed into a counterpart. She serves as a constant reminder that without the gift of immortality, I am destined to wither like all mortals. Time escapes no man except the one whom the hourglass cannot affect."

"So, the hag…I mean the elderly woman," Parry corrected. "Her purpose is to teach you the same lesson you were trying to teach me?"

The Maiden nodded. "This is why I so desperately wanted you to understand. I shall always be flawless so long as I remain a counterpart, but I cannot escape what could have always been. She is there, day after day, year after year, taunting me. You, as a mortal, have the ability now to age gracefully and carry what matters most in your heart. By the time you reach the end of your life, the physical will no longer matter. You will be surrounded by love, happiness, and fulfillment. That is the most beautiful thing of all."

Parry leaned against her friends, who hugged her tightly. She didn't have to be alone anymore. She was loved by so many people. She thought of Hunter and his soft lips. The passion they had shared. Did he feel the same? She envisioned asking him out on a date when they returned home. It felt nice.

"Ganymede, Cerus," the Maiden said, addressing her allies, "do you feel any differently now that you've witnessed my other form?"

The Aquarian and the Taurus burst into a babble of reassurances.

"You, my darling, are perfection!"

"All the hags in the world could not change the way I feel about you…I mean…elderly women."

"You are a divine being…a vision!"

"You should see *my* other form!"

The Maiden raised a hand to silence them, but she was smiling with bright eyes. "How fortunate I am to have such loyal friends."

Parry felt the same. She turned to Ambrite and Slade, who were slowly lifting themselves off the stone floor. They held out a hand each and pulled her up. Without thinking, she faced Ambrite and spoke before losing her nerve.

"I know you're going to ask, so here it is. I slept with Hunter. I shaved my hair to look like yours so he would be more interested in being with me. At first, I was trying to prove that I wouldn't die alone, but…I really like him. He's sweet. I hope you don't mind?"

Ambrite stared at Parry in shock. Clearly, she hadn't been expecting her answer. Slade just looked uncomfortable and awkward.

"I'm sorry," Parry added. "Please don't hate me."

Ambrite shook her head in disbelief, but she didn't appear angry or disappointed. "I don't hate you, Parry," she said. "I'm just surprised. Hunter has been pining after me for so long. I've been really worried about leaving him and starting a new life with Wasabi here, but if you promise to take care of him, I'll feel a lot better."

Parry nodded gratefully and took Ambrite's hands in her own. "I promise…that is…if he feels the same way and even wants me around when we get back."

"He will." Ambrite squeezed her hands. "This may be the lesbian talking, but I think you look way hotter now than you did before. You have some serious hardcore sass happening."

"You know, I don't hate it." Parry flushed. "I actually really like it. Plus, the low-maintenance factor is a huge bonus. I never realised just how much work and time I put into styling my hair each day. I could've been doing something more productive…"

"Absolutely!" Ambrite agreed.

"Like perfecting my contouring." Parry beamed.

Ambrite let go of Parry's hands and patted her on the back. "Close enough."

At the sound of Slade clearing his throat rather dramatically and loudly, the two girls turned to face him. He sounded like an old man during an allergy attack. Ganymede had his fingers in his ears and a pained expression on his face.

"I'm so glad that everything has been resolved," Slade began, "but we need to work out where Graham is and get to him pronto. I'm concerned that he won't be there anymore by the time we arrive."

"I agree with the mortal." Cerus nodded. "Maiden, you mentioned a mine? I believe I know where he might be."

"Where?" Parry, Ambrite, and Slade chorused.

"Well" – Cerus puffed up his bulky torso – "the only one I know of in this galaxy is on Liria. It is filled with precious gems and ingots for the workers to extract."

"Liria," Ambrite murmured. "Garth mentioned that place. Isn't that where Charlie's father is? Why would Graham need to go to a mine? It seems really odd."

"Who knows what that horrible imposter has him doing?" Parry shook in anger. "He could be a full-blown slave now. If he's trapped down there, labouring his beautiful muscles away, we need to rescue him."

Slade turned to Ganymede, who was smiling with impressively white teeth. "I'm guessing it isn't too far away for your Aquarian Air?"

"Correct, little human," the counterpart sang. "Liria is only a three-hour flight aboard the Aquarian Air. I do have some use after all!"

"Hallelujah," Cerus huffed drily.

Ambrite shot him a *Don't be a bully* look.

"Come." Ganymede strode to the centre of the Coloured Cavern. "Let us waste no more precious time. I will ensure safe passage from Bastion to Liria and back."

The group gathered around Ganymede as he held the urn out in front of him and muttered a string of words in an ancient language. Parry felt the air pressure take a dramatic dive. The tiny little stones on the cave floor danced and bounced as the Coloured Cavern whirred and thrummed with power. The urn started to ooze wisps of azure light and mist, signifying its excitement at finally being used.

Parry shivered against the howling wind whipping through the insulated cave. Slade and Ambrite were rubbing their arms in discomfort. Ganymede smiled at everybody. It was time to unleash the Aquarian Air. With both hands, he began to turn the urn towards the entrance of the Cavern of Grey when several voices shouted at him to stop. Ganymede let out a terrified squeal, nearly dropping the urn for the second time in shock. The momentum of increasing power died instantly, and the room returned to its comfortable temperature. The light and mist faded as quickly as it had poured out.

It took Parry a second to realise that an unlikely band of characters had formed around the entrance, directly in line with where the Aquarian Air would have been unleashed. Before her stood Danni, Charlotte, Reilly, Drew, Hannah, Chiron, Charlie, Karki, Castor, Pollux, Sirena, and Calypsee.

"Are you going to Liria?" Danni pleaded. "Please bring us with you!"

"How did you know we were going to Liria?" Cerus demanded.

Chiron let out a pompous laugh. Parry was surprised to see his hand lightly touching the small of Reilly's back in a very protective manner.

"Calm yourself, bull. We are simply going to alert the child's father of what has happened and reunite them."

At the mention of his father, Charlie leapt in the air with a loud cheer. Karki giggled and clapped her hands in delight. Parry noticed a small smile forming on the Maiden's lips. A happy child could melt the heart of any human, counterpart or no.

"This will be difficult," Ganymede tutted. "With our new additions, the Aquarian Air will have to hold eighteen of us. I hope nobody minds getting up close and personal?"

Parry watched Reilly and Chiron exchange electrically charged looks.

"I don't think all of us mind." She winked in their direction. Reilly blushed and tore her gaze away from the counterpart.

"Hang on," Slade interjected. "Does Aquarian Air not hold unlimited people? It's air!"

"Oh, you sweet, simple boy." Ganymede tutted. "Once released, the Aquarian Air becomes an air wave. If you stray too far off the edges, you will plummet to your death. It is that simple. Also, the air wave protects you during space travel. Navigate outside of its boundaries and say good-bye to your precious life."

"What could go wrong?" Ambrite muttered sarcastically.

Everybody looked nervous except the counterparts and Charlie. Parry could tell some of them were close to backing out.

"Okay, Mr. Fancy," Charlotte spat rudely. "Can you make sure that none of us go outside these boundaries? I'm guessing you will be the only one who can see them?"

Castor and Pollux snickered in approval. Whatever Parry felt about the Maiden, she was glad the delicious yet awful twins weren't her counterparts. They were far too obnoxious, in her opinion.

Ganymede stared down at Charlotte as if she were no bigger than a bug. His withering glare made her break eye contact. "Yes…I am the only one who can see the boundaries. I propose that four counterparts volunteer to sit at each end so that you humans don't overstep the limits. I am happy to be one of them."

"I will gladly protect my friends." Karki raised a tiny hand.

"As will I," Chiron added, addressing Reilly more than anybody else.

"I feel I have much to atone for." The Maiden nodded. "I will keep you all safe."

Parry nodded at her counterpart. She appreciated the gesture.

Ganymede stamped his foot in earnest. "Let us be going, then. We have three hours of travel ahead of us, which may not seem like much, but if you are hungry or need to use the bathroom, it could be quite a nuisance. I suggest you all quickly adhere to your needs now or forever hold your peace."

The Astro A Team all looked at one another.

"Five minutes!" Danni called, and they raced off back to the Mission Base to refuel.

It was completely empty. There were no signs of Asterion, Garth, or any of the other remaining members. The buffet, however, was fully stocked with fresh hot food for the taking. Mini pizzas, burgers, chips, sweets, drinks, and more were arranged in perfect piles with brown paper bags and tongs on the counter for take-away service.

"Man, am I going to miss this place, if only for the food," Drew groaned in hunger.

"So we don't waste any time" – Danni grinned – "would you and your girlfriend make up bags of goodies for all of us to take whilst some of us go…adhere to our needs?"

"Sure!" Hannah beamed. "Come on, Charlie, let's get you some food."

Parry walked with Danni, Ambrite, and Reilly to the bathroom. She leaned in close to the Gemini. "Are we really going to go without Brodie, Ronan, Crawford, and Hunter?"

Danni turned to her with a stricken expression. She had seemed fine up until this moment. "I'm worried about Ronan," she sighed. "I haven't heard from him since he went to see Aegipan. Before we found you guys, we went to Slade's Coloured Cavern to see if Ganymede was there. Well, the rest went. I ran to Ronan's, but it was empty. I'm sure they are both fine, but I'm scared he's going to be upset once he learns we left without him."

Parry nodded. The girls stepped into the bathhouse and locked themselves into different cubicles. After a minute of awkward silence, Ambrite spoke in a reserved voice.

"Do you think Wasabi is okay?"

Parry heard a flush and the banging of a stall door. Somebody was now washing her hands. She could smell the coconut soap from the dispenser.

"Yes, I have no doubt, Amb," Reilly responded over the gushing water. "She's gone to the valley to negotiate with the Unsigned. We can't interrupt this important mission. By the time we get back, she won't even know we were gone."

"You sound pretty optimistic," Parry heard Danni say as a second figure flushed.

"Well, I hate to sound naïve" – Reilly's voice carried throughout the bathhouse – "but what could go wrong on a planet like Liria? It's where Charlie's father works. Plus, we have the counterparts to protect us."

Parry flushed and walked out at the same time as Ambrite. Reilly and Danni stepped aside as they joined them at the sinks.

"Yeah, but not all of us have a handsome centaur to keep us safe." Ambrite wiggled her eyebrows.

Reilly bit her lip, cheeks reddening. She wiped her wet hands vigorously on her skirt.

"We are not judging you, girl." Parry smiled. "He is gorgeous. I totally get the appeal, horse man or not."

Reilly met eyes with Parry, her blush deepening. "I actually don't know what to tell you guys without sounding ridiculous. Every time I'm about to say something, I stop myself because it's so stupid. What do I say? We are taking it slow? Um, we are hopefully getting off this planet soon, so how slow can we take it? We are dating? Where is he going to take me? Bastion is basically a ghost town now. This is not exactly the most conventional relationship."

"Understatement!" Ambrite laughed. "But who am I to judge? I'm immortal, and my hopefully soon-to-be girlfriend's name is Wasabi. Do they even eat that here? Do they even know what that is?"

"I'm not even going to get into my love life," Parry said, eyes downcast. She refused to make eye contact lest they begin asking her questions.

Danni threw her arm around Reilly, a huge grin on her face. "Well, girls, I wish I could share, but Ronan is the man! No complaints here."

Ambrite mimed sticking two fingers down her throat and gagging.

Reilly bumped Danni playfully with her hip. "Yeah, we see the way you two moon at each other. It makes us sick, but we're happy for you both."

"Before I forget," Parry interrupted. "We are going to Liria because we believe Graham might be there…"

Danni and Reilly rounded on both girls, faces startled. They both spoke at once.

"Why did you wait so long to tell us?" Reilly spluttered.

"How can you be sure?" Danni frowned.

Parry looked at Ambrite, who silently gestured for her to explain. "My counterpart has the ability to use her mirror and see where people are at that exact point in time."

"Oh, like in *Beauty and the Beast*." Reilly beamed.

"I guess?" Parry shrugged. She had never been a big fan of Disney, but she wasn't about to voice that unpopular opinion. "Anyway, she saw Graham sitting in a mine, drinking water from a bottle. Cerus told us that the only mine he knows of is on Liria. It's where the workers, like Charlie's dad, get their goods."

Reilly seemed satisfied with the news, but Danni's face went ashen.

"Now I feel even worse about leaving without all of us," she moaned. "What if we come face to face with Milo and don't have the resources or numbers to stop him?"

"There's nothing we can do," Reilly said. "You looked for Ronan; he wasn't there. Wasabi is doing important stuff, and Asterion and Garth aren't back yet from Cassius. Let's just go and see what we find. It's not fair to keep Charlie from his only surviving parent."

The four of them walked out of the bathhouse into the empty Mission Base. Parry noticed what looked like Drew's foot disappearing into the Cavern of Grey. It felt so quiet and empty. She cast a glance at Hunter's still unmade bed. Not that long ago they had been fervently intertwined, mouths hot on one another, moving together as one. The thought made her insides wriggle. He had known just what to do.

"Let's go catch up," she squeaked, still torn between reality and her memory.

They raced through the dark Coloured Cavern until it eventually opened up into the ethereal parlour of the Maiden. Everybody was standing in the centre again, circled around Ganymede and his urn. The girls made their way over to the crowd.

"Come now, what took you so long?" Ganymede scowled. "We are leaving this time, no exceptions."

Parry hugged herself tightly in anticipation right before the Coloured Cavern dropped several degrees in temperature. Everything rattled and shook as the urn spewed mist and light once more. Ganymede turned it towards the entrance, much faster and less ceremonial this time. At the pinnacle of power, he shouted something in an ancient language, which caused the urn to expel every bit of Aquarian Air trapped within it. To the untrained eye, it would appear nothing had happened, but Parry could just see the faint outlines of what looked to be a giant mattress floating and waving in the room.

"Counterparts, please seat yourselves at the four corners," Ganymede commanded. Karki, Chiron, the Maiden, and, lastly, Ganymede seated themselves at the edges of the air wave. It was incredibly strange seeing them float on nothingness. The Astro A Team, plus Charlie, who nestled himself in Hannah's lap, stuck as close to the centre as possible. Reilly was the only one who moved near Chiron.

Ganymede nodded at them all with respect. Parry felt strangely honoured to be a part of the mission.

"To Liria!" the counterpart cried.

The air wave took off with a whizzing *whoosh*. It had zipped through the Coloured Cavern and out of the Mission Base before Parry could blink an eye. She closed her eyes, hugging her knees as they hurtled towards the stars and out of the atmosphere. This form of travel felt twenty times faster than flying via airplane.

She could hear Drew handing out rustling brown bags of food to everybody. Somebody nudged her, but she just shook her head and waved it away. She was much too queasy and unsettled to think about eating. There was something extremely confronting about coming face to face with the stars this easily when organisations such as NASA had to spend years preparing for one visit to the moon. It felt wrong.

A collective gasp from her friends indicated that they were no longer on Bastion. Screwing up her courage, she squeezed one eye open…and then two. The air wave was floating, at a much softer pace, through a vast galaxy of glittering lights. It was overwhelming and altogether humbling. A lump formed in her throat and unexpected tears splashed onto her cheeks. She knew in that very moment, no matter what happened, she was the luckiest girl in the entire universe. She wasn't alone. She wasn't going to age into a withered old crone. She, Parry Mason, was a beautiful human being…inside *and* out.

Chapter 16

A Piece of the Puzzle

"I hate to be a downer" – Brodie sighed for the umpteenth time since setting foot in the Place of Pages – "but this seems ridiculously impossible. Not just impossible…but ridiculously so."

Equas hadn't spoken to her once since they had opened the enormous tome outlining every registered and known planet in each registered and known galaxy. At first, Brodie had been hopeful it wouldn't take long after their search was narrowed down to a single galaxy, Hyrin – but that large glossy heading had close to three hundred planets listed underneath, with detailed descriptions of each. Equas ignored her, trailing a stony finger down each dot-point. Brodie watched in fascination as her counterpart somehow absorbed the information written on the brittle pages and relayed it to her brain. Equas paused frequently, finger gently tapping every now and then to ensure she didn't miss anything. Brodie wanted to lean in close like she would with a study-buddy, but unfortunately, her companion was too stony to rub shoulders with. She could barely make out any of the words. It made her feel useless. Letting out her most exaggerated sigh yet, she grabbed Equas's finger a little too forcefully before it drifted to the next planet. The counterpart lifted her heavy head in confusion, looking slightly to the left of Brodie.

"Is something wrong?" Equas rasped.

Brodie shook her head before realising Equas couldn't see her.

"No, it's just that I'm not helping at all. I want to know what's going on. What have you learned? Are we any closer to solving this thing? Can I do something…anything at all?"

Equas hung her head in what appeared to be shame, although Brodie imagined it would be difficult holding up something as weighty as that, even at eye level.

"I apologise, Brodie. As you can see, I am visually challenged, so reading a book is not a simple process for one like myself. It takes a strong degree of concentration. Also, I sense your discomfort at my hard exterior. You do not wish to look over my shoulder. I understand. However, with those two factors combined, it makes this task a one-person job."

Brodie, still holding Equas's finger, released it and patted her rocky hand. "I get it, but can you see how stuff like this plays into my insecurities of feeling like I have nothing to offer? At least give me regular updates."

Equas nodded very slowly. "I apologise," she repeated. "What I have done, with my existing knowledge, is mark all of the planets that I know to be either currently inhabited with citizens, filled with noxious gases, too small to reside on, or infested with dangerous beasts and flora. Then, I have…"

"Sorry," Brodie interrupted. "Marked how? The pages look the same, and I can tell this place has a zero-tolerance policy on marking up these precious books."

Equas flipped to the very back of the book, which held excess blank pages. Brodie could make out a faint list scrawled in elegant silver typography detailing which planets Milo and Graham couldn't possibly be on.

"Are you allowed to do that?" Brodie asked, wide-eyed.

Equas tapped her finger once more and, like magic, the list disappeared. "There is no permanent damage this way," she explained. "Now that I have my first list, I can tap the planets remaining and move them into a second list, which will be nicely narrowed down. Once we have our two lists, you can tell me all you know about Graham, Milo, and last evening. It may provide some sort of clue."

Brodie felt a rush of respect for her counterpart. She was so calm, efficient, and organised. There was just one hitch in her plan.

"Hmmm, so last night I was knocked unconscious by Milo," she muttered. "I'll do my best to remember what happened beforehand, but I might not be the person to interview."

Equas turned to look in her direction. "I believe you are the most ideal person to interrogate. You were there before the others. Your intuition led you to follow your friend. I value your account of the events that transpired more than anybody else's."

Brodie flushed. It felt nice to be treated with such importance. She wasn't sure if Equas meant what she had just said or was simply trying to make her feel better, but either way, it worked.

"All right, you do your second list thingy and I'll start thinking about what happened before I was thrown halfway across the room."

She closed her eyes and drifted back to the evening before. She remembered following Graham up the spiral staircase to the roof of Constellar, a lovesick smile plastered on his face. The air had smelt off, as though pre-empting the many deaths to come. A figure in a long maroon robe was hidden in the shadows. Brodie had just assumed he was Serket, the Scorpio counterpart. She had watched Graham embrace him with so much passion and adoring love, it had seemed forced – almost manipulated. The imposter was calling him 'my darling' and 'my love'.

At the precise moment that Milo had said, "No matter, my babies will find them and finish the job wherever they are," Brodie had stepped into their line of sight without thinking. She had tried to warn Graham to move away from him, but an invisible force had flowed through her friend that would not waver. He had attempted to assure her that this man was his everything, but nothing had ever felt so wrong. Her heart sank at the memory of Graham's involuntary smile. His beautiful eyes had looked so hopeful as he declared, "This is the love of my life, Brodie. His name is Serket, and we are going to live on this new planet he made just for us."

Brodie's eyes flew open. Maybe it was nothing, but the wording Graham had used provided a potential clue. She put a hand on Equas's hard shoulder.

"I'm sorry to interrupt you, but I remembered something that may be important."

Equas paused her page-tapping and nodded encouragingly.

"Graham said something about him and Milo living on a new planet made just for them, but we also know that a zillion scorpions were unleashed onto Constellar last night. Where the hell did they come from? Is there a planet on your list that is home to those creepy monsters?"

Equas didn't respond for several moments. Brodie bounced in her chair, eager to learn if she had hit the jackpot.

"The unfortunate thing is," Equas said softly, "Serket would have known about a planet like that due to his creature connection. We are now no longer in a position to ask him. Looking at this list, there are fifty-five planets that could be Graham and Milo's new home, but it seems entirely foolish to visit each one when time is of the essence."

Brodie let out a heavy sigh. "Do none of the planets have clue-type names like Scorpius or Milo's Pad?" She had meant the last one as a joke, but her counterpart didn't laugh.

"The names do not relate in any way," Equas rasped. "Trust me, I have already scanned them for relevance."

"Why is our planet called Bastion?" Brodie asked, momentarily moving away from the subject.

"Bastion is another term for 'defender'," Equas explained. "We twelve are meant to symbolise a stronghold for the galaxy Hyrin. It is our responsibility to support the stars and keep order. As you can see…it is working well."

"Was that sarcasm?" Brodie grinned. Equas shrugged weighted shoulders. "So we're back to square one…" Brodie groaned, her shoulders slumping.

"Not necessarily." Equas shifted in her seat. "You raised a very interesting point regarding Milo's creatures. They would require a certain terrain or habitat, rather, to thrive on. There are a few planets listed here that have sub-zero temperatures; therefore, they can now be eliminated from the rest."

Nervous energy coursed through her veins. It felt like they were close. A small, insecure part of her wanted to be the one to solve the mystery of Milo's location and prove her place in the Astro A Team.

"I don't know what scorpions in the Hyrin galaxy are like, but back in school, we learnt that they prefer dry places like the desert…and the dark! They love the dark."

Equas bobbed her head in agreement, tapping various planets on the page. "It is the same in Hyrin. This may explain why they were much more powerful during the battle at Constellar. It took place in the deepest part of the night."

Brodie wanted to say something lame, like that they made a good team or *Libran powers, unite!* but she held back. Equas didn't seem like the high-fiving, fist-bumping type.

"I guess the obvious thing to do now is to narrow down all the planets that have a dry or dark landscape. That must be where Milo is hiding. He would want those creepies close just in case."

"I will need to research each of their profiles," Equas agreed. "Give me a few moments to concentrate."

Brodie watched her counterpart in silence as Equas flipped back and forth between the pages of the giant tome, feeling for each description and tapping when she located a potential candidate. She wondered how Ronan and Aegipan were faring. She didn't envy the Capricorn and his crusty old counterpart. If she strained her hearing, she could just detect their whispering down the hall. For the first time in hours, she also thought about Slade. How was her brother? What was he doing? They had always been best friends, ever since they were toddlers. It felt strange to be working on a serious mission separately. There was so much uncertainty surrounding Graham's fate and their journey back home, it made Brodie's stomach gurgle nervously. Equas looked up at the sudden sound, then straight back down to her work. Brodie couldn't think about those things now. She needed to keep a clear head and contribute as best as possible.

After what felt like an eternity, Equas made a sound resembling a choking bird.

"What the hell was that?" Brodie jumped.

"I have done it." Equas forced a warped smile to her stony façade. "I have limited the search to only two possible planets, Corathinia and Malvolt. Both possess dry, arid landscapes that are devoid of any life as far as we know. Not a single thing can grow on either of them, hence the lack of civilians, flora, and fauna. The single difference between them is that Malvolt is eternally dark due to its positioning in Hyrin, whereas Corathinia is lit by neighbouring planets. Milo's creatures could exist comfortably on both. It is up to us to choose the correct planet, as they are situated at opposite ends of the galaxy."

"Great work!" Brodie cheered triumphantly without a thought for any of the others studying. "We need to find the others and take a vote."

Having pushed her chair back, Brodie stood and stretched her aching limbs. Equas remained seated.

"Come on," Brodie urged. "Let's grab Aegipan and Ronan and head back to the Mission Base."

"They are gone." Equas shook her heavy head. "The majority of your friends have left for Liria. I sense it. Garth and Asterion are still on Cassius, tending to important work. Wasabi lies in the valley, and Hunter and Crawford are with their counterparts."

Before Brodie could protest, Ronan and Aegipan sidled up behind her.

"We heard you yell." Ronan grinned. "Tell me you have good news for us."

"Such noise in the Place of Pages," Aegipan grumbled. "It is most unbecoming."

Brodie stuck out her tongue at the wide-eyed goat. "We have good and bad news. The good news is Equas discovered the only two possible planets in Hyrin that Milo and Graham could be on."

It could have been a trick of the light, but her stony counterpart appeared slightly smug at Brodie's confession. Aegipan looked pea-green with envy.

"Amazing!" Ronan leaned forward and clapped Equas on the shoulder only to wince and clutch his palm in pain. "What is the bad news?" he groaned.

Brodie inhaled deeply. She didn't know Ronan overly well, but if he was anything like Slade…well… "A big chunk of the Astro A Team have left for Liria already. I'm not sure how, but Equas can sense it. Apparently, Hunter and Crawford are still here, but the rest are gone, and I have no idea when they'll be back…"

Ronan stared at Brodie, expressionless. He turned to Aegipan with a hint of steel in his tone. "Did you know?"

Aegipan looked everywhere but at him, forcing Ronan to take a step forward and breathe the same air; such was their close proximity.

"Did you know about this?"

"Yes," muttered the goat. "I sensed it as well. I didn't want to distract you from the fine work we were doing. *We* learnt how Milo absorbed Serket's powers and killed him." With that last declaration, Aegipan threw a smarmy look at Equas, who appeared bored.

"I don't care about any of that," Ronan hissed. Brodie moved to calm him down, but the Capricorn stepped even closer. "You let Danni leave for another planet without telling me? Oh, I am going to kick your bony butt."

Aegipan bleated in terror, causing a few shadowy figures to look up and shush him.

"Don't make me use my ability on you, boy," he squeaked. "I will do it."

"I'd like to see you try," Ronan snarled.

"Stop it!" Brodie interjected, standing in between them, palms flat on their chests. "Ronan, I get that you're upset, but starting a fight in a library, of all places, isn't going to achieve anything. I'm sorry Danni left without you, but I'm sure she had her reasons. She will be fine. Once they get back, we can all go together. I hate to admit it, but Aegipan is right. You and I had important work to do here and didn't need the distraction. Let's wait for them in the Mission Base. Trust me, I'm not happy that Slade isn't here either, but what can I do?"

Ronan nodded, looking slightly ashamed. Aegipan watched him warily with beady eyes under his spectacles. Equas was staring off into space.

"I have to say something that I never would have said before I met Danni." Ronan smirked. "You are a classic Libra, Brodes."

"How so?" Brodie said.

"You're a peacemaker." He smiled warmly. "You hate conflict and you aren't afraid to set things straight."

"I guess I am!" Brodie laughed.

Equas, having returned to reality, looked up in Ronan's direction. "The boy is wise, Aegipan. You would do well to learn a thing or two from him."

Aegipan's face turned black, but before he could begin screaming, Brodie cut him off.

"As I said earlier," she said hurriedly, "let's head back to the Mission

Base ready for a debriefing."

Equas slowly stood as Aegipan began creating a portal in one of the dark empty stacks.

Brodie watched Ronan stare wistfully at the shelves of mystical tomes. She felt the same pang of loss.

"I am going to miss it here too," she whispered.

"I just wish I could've shared it with Danni," Ronan murmured. He stroked one of the leather-bound spines, savouring the touch of ancient knowledge.

"Well, maybe if you don't aggravate your counterpart too much" – Brodie wiggled her eyebrows – "he might let you take her here after we save the day."

The portal shimmered and waved, inviting them to enter. Equas and Aegipan had already disappeared inside.

"Just be thankful your counterpart isn't a stubborn old goat." Ronan grinned, staring at the black space before him.

"Yeah, I'm pretty lucky," Brodie said.

Together they stepped through the unknown, leaving a place they would never forget for the rest of their lives.

*

It wasn't easy leading a revolution, a whole community of people depending on just her. There was a lot at stake, and if she couldn't deliver on her promises, guess who would get the blame. On the way back to the Mission Base, Wasabi recited the terms of the Unsigned over and over in her head. Occasionally, she said them aloud. Bastion was a ghost town; who could possibly hear her or even care?

"One," she muttered. "Asterion bans the colour system. If Constellar is rebuilt, there must be only one male and female bathroom for everybody to use. Two, the Unsigned get to choose which empty houses they want. Mr. Arthurton will receive top medical care. Three, this will all be done on a trial basis. If it does not work out, the Unsigned will move back to the valley."

Every time she pictured delivering her epic speech, metaphorical snakes slithered through her nervous system. These were big demands for a planet that had always run the same way. But then again…nothing this disastrous had ever struck Bastion before. This seemed like as perfect a time as any to make lasting positive changes.

Her heart beat faster as the entrance slowly approached. Wasabi was nervous about her message, but she recognised with a small smile that some of the adrenaline was in anticipation of seeing Ambrite again. At the very least, she would have her support. Things had moved quickly between the pair of them, but trauma had a way of doing that. Once one bypassed the surface-level 'getting to know you' stuff and endured a near-death experience, one tended to bond quickly with the other victim.

Wasabi had envisioned many scenarios taking place once she entered the Mission Base, but not once had this one crossed her mind…

It was empty. Devoid of any life, noise, or indication that people had ever been there before she left. She made her way to the buffet counter, stomach rumbling from lack of food. The trays were virtually empty save for a few mini pizzas. Wasabi wolfed them down without any hesitation. A moment later, she winced at the sudden heat burning in her chest.

"Shit!" she yelled, pounding her sternum with her fist.

"Try not to act that way on your first date," someone said from across the room.

Wasabi spun around to see the one person she had hoped to avoid. She suspected the feeling was mutual.

"Sorry." She blushed, leaning against the counter in a forced casual stance.

She watched Hunter bridge the gigantic gap between them. He looked like he had been running a marathon. His hair was soaked, and his clothes clung to his body like their life depended on it.

"Is there a pool here that nobody told me about?" Wasabi wrinkled her nose.

He didn't laugh, but she saw his lip turn slightly upwards. "Some would call it a pool, others a death trap."

"Right…" She shook her head and turned back to the buffet. After plucking a plastic cup from the tray, she poured herself a bright pink drink that tasted like liquid strawberry jam. It wasn't awful, but the aftertaste made her grimace. "Want some?" She thrust the half empty cup in his face.

"Not after the face you just made." Hunter frowned. "I was feeling a mini pizza, but you scoffed them all, so thanks for that…"

Wasabi felt slightly guilty, but her remorse quickly transitioned into annoyance. She positioned her hands on her hips and looked him square in the eye. "You really don't like me, do you?"

Hunter sidled past her, picking at a few burnt hot chips nestled in the corners of the silver trays. "Well, now that you've said it, I don't have to."

Wasabi felt her heart ache and tears start to prick her eyes. Despite her tough exterior, she was extremely sensitive. It hurt that a complete stranger detested her so openly. She turned away so he couldn't see just how much his words had affected her.

She heard him smack his lips and wipe his greasy hands on his pants.

"I have to go change. Lovely seeing you again," he sneered.

Wasabi watched him stroll over to his closet and strip down to his underwear. The rippling muscles and smooth skin did nothing to her insides, but she couldn't deny how handsome he was. If Ambrite had been interested in boys, she would certainly have gone for him. The thought made her irrationally jealous. Shaking her head, she walked over to him. This encounter, despite its awkwardness, presented valuable opportunities that she shouldn't waste.

She sat on the edge of his rumpled bed as he pulled on a pair of red swimming trunks and matching tank top. He was dressed as if going to the beach, not saving a planet in peril. As he knelt to change his shoes, he noticed her eyeing him patiently.

"Uh…what are you doing?"

Wasabi didn't flinch under his calculating stare. "I am not leaving until you and I make amends. You have just admitted that you do not like me despite not knowing anything about me. Now, I understand that you're upset. Your best friend has knocked the light out of your stars. Not only is she not interested in you romantically, but she's also decided to remain on Bastion long after you leave. That sucks hard, but I ask you this: is any of that *my* fault?"

Hunter slowly stood, not taking his eyes off her. She had never been great at understanding the male species, but there was no doubt in her mind that he was feeling conflicted.

"It's not your fault," he sighed, running his hands through his damp hair. "I'm just having a really hard time coming to terms with everything…"

Wasabi nodded sympathetically.

"You have to look at things from my point of view," he continued, exasperated. "We have been best friends for months. She knows everything about me and I know everything about her. We've shared so much pain and heartache, it's ridiculous. We even saw the same counsellor! I get that she doesn't feel the same way about me, but in less than a day, she already looks at you the way I have wanted her to look at me ever since we met. Can't you see how that kills me?"

Wasabi opened her mouth to respond, but he cut her off, the pain pouring from his lips.

"And now she is going to live on a planet that I am never going to return to…ever. It's not like I can just hop in a car and road-trip to her new digs. She will be living in another galaxy! I have lost the most important person in my life, and I can't help but hate you a little for getting everything I wanted. It's just not fair."

Wasabi bit her lip, suddenly unsure how to continue. Trusting her instincts, she patted the bed, gesturing for him to come sit beside her. Her adoptive parents hadn't always known what to say, but they'd been wonderful at comforting her without words. A squeeze of a shoulder, a heartfelt smile, a silly joke…all those things went a long way.

To her surprise, Hunter slumped next to her, their sides pressing together. She wrapped an arm around his shoulder tenderly. Feeling him stiffen, Wasabi readied herself to pull away, but after a moment, he relaxed into her warmth.

"I am so sorry, Hunter," she whispered.

"I feel like such a baby," he groaned. "Like a kid throwing a tantrum because the neighbour's kid gets to ride a brand-new mountain bike and he's stuck with the tricycle."

Wasabi giggled. "I've never heard that analogy before, but it sounds slightly sexual. Who is the tricycle?"

Hunter pulled away awkwardly, scratching at a dry patch of skin on his cheek.

"That came out wrong," he mumbled. "I…well, the reason Parry and I weren't at Constellar when shit went down was because we were here."

"I know," Wasabi said. "You were very drunk, and she helped you get home safely."

He began to scratch harder now, nails leaving a rash where they had raked his face repeatedly. Wasabi grabbed his hand to stop him. He gave her a grateful nod and placed his hand in his lap.

"That's not what happened. I mean, yes, I was stupidly drunk, but we both left Constellar knowing what would happen when we got back."

"Oh no…" Wasabi's eyes widened as she put it together.

"Yeah…"

Wasabi suddenly jumped up with a horrified expression. "I'm sitting on your sex bed, aren't I? Please tell me the sheets have been washed!"

Hunter stood and faced the scene of the crime with a mischievous grin. "Sorry, the maids haven't been by yet for turndown service. Honestly, I am going to write a letter about the hospitality here."

Wasabi glared at him, edging further away. He laughed and then stepped towards her, looking slightly more serious.

"Hey…um, I just want to say sorry, and all I ask is that you take good care of her. No words will ever describe what that human means to me."

"I will." She softened. "I barely know her, but I can already see how special she is. I won't let you down, Hunter, I promise."

They smiled shyly at one another. Wasabi turned, ready to sit on Ambrite's bed and wait for her, when the sound of footsteps thundering from different points of the Mission Base stopped her in her tracks. Wasabi noticed Hunter scanning the room, resting a hopeful gaze on the entrance to the Cavern of Green.

At the exact same moment, Brodie emerged from the Cavern of Blue and Ronan from the Cavern of Black, their counterparts trailing behind them.

The pair met in the middle and raced over to Hunter and Wasabi, breathless.

"Hey." Hunter waved. "Where is the rest of the gang?"

Ronan and Brodie exchanged glances. They gestured for one another to go first, laughed, began talking at the same time, and finally agreed that Brodie should deliver the news. Wasabi watched them in fascination.

"So," the Libran began, "it turns out that the rest of the Astro A Team have gone on a little quest without us to Liria. We have no choice but to wait here until they return."

"What?" Wasabi and Hunter echoed.

"Yeah, I wasn't happy about it either." Ronan frowned.

"Why would Ambrite leave without telling either of us?" Wasabi wondered. Her stomach began to churn, either from eating one too many mini pizzas or from dread.

"It may have been a matter of urgency." Brodie shrugged. "We don't know that they didn't come looking for us before they left."

"I'm guessing Asterion and Garth aren't back yet?" Ronan asked.

They shook their heads in silence. An uncomfortable tension hung in the air. Wasabi put it down to a feeling of hopelessness. Neither she nor anybody else in the room could do a single thing about their situation.

"Where have you guys been?" Hunter broke the moody stillness.

Aegipan jumped in before either Ronan or Brodie could explain. Wasabi found the little goat to be cute in an elderly grandpa-ish sort of way.

"We have much to explain, but as I would rather not repeat myself, perhaps it is best that we wait patiently. A formal meeting must be held regarding the information we obtained. It may not be disclosed until the morrow."

Wasabi was surprised at her ability to understand the counterpart's words. He was so proper. Glancing at the purple doors, she let out a loud sigh.

"What is it?" Hunter asked with more affection in his tone than before their conversation.

"Time," Wasabi replied. "It moves differently here. Sometimes faster, sometimes slower. It was about mid-afternoon when I arrived here from the valley. Aegipan is right. We might not get to talk to them until tomorrow. Let's just hope nothing happens to them between now and then."

"So we're supposed to just sit here and do nothing?" Hunter scoffed. He whirled on the counterparts with menace. "Get us to Liria right now. Come on, open a portal or something."

"Hunter." Wasabi glared.

The stone woman didn't appear too put out by Hunter's sudden demands. Aegipan, however, became very twitchy and bristly.

"Listen here, young man. I will not be ordered about on *my* planet! The truth of the matter is we cannot create a portal to Liria. Your friends would've been transported via Ganymede's Aquarian Air. The journey will take them three hours each way. Should Garth return before they do, he might consider opening up a portal, but until then, I suggest you sit down and mind your tongue!"

Wasabi held her breath as electrical anger crackled between the pair. She would never say it aloud, but Aegipan was right. There was nothing they could do.

In true Hunter fashion, the boy let out a growl and stalked off into the bathrooms. This was becoming a pattern for him. Aegipan snorted and disappeared into his Coloured Cavern.

Brodie, Ronan, and Wasabi shared uneasy smiles. Equas knocked herself gently against Brodie before also leaving the Mission Base.

"Apparently Crawford is still here," Ronan said. "Should we tell him what's going on?"

"Why not?" Brodie laughed. "What could go wrong, walking into a lion's den?"

*

The minions had rendered all of the workers unconscious. The Scorpios on the list had been carried onto the aircraft and thrown into a dark corner without a care. Graham had felt his stomach lurch as the two ferrymen at the docking zone were attacked and stung multiple times. The rest of the workers were left in the cave, trussed up like turkeys. To his rage, the minions had also forcefully shoved him into the aircraft and locked the only entrance/exit. They had left him to scavenge for the remaining animals in the mountains, clearly unafraid of Milo's impending wrath at hurting his most loyal companion. They had been gone for what felt like an eternity. Graham stared at Issac's drooping face and closed eyes with overwhelming guilt. They hadn't known each other long, but Issac had been good to him, trusted him. He had betrayed him by extending the distance between him and his family for longer. He would never be forgiven, but if he kept Issac safe and ensured his speedy return to Bastion, maybe he wouldn't be hated. Tears pricked at the corners of his eyes. He turned away hurriedly and stood from the spot where he had been pushed.

The inside of the aircraft was cold, enormous, and hollow. Graham forced himself to pace the dimly lit cargo room to keep from going mad. He wasn't overly hungry, but he hadn't eaten since the buffet and needed to maintain his strength. He discovered a bag of lightly salted crackers and a bottle of carbonated orange drink in one of the foot lockers. He ate and drank slowly, settling his stomach. Around him lay the logs of Glarafae, the vats of sap, the sacks of iron and silver ore, the melting pot, and the two gold bars nestled behind a small crate. For little minions, Graham had never seen such strength. They had managed to cart all of the items on the list to the aircraft with ease and speed. If only moving guys back home were that efficient. A strange wave of motion sickness overtook him despite the fact that he wasn't moving as he thought about Maltin's Tanning Salon back on Earth. He closed his eyes and pushed the images away, willing the food and drink to stay down. No sooner had they disappeared than his gut returned to normal. Graham was beginning to sense a pattern. If he thought about his former life and friends or questioned Milo's authority, pain and sickness would appear. Nothing made him unhappier than the thought of displeasing the love of his life. He vowed to remain in his good books moving forward. Sinking by the logs of Glarafae wood, Graham let his eyes grow heavy as daydreams of his reunion with Milo helped him drift away.

He awoke with a start at the sound of the gigantic aircraft door opening. Having scrambled to his feet, Graham stood aside as the minions threw species after species of animals on the cargo room floor. Everything was dead, lifeless eyes staring into nothingness. The advantage of having a fatal stinger was that little mess was made in the murdering process. The beasts resembled boars, stags, cows, fowl, and foxes but with slight differences. Some had green ears instead of brown; others possessed spiky antlers that zig-zagged instead of curved. The birds' plumage shimmered like the sun reflecting off the ocean. Graham had never been a huge meat-eater before, but seeing his dinner before him, displayed in all its deceased glory, was enough to turn him off for life. He wanted to believe this amount of food would last them several months, but after witnessing the minions feast at breakfast, he would be surprised if it survived the week. At the very least, everything that had been gathered today would regenerate after a short amount of time.

The minions glared at him as they kicked the animals with their feet, moving them into places that would create more space for them. He glared back, hating them with every fibre of his being. Milo would hear all about their insolence and brutality. Graham would demand they be punished, and he would be sneering front and centre as they received their just retribution.

One of them shouted in a voice that made Graham's blood run cold. It was full of decay and monstrosity. All of the aircraft's lights switched on, blinding Graham momentarily. He stole a glance at the workers, but neither the noise nor the brightness woke them. The engines whirred as the shuttle powered to life and rose into the air. It was time to return to his new empire. Graham huddled closer to Issac, away from the minions cackling and sneaking pieces of raw meat to chew on. He reached out a hand to cup the kind man's chin. This was a big mistake, because a mere second later, Graham clutched his head in agony and screamed before the room turned black.

*

It was extremely uncomfortable flying via Aquarian Air. Danni's back was aching. She couldn't stretch her legs out due to the seventeen other passengers crowding her space, and if she tried to lean back on her elbows, she was hit with an overwhelming slap of vertigo. They had been flying for what felt like hours, and in all that time, not a single word had been spoken. Charlie had fallen asleep in Karki's lap, Drew was stuffing his face without a single care, Hannah, Slade, and Parry were gazing at the magnificent display of stars before them, Reilly was fused to Chiron's chest as he stroked her hair lovingly, Charlotte was pulling off her fake nails, Ambrite was tapping her fingers against her knee to an imaginary tune, the Maiden, Ganymede, Cerus, and the two mermaids were looking at Drew in disgust, and Castor and Pollux were engaged in a silent thumb-war that never seemed to end. Neither of them could accept a loss, so they continued to challenge each other to rematches.

Danni glanced over at her paper bag filled with hot food, which was probably cold by now. She couldn't bring herself to eat any of it thanks to the morbid thoughts running through her head, the main one being *What if we don't all come back from Liria?* She would never voice her concerns out loud, but what if she never saw Ronan again? What if Milo killed Graham right in front of them for daring to seek him out? What would happen once they found Charlie's father and he realised his wife was dead? It was all too much to bear. She turned to Charlotte, still picking at her hot pink acrylics, and grabbed one of her hands for comfort. It felt strange, this sisterhood they were trying to manufacture. She expected Charlotte to push her away or make some snarky remark, but to her surprise, she clasped it back firmly, meeting her eyes shyly.

"Are you okay?" Charlotte whispered, seemingly conscious of Charlie sleeping near her.

Danni shook her head, the panic swishing at the bottom of her stomach, threatening to rise and overflow everything.

"It's going to be fine," Charlotte reassured. "We don't even know if Milo will be there. Our main task is to find Charlie's dad and bring him home."

"It's just that," Danni whispered back, "I feel responsible for all of you guys. I started this group, and now we are heading to some unknown planet that could be dangerous. It's bad enough that we lost Graham. I won't be able to live with myself if anything bad happens to anyone else."

"Drama queen much?" Charlotte rolled her eyes.

"I'm serious," Danni hissed. "If it weren't for me, none of you would be here. I am the sole reason…"

"Oh, please," Charlotte interrupted. "We are not children following our mother's orders. We are basically adults and make our own choices. You think you made all this happen, but we would've come whether you wanted it or not."

Charlotte's words were oddly comforting. At the very least, they took a minute amount of pressure off Danni's shoulders. Still, she chewed on her lip until Charlotte swatted at her face as if she were banishing an obnoxious gnat.

"Stop that," she scolded.

Charlie woke with a start but closed his eyes once Karki began crooning a soft lullaby. Reilly sat up from the arms of her hunky centaur and grinned. Drew let out a chuckle, sucking the salt from his fingers with irritating sound effects. Ganymede's face turned black. He looked ready to throw the poor Piscean off the air wave. The twins released thumbs, shaking their hands shamefully at Danni and Charlotte. They didn't seem to grasp that it was perfectly normal to squabble with a 'sibling'.

"Dan's chewing her lip." Drew frowned. "That can only mean she's trapped inside her already crazy head."

"Thanks, Drew." Danni glared although she was secretly pleased that her best friend knew her so well.

"What's up, Dan?" Reilly straightened. Chiron unlocked his firm grip from her waist, planting a quick kiss on her head before she could wriggle out of his lap. Danni smiled as Reilly's cheeks bloomed with a reddish hue.

"Nothing," she murmured, embarrassed that the entire crew were now focused on her neurotic behaviour.

"Oh, so you can tell Charlotte but not me? Your best friend?" Reilly scowled.

"Hey!" Drew and Charlotte cried in unison.

Danni inhaled sharply. "Fine. If you must know. I was just telling Charlotte that if anything happens to any of you, it's my fault."

All at once, the deafening silence transformed into chaotic protests from her friends. Even the counterparts chimed in with their two cents.

"Absolute nonsense," Ganymede huffed. "*I* am solely responsible for your safe passage between Bastion and Liria. If a tragedy occurs, *I* will take ownership."

"Now wait just one minute." Chiron thrust out his sculpted chest. It wasn't difficult to see why Reilly liked him so much. "You may be the keeper of Aquarian Air, but I did not see you lift so much as a finger in the battle at Constellar. If I hadn't been there, my poor love would've perished." He gestured to Reilly, who looked ready to melt into a puddle of mush. "You think yourself so grand, Ganymede, but some of us are far better protectors, and you know it."

If Danni had been panicking before, she was now ready to self-combust. "Can we please not turn this into some macho constellation crap again? The last thing I want is a full-on brawl that's going to send us off this air wave."

"Danni's right," Reilly said. "What you all don't seem to realise is that you are useless alone. Together, you are powerful. Only when you are united can you properly protect us and Bastion and save Graham from Milo. Stop trying to one-up each other. It's childish and stupid."

"But you are the one who came up with the idea of the competition." Sirena narrowed her perfectly sculpted brows.

Reilly let out a shrill laugh. "Man, for almighty rulers of the stars, you guys sure are thick sometimes."

Chiron began laughing along with her but stopped when he realised he was part of the joke. He turned to her with a face full of concern. "Do you also find me simple, my love? I have always prided myself on my wisdom. It is what Sagittarians are known for."

Danni felt immediate sympathy for her best friend, who she could tell was choosing her words carefully. The counterparts watched with bated breath, lapping up the awkward moment.

"N—no," Reilly stammered, placing a hand on his muscled forearm. "I don't find you simple, but I do believe that you all have very high egos…healthy egos, though!" she added as Chiron hung his head, crest-fallen.

"It's like witnessing a train-wreck," Danni heard Drew cluck caringly to Hannah.

"I think what Reilly is trying to say is you all jumped at the chance to compete against each other purely to see who would win instead of focusing on what really matters," Ambrite piped up. "Victory is so much more important to you guys than working together as a team. You might not think I know much, lowly human that I am, but I spent the last few months learning to get along with eleven different personality types back home, so I know a little something about this subject."

"Yeah," Parry said. "Do you think I liked everybody in the Astro A Team when I first joined? Some of you were so annoying, not to mention terrible dressers, and…"

Charlotte's withering gaze stopped her mid-sentence.

"The point is" – Ambrite rolled her eyes at the flushed Virgo – "we were able to put aside our differences to do what is right for our friend. Furthermore, we came here in the first place to help unite you all so you would keep producing starlight. Now we have bigger problems, so can we just put aside this petty competitive bullshit and get to work?"

"Strong words coming from a girl who was ready to leave the group after your leader kissed the Aquarian boy," Calypsee sneered. "I mean, I don't blame you, of course." She turned to Danni now, who shrank back, wishing to never be reminded of her betrayal again. "He *is* super cute."

Slade choked on his hot chips.

Drew let out a dramatic snort. "Oh, you merbabes never give up, do you? It's like all men are fish food! I for one am tired of being treated like a sex object. Slade, you with me?"

Slade wiped tomato sauce off his chin, clearly humiliated by the lusty mermaid's attention.

Danni was about to poke Reilly and apologise for her rotten behaviour with Slade again, but Reilly was too busy being locked in a lovers' stare with Chiron. Danni screwed up her face. Nobody was ever allowed to tease her and Ronan again. She had way too much ammunition.

"I'll be the first to admit that I'm not perfect," Ambrite continued. "I was really angry at Danni, but when I came here, I realised she was a really good person who deserved a second chance. We all did. I have never fought to be group leader or been jealous of Danni's position. You know why? Because she doesn't act like she's superior to the rest of us. We are a team. Why not take notes, hmm?"

The stars whizzed by them in a blur. It felt like they were hurtling through Space Mountain at Disneyland. Danni knew she would never be able to grasp the reality in front of her at that very moment. If only Ronan could have witnessed it with her...

Ambrite's speech had rendered the passengers of the Aquarian Air silent once more. A few of the counterparts seemed lost in thought, taking in her words. Others, like Castor and Pollux, were arm-wrestling with pained expressions.

Ganymede stood suddenly with an air of authority. Danni smiled. He was loving being in charge.

"I sense that we are not far from our destination. Please ensure you collect all your belongings and tidy any messes you have made." He directed his last request at Drew, who had treated the air wave like it was a movie theatre.

The Piscean boy stood on shaky legs, looking extremely uncomfortable. "Guys...I ate a lot of food, and my stomach just can't wait until

Liria. Can you all turn around so I can unload? Who has some toilet paper I can borrow?"

*

"Honestly, how long do they need to talk this over?" Garth sighed impatiently, sipping a decadent drink he had been handed in the employee lounge.

"We have just asked them to hand over a chunk of their population. Do be reasonable, Garth," Asterion replied, nibbling on a spongy pink biscuit filled with purple cream. "Mmm, these are delicious! We must stock them back on Bastion."

The pair had been waited on hand and foot the moment they left the boardroom. Garth couldn't deny the level of service was top notch.

"Or" – he sat up straighter – "we could hire some of these lovely waitresses to…"

"I said no," Asterion snapped. "It's bad enough watching you moon over Sirena and Calypsee. I will not subject these poor women to your hot-blooded whims."

"What an interesting way to say 'charms', my lord." Garth chuckled. He slurped at the dregs in his cup before crumpling it up and throwing it into a bin behind him.

Asterion signalled to a slender waitress with a raven-haired bob and ruby lips.

She knelt by his side, beaming. "How can I help you, sir?"

Her honeyed voice sent a shiver down Garth's spine.

"Another pink biscuit if you would, my dear?" Asterion patted her arm.

She nodded, gliding towards the food station. Garth's eyes followed, his tongue practically dragging on the floor.

Asterion shook his head, disgusted. "You're a pig."

"Maybe." Garth removed his hat. "But this bird's gotta fly."

Much to Asterion's chagrin, he stood and prowled over to the unsuspecting waitress. He was just about to deliver his smoothest pick-up line when the doors to the boardroom opened.

"Ah, there you both are," Hammond huffed, looking even more exhausted than before. "We are ready for you now."

Jimnian, Marlin, and Nivil stood behind him, scowling at their guests.

"Two more minutes." Garth signalled with his peace fingers and turned back to the waitress, who was now staring at him blankly.

"Garth!" Asterion warned.

"Fine," Garth said with a pout. He gave the waitress a quick kiss on the back of her hand before stomping into the boardroom like a child denied candy before bed.

Asterion followed behind him, settling into the same spot as before. The Council members stood in front of the chart, arms crossed and bodies rigid.

"We have discussed the matter at length," Hammond said, jumping straight to the point. "I won't lie; the voting was not unanimous."

Garth resisted the urge to snort. He knew Jimnian and Marlin would have protested any demand made by him and Asterion purely from irrational hatred.

Asterion sat patiently, content from his earlier feed.

"We are willing to adhere to your request. However, there are a few terms to be agreed upon first." Hammond steepled his fingers.

"Naturally." Asterion nodded as though he hadn't been expecting anything less.

Hammond plucked a sheet tacked to the chart filled with illegible scribbles. He held it slightly away from him, eyes squinted. "Condition number one: *we* select the citizens from Cassius to be deported to Bastion. You do not have free rein to take our finest men and women."

"I perfectly agree, Hammond." Asterion bowed solemnly. "We are not looking for an elite class of people, just those willing to work and exist on a planet that sorely needs more life."

"Yes, well, that brings me to my next proviso." Hammond glowered, clearly irritated by Asterion's lack of defensiveness. "The citizens we choose must be willing – key word *willing*, Asterion – to live on Bastion. We are not forcing anybody off this planet. It is their home, and to uproot their lives without their consent is grotesque."

"What kind of people do you think we are?" Garth raised his eyebrows. "No, scratch that, don't answer it." He was not about to open the room up for discussion on *that* topic.

"I think what Garth is trying to say," Asterion said, "is that we would never take anybody from Cassius who wasn't interested. We are seeking those who wish for a fresh start. An opportunity to live somewhere new and make a difference."

"And if no one should agree, hmm, what shall you do then?" Jimnian questioned haughtily.

"Then we shall take our leave and seek help elsewhere," Asterion replied, expressionless. Garth ground his teeth as Marlin and Jimnian shamelessly exchanged triumphant glances.

"But know this," Asterion continued. "If any of the citizens are threatened to remain on Cassius or dissuaded in any way, shape, or form, Garth and I will know. You have now seen the power of his dragon pendant. We have eyes watching, and they will alert us the moment foul play arises."

Garth resisted the urge to dance on the table as the smirks vanished from the Council members' faces. They had bought Asterion's lie. Only the two of them knew the limitations of the dragon pendant's power, and it was going to stay that way.

"Any more conditions, Hammond?" Asterion smiled.

The Council President looked defeated. Whatever reactions he had been expecting and hoping for, this clearly hadn't gone his way.

"Uh…a review period will be conducted over the course of six months. Homes will not be sold in the event that our people are unhappy on Bastion."

"That is fair. However, I have complete confidence that each and every one of them will thrive on our humble planet," Asterion challenged, a twinkle in his eye.

Garth knew it was petty, but he unleashed a fully-fledged Cheshire Cat grin at the four disgruntled men before him. They could not renege on the deal now.

"Very well," Hammond grumbled. "I will ask my receptionist to draft the necessary documents, sign them, and courier them to you for approval. Now, please, kindly leave and do not return unless there is a dire emergency. I cannot stand the sight of you both a moment longer."

"Nothing would make me happier," Garth retorted. "Quite frankly, I need a steam and scrub after being surrounded by you stuffed…"

"Your hospitality has been greatly appreciated." Asterion cut Garth off, placing a firm hand on his shoulder. "You can rest assured we will treat your citizens with warmth and welcome."

None of the Council members spoke, nor did they extend their hands to shake. They merely turned away and began talking in dramatically loud voices about the findings on their chart. It reminded Garth of snooty teenage girls trying to exclude the nerds.

Asterion opened the boardroom door, gesturing for Garth to exit first. He grasped Garth's shoulder tightly again before he could scurry over to the leggy waitress. They made their way to the steel levitator in silence.

"Where to, gentlemen?" the tinny voice probed.

"Ground floor," Asterion replied.

They emerged into the blinding brightness of the foyer. Asterion sidled over to the front desk, where the receptionist, refusing to look at either of them, stared intently at something on her screen.

"Excuse me, miss?" Asterion tilted his head.

The receptionist tore her eyes away from the computer as though it was painful to do so. She met his gaze with an unimpressed look. "Yes, how may I help you?"

"Hammond mentioned you would courier some formal documents over to Bastion once they were drafted up. I just wanted to let you know…"

"Council President Hammond," she interrupted rudely, glasses balancing on the edge of her pointed nose.

"I beg your pardon?" Asterion leaned closer.

"You referred to him as Hammond." The receptionist spoke slowly, like she would to a child. "It is Council President Hammond."

Before Asterion could apologise, Garth pushed in front of him, hands splayed across the desk.

"Hammy Ham mentioned that you would courier the papers, so we just wanted to give you the postal address specifically used for matters such as these." He pulled out a piece of paper, plucked a pen from her workspace, and wrote it down. Garth struggled not to laugh at her horrified expression. "Be a dear and make sure it arrives there, won't you?"

With that, he pulled Asterion outside and power-walked him into the waiting aircraft.

"Garth?" Asterion turned to him once they were finally seated and ready to take off.

"Yes, my lord?"

"Remind me to promote you someday…"

Chapter 17

A Dead End

Hunter wondered how a jungle could be so alive yet so empty at the same time. All around him a symphony of squawks, roars, grunts, and chatters rang throughout the deep green forest. The damp earth beneath him trembled as though at any moment, a stampede like the one in *Jumanji* could race through and knock him and his friends out of the galaxy. His senses were on overdrive, yet not a single living creature emerged. It reminded him of a natural history museum he had visited once when he was a boy. When his parents weren't watching, he had wandered into an exhibit modelled on the Amazon rainforest. The soundtrack of animal sounds had played on an obnoxiously loud loop, but it hadn't bothered him. He had thrown his arms around a stuffed spider monkey perched on an information board and tried to drag it home with him. The museum staff and his parents had been none too pleased. This was back when they actually cared and his dad could leave the house without getting high first.

The Cavern of Gold was incredible, besides the sweltering heat. Hunter had just left what he thought was the hottest place in existence only to end up sweating profusely from the dense humidity once more.

"I get it, I'm a fire sign," he growled to no one in particular.

"Huh?" Wasabi trudged beside him, panting.

He glanced over at the eccentric girl before him. Less than an hour earlier, he had hated her with a burning passion. Now, he was rapidly starting to change his mind. She had made him realise once and for all that it would never happen between him and Ambrite. For the first time in a while, he felt ready to let go of her…but not before having a heart to heart first. Somewhere amidst the chaos of saving Graham, he would get her alone to make sure their friendship was solid. They were not going to live in two completely different galaxies with any unfinished business between them. A large part of him, bigger than he realised, really wanted to take Parry on a date when they got back home, but he was worried she would feel like a rebound. If they were going to try to make it work, he had to do things right. He had to promise that he would not hurt her or treat her as a way to get over somebody else like he had the night before. The beautiful Virgo deserved better than that.

"I was just complaining about the heat," he replied. "The Cavern of Red is literally in the middle of a volcano, and now I'm in the muggiest jungle known to mankind."

Wasabi let out a good-natured laugh. "Well, that's unfortunate, isn't it? Fire signs attract heat." Her smile faded, replaced by a thoughtful quirk of her lips. "I know that it shouldn't matter, but I've always wondered what my zodiac sign is. I look at you guys and think, what traits do we have in common? In all honesty, I feel the closest to Ambrite, not just because…you know…but because she's creative and independent like me. Does that make me a Taurus?"

Hunter shrugged. "I would ask Danni when she gets back. She's the expert on all things astrology. When I first met her, she claimed to know people's signs just by talking to them and getting a feel for their personality. I'm sure she could narrow it down for you."

When they had first met in Dr. Yates's office, Hunter had thought

Danni to be the strangest and most irritating person on the planet. He had resisted her offer of friendship for so long because he was afraid of allowing new people into his life who could hurt him. She had shown him that some humans were worth opening up to. That goodness did exist if one was ready to receive it.

"She sounds like a witch. A good one," Wasabi added hurriedly.

"Who's a witch?" Ronan sidled up beside Hunter. Brodie fell into step next to Wasabi. The four of them crunched through the wild forest, and for just a moment, Hunter felt like he was back home on a fun all-day hike with his friends.

"Your girlfriend." Hunter laughed. "I was just telling Wasabi that Danni should be able to guess her zodiac sign."

"If anybody can, it's her," Ronan said wistfully.

"Hey, she's going to be okay." Brodie patted him on the back.

He gave her a small smile in return but didn't look convinced.

Hunter was surprised to feel a twinge of jealousy. If he knew Danni, she would be just as worried about Ronan. Their relationship seemed so…effortless. Would he ever have that kind of thing with Parry?

"Does anybody else hear a waterfall?" Wasabi interrupted Hunter's train of thought.

The group stopped dead in their tracks and listened. Sure enough, Hunter could hear a peaceful roaring in the distance. The sound immediately relaxed him. He was pretty certain people back home meditated to waterfalls, ocean waves, birds chirping, thunderstorms, and pan flutes. Nature had the best soundtrack.

"Waterfalls equal water, and that means I'm going for a dip!" Brodie cheered.

Hunter wanted to protest that they should probably look for Crawford first, but the smell of his sweat made him relent.

Just beyond the condensed thicket, a crystal-clear lake lay before them. Unlike the volcano, this body of water promised cool refreshment. Hunter pictured himself diving deep into the icy pool and swimming for the waterfall on the other side. From where he stood, it looked like there was a hidden cave beyond the curtain of running liquid. A cliff ran just above the rocks, overlooking the vast jungle. No wonder they hadn't seen Crawford in hours. If this were *his* Coloured Cavern, he'd never leave.

Ronan, Brodie, and Wasabi began wriggling out of their sticky clothing. Hunter was about to do the same when a booming voice rang across the area.

"Humans should look before they leap," it warned.

The group spun around, trying to locate the anonymous speaker, but there was nobody in sight.

"That sounded like Crawford's counterpart," Brodie whispered. Her midriff was now exposed, revealing a glinting sapphire navel ring.

From the edge of the clearing, where they had just emerged, a boy with brilliant orange hair stood with his arms crossed.

"Hang on. That was my bartender at Constellar," Hunter breathed out, rubbing his eyes.

The boy had been wearing a tight red bodysuit, black shades, and a superior attitude. He remembered being served many strange-looking and -tasting drinks that had led to him hurling outside the club. He remembered Parry walking towards him, looking ravishing as hell.

"What are you talking about?" Wasabi hissed. "He was at the Mission Base, remember? Oh…right."

Hunter had seen the counterpart only as a lion right before he had stormed off to the bathroom due to Ambrite's shocking reveal.

"Yeah, and he wasn't at Constellar when we were fighting the scorpions," Ronan added before screwing up his nose. "Did you say bartender?"

"Your words may be soft, but my ears still hear," the boy growled.

"Where is Crawford?" Brodie raised her voice, clambering clumsily back into her clothes. The rest followed suit.

"He is training in my cave," he responded smoothly. "You do realise you were about to swim in crocodile-infested waters?"

Hunter swore the lake had been empty at first, but now he could see a dozen or so spiky green tails wading near the shallow entrance. He backed away, even though they couldn't possibly reach him from where he was standing.

"They were not there before," Ronan shouted, echoing Hunter's thoughts.

The counterpart rolled his eyes rather rudely. "Actually, they were. You were just so overcome with the desire to lower your body temperature that you missed them."

Hunter wanted to argue that he and his friends would've definitely noticed an army of crocodiles, but Wasabi cut him off before he could.

"What do you mean, Crawford is training? Can we see him?"

"I am letting him lead this mission to save your friend." The boy uncrossed his arms and began walking towards them. "His first order was to be taught basic combat and predatory skills. Heroes require courage, and Crawford was in short supply of that when we met."

"Well, all the courage in the world isn't going to make any difference." Wasabi tilted her head. "The majority of the Astro A Team have left for Liria, and Asterion and Garth still aren't back yet. We, however, have a pretty solid idea of where Graham might be, so let us collect Crawford, take him back, and wait for the others to return. We are not leaving without him."

Ronan and Brodie still hadn't told them what they had learnt, but the counterpart didn't know that.

The boy narrowed his eyes at Wasabi, but Hunter detected a hint of respect beneath it all.

"Very well. If you are able to swim across this lake and enter the cave in one piece, I will allow you to interrupt Crawford." He smiled, baring straight white teeth with alarmingly sharp incisors on either end.

Hunter knew better than to underestimate the odd teenager. A ferocious lion lived within, waiting to burst forth and devour. "So what you're basically saying is," he ventured, "turn around now or be killed. Is that pretty much the gist of it?"

As if in response, the crocodiles swimming below rushed to the surface, reptilian eyes glowing gold, with globs of saliva hanging from their jaws. They thumped their tails excitedly, sending splashes of water into the air and down onto the group. The spray would've been refreshing if the group hadn't been so terrified.

"What do we do?" Brodie shivered.

"Call his bluff?" Ronan smiled weakly, his face turning pale.

"No way!" Wasabi shook her head. "I am not risking my life just to see Crawford. He'll come out of there when he's good and ready. He can't train forever."

The counterpart watched their debate with a wicked grin. Hunter wanted to punch him square in the nose, but that would probably be the last thing he ever did. On the other hand, would Asterion and Garth allow them to be harmed? The thought made him say something he immediately regretted.

"I'll go," he said, pulling his shirt off.

"Hunter, no!" Wasabi grabbed his arm. Brodie and Ronan stared at him with gaping mouths.

Hunter turned to his friends, a mischievous glint in his eye. "Guys, I'm going to be just fine, you'll see. Wait here for me. I'll bring Crawford back straight away."

"Are you absolutely friggin' nuts?" Ronan shouted. "Are you not seeing what we are? Those crocs will make mince out of you!"

Hunter didn't want the counterpart to know how confident he was, so he answered Ronan with a wink and a slap on the back.

Before they could yank him back, Hunter kicked off his shoes and socks. He made a finger gun at the smirking counterpart and dove head-first into the only patch of water not crowded by salivating crocodiles.

The lake was heaven on his skin. For just a blissful moment, Hunter was submerged entirely, the only sound coming from the gentle cascades of the waterfall. As he surfaced, the screams from his friends hit him at full force. He wiped droplets from his eyes only to discover a multitude of hungry crocodile eyes facing him, poised to strike.

The counterpart shook his head in disappointment as if to say, *Poor foolish earthling.*

It was at this moment Hunter began to panic. He did the only thing instinct would allow. Refusing to look back, he swam with all his might towards the cave, praying that he had been right. He could sense them gaining on him, hear them gnashing their teeth in anticipation. He zig-zagged through the water, hoping to avoid even the tiniest nip. His strokes were powerful, and his legs kicked as if there were a giant spider resting on them. He could hear Brodie, Ronan, and Wasabi yelling at him, "Watch out!" and "Go, go, go!"

The entrance to the cave behind the waterfall was in sight. If he just maintained momentum, he could reach it a millisecond before the predators did. He was just about to pass through the curtain of streaming water when his flailing left foot struck a large and pointy embedded rock. A flash of blinding pain washed over him, giving his pursuers the advantage. With throbbing, bleeding toes, Hunter turned to accept his fate. There was no way he could reach the entrance before them now. The pack of crocodiles, further incensed by his cut, opened their mouths as wide as possible to take a hefty chunk of flesh.

Hunter felt more ashamed than fearful. His idea had been absolutely ridiculous. What did this counterpart care whether he lived or died? He was the king of the jungle. Asterion and Garth had no control over his domain. He closed his eyes tightly, wishing he had gotten to say goodbye to Ambrite first. She would never know just how sorry he was. In his final seconds, he tried to focus on the sound of the relaxing downpour behind him. At least he would die in a beautiful place.

As the mist sprayed his face, Hunter began to wonder why he hadn't actually died yet. With every ounce of willpower, he forced his eyes open to a scene too bizarre to believe. The crocodiles were mere inches from his nose, mouths still ajar and breath stinking of rotten carrion, but… frozen. Not a single one twitched or moved. Hunter felt his heart slide up his chest. He wasted no time swimming past the waterfall and clambering onto the cave entrance, his two largest toes still bleeding. He could hear Crawford grunting and panting somewhere amidst the darkness. It sounded like he was in a boxing ring, punching at an imaginary opponent. Before he could venture further, Crawford's counterpart stepped in front of him, appearing from out of nowhere.

"Well done, young man." The boy quirked an eyebrow. "You showed impressive courage back there. Not one of your friends would've dared to brave the lake. But I must ask, why so foolish?"

Hunter winced, his toes pulsing in agony. He pointed to them with desperation, but the boy merely shook his head.

"I am not your counterpart; therefore, I cannot heal you. I would recommend wrapping it up in something for the time being."

"Do you have a first aid kit lying around?" Hunter groaned.

"What need would I have for a medical kit?" The counterpart scoffed. "Be resourceful. Be true to your name – Hunter. Hunt for something else."

Hunter resisted the urge to punch the boy in his smarmy face. He turned away from the cave and hobbled over to a path that led up to the cliff. Luckily, he did not have to go far. Leaning against the trunk of a small tree, Hunter grasped the leaves of a thick rubbery plant and pulled them off. Lowering himself gently to the rocky floor, he used the leaves to staunch the wound, wrapping them around his toes. The counterpart watched with a mixture of amusement and respect. Thin strips of bark hung loosely above Hunter's head, which served as a makeshift bandage to keep everything together. It was rough and completely unsustainable but better than nothing. After using the trunk to pull himself to his feet, Hunter limped back to the counterpart.

"To answer your question" – he exhaled, slowly daring to put weight on his injured foot – "I was 'foolish' because I knew you would never harm me. You might be an almighty, immortal counterpart, but with one of us already missing, you would be a damn fool to kill me off too. Asterion and Garth would have your big shaggy head."

The counterpart shrugged in defeat. Hunter had hit the nail on the head.

"You are wise and brave, Hunter McGowan. There is no doubt you possess the most positive traits of a fire sign. The ram would be proud of your impulsive actions; such is befitting an Aries. I am not sure if we have been introduced, but my name is Leonis, and, yes, I was your bartender that night at Constellar. I am not one to miss out on all the fun."

Hunter was pretty certain Leonis was the most twisted of all the counterparts. His idea of fun was serving ridiculously strong alcoholic drinks to teenagers and daring them to swim in crocodile-infested waters. Poor Crawford had his work cut out for him.

"Can I see Crawford now?" Hunter sighed wearily. "We really need to get him back to the Mission Base so we're all ready to leave once everybody else returns."

Leonis looked irritated, as though he were hoping Hunter would stay and 'play' for a while longer. "He is not even close to finishing his training, but I will allow it, provided I see the same sort of bravery from him that I did with you before."

What did Leonis expect Crawford to do? Take on Milo and all of his minions singlehandedly? His friend had a tough road ahead if that was the case.

"Yeah, no worries. We will swap battle scars once all of this is over." Hunter rolled his eyes. He staggered back towards the cave with Leonis in tow. His foot felt marginally better thanks to the pressure from the leaves and bark. Hopefully Ares would heal him properly once he got back.

Entering the cool, dark cave, Hunter heard Crawford's grunting once more. A little ways in, a flicker of orange danced in the centre, illuminating his friend's shadow on the craggy walls. From the way it moved, Crawford looked like he was indeed punching at an invisible foe.

"Crawford?" Hunter echoed. The shadow froze, looking monstrously large on the ceiling.

"Hunter?" Crawford rasped in reply. "What the hell are you doing here?"

"Come here, buddy, and I'll tell you all about it." Hunter squinted in the blackness. He didn't dare walk any further lest he hurt his other foot.

"No," Crawford replied. "This is a test from Leonis. He just wants to make sure I'm committed to my courage, and I am, so leave me alone."

Hunter was dangerously close to losing his patience. He had nearly – well, sort of – died trying to get to Crawford, and his toes were fused together with a bundle of nature. This was no time for games.

"Crawford, this is Hunter," he said, gritting his teeth. "We are pals. We live in Juggler's Corner. You rake the leaves at Bouquet Reserve and enjoy playing basketball with Drew. Oh, yeah, and you hooked up with Charlotte whilst two-timing Danni. Remember that?"

Crawford let out an impressive growl. He truly was a Leo. "You have no right to keep using that information against me. Danni and I are cool now. The past is the past. I get that it was a cowardly thing to do, but how am I ever going to redeem myself if you keep hanging it over my head?"

Hunter turned to Leonis with wild eyes. "Can you please tell him it's me? I'm tired of this crap. He's convinced you're manipulating him."

Leonis looked like he was fighting back laughter, but he trotted forward on lithe legs and called into the centre of the cave, "Crawford, this is Leonis. Hunter has come here with a message for you. If you do not stop your training this instant, I will pounce on you when you least expect it in my lion form."

The cave went silent save for crackling flames. A moment later, Hunter heard feet shuffling towards him. A handsome face covered in grime emerged into his field of vision. Crawford had the appearance of somebody who had been living in the wilderness for at least twenty years. His clothes were ripped in patches, and his curly hair was matted with dirt. He had a big bruise forming on his left cheek and red, raw knuckles.

"Dude," Hunter breathed, "what the hell has he done to you?"

Leonis cleared his throat in irritation. "*He* has made your boy into a man. We both agreed that he was in no state to save Graham without some formal physical training first. Crawford needs to build up stores of strength, endurance, resistance, and agility. He has much to prove."

"It's cool, bro." Crawford grinned. "This isn't dangerous or anything. Think of it as some serious sensei shit."

"Have you looked in a mirror lately? I'm afraid if you train any harder, you'll drop dead. Come on, dude. We have to get back to the Mission Base."

"Why, what happened?" Crawford's face fell. Hunter noticed his feet were completely black. The kid needed a thorough washing.

"I'll explain everything once we get out of here. Brodie, Wasabi, and Ronan are waiting. Come on."

"Why just them? Where are the rest of the group?" Crawford tugged at his torn shirt.

"You'll find out. Let's get going. You need to clean yourself up and get into some new clothes."

Crawford glanced at Leonis as if to gain his permission. The counterpart nodded and strode towards the exit, vanishing the instant he was outside the cave. Crawford inhaled sharply. He looked relieved.

"Did you see any crocodiles when you crossed the lake?" he asked. "I encountered one on my first visit here. Luckily, I didn't notice it until I was out of the water."

"I may have spotted one or two." Hunter grinned. "It's those damn rocks that are the real villains in this story." He lifted his bandaged foot. Crawford blanched.

"Ugh, you should probably get that looked at. I don't want to see what's under there, but I can guess it's pretty nasty."

The boys carefully made their way out of the cave and down to the water. Crawford helped Hunter hobble his way to safety. At the edge, they slipped into the lake and swam to the opposite side. Not a single crocodile in sight. Hunter could see his friends scanning the water anxiously. When they saw the boys paddling towards them, they jumped up and down and waved their hands.

"Why are they acting like we've been missing for ten years?" Crawford splashed. Hunter noticed he was leaving trails of grime behind every stroke.

"They were worried about me. I'll tell you later."

They reached the end and were helped up by Brodie and Ronan. Wasabi flung her arms around Hunter, which surprised them both.

"I'm so glad you're okay." She smiled, releasing him. "Don't ever jump into crocodile-infested waters again."

"Yeah," Ronan agreed. "Talk about Russian roulette. You really know how to give a guy a heart attack!"

Crawford turned to Hunter, frowning. "Infested? You said one or two."

"I guess I lied." Hunter shrugged. He began throwing on his sticky, sweaty clothes. "I knew that Leonis wouldn't kill me. Asterion and Garth would banish him to the ends of the galaxy if he did. Sure enough, I was right."

"Still…" Brodie eyed Crawford's shabby appearance. "That could've gone so badly."

Crawford caught her staring and scratched at his matted locks in humiliation. "I need to shower…"

"Understatement!" Hunter punched Crawford on the shoulder. "Don't worry, I do too. Let's get out of this place. I may be a fire sign, but I am well and truly over the heat."

*

The second Reilly stepped off the air wave, she knew something was wrong. It was quiet…too quiet. According to Ganymede, a worker was supposed to greet them at the docking station, but nobody did. The entire area was empty.

"Something is afoot," Ganymede sniffed. "We must investigate. Milo may have already passed through here and wiped out every civilian in sight."

"This planet seems massive. Does anyone know their way around?" Reilly asked, stomach churning. Even with a strong, masculine centaur by her side, she felt uneasy. Chiron, sensing her fear, slipped his hand in hers. His grip was firm but gentle. She smiled at him weakly.

"It may seem large, but there are only three areas one can visit," he replied. "We can search either the Glarafae forest, the mines, or the mountains. Dare we split up?"

"Hang on," Ambrite interjected. "When the Maiden looked in the mirror, she saw Graham in the mines, so that's where we should *all* be heading. Now, how do we find them?"

"Who made her leader?" Reilly heard Sirena whisper to Calypsee. Her beautiful sister shrugged in response. They looked completely out of place in matching sea-green rompers and stiletto boots.

"The mines are to the right." Cerus sniffed the ground. "I can smell dirt and metal."

Reilly wondered what the majestic bull looked like as a human. She had a feeling he was ridiculously handsome. The inappropriate thought made her stomach churn. Just because her boyfriend was half-horse did not suddenly give her the right to fancy other beasts.

"Let us make our way there, then." Ganymede pointed in the direction of their destination. He took ridiculous, haughty strides that made him appear as though he had a pole up his...

"Whoa!" Drew shouted, causing Reilly and several others to jump.

To the left of his feet was a male figure in uniform lying unconscious on the ground. At least she hoped he was unconscious.

"It's a docking station officer," the Maiden said with a gasp, approaching him slowly as though he might attack her at any moment.

"Is he dead?" Charlotte breathed out.

Reilly gestured at Karki, who immediately nodded and shielded Charlie from view. She didn't want the child to become even more traumatised than he already was.

"Is Papa here?" he whined. The kindly counterpart brushed his sandy hair back from his forehead and kissed it. Charlie flushed and burrowed his face into her dress.

The rest of the group crowded around the lifeless officer. Castor and Pollux took turns prodding and lightly kicking at the body until they were pulled back by Chiron, who was glaring at them furiously.

"Have some respect," he snarled. The twins bared their teeth in response.

"This man is not dead," Ganymede professed. "He is breathing, but the air is shallow. I am certain this is the work of scorpion poison. Serket could paralyse a victim with his venom in seconds. He may not regain consciousness for hours. Maybe days. At the very least, this confirms Milo was here on Liria, but he is long gone by now."

"That does not necessarily mean that Milo was here," said the Maiden. "It could have been his minions doing his dirty work for him. The mines will reveal the answers we seek. Let's stick together just in case we are not alone." With that, she lightly stepped over the officer as though he were a piece of driftwood.

Reilly shivered. It had seemed like a great idea at the time to travel to Liria, but now that they were there, she felt incredibly unprepared and frightened. She just hoped the counterparts would protect them should they encounter any enemies along the way.

"Hey." Danni brushed her arm. "You okay? Is it my turn to comfort you?"

"I'm all right." She nodded. "Just seeing that poor man has made me realise that we may be in over our heads. I'm starting to think we should've waited too…"

"I'm glad someone understands," Danni muttered.

"Are you both sulking now?" Drew suddenly appeared, arms slung over both their shoulders. "Look, we are here now, so let's make the most of it. There's no point questioning whether this was the right choice or not. Plus, if we could tackle an army of scorpions and take down Ichoris, we can do anything."

"Actually, Karki took down Ichoris," Hannah chimed in. "If it wasn't for her, we would've died."

"Please, baby, I'm trying to make a point," Drew groaned.

Hannah laughed and kissed him on the cheek. Reilly felt a surge of gratitude for her friends. They always knew how to lighten the mood.

The counterparts marched ahead whilst the humans trailed behind, hyper-alert to every sight and sound. Charlie was the only excited individual in the pack. He hopped and skipped, singing, "Daddy's here, Daddy's here." Karki kept glancing behind her, beaming at the lively boy and Hannah.

Reilly knew they were approaching the mines when the ground became rocky and sparse, devoid of its prior green lushness. A gigantic earthy entrance greeted them as they rounded a large red boulder. The gaping, silent black hole did not look inviting in the slightest.

"Um, can someone say creepy?" Charlotte paled.

"Ugh, you kids are babies." Calypsee rolled her eyes. She sashayed into the mine with Sirena right at her heels. The counterparts, minus Chiron, made their way forward fearlessly. The centaur turned to Reilly with a look of apprehension. She knew what he was going to say before he said it.

"I think it's best that you wait out here," he declared. "I nearly lost you once to scorpion poison. I don't want to take that chance again."

Reilly opened her mouth to object, but Ambrite stepped forward, eyes blazing.

"Why did you even let her come if you were just going to keep her from all the action? Graham is our friend, not yours. I think we should all be together."

Chiron looked at Ambrite as if she were a disgusting squished bug he had just found under his horseshoe. "Please do not discuss things you know nothing about." He glared. "I am not denying that my love is capable of looking after herself. I am merely trying to protect her from the close proximity of the mine walls. She is more likely to get stung in there than she is in an open space."

Ambrite stood her ground in true Taurean fashion. Reilly couldn't help but agree with her friend.

"I repeat, why bring her, then? You knew we were going into the mines. Was your plan this whole time to keep her caged out here whilst you played the hero? So what if she gets stung? Sorry, Reilly," she said apologetically. "You are her counterpart. Save her again. No biggy."

"Can I speak to him privately, please?" Reilly interrupted before things got out of control.

Ambrite shrugged and stormed into the mines. The rest of the group ran after her. Chiron leaned against the entrance, scratching his neck nervously.

"Did I displease you, my love?" he murmured.

"No," Reilly answered gently. Without thinking, she placed her hands on his chest and kissed him firmly on the mouth. He tasted like pine and fir and Christmas all rolled into one. He moaned and fisted his hands in her wild hair. Never in all her life had she been kissed like this. She didn't understand how somebody could be aggressive and gentle at the same time. She couldn't comprehend this level of passion. It was enough to make her see stars when they finally broke apart, panting but smiling like idiots.

"I see you are not so angry with me after all." Chiron grinned, his perfect lips slightly swollen.

"I know you were just being protective of me." She traced his collarbone with her finger. "I like it…"

"But?" He raised an eyebrow.

"But Ambrite is right. I'm going whether you approve or not. Graham is our friend, and we need to rescue him as a team."

Chiron took both her hands in his and kissed the tips of her fingers. Reilly knew in that moment that no man back on Earth would ever measure up again. Maybe she could stay on Bastion with Ambrite…

"I understand." The centaur released her. "Nevertheless, I am going to stick quite close by you just in case."

"I'm fine with that." She laughed.

They strolled into the musty mine, which had now been lit with torches. The air was oppressive and humid. Reilly swallowed, her claustrophobia niggling at her nerves. Fear told her to race back outside into the open air, but she had just told Chiron that he would not hold her back from searching for Graham. She could hear the group in the distance talking in hushed tones. Relieved that they had waited, she dashed forward to find them examining something on the left wall.

Reilly's stomach lurched. She wanted to believe it was paint or tomato sauce, but the thick streak splashed against the dirt was unmistakeably blood.

Karki grabbed Charlie once more and thrust him behind her back. He was nearly taller than her, so this didn't do much.

"Is that…" Danni trailed off.

"Yes," Ganymede whispered. "Perhaps a worker put up a struggle and was punished or worse…"

"Han, maybe Karki and one of us should stay back with Charlie," Reilly murmured to her cousin. "What if that blood is only the beginning of what we will find? The kid has been through enough."

Hannah nodded, her mouth forming a thin line of worry and fear. "I'll stay with Karki. The rest of you go on ahead."

The rest of the group didn't need an explanation. They understood that Charlie risked being exposed to something traumatic should he venture further into the mines. The boy, however, did not share the same view. Charlie burst into tears when he realised he wasn't joining them.

"Papa!" he howled, making the walls tremble.

"Ugh, make that thing stop," Castor groaned, blocking his ears. Pollux mimicked him, screwing up his face.

Reilly, Hannah, and Karki knelt before him, rubbing his shoulders and stroking his hair. The affection and attention of his three favourite girls made him stop wailing, although he continued to gulp and sniff.

"Charlie, I promise we will find your papa." Reilly hugged him. "We just need you to stay here with Hannah and Karki in case there is something dangerous down there. Can you keep watch here? We need your eyes and ears on alert."

Charlie nodded, the muscles in his face starting to relax.

"Wow, Charlie." Karki gasped. "You've just been set your very first important quest. That is quite an honour for a boy your age. Well, there is no one I trust more than you to keep a lookout."

Charlie puffed up his chest proudly. Reilly shot Karki a grateful wink.

With that, she and the rest of the group journeyed deep into the muggy mines. Cerus led the way, his nose guiding him towards any detectable scent left behind by Graham. According to Parry, they both wore the same perfume. Several times, the path forked into two or three tunnels, causing them all to stop and wait as Cerus nuzzled each entrance, thus creating a process of elimination.

At one point, Slade accidentally brushed against a plant with arrow-shaped leaves. Yelping in pain, he watched in horror as his entire left arm broke into red-hot rashes. Ganymede heaved a sigh and strode over to heal him. For the rest of the trek, the group stuck to the centre, treading carefully and avoiding anything that looked questionable.

Reilly noticed her breathing had started to become laboured as they descended deeper and deeper. Bile rose in her throat, and she struggled to keep her lunch down as the mine shaft narrowed.

"I am getting closer to the scent," Cerus huffed. "I am fairly certain it is just a few paces away."

Reilly noticed the path widening slightly up ahead and quickened her pace, eager for more breathing space. To her relief, the trail opened into a vast circular room filled with crude holes in the walls. To her dismay, about forty workers were bound in clusters all around the room, their heads slumped and eyes closed.

"What the hell?" Drew breathed. "Are they all dead?"

"No," Chiron replied delicately. "They were stung, much like the officer back at the docking station. The ore and jewels have been completely mined and won't regenerate until tomorrow. It looks like Milo got what he came for."

"Here," the Maiden's silvery voice rang out. Everybody turned to see her standing by a wall, pointing to the floor. "This is where I saw Graham in the mirror. He was sitting right here, drinking from a bottle."

Cerus trotted over to where she stood, sniffing the ground and grunting. "Yes, you are indeed correct, Maiden. The scent is strongest here. He rested here for only a few minutes, but it was enough to leave an imprint."

Reilly watched Parry walk over to her counterpart, tears spilling down her cheeks.

"I was really hoping he would be here," she cried softly. "I am trying to be strong, but what if this is a dead end and we never find him?"

"We will, my sweet," the Maiden crooned gently. She placed a dainty arm around the girl's sagging shoulders and squeezed her closely. Parry, clearly surprised by the Maiden's sudden warmth, stared at her in awe.

"Well, at least we know he was definitely here," Danni offered. "As Chiron said, all of the goods have been mined, so they were successful in their mission."

"Yes, but what do they need them for? That is the question," Calypsee countered.

None of them spoke for several moments. Castor and Pollux broke away to explore the circumference of the room. The Maiden and Parry dashed over to the unconscious workers, eager to learn more information about the attack. Reilly looked up at Chiron, the memory of his luscious lips still upon hers. Catching her gaze, he flashed her a smile that made her knees weak.

Ambrite, Charlotte, Drew, Slade, and Danni dug around the place Graham had sat, hoping to find something that would point to his whereabouts. The rest of the counterparts surveyed the space with sombre expressions.

"It's hopeless." Danni broke the silence, throwing her arms up in frustration. "There's nothing here. Not even the water bottle he drank from. I hate to be negative, but I don't feel any closer to finding him."

Reilly couldn't help but agree with her best friend. This mission had not been successful.

"Guys!" Parry called unexpectedly from the centre of the room.

The group filed around five workers all tied together and gagged with duct tape.

"What is it?" Sirena asked excitedly.

"Look at all of the workers." Parry gestured around the room. "What patterns do you see?"

Reilly surveyed each collection of workers but couldn't see any 'patterns'.

"They're all men?" Ambrite frowned. "Where is the equality…?"

"No," Parry moaned. "Look at what they are wearing."

Reilly didn't register what Parry was saying at first. The workers were kitted out in cotton overalls with various shirts, t-shirts, and jumpers underneath. Some wore woollen caps on their heads. Mostly all of them wore black fingerless gloves. Not a single one was without steel-capped boots. Then it hit her.

"Oh…" she exhaled. "Of course! Garth said all the workers were from Bastion. They are wearing coloured overalls according to their signs."

"Yes!" Parry exclaimed. "And which colour is missing?"

Reilly didn't need to look around the room to know the answer. "Scorpio…"

"So Milo has taken all of the Scorpio workers from Bastion and left the rest," Ganymede deduced. "What, is he planning on building some sort of army?"

Danni grabbed Reilly's arm, making her jump. "Do you remember what Milo said before he took Graham away? He said he was going to live on a faraway planet with only those born under the sign of Scorpio."

"Fascism," Cerus grumbled. "We may think ourselves superior, but none of us would ever create an empire under one sign."

"All right, here's what we know so far." Danni stepped forward. "Milo has abducted Graham and taken him to an unknown planet where he plans to establish a world just for Scorpios. He has taken all of the resources from this mine, I'm guessing to build stuff with, and the workers are going to either assist him or be forced to live there as new civilians… or both."

"What about Charlie's father? Is he in this room?" Slade inquired.

"Yeah, we didn't think this through…" Drew chuckled. "With Charlie back at the entrance, how are we supposed to identify the dude?"

"Let's revive all of the workers we can," Chiron ordered. "Unfortunately, the Librans, Capricorns, Leos, and Aries will have to remain unconscious for now."

Cerus let out a bellow which sounded like either a mocking laugh or an offended cry. Everybody, including the counterparts, stumbled in shock.

"You seem to forget, pony-boy, my ability allows me to heal any sign. Watch and be amazed."

Cerus pranced around the room, working his healing magic as if he were performing a ballet. Reilly bit back the urge to laugh.

"He really is very good." Slade rubbed at his lip with his sleeve.

For a big creature, the bull swished his tail back and forth very gracefully as he weaved in between the clusters of workers. Once the ritual was complete, he loped back over to the group.

"And now time to change…" He smirked.

To Reilly's amazement, the bull transformed before her very eyes into a round, short gentleman with a receding hairline. He was not what she would call eye candy. It was probably for the best that another animal didn't set her heart aflutter. The rest of the counterparts were already in human form, giving them enough time to look normal as all around the room, the men started to awaken. They gawked at one another, dazed and confused.

"Quick, let's release them from their bonds," the Maiden urged.

The team dashed over to different groups, removing the duct tape as smoothly as possible first and loosening the knots second. Reilly received many nods and exclamations of gratitude from the weary workers. The mission no longer felt like a failure. They had saved many innocent men.

"Is any of you father to a boy named Charlie?" Reilly shouted, helping some of the men to their feet.

A frantic voice sounded from the far right side of the room. "Charlie! Please…I know his father!"

Reilly raced in the direction of the anonymous voice and found herself face to face with a man sporting floppy red hair and freckles. His clear blue eyes danced over hers with concern. He wore forest-green overalls with thick leather boots.

"You know Charlie's father?" Reilly demanded.

"Yes," the man replied, his eyes watering. "Issac Venturion. He's a friend of mine. This kid and a bunch of disgusting-looking man-like scorpion monsters took him and the other Scorpios."

The rest of the group began to assemble behind Reilly. The worker gazed at them all mistrustfully.

"It's okay," Reilly soothed, reaching out to rub his arm. "They are friends. Charlie is here, at the entrance to the mine. We need to get some information from you about what happened."

"You brought Charlie here?" the man exclaimed, his expression turning from suspicious to terrified.

"Yes, but he's perfectly safe." Ambrite stepped forward. "We have friends guarding him. We were hoping to find Issac and bring him home. A lot has happened back on Bastion, but we don't have time to explain."

"Can you please tell us everything that happened?" Danni added. "Any detail, no matter how big or small, will help."

The man, still wary of the company before him, walked to a quieter part of the room and gestured for them to follow. Once they were out of earshot of the other workers, he began to speak.

"Honestly, it all happened so quickly I'm still struggling to process it. I was extracting some ore when Issac walks into the mine with this young fellow and tells me that he's helping him collect supplies for this new kingdom called Maltin?"

"That's Graham's surname!" Parry gasped.

"Graham is the 'fellow' you mentioned," Slade explained, seeing the confusion flickering across the man's face.

"So he isn't royalty?"

"No." Parry's lip trembled. "He's just a regular teenager and my best friend. Graham was kidnapped by an evil imposter named Milo and manipulated into doing work for him. Milo obviously sent him here to capture all the Scorpio workers and bring them back to wherever he is hiding."

"That makes more sense." The man tilted his head thoughtfully. "Issac had literally just finished telling me how important this Graham was when his vile minions attacked us. They tied us up and gagged us. Their venom knocked us right out. It was terrifying."

Reilly's heart went out to the poor dazed man before her. He was still so shaken from the event. "What do we call you?" she interrupted. "I'm Reilly."

"Oh, you can call me Mads. My full name is Madslow. Is my family safe?"

Reilly didn't know how to answer. The truth was she didn't know if his family was safe or not. Many had died at Constellar, but a good number had survived, and some civilians hadn't been there at all.

"Did your family ever go to Constellar?" Danni said, breaking the silence.

"No." Mads shook his head. "I have a wife who is paralysed from the waist down. My sister lives with us and cares for her whilst I'm at work. My daughter is only six."

Reilly exhaled. She didn't want to get his hopes up, but if they had stayed at home, it was likely they were still there.

"Constellar was attacked by a man named Milo last night," Danni continued. "His scorpions killed many people, and unfortunately, Issac's wife was one of them. I saw it happen…"

Danni broke off, tears welling in her eyes. Reilly rubbed the small of her back. She couldn't resist glaring at Castor and Pollux, who, for once, looked guilty as hell.

"Ella," Mads whispered, his hands shaking by his sides. "Oh, that's simply awful. Poor Issac… Poor Charlie! Wait, does that mean my family *are* safe?"

"We cannot say for certain." Chiron lowered his voice. "If they were not at Constellar, there is a chance, but we have not inspected all of the houses on Bastion yet. The scorpions could've attacked. It is unknown."

Mads turned a sickly shade of green and clasped Reilly's hands with such force that she yelped. "Please, take me back home now. I need to see if they are okay."

"What about your aircraft? How did you get here in the first place?" Chiron protectively but gently loosened Mads's grip on Reilly. He massaged her palms in such an intimate way that Mads blushed and stepped back.

"We all came in a carrier that will not pick us up for another couple of days," he explained. "We've been spending our nights at a shelter near the docking station. Not all of us can afford the hotels on small nearby planets."

Reilly saw Ganymede's face contort. She could tell he was about to say something incredibly rude.

"What if," she intervened, "we bring you back with us but not tell the others about what happened on Bastion? We don't have the room to accommodate all of you, so if they can sit tight, we can brief them on everything that happened on our return."

Mads looked like he was about to be sick. Reilly knew the situation was less than ideal, but how could they fit that many workers onto the Aquarian Air?

"These are my brothers," he croaked. "Not literally, obviously, but we have worked together for years. I know all of their families. To think that I would leave them behind, even if just for a day, it doesn't feel right…"

"Would Asterion let us borrow his aircraft?" Ambrite turned to Ganymede. "If so, we could send for everybody once we get home."

"Asterion?" Mads gaped. "You know him?"

"Long story." Ambrite grinned. "So do you think he would let us?"

Ganymede closed his eyes in pompous thought. It was highly evident that he loved being the centre of attention. He flicked them open after several minutes of silence. "I propose this. Mads, you will remain here with the other workers and not breathe one word of what has happened back on Bastion lest you start a riot. Understood?"

Mads nodded, a mixture of awe and horror in his gaze.

"What we have gathered here today is that Graham and Milo's minions visited Liria and collected supplies for the new kingdom Milo is building. This empire will be home to Scorpios and Scorpios alone. What we don't know is where this planet is located. The most optimal move is to return to Bastion and collaborate with Asterion and Garth. I have seen the carrier, and it is large enough to transport all of us plus the workers. The moment we pinpoint Milo's new location, we set off for Liria, collect the workers, and journey to our destination. If they wish to help us fight, more's the better. If they do not, they can sit in the carrier and wait until we are victorious. Make no mistake, we shall triumph. Once we have rescued Graham, vanquished Milo, and destroyed his foul monsters, we fly home to Bastion and reunite the workers with their loved ones…if they are still alive, that is."

"Very sensitive," Ambrite muttered.

To Reilly's surprise, all of the counterparts and her friends nodded in agreement. There really was no better option. It was too much energy and effort for Garth to create a portal to Liria for that many people and then another one to an unknown planet. He needed to conserve his strength. The aircraft was the way to go. Plus, Ganymede had raised an excellent point. Perhaps the workers, fuelled by rage about what had happened to their families, would help them in battle.

"How long will all of this take?" Mads sighed.

"It will take us three hours to fly home," Ganymede said. "Once we arrive, Asterion and Garth should be back from their mission on Cassius. Surely, with all of our brains combined, we can discover the location of Milo's whereabouts. The second we do, we travel back to collect you and the workers. In the meantime, do not under any circumstance tell them what has happened. They will not see reason. We shall brief them once we return."

Reilly noticed that some of the other workers were looking over at them. They had to get going before one of them became suspicious.

"Mads," she whispered, "tell them whatever sounds convincing. We will come back for them. Also, please don't feel you have to fight. This is a lot to—"

"I will fight," Mads said, a steely resolve in his tone. "They will too. It will be an honour to serve Asterion and avenge all that has been lost. It is the least I can do for Issac, Charlie, and Ella."

Castor and Pollux strutted forward and slung their arms around Mads's shoulders, regarding him with a cool intensity.

"We respect you, human," Pollux said, "the way you speak of brotherhood and your willingness to fight for a good cause. You are welcome in our training area anytime."

Castor grinned and began swinging his fists into the air. "I am eager for a new opponent. My brother is becoming weak in his age."

"Weak?" Pollux growled and leapt onto Castor. The pair began laying into one another, much to the shock of the other workers.

"Human? Oh my…" Mads breathed. "Are they the Gemini counterparts?"

"And on that note," Drew shouted, "it's time to go! Mads, pleasure meeting you, buddy. Remember the stuff and things, okay?"

The group, including Castor and Pollux, who were dragged by Sirena and Calypsee, fled from the large cavern without looking back. Reilly could hear the shouts of several workers, confused by their sudden appearance and disappearance. She kept her head down, desperate to quell the nausea rising in her stomach, as she navigated through the smaller, darker, and hotter spaces of the mine. Chiron stayed close but didn't interfere with her process. He was perfect. She breathed a sigh of relief as they rounded a corner and were hit by the natural light of Liria. Charlie, Hannah, and Karki were working on a strange dance that involved flapping their arms like a chicken. Charlie was giggling and stomping his feet with enthusiasm.

"Honey badger!" Drew exclaimed, kissing Hannah like he hadn't seen her in seven years. Charlie stopped dancing and frowned at them in disgust.

"How did you go?" Karki asked. Her bare feet were black, but she didn't seem to care.

"We have to get back to Liria now," Reilly urged.

Hannah broke apart from Drew with a look of concern. Her lips were plump and flushed. "Is everything okay?"

"We'll explain on the way." Sirena yawned. "We have to do something to pass the time, right?"

Chapter 18

Aligning the Signs

The journey back was much faster. The counterparts and humans actually spoke to one another this time, making the experience almost…pleasant. Ambrite mainly listened, observed, and pondered. She was stuck in a very strange place. A place of unknown. Every second that passed drew her closer to saying goodbye to all of her friends and life back on Earth. This gigantic decision had sparked a question: what was she?

If she was immortal, did that still make her human? She certainly wasn't a counterpart. Where did she fit in on Bastion? What would she do for a living? She loved the idea of being Wasabi's assistant at the tattoo parlour. If Constellar were ever rebuilt, maybe she could learn to DJ as well. Would Wasabi resent her as they grew older, knowing that as she aged, Ambrite would remain the same? If she spent too much time dwelling on the logistics, she would drive herself mad. At this stage, it was just best to live one day at a time.

She couldn't deny the big part of her that couldn't wait to see Hunter and have a proper discussion with him. They had to have it out once and for all. Parry's revelation of their sleeping together had reaffirmed that Ambrite had zero romantic interest in him. She had not felt jealous in the slightest. In fact, she thought they would make a pretty good couple back home, provided Parry didn't revert to being a superficial bimbo. It was going to be painful, watching him leave, but Ambrite knew that what she and Hunter had was extremely special and rare. It was a true friendship that would last the test of time.

Bastion was completely dark by the time they returned. Ambrite had no concept of time on this planet, but what she did know was that a whole day had officially passed since Graham had been captured. Truth be told, it felt a lot longer. The air wave dipped and descended towards the entrance of the inconspicuous Mission Base. Ambrite's heart rate sped up at the thought of seeing Wasabi again. She knew they didn't make girls like her back home. She anticipated their first kiss, imagining Wasabi tasting like bubble-gum.

"You don't realise how much you miss a toilet until it's not available to you," Drew groaned, killing Ambrite's fantasy and hugging his stomach.

"How do you need to poop again?" Ambrite sighed.

"I'm a nervous flyer, sue me!" Drew bit back.

Hannah fussed over her boyfriend, rubbing his swollen belly and whispering sweet nothings. Ambrite fought back a fountain of vomit. She was all for romance, but those two needed boundaries.

Ganymede stood, giving him the illusion of levitation. He used his arms to direct the air wave onto the floor of the Mission Base. Drew leapt off mid-air and raced to the bathrooms, prompting an angry growl from the Aquarian counterpart.

From where she sat, Ambrite could see Hunter, Wasabi, Ronan, Crawford, Brodie, Asterion, and Garth talking amongst themselves in the centre. The remaining counterparts lingered nearby. It took all her willpower not to run into Wasabi's arms. Instead, she stepped off the air wave and strode as casually as possible over to her friends.

"Hi, y'all!"

The team jumped, breaking apart to see who had spoken. Wasabi's face broke into a gigantic smile. To Ambrite's delight, she threw herself at her with a tight hug and kiss on the cheek. Hunter flushed the same colour as his clothing and waved at her timidly. She returned the wave with a warm grin.

"You have returned, young immortal." Garth tipped his hat. He muttered a strange language to himself, and the two thrones reappeared close to where they were standing. Asterion sat himself comfortably in the larger one and gestured for Garth to join him. Ambrite watched as everybody around her reunited. Ronan swept Danni into a long, passionate kiss. Drew high-fived Crawford. Brodie squeaked and embraced her brother. Slade held her by the shoulders, trying to determine whether she was hurt or not. She swatted him away with a laugh. The counterparts barely acknowledged one another, but none of them left the Mission Base. Ambrite felt Hunter standing nervously on one side of her, with Wasabi gripping her hand on the other. It felt nice to have them both so eager for her time and attention. She turned to her super cute girlfriend, heart thumping with excitement and desire.

"I missed you," she whispered. "I cannot wait to hear all about your adventures lately, but do you mind if I chat to Hunter first?"

Wasabi nodded happily. "Yes, absolutely! Go easy on him. He's a great guy." The pair smirked at one another good-naturedly.

Before Ambrite could question this new development, Wasabi leaned in and pressed her lips against her mouth. It was only brief but powerful. Ambrite felt her knees weaken. She wanted more, but Wasabi walked away in a maddeningly sexy swagger.

"Wow," Hunter said. "If that isn't the very definition of chemistry, I don't know what is."

Ambrite was surprised to hear him sound so sincere. She studied his face suspiciously, but he showed no signs of jealousy or anger. Gently, she took his hand and pulled him towards her bed. They sat down, knees touching, and faced one another.

"So…you no longer hate me, then?" Ambrite began anxiously.

"I could never hate you." Hunter shook his head sadly. "I've been an absolute tool, and I'm so sorry for the way I treated you. It makes me sick to think I acted like my father."

His last words hit her square in the chest. She felt herself physically recoil. Hunter may have acted immaturely, but he could never come anywhere close to his deadbeat father. She remembered the first time they had laid their souls bare, both of them sharing stories regarding their negligent parents. His confession had torn her apart. No child should ever have to walk in on his father injecting himself with hard drugs. That image alone had left a deep wound that would take years to heal. Whatever Hunter thought he was, he was not a monster.

"How did you act like your father?" She took his hands in her own and squeezed them.

"I was forceful, not physically but emotionally. I expected you to feel the same way I did. I pretty much demanded it. How does that make me any better than him?" Hunter refused to meet her gaze, lip trembling. She could feel the wounds beginning to open.

"Hunter," she soothed, "you cannot possibly compare your behaviour to his. I get it. I understand. I'm super stubborn too and probably would've reacted the same way. I admit it wasn't your finest hour, but it didn't take you long to come around. You've had a lot to absorb in a short amount of time…"

They sat silently on the bed, content to finally feel the peace flowing between them after so much tension. Ambrite was on the verge of tears. She didn't know how she was going to cope without her best friend. As if reading her mind, Hunter laid his head on her shoulder.

"Just answer me this one thing… Will you miss me?"

Ambrite folded her arms around his muscular frame. She breathed in the scent of his messy hair, trying to store it somehow in her memory.

"I am going to miss you so much," she murmured. "You're my best friend in the whole world and nothing will ever change that. No amount of distance will break this bond, boyo."

He let out a muffled laugh against her. She could feel him trembling from emotion. This was normal. This was them.

"I approve of your taste in girls, by the way," he added.

"Funny…I was going to say the same thing."

Hunter pulled away from her quickly. She had never seen him so jittery before.

"Did she tell you?" He spoke in a hushed tone.

"Yes." Ambrite laughed. "What are you, twelve? Is it really some huge secret?"

"Well, kinda. We don't know what we are yet. At the time, it felt like a drunken hook-up, but I think she has real feelings for me and I'm… not sure."

"She does." Ambrite smiled. "She thinks you're sweet and promised to take care of you once you get back home. I think this whole experience has really changed Parry. She's actually quite deep. Give her a chance, won't you?"

Ambrite watched Hunter search for Parry in the crowd. She saw his eyes finally settle on a slim figure with cropped hair and an edgy figure-hugging outfit. His nostrils flared in approval.

"I think I can give her a chance." He grinned. "Man, she's beautiful. I mean, she's always been gorgeous, but it was in a 'I know I'm all that' kinda way. Now, she's confident and sexy. Did I mention she's wild in the sack?"

"Too far." Ambrite screwed up her nose. "I don't want to know about that part." She slumped against his side with an exaggerated sigh. "Ah, how am I going to keep in contact with you guys? I want to know if you end up marrying and having a billion babies."

Hunter shoved her gently. "Now who is going too far? Let's just see how the first date goes. In all seriousness, though…" He paused to rub his nose. Ambrite was used to this anxious gesture of his. "I wonder if Garth or Asterion could allow us somehow to keep in contact. Like an alternate reality video chat or something."

"I would like that." Ambrite nodded. "It's going to be hard enough, adjusting to eternal life on a new planet. The transition would be much easier if I could still talk to my friends every now and then."

"What's it like?" Hunter asked, tone serious.

"What's what like? Being a lesbian? Amazing!"

"No." He grinned. "Being immortal. How does it feel to know you are never going to die?"

Ambrite stiffened. It was still such a fragile issue for her to comprehend. For one thing, it had been forced upon her. She had not asked for this. For another, the thought of an endless life felt incredible and terrifying at the same time. She said the first word that came to mind. The same word that would always come to mind.

"Lonely…"

*

Ronan didn't know whether to yell at his girlfriend or keep kissing her. He decided to go with the latter. The moment she appeared, he had whisked her into his arms and familiarised himself with her tasty lips. He knew he was being slightly melodramatic. After all, they hadn't been separated for that long, and yet…it had felt like a lifetime. When they finally broke apart, he was pleased to see her breathless and flushed.

"Missed me, hey?" Danni grinned, pressing her forehead against his.

"Just a little." He shrugged, returning the grin. "I wish you hadn't left without me, though…"

Danni's face fell. Ronan immediately felt guilty. His intention hadn't been to upset her.

"We tried looking for you," she explained, biting her lip. "I admit it was a last-minute, rash decision, but you'll be pleased to know it won't ever happen again."

"Danni," Ronan said, then kissed her lightly, "you don't owe me any explanations. I am not your keeper; I was just worried about you. I love you."

It still felt strange to be uttering those three words to somebody unrelated to him. Ronan had never said them before Danni. He was fairly certain she had never said them before either. Crawford and Slade didn't count. He had to tell himself that in order to keep himself from punching both of their lights out. It was stupid and irrational, but wasn't that love?

"I love you too." She nuzzled his nose. "I am never going to get tired of hearing you say that."

They swayed in place for a while, cuddling, kissing, and making everybody else want to puke. It would be so much better when they were back on Earth and he could actually have some privacy with her.

"Tell me everything you found out," he murmured against her ear.

At that moment, a sharp piercing whistle sounded across the large room. Ronan spun around to see Garth ushering everybody to the foot of the two thrones. It was time to debrief.

"Come on." Danni took his hand. "We can share our adventures with the group."

They settled themselves onto the cold stone floor, still holding hands. Hannah and Drew sat beside them with a smile. Ambrite followed, leading Wasabi gently into her lap. Ronan noticed that Chiron was trying to snuggle up to Reilly, but she looked supremely uncomfortable. Asterion and Garth were eyeing them warily.

"They are head over heels for each other," Danni whispered, noting his confusion. "She's just worried that public displays of affection will get them into trouble with the powers that be."

"I thought the counterparts were the powers that be," he whispered back.

"Can everybody kindly shut their mouths, please?" Garth boomed. "I see all the couples have paired off… How sweet." He looked like he had just bitten into a lemon. "Chiron! I've noticed you and the young Reilly are fighting your sexual urges like some pre-pubescent virgins. How do I put this delicately? …Keep it in your pants!"

"Garth," Asterion chided, despite not looking too pleased either.

Ronan felt supremely sorry for Reilly, who was blushing furiously. Chiron looked ready to loose a thousand arrows into the Chief Advisor's face.

"What? Don't you agree this relationship is a tad mismatched, if not forbidden?" Garth whined.

"Hey!" Reilly shouted, hands on hips. "I am not a child, and you are not my mother. How dare you have input on my relationship?"

Garth jumped up on his throne with a glower. Nobody else dared speak or move.

"Garth," Asterion repeated calmly, tugging him back down. "Perhaps this is a discussion for another day, hmm? Do remember that whatever this is…it's temporary."

That was apparently the wrong thing to say. Reilly let out a shriek that startled even the stoic Equas.

"Oh, so you think that this is just a phase, huh? Let's not bother with Reilly and Chiron because soon she will be back on Earth and will never see him again. Well, what if I decide to stay too?"

Danni and Drew both let out a gasp. Ronan saw the pain in his girlfriend's eyes. He wasn't sure how to comfort her.

"Are you serious?" Danni gaped at her, tears forming.

Reilly looked just as surprised as everybody else by her outburst. Clearly, she hadn't thought this plan through. "I don't know," she murmured. Chiron rubbed her shoulders with a satisfied smirk. "I finally find an amazing guy and he just happens to be an almighty counterpart slash centaur on another planet. My Facebook relationship status would totally read 'It's complicated'. How am I supposed to give him up?"

"Reilly," Asterion said, "let us not discuss this now. I think we can all agree there are more important matters at hand here. We need to rescue Graham and bring Milo to justice. Now, from talking with the group that didn't go to Liria, it appears that some progress has been made. I believe a debrief is in order. Use this time to make your decision. You are of course welcome to remain on Bastion with Ambrite, but know that a relationship between a mortal and a counterpart is quite difficult. There is much to consider."

Reilly looked as though she wanted to keep arguing but thought better of it and sat down. Chiron stood behind her, his firm legs pressing into her back. Danni looked deathly pale and slightly green. She was not ready to lose her best friend. Ronan kissed her cheek, but she remained frozen in place. Drew sulked against Hannah and glared at Chiron every so often. The three were a tight group; it would be painful to break them up.

"Wonderful," Asterion exhaled. "Firstly, I would like to hear from Ronan and Brodie, who visited the Place of Pages with their counterparts. They were very successful in their mission. Ronan and Aegipan discovered the source of Milo's powers, whilst Brodie and Equas may have located where Milo took Graham. This is absolutely fine work, and I commend you all on your efforts."

Danni unfroze and gazed at Ronan. He grinned and threw his hands up in a *Who, me?* gesture. She returned the smile and hugged him. It was such a nice feeling, knowing his girlfriend was proud of him. He stood and walked over to Aegipan, who was struggling to swallow a silver spoon he had found by the buffet.

"Do you want to take this one?"

Aegipan shook his head and choked. He inclined his head towards Ronan, indicating that he should take it away.

"Okay, well, Aegipan and I studied a book that I believe was called

Florae & Faunae of the Hyrin Galaxy. It lists every possible plant and species found in just this galaxy alone. To be honest, Aegipan is the one who discovered…"

Ronan trailed off as the goat made a loud retching sound followed by a dramatic gulp. He had bested the spoon.

"As Ronan was saying," Aegipan interrupted with an air of arrogance, "most of the credit lies with me. Allow me to explain what I found."

Ronan nudged the bony counterpart square in the ribs. Aegipan let out a yelp.

"All right, all right, what *we* found! There is a plant, named *Venominulae mortalis*, which exists solely on a planet bordering on Hyrin's outer rim called Darkstrom. It is extremely deadly. One taste and your heart will stop. Milo extracted this plant with the intention of killing Serket. However, as we all know, it would take a lot more than that to annihilate an immortal."

"'Annihilate an immortal' is a total oxymoron." Ambrite rolled her eyes.

"I agree." Aegipan tilted his head. "However, Milo found a loophole, and it involved another substance… Mamboa venom."

"That does not sound good." Crawford gulped.

"It isn't, young lion," Aegipan agreed. "The strangest part is the lengths and risks Milo took in order to harvest it. You can find Mamboa only on Mt Fosso, which is located on a planet named Ravine. Not a single being is foolish enough to go there. Their venom will paralyse you instantly. I will read you a passage that I copied from the book."

Aegipan produced a piece of paper. From where, Ronan did not know. His spectacles slid further down his nose as he narrowed in on the specific text of interest.

"Mamboa venom, if combined with a specific lethal substance, has the ability to melt blood both mundane and superior. If harvested, the vitals can be ingested, with supernatural results depending on the victim. The trace elements found in the victim's contaminated blood contain magical properties. The rest of the venom will dissolve the victim's insides, leaving an empty husk."

"So Milo combined that deadly plant with the venom and used it on Serket?" Parry mused.

"How did that guy live to tell the tale, honestly?" Drew huffed. He appeared to still be on edge from Reilly's announcement.

"Greed and power do not live on the plane of rationality. They can take a man very far away from himself." Aegipan stuffed the paper back into thin air. "What we do know is that Milo absorbed Serket's abilities without any consequences upon murdering him. The venom in his scorpion tail refills itself. He will be extremely difficult to destroy…if he can be destroyed at all."

"This is why it is imperative that you all work together," Asterion urged. "Align with one another. Use your combined forces and take down the true enemy."

"Yeah!" Garth fist-pumped the air.

"Can I ask something?" Ronan raised his arm. He normally hated being in the spotlight, but something Aegipan mentioned in the Place of Pages had stayed with him.

"Indeed, Master Tate." Asterion bowed.

"Aegipan told me that even if we do manage to overpower Milo, killing a counterpart is a very serious thing. Not only that, he needs to be replaced. Is this true, and if so, how do we go about replacing him?"

An uncomfortable silence fell over the Mission Base. It confirmed to Ronan that eliminating Milo wouldn't be as simple as he thought. There would be hesitations, a moral code broken.

"I have the ability to initiate new counterparts," Asterion answered. "I did it for my two sons."

He gestured towards Castor and Pollux, who glowered in his direction. They had never forgiven Asterion for mating with their mother, Leda, who had died in childbirth.

"Okay, so you could initiate a new Scorpio counterpart," Ronan continued. "But who would it be? Once we rescue Graham, he isn't going to want to stay here. At least I highly doubt he will. And how do our current counterparts get past the guilt of having to kill one of their own in the first place?"

"Papa is a Scorpio!" Charlie squeaked in delight. "Papa could do it!"

Ronan expected the counterparts – or at least some of them – to scoff, but to his surprise, they looked thoughtful.

"We have much to tell you about our trip to Liria, my lord," Calypsee purred adoringly. Ronan noticed Garth squirming in his seat. "The boy's father has been…" She trailed off as Karki blocked Charlie's ears. The Cancerian gave her a thumbs-up to continue. "He was captured by Milo along with every other Scorpio worker. Perhaps one of them, once brought back home, could be considered?"

"I don't wish to speak for all of us…" Ares trotted forward.

"But you will," muttered Cerus to Ganymede.

"But I will." Ares grinned. "If we could find a suitable and worthy replacement of Serket, I would not be as hesitant to vanquish Milo. After all, he has not assumed his status in the traditional sense. He forced his way in and murdered one of us to do so. I understand that killing another counterpart is not favourable, but surely, he is the exception of all exceptions? Are we honestly supposed to offer mercy to this monster?"

"Ares is right," Equas rasped. "We cannot be expected to just apprehend Milo and bring him back to live with us in peace. He will not comply. He seeks ambition and power over everything. Furthermore, Serket deserves justice. He should be avenged."

Everybody in the room murmured agreement. Ronan had grown quite fond of the stone lady during his adventures to the secret library. She was tough but fair. Aegipan, on the other hand, was an arrogant kook, but still, he would miss him once this was all over.

"What of the other workers?" Asterion probed. "There aren't just Scorpios on Liria."

Danni wriggled uncomfortably next to Ronan. Clearly, there was more to the story.

A deliberate cough from Brodie caught everybody's attention.

"Before we go into that," she said, "Equas and I haven't shared what we discovered in the Place of Pages. You need to hear this first."

Equas shuffled over to Brodie, and they took turns gesturing to one another on who should speak. Thankfully, Brodie won. Equas was by far one of the better counterparts, but her gravelly voice still set Ronan on edge.

"Equas and I searched through this ginormous book that lists every single planet in the Hyrin galaxy. You would not believe how many there are. It was a real process of elimination, but we narrowed it down to two potential locations."

"How can you be so sure either of the two is a true contender?" the Maiden asked doubtfully.

"Good question." Brodie beamed. "Milo's scorpions. Basic science tells us that scorpions thrive in arid, dry land. There are so many planets in the Hyrin galaxy that have sub-zero temperatures or are just filled with water. We were able to narrow it down quite nicely. Not only that, Graham mentioned living on a new planet with Milo. This meant we could also cross off ones that were already populated or uninhabitable due to the dangerous species living there."

"Excellent work, detectives!" Drew tipped an imaginary hat. "So, where are we jet-setting off to next?"

"Corathinia or Malvolt," Equas rasped. "They both possess conditions perfect for Milo's minions. The only issue is they are on completely opposite sides of the galaxy."

"From what I've heard, Malvolt is entirely in the dark, is it not?" Asterion frowned.

"Yes, and Corathinia is lit by neighbouring planets." Equas nodded. "If I were Milo, Malvolt would be the better option."

"Unless he is hiding in plain sight?" Garth questioned.

"Ah, now this is where I am the most useful." The Maiden smirked. Ronan watched her glide over to the centre of the room, her lithe figure bathed in a grey silk dress. She was undoubtedly exquisite.

"Ouch!" Ronan cried as Danni's elbow jammed into his ribs. He turned to see his girlfriend assessing him with raised eyebrows.

"Eyes on me." She grinned.

"You're cute when you're jealous." He laughed.

The Maiden's lips quirked slightly. She was used to the attention. She lapped it up with gusto. "My mirror shows where somebody is at that exact point in time. It was how we knew to look on Liria for Graham. If Malvolt is dark and Corathinia is bright, surely we will notice this?"

"Not if Graham happens to be inside," Sirena sneered.

Ronan could sense the hostility coming off her in waves. She and Calypsee were gorgeous, but they didn't exude perfection like the Maiden did. It was like being back in high school.

"I shall look and report back." The Maiden ignored the mermaid. With that, she vanished in a puff of perfumed mist.

Wasabi stood. "Whilst she's gone, I'd like to share my progress report with the citizens of the valley."

"Ah, yes." Asterion smiled. "Thank you, young lady. How did you fare?"

"There are four conditions…" Wasabi tapped her feet nervously. "One, the colour system needs to be banned once and for all. Should Constellar be rebuilt, there is to be only one male and one female bathroom for everybody to use. Two, the Unsigned get to choose which empty houses they want. Some of them have children, so that needs to be taken into consideration. Mr. Arthurton will move in with one of the families and receive top medical care. Three, the move will be purely on a trial basis, so please leave the homes in the valley as they are. If they feel it isn't working out, they must have the option to move back home."

Ronan kept flicking back between Asterion and Garth. They looked deep in thought.

"Finally," Wasabi exhaled, "the word 'Unsigned' needs to be banished forever. It divides us…"

"It's funny." Garth's eyes shined with tears. "I was marked as an Unsigned the moment I was born, yet I never really realised how isolated I felt until you spoke, Wasabi. If Asterion is happy with these terms, I am too."

Asterion laid an affectionate arm on his friend. "I am quite happy to meet these terms. To be honest, I have always found the whole thing ridiculous, but I was trying to keep peace with the elders. By the way, they all perished at Constellar. It is unfortunate, but perhaps their deaths pave the way for new beginnings. Whilst you were on Liria, Garth and I took inventory of the available homes and living citizens remaining. There are actually more than we thought, which is positive. We shouldn't need to import too many from Cassius."

"What? It's time you told us what you were doing over there," Ambrite demanded.

Asterion and Garth took turns explaining their mission to the group. Everybody laughed at Garth's theatrics and obvious distaste for the Council members. Ronan wished he could've seen the looks on their faces when Garth replayed what had happened at Constellar.

"Those stuffed shirts were positively owned!" Garth crowed victoriously. "Oh, it was the best. I have already replayed it on my pendant five times."

Asterion chuckled. "In short, we have been provided with similar conditions. The citizens on Cassius will be handpicked by the Council and must be willing to live and work here on a trial basis. A contract is being drawn up as we speak."

Wasabi grinned, showing a full mouth of teeth. "Thank you so much. This means more to me than you will ever know. It's hard enough not knowing who your parents really are, but being treated like an outcast your whole life hasn't been fun. To think that we can be treated like normal people now…well, that is just awesome."

"My girl has such a way with words," Ambrite whispered to Danni. Ronan struggled not to laugh out loud.

At that moment, the Maiden re-appeared in a new outfit and spiky stilettos. She was adorned in a stunning silver halter-neck dress, and her scarlet hair was perfectly wrapped up in a bun. She looked like a goddess. Ganymede let out a sound like air escaping from a balloon. He immediately tried to turn it into a manly cough.

Garth waved. "So, my dear, what did you see in your mystical glass mirror?"

"I would rather not say," the Maiden mumbled, turning a surprising shade of red to match her tresses.

Aegipan gasped. "That blush is the colour of cardinal sin. She must've caught Graham in flagrante with his captor."

"English, dude?" Hunter sighed.

"My counterpart saw Graham and Milo getting physical," Parry answered on behalf of the goat.

"Oh." Hunter flushed and turned away. Ronan noticed Parry's eyes lingering on the back of Hunter's head for several seconds.

"The point is I saw nothing of import," the Maiden snapped.

"We can try again later, my dear." Cerus nudged her lovingly.

"There is no time." Charlotte crossed her arms. "We told Mads we would come back for him and the workers." She marched over to the thrones and placed her hands on either side of Garth's, levelling an intimidating gaze at him. The Chief Advisor sat back in alarm. "We need your aircraft. We are going to finish this once and for all. Whenever everybody is ready, we are going to pick up those poor men from Liria and ask them to help us fight against Milo. They will do it once they learn about what happened here. We are then going to pick a planet and fly there. Graham may be having a hot and heavy moment right now, but he has been manipulated long enough. Let's end this crap so we can all go home. Understood?"

"Yes!" Danni exclaimed, making Ronan jump. He hadn't thought it possible, but the pair had somehow formed an understanding. They were a long way from making friendship bracelets, but at least they weren't tearing each other's throats out.

Garth released Charlotte's grip on his throne with a wary eye. "I appreciate your candour, young Gemini, but we don't want to do anything rash here…"

"Rash?" Charlotte exclaimed. "I never wanted to come to this stupid planet in the first place, let alone be a part of this dumb group. No offence, guys." She gestured placatingly to the Astro A Team, who glared back. "I was forced against my will to travel through space and time to this godforsaken cave. My boyfriend dumped me, and I had to fight off disgusting scorpions on the roof of a nightclub. My wardrobe consists of the worst colour in the world, and I have to share a bathroom with a bunch of other girls. I have never had to do that in my life! So don't tell me this is rash. We are getting on that aircraft, rescuing those poor workers, and saving the one person in this galaxy who has any fashion sense aside from me. Understood?"

"Hey!" Parry and Drew called out simultaneously, bruised by the fashion comment.

With that, Garth jumped up from his throne, rubbing his hands together. "Well in that case, what are we waiting for?"

"Really, Garth? A child's tantrum is all it takes?" Ganymede huffed.

"Yes, pretty boy," Garth replied drily. "If we are going to take on an evil imposter, I have to make sure these kids have fire in their blood. This isn't going to be easy, but it must be done, not only to save Graham but to show Milo he does not mess with the stars. He has taken enough from us. It's time for some serious retribution!"

*

Despite the rough ride back and a throbbing migraine, Graham was happy to see Milo in an overly good mood. He had been certain his master would punish him the moment they landed, but instead he was being…rewarded? No words were spoken. No harsh reprimands. Milo's strong hand grasped his and dragged him upstairs into the beautifully decorated room he had woken up in. Graham braced himself for more mind-melding torture, but Milo had other plans. He pushed Graham gently onto the four-poster bed, meeting his mouth with a soft, wet longing. Graham let out a groan of surprise and pleasure. The silk sheets cushioned them as they rolled around the mattress, gripping each other's hair and kissing with an intensity Graham hadn't known was possible. The passion was making him heady. It felt like they could go on for hours this way and it still would never be enough. When they finally broke apart, Graham was breathless with euphoria.

"Wow." He shook his head in disbelief.

"You are welcome." Milo smirked smugly, propping a burgundy pillow up behind his back.

Still drunk on Milo's affection, Graham inched forward and laid his head on his firm chest. Milo brushed his fingers against the nape of Graham's neck, making him shiver.

"I thought…well, I was worried you would be angry with me," Graham murmured meekly.

Milo sat up, eyes flashing coldly. Graham flinched, shuffling backwards.

"Make no mistake, my love, I am not pleased with your momentary lapses in judgement, but overall, we achieved our goals, and I am nothing if not an optimist."

"Uh, so where did you put the workers?"

This was apparently the wrong thing to say. Milo leapt off the bed, the anger radiating off him in waves.

"Why?" Milo barked. "Do you wish to rescue them? Set them free? Do not think I didn't sense your little friendship with Mr. Venturion. I swear upon all the moons and the stars, Graham, that if you even dare try…"

"I won't, I promise!" Graham cried helplessly. "I just wanted to make sure they were comfortable. I am not going to interfere, but I need to know they won't come to harm. Please don't kill them once this is over. I'm begging you."

Milo appraised him with unblinking eyes. He slowly shrugged on his black cape without looking away. Graham felt smaller than a pea.

"Oh, darling." Milo laughed harshly. "You have so much to learn about running an empire. What you must understand is that we have an image to uphold. The only way to get what you want is through intimidation and fear. If you coddle the workers and give them lavish lodgings and privileges, they will never respect you. If you show them power, you will achieve excellent results. I promise to use death as a last resort, but if they defy me, I will single out a worker and make him an example to the rest. It is the only way they will learn. Do you understand?"

Graham's stomach roiled and his palms felt unnaturally clammy. Once again, he was torn between wanting to please Milo and wanting to protect the workers at all costs.

"Do you understand, Graham?" Milo repeated, his voice increasing in volume and strength.

"Yes, I understand," Graham whispered, looking down at his slick hands.

Milo let out a sigh and sat back down on the bed, brushing a tendril of Graham's hair behind his ear. He desperately needed a haircut when he got back…to wherever he came from. His past was becoming more and more blurry.

"Now, darling, you must be famished from your big adventure. Shall we go downstairs to the buffet? My minions will be detained until you have had your fill; otherwise, you won't get so much as a crumb. Tomorrow, the real work begins."

Graham nodded and made his way towards the bathroom. "I'll meet you there. I'm just going to shower. The mines weren't exactly clean."

Milo pressed a kiss against his forehead. It felt comforting and patronising all at the same time.

"Don't be too long, sweetheart," he purred, black cloak billowing as the bedroom door closed.

Graham gulped and raced to the bathroom, where he knelt beside the toilet to retch. It had all been too much. The trip to Liria, the ambush of the workers, the pressure, his throbbing head, and even the passionate moment with Milo. Wiping his mouth, Graham stood shakily and flushed. He didn't even remove his clothes as he stepped into the steaming hot shower and wept.

*

Finally, things were moving at a pace satisfactory to Charlotte. Everybody, Asterion and Garth included, was piled into the silver aircraft, flying towards what mattered. Their first stop was Liria. From there, they would visit Corathinia. Malvolt did seem the more likely option, but Corathinia was closer in distance. It would make sense to check it out first. Should Corathinia prove to be a dud, they would set course for Malvolt and take Milo and his minions by surprise. Charlotte only hoped they wouldn't be too late.

She had dressed sensibly this time. Charlotte looked down at her mustard jeans and zip-up matching hoodie. They were warm, stretchy, and comfortable. She made a solemn vow that this would be the last time she would ever wear yellow. She never wanted to see that particular shade in fashion ever again. It filled her with joy, knowing that the colour system would be banished from Bastion once things had returned to normal. It had seemed like such a stupid rule to her from the beginning. Back home, people would just ask what her sign was…and even then, it wasn't that common a question.

Thinking about Juggler's Corner left a lump in her throat. What would her life be like once they returned? Would the twelve teenagers she had saved the universe with ever want to see her again? Would they all just go their separate ways? The thought made her sad. This was the first time in her life that she'd had real friends. Not that the majority of them would her call her a friend, but still, she felt like she finally belonged to the Astro A Team.

At the very least, Danni had started to warm to her. Their relationship had started off quite rocky, for want of a better word. She had made Danni's life a living hell. Firstly by seducing her boyfriend, who had ended up breaking Charlotte's heart as well, and secondly by ruining her friendship with Reilly by filming a forbidden kiss between Danni and Slade. Their first encounter with Castor and Pollux had been disastrous, to say the least. Charlotte had passed out and Danni had been almost killed by the angry Gemini twins. Only now could Charlotte see the light at the end of the tunnel. She and Danni were finally working as a team, and she actually wanted to save Graham as much as the rest of them did.

Charlotte gazed at Crawford with fresh eyes. The delicious boy she'd had to have back home was no longer appealing to her. Sure, he was still gorgeous, but their love, if she could even call it that, had been tumultuous from the beginning. It had bloomed from deceit, lies, and manipulation. Her next romance would be natural and without taint.

As during their first trip to Liria, they zoomed through the stars in silence. Their aircraft would take slightly less time to arrive than the Aquarian Air had. Charlotte noticed that most of the group looked slightly queasy, and she knew with absolute certainty that it had nothing to do with motion sickness. They were scared and unsure of what was to come. It felt unlikely that they would get out of this battle alive. They had been lucky at Constellar, but so many of the citizens had not been. It would be a fight to the death. Charlotte stretched out her legs for the umpteenth time in that first hour of travel. She was restless with the need to take action.

"Shouldn't we formulate some sort of plan?" She turned to Garth and Asterion, who were sitting comfortably in their plush seats behind the pilot. They were whispering like two children after lights out.

"I was thinking we would just wing it." Garth winked, placing his arms behind his head.

"Any ideas, young Gemini?" Asterion leaned forward.

"Not really." Charlotte pouted. "I guess it's hard to come up with anything until we scout the location."

"Wow, scout the location?" Someone behind her chuckled. Charlotte turned to see Crawford grinning at her. "Since when did you become the war tactician?"

Charlotte felt her face get warm. They hadn't spoken since he had yelled at her at Constellar and ended their relationship.

"Well, at least I'm trying," she snapped defensively. "I don't see anybody else taking this as seriously as I am."

Crawford settled himself next to her. She stared at him in surprise. Garth smiled and returned to his hushed conversation with Asterion.

"Can I help you?" Charlotte squeaked, crossing her arms in front of her chest.

"Charlotte," Crawford began calmly, "I want to apologise to you. I said some pretty awful things to you that night at Constellar. It wasn't cool, and I just want to clear the air in case…well, you know?"

Charlotte wanted to scream and throw her fists against his chest in rage, but his even tone and kind eyes kept her diplomatic. "As I recall, you called me a whinging brat and said everybody hates me," she sniffed.

"I know." Crawford looked miserable. "I didn't mean it. I promise.

You are not a whinging brat, and we don't hate you. Granted, you haven't made the best choices…"

"And you have?" Charlotte retorted. "You had control that night of the dance. You didn't have to kiss me. You didn't have to break Danni's heart. You certainly didn't have to start dating me afterwards. Don't act like you are completely innocent in all this."

"I'm not," Crawford sighed wearily. He suddenly looked older, as though this adventure had aged him. "I have learnt a lot about myself in this short time here…"

"And let me guess." Charlotte cut him off rudely. "After a journey of soul-searching, you've realised you want me back. Well, you can forget it. I would rather date the goat."

Crawford blushed, biting his lip awkwardly. "I actually don't want you back. That's not what I was going to say at all."

"Oh," Charlotte replied, slightly stung and surprised.

"Yeah…" Crawford muttered. The silence hung between them like an ugly black cloud. "I wanted to tell you that my counterpart opened my eyes to lots of things. I realised that I'm a coward and don't handle confrontation well."

"No kidding," Charlotte scoffed, but she immediately regretted her words, as a flash of hurt crossed Crawford's face. "I mean, tell me more. What led to this epiphany?"

"Leonis, my counterpart, said I didn't handle this whole Danni thing and our relationship well. I was cowardly and dishonest. You were right. I didn't have to kiss you that night. I acted dishonourably, which is basically a giant slap in the face to Leos everywhere. I strung you along, and when I finally confronted my true feelings, I treated you terribly instead of just doing the right thing in the first place."

"Wow." Charlotte hung her head. "It sounds like you never cared about me at all." Tears threatened to flow down her cheeks. She knew most of this had been her fault, but still, it would have been nice to know

Crawford's feelings for her had been real.

"No." Crawford shook his head, grabbing her hand. Charlotte recoiled slightly but didn't push him away. "I did. I really cared about you. Don't take this the wrong way, but I feel like I'm the only person who has seen you for who you really are. You're sweet, Lottie. You have a big heart, and when you show it, you really fulfil the Gemini stereotype. Two sides."

Charlotte flushed at the mention of his intimate nickname for her. If anybody else had called her that, she would've punched them in the face, but Crawford made it sound so familiar.

"Look, I'm sorry for all of the pain I've caused." Charlotte's lip trembled. "I have been an absolute bitch. Not just to you but to everyone else. I don't want to get back together, but promise me that you will at least be my friend when we get back home. I'm going to have nobody…"

"You're not going to have nobody." Crawford laughed softly. "The Astro A Team will always be there for you."

Charlotte nodded meekly, but she wasn't so sure. They would ditch her the second they could. Why would anybody want her around? She wouldn't want to be her own friend if given the choice.

At that point, the pilot shifted in his seat and threw up two fingers. "We shall be arriving at Liria in just under twenty minutes."

Garth and Asterion stood and made their way to the back of the aircraft, where the main exit door was located. Charlotte followed behind Crawford and the rest of the group, her heart in her throat. She had just been there, and yet she was filled with nerves. She tried to ignore the little voice in her head that kept repeating, *One-way ticket.* Everybody stepped outside into the cold, frigid air. Once again, Karki volunteered to babysit Charlie in the aircraft. They waved with encouraging smiles on their faces as the pilot rose into the air to park the aircraft somewhere more suitable. Charlotte noticed the docking station officer was still lying unconscious on the ground.

"We probably should have covered him with a blanket or something."

Danni laughed without humour. Charlotte couldn't help but agree. Chiron lifted him onto his back and trotted towards the shelter where the workers lodged after a hard day of labour. Once he returned, the group took off towards the mine in a hurry. The journey took them half the time now that they were no longer scared or unsure what could ambush them at every turn. When they reached the gigantic cavern, Charlotte was relieved to see the workers huddled together in the centre. Mads jumped up and rushed over to them with a shocked expression.

"You didn't think we would come back, did you?" Drew grinned.

"I'm not going to lie… I had my doubts." Mads loosed a breath.

Reilly stepped forward and took Mads by the arm, gently manoeuvring him towards the rest of the workers. "We really need to get a move on," she murmured. "Let's brief the workers here so we can get going."

Mads nodded and clapped his hands to get the workers' attention. They were already alert, throwing curious glances between the diverse company standing before them. Charlotte stood by Crawford and Danni, feeling relieved that she was on good terms with both of them over everyone else.

"Listen up, everybody," Mads called, his voice carrying within the large room. "Thank you for being so patient. I am sure you have many questions, but for now, I ask that you just listen and save them until the end." Mads took a deep inhale. Charlotte noticed his hands were slightly shaking at his sides.

"These good people travelled from Bastion to deliver a very important message. Unfortunately, when they first arrived, their mode of transport was too small to bring us back, but now they have a proper aircraft to take us all home. Basically, whilst we have been toiling, Constellar was attacked by an evil man named Milo and his scorpion minions. Many people perished…"

The men stared at Mads, frenzy in their eyes as they took in his emotional delivery. Charlotte could tell it took all of their willpower not to drown him in questions.

"I don't know if Livia, Penny, and Annie are alive. The same goes for your families... I'm so sorry."

Charlotte sucked on her bottom lip, desperate not to cry. Her heart was bleeding for Mads and the workers, who had all turned ghastly shades of white. Hannah was sobbing soundlessly into Drew's shoulder.

"The boy you would have seen before we were attacked belongs to this party," Mads continued with ragged breaths. "He was kidnapped and manipulated by Milo. They have taken what they need from Liria – alongside our Scorpio brothers – back to an unknown planet where that bastard is residing." He spat the last words with venom. "Before we return to Bastion, we have been offered the opportunity to fight back with these brave people and take down the monster who destroyed our home. Who is with us? Also, please do not feel obligated to join our army. If you do not wish to, you are welcome to wait in the aircraft."

Charlotte smiled. Mads spoke so politely and eloquently. Had she been in his place, she would have delivered his speech with much more demand and fury. She watched with bated breath as, one by one, the workers stood and slammed their mining tools on the ground with conviction.

"We will fight, brother. Of course we will fight!" a bearded bald worker shouted.

The rest of the men yelled in agreement. Mads beamed with shining eyes. The Astro A Team, the counterparts, Garth, and Asterion nodded with excitement.

"Thank you, good gentlemen." Asterion stepped forward. "Bastion will not forget your valour and bravery. I am extremely sorry that I cannot reassure you about your families. Just know they will be very proud of your efforts. Now, we must get going. Truth be told, we are not completely sure where Milo is located. We will stop at Corathinia first. Failing that, we will head straight to Malvolt. Please bring all of your equipment. You never know what we may need."

With that, he turned on his heel and strode out of the room with Garth following close behind. Drew, Ronan, Crawford, Hunter, and Slade began helping the men with the tools and potential implements of destruction. There was a fervent energy in the air. A mix of comradery and lust for war. The workers were running on pure adrenaline, rage, and vengeance. This was the best time for them to strike. Charlotte wasn't fooled, however. She saw them exchanging looks of despair and misery. They were putting on brave faces but close to cracking. This mission would hopefully serve as a welcome distraction and a way to channel all their conflicting emotions.

"Charlotte, are you coming?"

Charlotte's head jerked up at the sound of Danni's voice. She had been standing in the room by herself, somehow missing everybody else's exit.

"Oh, yes…sorry." She hurried alongside her Gemini twin.

*

It felt like the middle of the night, but it was hard to tell on an eternally dark planet. Graham knew he would be royally punished if caught, but he just had to know Issac and the other workers were safe. Milo slept soundlessly next to him. He appeared to be quite a heavy sleeper. Graham slid quietly off the sheets and tiptoed out of the partially open bedroom door. He made sure to take each step downstairs with careful soft footing.

As he reached the landing, he heard something akin to a pig with a sinus infection. Graham realised just in time that he had been about to walk into a minion on guard duty, snoring rather obnoxiously. Graham ducked behind the large kitchen counter, reminding him of his first morning. Had that been just the day before? It was so difficult to judge time there. Graham army-crawled along his belly across the length of the counter. When he reached the other side, he moved swiftly in the shadows to the door leading outside.

Graham screwed up his eyes in panic as he slowly pushed down the handle and crept out into the warm dusty air. He could see the path leading down to the docking station. Milo wouldn't have been stupid enough to house them in the aircraft, their only means of escape. Turning left, Graham crept alongside the perimeter of the warehouse, eyes darting in the direction of any unfamiliar sounds. He avoided all of the craters, aware that the minions would be sleeping in clusters within the grooves of the planet. There were no discernible structures in sight. Where could Milo be hiding fifty-something workers?

A flash of silver caught his eye beyond a rocky outcrop in the distance. It took several seconds for his eyes to adjust before he realised it was a gigantic stack of the ore that they had taken from the mine. His heart leapt in hope. Surely the workers would be placed near their building materials? The darkness of the planet gave Graham the camouflage he needed to race along the arid landscape towards the metals. As he neared the ore, he noticed the rocky outcrop was actually a small dark cavern. A howling hot wind whipped through his hair, leaving a ghostly echo. The cavern was barely bigger than a tool shed.

Graham crouched to avoid hitting his head on the jagged ceiling. He couldn't see more than a foot in front of him, but he could hear a mild whimpering. Amidst the wind, it was barely noticeable. Graham had to strain his ears and allow the sound to repeat several times before he was certain he wasn't alone in the cavern. He trudged slowly forwards, his breath catching in his throat when he noticed a familiar long blond ponytail attached to a man sitting against the wall, limbs tied and mouth gagged.

"Issac!" Graham hissed, rushing forward.

He couldn't see any of the other workers, but from where he stood, the cavern appeared much deeper on the inside than on the outside. Issac looked up at him with tear-stained eyes and a drooping expression. Graham removed the gag and pressed his palm firmly against Issac's mouth.

"Please don't make any loud noises," Graham pleaded. "If they catch me here, I'm dead."

Issac nodded to indicate he understood. Graham gently removed his hand and, without thinking, threw his arms around Issac's neck, silently weeping.

"I'm so sorry, Issac. I am so sorry." Graham shuddered. "I begged Milo not to harm any of you. If you guys do the right thing and follow his orders, you'll be safe. If you don't, he will kill one of you as an example to the rest. Just do the work, build whatever he wants, and before you know it, you'll be home with your family."

"Charlie," wheezed Issac, eyes bleary. "Ella. Please take me home."

Graham felt his heart sink. He had to help the workers. They were there against their will, away from their families. He loved Milo, but this was going too far.

"Issac, where are the other workers?"

"Scattered," Issac rasped.

Graham wished he had thought to bring water. They were probably extremely dehydrated and hungry.

"Some are further down this cave," Issac continued hoarsely. "The rest have been put in the bigger craters and other caverns. They didn't want us to all be together. What is going on, Graham? Why is your king so evil?"

"He's not evil," Graham cried, sensing the desperation in his tone. His head was beginning to throb painfully again. He wanted to tear it out of his skull.

Issac shifted uncomfortably. "Graham, this man has manipulated you, don't you see? There is nothing good about a person who tears people away from their families without any explanation or warning and trusses them up like prisoners on some wasteland of a planet. Please tell me you see that."

Graham grasped the sides of his head and let out a cry of agony. His vision blurred as he fought with all of his might to keep his last meal down. He clutched Issac's hand in fright.

"Graham, what has he done to you? I remember you reacting like this in the mine. This man needs to be stopped. Untie me and we can gather up the other workers. We may be small in number, but we have fighting spirit. In any case, I would rather die than submit to this monster and his disgusting, vile minions."

Graham swivelled to heave onto the cave floor. Never had the pain been this strong. He immediately felt better, his pain lessening to a dull ache. He stared into Issac's kind, concerned eyes. He knew he was right. The argument was sound, logical, and yet…he wanted to please Milo more than ever. The thought of disappointing him was almost too much to bear.

"Can you not just do what he says?" Graham groaned in misery. "Do the job and he will let you go."

Issac pressed his hands firmly on top of his. "Graham, do you honestly believe he is going to let us go after this? You know deep down that once our work is done, we will be eliminated. You know this."

Graham hung his head, defeated. He nodded slowly, biting his lip to keep more tears from flowing. The truth was undeniable.

"Let me go, and if I'm caught, I will not implicate you in any way," Issac urged. "I will lie and say I broke free somehow. I can leave you out of it. Just do this for me, please. I have a family that needs me…and I need them."

Standing shakily to his feet, Graham leaned forward and ripped the ties from Issac's hands and feet. They were not difficult to loosen, but there was no way Issac would have been able to reach them himself. The worker rubbed his raw red wrists in pain and allowed Graham to pull him up.

"Thank you, Graham." Issac squeezed his hand. "You've done the right thing. Now, go back to sleep before Milo realises you're gone. I'll take it from here."

"Okay, good luck." Graham moved towards the entrance but stopped short when a familiar figure in a flowing black cape blocked his exit. Graham felt his entire body freeze.

"Well, well." Milo's eyes flashed deviously. "What do we have here?"

*

Corathinia was not what Drew had expected. It immediately reminded him of a dystopian zombie game he'd been addicted to back home… minus the zombies. The planet was completely deserted, ridiculously hot, and unusually bright. Brodie had told them that Corathinia was lit by neighbouring planets, but that didn't make it any less creepy. The wind was so harsh, Drew had rashes on his arms within five minutes of walking through it. He wished he had brought something with long sleeves. He would pick the heat over the pain any day.

The group, workers included, trekked across the arid wasteland, keeping their eyes and ears open. Parry had brought along one of Graham's silk maroon scarves for Cerus to sniff and track. Cerus inhaled deeply against the material before turning around in a circle to match the scent. After several seconds, the bull shook his head.

"Do we go back?" Drew asked a little too eagerly, rubbing his red arms.

"Not yet," Asterion called back from the front of the group. "This planet is quite large. Let's be absolutely sure before we board the aircraft."

"Great," Drew huffed. Hannah leaned in and kissed him on the cheek. She was always there for him. He had to stop himself from proposing to her every second of every day. Like a classic Pisces, he was a true romantic, in love with love. He noticed Sirena and Calypsee glaring at both of them. He responded by poking out his tongue at them. Just let them try to overthrow his queen again.

The workers stopped in the middle of the path and sat down to eat the ridiculous amount of food Garth had taken from the buffet inside the

Mission Base. Drew had never seen a more ravenous pack of vultures. They slurped and chewed and grunted as they devoured everything in sight. The Astro A Team just stared at them in disbelief whilst the counterparts turned away in disgust.

"So, I assume we are on a break?" Cerus sighed loudly. "It's not like we are on a time-sensitive mission or anything…"

"Patience, dear Cerus." Asterion clucked his tongue. "These workers need their strength. Who are we to deprive them of fuel when they have so selflessly volunteered to fight with us? I personally would like to take this moment of respite to scout out our surroundings."

Cerus swished his tail in irritation. The Maiden patted his rump sympathetically.

"I do not approve, either," Drew heard her murmur. "For starters, this wind does not agree with my hair."

Drew bit back a laugh. No matter how strong the gusts, the Maiden's hair moved barely an inch. Hannah spat out a wad of her own locks for the fifth time in several minutes.

"How dare she complain?" she moaned. "This is ridiculous."

"Cutting my hair was the right choice." Parry beamed. "I have finally found a reason to keep it this way."

"I hope you do keep it that way." Hunter sidled up beside her. Parry flushed furiously in response.

The sexual tension between the two was palpable. If Drew didn't know any better, he would've sworn something had gone down that fateful night Graham was abducted. Hannah would know. Girls talked. Plus, they had this heightened sense of awareness. They were so much better at reading signals and body language.

Asterion and Garth had wandered off into the illuminated dusty path to the north. The counterparts had split up to tackle the east and west. The Astro A Team had been left behind to babysit the ravenous workers.

"Just because we don't have the ability to make starlight, doesn't mean we are useless." Ambrite glared in the direction of the workers. "We are perfectly capable of exploring this shithole of a planet."

Nobody argued with her. They were all imbued with a restless energy to prove themselves.

"I don't think they are going to find anything here, anyway," Brodie said, ever the diplomat. "It has to be Malvolt. Once we find Milo, we will be fighting with the rest of them."

"Yeah," Drew exclaimed, sounding braver than he felt. "This time, we will be armed with some more impressive weapons… No offense, Wasabi."

Wasabi shrugged, seemingly unoffended. Castor and Pollux had loaded the aircraft with every deadly instrument they could find from the Cavern of Yellow.

From way off in the distance, Drew could make out two figures dragging a third towards them. At first, he thought it was one of those blurry desert mirage things, but as they got closer, it was undoubtedly Asterion and Garth holding fast to a leathery black lump of a being.

"What or who the hell is that?" Reilly whispered.

"It kind of looks like a…scorpion?" Ronan narrowed his eyes.

At the sight of the mystery prisoner, the workers jumped up, grabbing their tools and brandishing them. They yelled and made moves to charge. Asterion held up a hand, halting their advances.

"Please remain where you are," he bellowed. "As soon as the rest of the group returns, we will interrogate the minion."

"You were right, dude." Drew turned to Ronan. "It's a scorpion in a really gross human form."

The counterparts slowly trickled back in, looking irritated that they hadn't been able to find anything. Drew watched in amusement as they naturally gravitated towards their human counterparts. The twins automatically stood behind Danni and Charlotte, Ganymede behind Slade, and so on. He felt his girlfriend tense up as Calypsee and Sirena took their place behind him as well. The mermaids would have made really cool counterparts if they weren't so…lusty.

Garth threw the scorpion rather roughly on the ground. The scorpion hissed up at him but didn't make any moves to stand.

"Does anybody know how to speak villain?" Garth called to the group, rubbing his hands together in disgust.

"We can." Castor raised his hand. Pollux nodded eagerly in confirmation.

"Are you serious?" Garth raised his perfectly sculpted eyebrows.

"We rule under the sign of language and learning. We understand every dialect ever created." Pollux fixed Garth with a withering stare.

Drew couldn't help but envy the arrogant twins. If he could have had one superpower, it would have been to understand and speak every single language in the world. That included Klingon, pig Latin and Elvish.

"Fine." Garth pouted. "Please get this creature to talk and get some information out of him."

Castor and Pollux exchanged devilish smiles. Without warning, Pollux tackled the already kneeling scorpion and punched him square in the face. Drew watched in fascination and horror as the counterpart slugged him over and over whilst Castor cackled gleefully. The workers cheered.

"Okay, that's enough!" Asterion boomed, face black.

Pollux frowned but stopped pummelling the poor prisoner. Holding his arms behind his back, Castor began speaking in a deeply disturbing manner. The words were harsh and clipped. They sounded remarkably like a cat coughing up giant fur-balls. The scorpion glared at Castor in silence until Pollux began twisting his arms in an unnatural position. The minion screamed in pain and began chattering rapidly in the same awful language.

Everyone waited to hear the translation. Castor turned to the group with a haughty smirk.

"You are so lucky to have Pollux and me," he declared smugly. "What would you do without our gifts?"

"Yeah, yeah," Garth groaned. "Spit it out, pretty boy."

"I asked the minion if he had brothers, and, if so, where the majority of them resided. I also asked him if he knew Milo and anything about Graham. He told me that he was banished here after refusing to comply with an order from his master. He didn't say Milo's name, exactly, but I assume that was whom he was referring to. He is the only one of his kind on Corathinia. The rest of his brothers do indeed live on Malvolt, where their master is currently building some sort of empire. He said there is a boy captive there."

"Great!" Garth exclaimed. "That's all we needed to hear. Let's go."

The scorpion began speaking again in loud, urgent tones. Castor frowned. Pollux released the minion's arms.

"What did he say?" Garth demanded.

"He said…" Castor took a deep breath. "If we set foot on Malvolt, we are all going to die. Milo cannot be stopped, and to even attempt such a dangerous mission would be foolish."

"Well, it would take a lot to kill us," said Aegipan. "The children, on the other hand…"

"You have such a way with words." Ronan rolled his eyes.

"Perhaps we should drop the children off at Bastion before departing for Malvolt?" the Maiden suggested.

"No!" Parry yelled. She looked so captivating in ripped grey jeans, with her bright red hair gelled and styled. "I am tired of being treated like a precious newborn. Graham is *our* friend, not yours. If we die saving him, so be it. I should have known something was up with him. I could have prevented his being abducted if I hadn't been so freaking self-absorbed. I want him to know that he is worth fighting for. He nearly left our group because he felt uncomfortable being gay. I am not going to let him think he is less than ever again. Now, let's not waste any more time. I am getting on that aircraft, and I'm rescuing my best friend. Who is with me?"

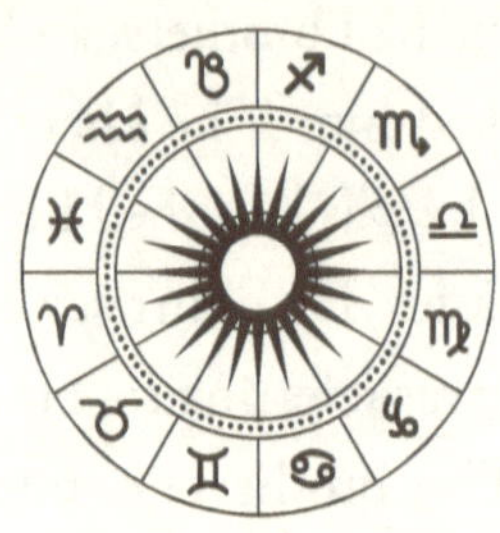

Chapter 19

Malvolt

Graham woke with a start. The first thing he noticed was the lack of silk sheets covering his body and decadent pillows cushioning his head. His joints ached, the taste of vomit burned in his throat, and his head felt like it had been flattened by a steamroller. He groaned, attempting to reach for something familiar in the dark, but all he could grope awkwardly was empty cold air. It took him less than a second to realise he was all alone in a dusty crater, bound and gagged. He had no strength to roll around, let alone attempt any sort of escape. Rolling onto his right side, Graham scanned his outdoor dungeon. There was not a single minion or worker in sight. He swallowed down bile in the fear that Issac had been murdered by Milo.

"Issac," he tried to yell, but his parched throat afforded him barely more than a whisper. He was completely useless and unable to help.

"Ah, you're awake." Milo's smooth, cold voice sounded from above.

Graham looked up to see his captor striding down the crater towards him, venomous scorpion tail waving behind him. The poisonous tip gleamed with red venom.

"What did you do to Issac?" Graham croaked as Milo came to a stop by his head. It hurt his neck to make eye contact, so he just stared at his shoes in terror.

"Issac, Issac, Issac," Milo repeated. "Is that simpleton all you care about?"

"He has a family," Graham rasped, using his forearms to move away from Milo. "All of the workers have families. We took them here against their will. The least we can do is treat them well before they are sent home."

"They aren't going to be sent home!" Milo yelled, stepping on Graham's shirt to keep him close. "Don't you get it, you idiot? I am their king. I am their emperor. They serve me, and once they have finished complying with my demands, they will be killed. If they beg to be my faithful lifelong servants, I shall consider keeping them here, but otherwise, they will die. I have tried to be patient with you, but you have forced my hand. A much higher dose is needed if I'm ever going to get through to you."

Graham's gut twisted. "Dose?"

Milo's scorpion tail whipped behind him like a poised cobra, ready to strike. Graham closed his eyes as the venomous point came hurtling towards his bare skin.

"Give in to me," Graham heard Milo whisper as his pierced skin began to burn. Graham let out one agonising scream before he lost himself completely.

*

If the aircraft circled Malvolt one more time, Danni was certain she would lose her lunch. There was no safe place to land that wouldn't alert Milo to their presence. They were going to have to pick a random section and hope for the best.

"Can we please just land?" she heard herself screeching hysterically at the pilot. Everybody turned to her in surprise. Danni was not coping well. She couldn't ignore the fact that she was essentially leading all of her friends and herself to their deaths. She didn't know whether to hug every single person, including the workers, or to just sit quietly. At eighteen years of age, she hadn't expected to go to war on another planet. At eighteen years of age, she had been hoping to fall in love, graduate from school, and travel for a year before pursuing further study. In any case, she had fallen in love, but it would be plain cruelty to rip him away from her before they had truly begun. She gazed over at Ronan with a heart so full it could overflow. Did he have to look so good all the time?

"We are going to land in the next twenty minutes," the pilot called. "I need to be absolutely sure I am not throwing you all into the midst of danger…more than you already will be."

With a groan, Danni stood and pulled Ronan to his feet. She dragged him wordlessly through the aircraft until they reached a dark unused cabin.

"What are we doing here?" Ronan laughed uneasily. "You're scaring me a little, Dan."

Inside the cabin was a bunkbed, window, and nightstand. It was extremely small and cramped, but Danni didn't care. Pushing Ronan onto the bottom bunk, she straddled him and began to take her shirt off.

"Woah!" Ronan sat up, grabbing Danni by the shoulders. "What are you doing? We are going to land any minute."

"Twenty minutes is more than enough time." Danni grinned, pinning him down with her legs.

"Danni, stop!" Ronan wriggled out from under her. "I get what you're trying to do here, but we are not having our first time in some bunk, scared that people could spring us any minute. When it happens, it will be completely private, romantic, and perfect."

Danni stared at Ronan for a moment before bursting into tears. Horrified, Ronan threw his arms around her, bringing her as close as possible. Danni felt extremely humiliated. Not only had she tried to jump Ronan in a very awkward way, but now she was crying like a lunatic.

"Ronan, don't you see why we have to do this?" She sobbed in his embrace. "We may never get an opportunity for a perfect evening. This might be the last time we are alone. I don't want to die not knowing what it's like to…you know?"

Ronan tilted her chin up so he could look deeply into her eyes. Thumbing her wet cheeks with his finger, he let out a sad laugh. "Danni, I love you. I love you so much that I would rather die than take advantage of this situation. We are going to make it through this, I promise."

"How can you promise something like that?" Danni wiped at her blotchy eyes with her sleeve. "We are on a life-threatening mission. It's not fair. We've only just begun, and I don't want it to be all over so soon."

Ronan ran his fingers through her hair and kissed her forehead. It was such a soothing gesture. Danni wished it would never end.

"I will protect you, Danni," he whispered. "You are going to go home. We are going to go home, and when we do, I will ravish you like crazy."

Danni choked out a laugh and a sob. "I will hold you to that."

Standing, Ronan offered his hand to Danni. She took it and allowed him to pull her up. Straightening her rumpled shirt, Danni felt her cheeks reddening at what had almost happened. They didn't even have protection. How had this been a smart idea?

"I'm so sorry for jumping on you like that, Ronan," she sniffed, not meeting his gaze.

Ronan encircled her with his arms and gave her another tender kiss on the forehead. She would never get tired of that.

"You don't need to apologise… It was pretty hot," he breathed against her.

"Really?"

"I'll be reliving it in my head for years to come." Ronan winked.

"I love your confidence." Danni nudged him with a small smile.

"Hey! Are you two decent back there?" Danni heard Reilly call from outside the cabin door. "We are about to land. Put on your clothes and let's go to war!"

Danni laced her fingers in Ronan's. Together, they made their way to the front of the ship, where the rest of the group were waiting. Danni did her best to ignore Drew's wiggling eyebrows, Charlotte's look of disgust, and Garth's finger guns pointed right at them.

"This is humiliating," she whispered to Ronan. "We didn't even do anything and suddenly we're the talk of the whole aircraft."

"Let them think all sorts of sordid thoughts," Ronan murmured back. "I'm enjoying this. Feel like quite a stud."

Danni playfully punched him in the shoulder. "Shut up."

"Attention, everybody," Asterion called. "We have just docked on the west side of Malvolt, which appears to be the most isolated place on the entire planet. None of us have ever been here before, so unfortunately, we have a strong disadvantage. We are also a big party, so trying to remain inconspicuous could be a problem. We need to scope out the area, stick to the shadows, and locate Milo's main fortress. Our main plan is to surround him and his minions on all sides and attack with the element of surprise. To my Astro A Team, please do not take on Milo by yourselves. This is a job for myself, Garth, and the counterparts. Understood?"

Everybody nodded in agreement, although Danni noticed Ambrite, Hunter, Parry, and Crawford looking disgruntled. They looked ready to take Milo down with their own two hands. The workers passed out their spare tools to the Astro A Team. Sighing, Danni glanced down at her pathetic rusty shovel. It didn't make her feel like much of a badass. Ronan was given a shovel as well, but his seemed a lot heavier and longer than hers. Drew brandished a shiny silver pickaxe with glee. He was much happier with his choice of weapon this time around.

"We were completely taken unawares at Constellar," Asterion continued, rolling up his sleeves. "This time, we are armed and ready with a clear purpose. We are united and strong. Milo does not understand concepts like friendship and love, but we do. Let that be the most powerful weapon of all."

The workers gathered in a circle and put their hands in together. Mads gestured for the Astro A Team and the counterparts to join in. It amused Danni to see the Maiden wrinkle her nose as she placed a dainty paw on a grubby worker's hand.

"On the count of three, we give our best but quiet battle cries," Mads whisper-shouted. "One, two, three!"

The group exploded in hushed howls, roars, whoops, and screams. The energy was electric. In that moment, Danni had no doubt that they could rescue Graham and return home safely.

*

Graham was there; Parry just knew it. The moment they stepped off the aircraft into the hot, dark wasteland, she could sense despair in the air. Corathinia had been empty, but it hadn't felt so…dead. Parry wiped the beads of sweat collecting on the back of her neck. She felt sick just knowing her best friend had been taken against his will to a place that would make a cemetery look like a cheerful place to hang out. Parry glanced over at Hunter, who was walking quite close to her, almost protectively. They had landed inside a large vacant crater that they had taken a long time to emerge from due to the steep incline. Parry had slipped several times on the gravelly rocks, causing Hunter to grab her hand. From that moment, he hadn't left her side.

"You don't have to fuss over me," Parry murmured, although she secretly wanted him to.

"I know I don't, but I want to." Hunter glanced over at her.

"I just don't want you to feel like you have a duty to chaperone me because of what happened. I'm a big girl. I can take care of myself."

Parry was doing what she always did, pushing people away when really, she wanted to keep them close. She was testing his loyalty and true intentions. It was immature, but she had never had a boyfriend before. An entourage of admirers, yes, but a boyfriend…no.

"I know you can take care of yourself," Hunter retorted. "I am not trying to sound like a chauvinistic jerk here, but I…care about you and want to protect you. Can you just let me?"

Parry's head jerked up. "You care about me?"

"Ah." Hunter turned red. "Yeah, I do. I wanted to ask you something, actually."

Parry felt her heart race. This seemed like such a strange conversation to have in the midst of a pitch-black planet as they marched towards potential death.

"When, if, no…when," Hunter stammered. "When we get back home, did you want to go on a date with me? No pressure, of course, just a movie and dinner, or we could just watch a movie at my place, or your place, not that I'm inviting myself over, but…"

"I would love to, Hunter." Parry smiled, happiness blooming in her heart. She had been so worried that her first time would be for nothing.

"You would?" Hunter grinned awkwardly. It pleased her to see the dimple on his left cheek dance. He really was super cute in a rugged sort of way. Much more handsome and striking than her pretty boy lemmings who all came from rich families.

"Yes, but…." Parry drew in a breath. She was afraid of Hunter's next answer, but she had to ask it. It would plague her forever if she didn't. "Are you…over her?"

Hunter stopped short, his expression unreadable. Parry immediately regretted her question. She had been so stupid. She should've given it more time. She shouldn't have pried. Now it was over before it had begun. Parry stood next to him, fixated on her scuffed boots.

"Let me put it this way." Hunter spoke slowly, as if every word had the potential to end the world. "Today, I woke up and she wasn't the first person I thought of. On the way here, I looked at her and Wasabi and I felt…happy. I like Wasabi. She's a super cool chick and they are actually really well suited. It took me a while to come to terms with everything, but I can honestly see it only getting better every day. I don't want you to feel pressured to date me. I'm a work in progress, and if you're willing to be patient, it won't be long before I'm back to my old self."

They began walking again. Parry was glad the dark shielded the gigantic cheesy grin plastered across her face. When had she become such a sap?

"I don't feel pressured," she replied softly. "I want to get to know you, and I'm very patient. Do you know how long it takes to get extensions? I am the queen of patience. Let's just take it slow."

Hunter let out a laugh. She felt his fingers brush against hers. It was enough to send electric shocks up and down her arm. It was enough to prove that she really liked him.

"Did I mention I dig your new look, and not because you look like someone else?" Hunter winked.

"You may have mentioned it," Parry said. She turned to face him, feeling the sudden urge to press her lips to his. Hunter stared hungrily at her mouth. Forgetting where they were, the pair leaned in. Just as they were about to meet in the middle, a hand grasped Parry's arm. Jumping, she whirled around to see a worker clutching his throat and choking, a festering black sore oozing on his neck.

"Oh no," she whispered. "They found us."

In that instant, scores and scores of scorpions emerged from all sides of the wasteland. Parry watched in horror as the infected worker fell to the floor, writhing for several seconds before his body froze and his eyes closed permanently. Screams could be heard in the dark. Shadows rushed by. Sickening thuds indicated that the workers, or her friends, were dropping like flies. Grasping hands, the pair streaked across the desert, desperate to locate a familiar face.

"Hunter," she wheezed. "Don't let go, please."

"I promise," he panted back. "Stay close to me, Parry. I'll protect you."

It couldn't end this way. If Parry was going to die, she had to at least see Graham one last time to know he was safe. Hunter let out a loud *oof* as he slammed into a minion with all his might, sending it sprawling to the floor. Parry watched as, without a moment's hesitation, Hunter stormed over to the dazed scorpion and stabbed it with his pickaxe right in the gut. Black guts spewed out of the minion's belly, covering Hunter's red shirt. Spinning the tool in his right hand, Hunter turned to Parry with a serious nod.

"It was him or me," he said by way of explanation.

"I don't know if I could do that." Parry shivered. All around them, shouts and fatal cries echoed in the dark.

"Parry, I need you to promise you won't hesitate." Hunter dropped his weapon and grabbed both of her hands firmly. The urgency in his tone made her recoil slightly. "The minute you pause is the minute it could be all over for you. Don't think, just act. These things took Graham. They want you and all of our friends dead. They killed men, women, and possibly children on Bastion. We have a duty to take them down and avenge the innocent people who lost their lives that night."

"I promise." Parry bit her lip.

Hunter released his hold on her, which was a relief and a shame at the same time.

"Come on," he said, picking up his pickaxe. "We need to find the others..."

*

Under normal circumstances, it would be much too early to ride her boyfriend...correction, ride *on* her boyfriend. But there was nothing normal about this situation, and the offer was far too appealing to pass up. For one, Reilly was much safer on Chiron's back than on the ground, where a scorpion could sting her for the second time at any moment.

For two, there was a certain strange intimacy that came with wrapping her arms around her man's neck as he cantered all over Malvolt, striking down enemies with his arrows. Some girls preferred flowers or a heartfelt poem, but the key to Reilly's heart was apparently a dashing archer who functioned as a partner and a noble steed. After what had happened at Constellar, Chiron hadn't wanted to take any chances. He had managed to revive her just in time on the rooftop. At the time, she had been so surprised to learn that he had actual feelings for her.

"Lower me!" Reilly shouted.

Chiron ducked just in time, giving her the opportunity to knock a scorpion off its feet with her shovel. Reilly cheered. This was a team effort, and she was no damsel in distress.

"Sagittarian power!" Reilly whooped.

Chiron let out a chuckle. "Remind me to teach you archery when all this is over, my love."

Reilly felt her heart sink just like it did every single time she realised she was going to have to make a huge decision. Stay on Bastion and live a life with Chiron or go back to reality with her best friends. The answer had been simple for someone like Ambrite. She had no relationship whatsoever with her parents. Plus, there was the whole immortal thing. Reilly, however, adored her family and didn't want to be the girl who gave up everything for a man she'd just met. Granted, he was no ordinary man, but still, how would her mother ever handle the loss of her child? It was a pretty selfish thing to consider, let alone go through with. She couldn't voice the decision that had already been made in her mind.

"Incoming." Reilly gripped her shovel tightly. Chiron dipped, but Reilly swung and missed her target. "Damn!" she growled.

Chiron trotted to a stop, whipped around, and headed back in the direction of the smirking minion. "Annihilate him, my warrior goddess!"

This time, Reilly swung with all her might and clocked the creature right in the head. She cackled in delight as its body went sailing over a small crater.

"This is oddly relaxing." She laughed. "I could totally get used to this."

In the distance, Reilly could see another dark figure standing in the midst of the ongoing battle. He looked taller than the other minions. There was something in the way he stood that set him apart from all of the other creatures. His stance was defiant, menacing, poised. Nobody dared go near him. Reilly could just make out an evil sneer and a wicked stare.

"Is that…Milo?" Reilly squinted. "Chiron, we should round up the other counterparts before we go charging over…"

"That's not Milo, darling," Chiron replied. "My vision is excellent. If I'm not mistaken, that is your friend Graham…"

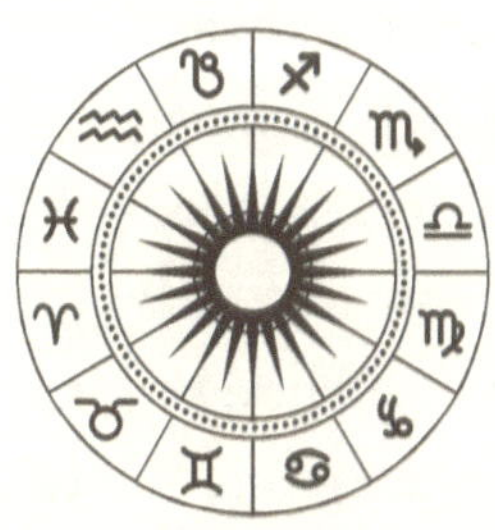

Chapter 20

An Act of Courage

Maybe it was all of the jungle training, or maybe it was the fact that he had just gotten closure with Charlotte, but Crawford was filled with a burst of renewed energy and a lust to kick some serious butt. Rather recklessly, he punched, jabbed, and kicked his way through a team of scorpions, dodging their venom left and right with a vengeance. He felt unstoppable. He felt invincible. This was his time to shine. Crawford was going to save the day. He was going to…

"What the hell do you think you're doing?"

A strong arm gripped his elbow and dragged him rather forcefully to the side of a small crater. Crawford attempted to yank himself free from Leonis's grip, but the counterpart just wasn't having it.

"Let go!" Crawford squirmed. "I'm on a roll. Isn't this what you wanted?"

"Ugh." Leonis rolled his eyes. "I cannot believe you still don't get it. How is throwing yourself into a pit of death brave? It is foolish and downright suicidal."

"What are you talking about?" Crawford yelled. "I have singlehandedly taken down six or seven of these bastards! What was the point of all that training if I'm not going to get to use it?"

Leonis released his grip from Crawford and fixed him with a withering stare. "The point," he growled, looking more animal than man, "was to give you the strength and courage to use your physical abilities in a safe, calculated way. Do you know how many times you were this close to being stung? Yes, I know I could heal you in two seconds, but that is not the solution. Healing takes energy. Be tactical. Be smart, boy!"

"Okay, okay." Crawford threw up his hands, knowing he was beat. "I understand. I just wanted to prove myself…"

Before Leonis could respond, one of the girls screamed Graham's name. Turning, Crawford saw his friends slowly approaching a darkened figure in the centre of the battlefield. The remaining minions lined up military-style behind Graham, ready to strike. There was no sign of Milo.

"Graham," Crawford breathed. "Come on."

The pair dashed over to where the rest of the group were standing, open-mouthed. Crawford understood their shock. Graham looked positively cutthroat in his stance and expression. Waves of hatred and rage were rolling off him, directed right at his friends and the counterparts.

"Graham!" Parry cried, running forward.

Crawford watched Hunter pull her back. Parry began sobbing and beating her fists against Hunter's chest, begging him to let her go, but Hunter didn't budge. The Graham before them all was not the one they'd met back home. This Graham had been tainted. Possessed. For one, he just wouldn't stop staring with eerie, emotionless eyes.

Asterion opened his arms with welcome. "Graham, we have come to take you home and away from this place. Please, son, your friends have been so worried."

For what felt like an eternity, nobody moved or spoke. The only sound came from Parry's whimpering against Hunter. Before Asterion could speak again, Graham began to twitch and jerk. Opening his mouth wide, he tilted his head and began to howl with laughter. Parry cried even harder, blocking her ears. It was a moment Crawford knew would haunt his nightmares for years to come…if he survived to sleep again.

"Graham, what has Milo done to you?" Danni's voice broke across the space. "We know you're in there somewhere. We love you. Don't forget who you really are!"

Graham continued to laugh maniacally as his limbs shivered and shook with more intensity. Crawford likened it to a demon wanting to escape its human shell. Milo must've injected him with a supremely large dose.

"What do we do?" Crawford turned to Leonis. "We have to do something whether you think that is stupid or not."

"It's not stupid," Leonis muttered quietly, eyes full of concern. "One move out of turn and the rest of his minions attack. We need to think critically."

Unfortunately, the Gemini twins had other ideas. Crawford watched them scream dramatic battle cries and, without consulting the group first, charge right at Graham and his monster army. Leonis slapped his forehead with his hand, letting out a tired groan.

"You are never allowed to complain about my reckless behaviour again," Crawford muttered.

Castor and Pollux barged straight past the unaffected Graham, strafing left and right as they mowed down the minions. The remaining workers were next. Brandishing their tools, the men, eager to avenge their families and fallen brothers, attacked with every limb and emotion.

"We need to help them," Leonis called to the group.

Crawford turned to his counterpart with his palm up. Leonis rolled his eyes but returned the gesture with a strong high-five.

"Let's do this," Crawford crowed, joining the chaos alongside everybody else.

This time, Leonis let him have free rein of the battlefield. Taking his advice, Crawford took on unsuspecting minions one at a time, dancing around them with precision in his feet. He even took it upon himself to shadow some workers who weren't thinking critically, as Leonis had put it. To his relief, there were no more casualties, and the fight was over in minutes. Not a single minion remained. The situation unnerved him. It had been too easy.

"Now is our chance to seize Graham and leave this place," Ganymede ordered.

As they were about to advance, Crawford heard Mads loose a breath and shriek, "Issac!" From beyond the carnage, fifty or so men marched towards Graham with the same crazed expressions and unblinking eyes. Judging by their maroon overalls, Crawford placed them as the kidnapped Scorpio workers. At the forefront, a man with long sandy hair and blue eyes led the troops. Issac stopped next to Graham with his army behind him. They were armed with all manner of sharp, pointy weapons.

"That's Charlie's father!" Reilly cried, clutching Chiron's neck.

At the mention of his name, Issac looked in her direction. His face contorted and his limbs twitched much like Graham's had.

"The poison," Aegipan growled. "Do you see how it infiltrates the system and confuses the victim? The real Issac is fighting underneath, desperate to be reunited with his son, but the venom ensures that he stays loyal to the master."

"Milo." Castor narrowed his eyes. "Where is the son of a bitch? Hasn't he done enough? Come on, let's keep fighting."

"No!" Mads pushed his way over to the scowling twins. "We cannot tear down our own brothers. They are victims just like your friend. Please, there must be some other way!"

Milo had presented them with an impossible scenario. If they tried to save Graham, they would be forced to confront the worker zombies and end up shedding innocent blood. If they turned around and left, nothing would be resolved. Milo would continue his reign of terror on Malvolt, growing stronger with more and more followers. Graham would live out the rest of his life a pawn in somebody else's game. They needed to cut the root off from its source. But where was he?

"Don't worry, Mads." Crawford grabbed his hand. "There is always another way. Everybody, listen up!" Crawford turned to the rest of the group. He felt a stirring inside him. The makings of a leader, a lion in charge of his pride. "Whatever you do, do not attack the workers. That is what Milo wants. We need to find him and finish him once and for all. His poison is controlling everything. If we can destroy his supply, we can return our friend and the good people of Bastion back to normal. I know it's not going to be easy, but together we are strong. Alone, we are nothing. Now who is with me?"

To his surprise, the group cheered, including all of the counterparts. Mads nodded at him in gratitude. Leonis clapped him on the back with a look that said, *Finally…*

*

Much as in a game of chess, the workers behind Graham didn't move unless their enemies moved first. They had been programmed to react but not to attack without provocation. The group were free to seek out Milo and destroy him, thus hopefully breaking the spell Graham and the workers were under. The only issue was locating him. Ronan and Aegipan huddled together to discuss what they had learnt about the poison from the Place of Pages.

"This is the time to strike," Aegipan bleated, despite being in human form. "The amount of poison Milo would've had to administer to not only Graham but these fifty or so workers would be enough to render him out of action for a while. He's hiding for a reason. He needs to replenish his stores."

"Could we not just wait for it to wear off?" Ronan said. "You mentioned that the real Issac and Graham are fighting underneath. Surely it won't be long now before they are back to normal?"

"There's no telling how strong the dose, when it was administered, and how long it will take for Milo to regenerate." Aegipan shook his head. "We need to find him now. He's going to be near impossible to kill, anyway. Best to take him at the only advantage we are going to get."

"Well, Asterion said only the counterparts are allowed to destroy him, so do the rest of us just babysit the zombies?" Ronan was surprised to hear the bitterness in his own tone. He wanted to feel useful.

"No, because if something goes wrong, you will need some of us to help fight. Our best bet is to split the parties, both counterparts and humans. Half will seek Milo. The other half will remain here, ready to defend."

Aegipan sauntered over to Asterion and Garth to explain. The pair nodded seriously and walked over to the rest of the group. They repeated the plan and then, just like in gym class, began nominating two teams featuring a mix of counterparts and humans. Ronan breathed a sigh of relief when he and Danni were placed in the same group. He didn't want to be away from her any longer. Alongside them, Parry, Drew, Slade, Wasabi, the Maiden, Castor, Ganymede, Sirena, Aegipan, and Asterion were tasked with searching for Milo. The remaining group consisted of Hunter, Ambrite, Hannah, Crawford, Brodie, Reilly, Cerus, Pollux, Leonis, Chiron, Calypsee, and Garth. Karki was watching Charlie and Equas, and Ares had volunteered to produce starlight back on Bastion. The workers refused to leave their manipulated brothers. Ronan figured that was the wisest choice, given Milo could just as easily brainwash them too.

Ronan felt a hand take his. He smiled at his beautiful girlfriend's worried but determined expression. It took all of his willpower to force the image of her taking off her shirt back on the aircraft out of his head. He knew they had made the right decision, but still, a big part of him wished he had taken her up on the offer. He couldn't wait to make it up to her once all of this was over.

"We stick together, okay?" He squeezed her palm.

Before Danni could respond, Drew grabbed both of their shoulders and whirled them around to face the front. "Look at Graham and Issac and tell me what you see," he whispered, excitement shining in his eyes. "Do you see it? Do you see it?"

At first sight, Ronan couldn't detect anything unusual…apart from the obvious, but on closer inspection, he noticed the two males were twitching in exact synchronicity. In fact, they were both…

"Oh my gosh," he hissed. "They are both signalling to the right. Do you think they are trying to tell us which direction to look for Milo?"

Ronan looked at them again. Now, he couldn't unsee it. Issac and Graham were tilting their heads to the right over in over in perfect time. It was, without a doubt, the creepiest thing he had ever seen.

"Yes." Drew stroked his chin. "Or…it's a trap. I think we should trust them, though. Let's gather the group and go right. We don't have time to question this."

The majority agreed that Graham and Issac were trying to help them out. After many fervent hugs, the group left the others to find Milo. They walked quickly and quietly, wary of any additional monsters or enemies that may have been lying in wait for them. It didn't help that Malvolt was so dark and foreboding. Ronan held on tightly to Danni's hand, keeping her close to him. He meant to deliver on his promise. They were going to get home safe and sound. Not just for her but to spend more time with his father and brother, Brandon.

Back in Juggler's Corner, Danni had helped Ronan's father come out of his garage and start living again. She had even prepared his favourite meal for dinner. For the longest time, Ronan had hated his mother for abandoning his family and had had the hardest time trusting any female, but Danni had changed all of that. She had unlocked the key to his heart by showing him that good people were out there. People who cared and wouldn't leave when things got tough or no longer suited their lifestyles. That was when he had known he was falling for her. There was a lot of love and happiness in their future just waiting for them.

"What are you thinking?" Danni whispered, running a finger over his knuckles.

"Just how lucky I am to have you." He smiled. He could tell she was beaming.

"I'm the lucky one," she breathed.

"Everybody!" Asterion hissed through the darkness. "I believe we have found something. If I'm not mistaken, that structure in the distance seems to resemble some sort of barracks."

Sure enough, Ronan could make out an almost warehouse-type building several metres in front of them. The closer they walked, the larger it got. Faint lights set in the sturdy walls flickered as if inviting them in. Ronan drew in a breath. If Milo was going to be hiding anywhere, it was in there.

"What is our plan of attack?" Drew smoothed his curls. "Do we just charge in there, guns a-blazin'…or, in our case, shovels a-blazin'?"

"No, young Drew," Asterion chided. "We proceed with caution and stealth. This is our one chance to take Milo by surprise and apprehend him. I spy a door up ahead. Let's circumnavigate the perimeter to see if that is the only entrance. Multiple doorways equal multiple opportunities."

"That's what she said," Drew muttered. Ronan chuckled, grateful for an opportunity to laugh a little.

Castor, Ganymede, and Sirena moved deftly and swiftly around the back of the warehouse. It was hard to believe that not that long ago, all of the counterparts had been fighting. In this moment, they moved as one, nobody trying to upstage or overtake the other. They returned several minutes later, nodding seriously.

"The doorway to the back has a path that leads down to Milo's aircraft," Castor relayed. "We tested it, and it opened without issue. I feel at least two of us should guard it in case he attempts escape. The last thing we want now is for him to disappear to another planet."

"Agreed," Asterion grunted. "Slade and Ganymede, please stand watch by the back entrance. Do not let Milo leave, whatever you do."

The Aquarians crept silently to their posting. The rest approached the front entrance, light on their toes. Asterion opened the door as softly as possible. Upon quick inspection, he motioned for everybody to follow inside, a finger pressed firmly to his lips, as if that were even necessary. The first thing Ronan noticed was an almost hipster-like modern dining hall complete with green plants, hanging lights, long tables, and a large kitchen. It reminded him of the trendy brunch places back home that served deconstructed food and different coloured lattes. Since when did an evil dictator have such nice taste? Across the way, he spotted the door Ganymede and Slade were guarding. Tucked away to the right was a staircase. The only unexplored place was up.

"Should we stock up on food?" Drew whispered, opening a cupboard in the kitchen.

"Drew, now is not the time!" Parry hissed, bouncing on the balls on her feet. "I just want to get back to Graham and make sure he is okay. Let's go!"

It was virtually impossible to ascend the stairs without eliciting some sort of creaking noises. The group kept stopping, breaths caught in their throats, but nothing happened. Would they really find Milo in his bedroom, sleeping off a venom hangover? The landing had one room, but this door was open and lit by a single candle. Much like the dining area, the room was beautifully decorated and modern. There was a magnificent four-poster bed in the centre draped in sheer burgundy netting with the silkiest sheets and pillows Ronan had ever seen. A door to the side opened up into a lavish bathroom complete with a clawfoot tub, brass faucets, and whitewashed walls. Illuminated by the thick waxy candle lay a piece of parchment with an inky black scrawl.

"A note!" Parry rushed forward and grabbed the letter, careful not to hold it too closely to the flame.

"What does it say, Miss Mason?" Asterion urged.

Ronan watched Parry's eyes dart over the parchment. With each line, her face progressively fell more and more until she looked up at them with watery eyes and a look of despair. Ronan's gut churned. She was about to present them with awful news.

"Um, it says…" Parry's voice trembled. "It says, 'Graham cannot be saved. Any attempt to restore his mental faculties will result in mass execution. This piece of parchment is triggered by touch. As you read this, every single worker and your friend have been programmed to attack. If I were you, I would escape whilst you can. Destruction is imminent. Sincerely yours, Milo.'"

With that, the bedroom door slammed shut, making everybody jump. Drew and Ronan attempted to force it open, but it wouldn't budge. Sirena forced everybody to stand back, her fingertips forming power-charged bubbles. They crackled and sparked upon impact, but the lock remained intact, just slightly charred.

"Oh, no." Danni bit her lip. "It *was* a trap. Asterion, do you think the other group will be okay? We need to get out now!"

Asterion gestured for Sirena, Aegipan, Castor, and the Maiden to line up beside him. Ronan and his friends sat back on the bed, careful not to get caught up in the mass of combined power that was about to be unleashed.

A blinding flash of light hit the room as Asterion and the counterparts threw everything they had at the enchanted door. Aegipan rubbed his temples, Sirena blew more bubbles from the palms of her hands, Castor flung spelled throwing stars, the Maiden froze the lock with an icy glare, and Asterion shot white beams from his fingertips. Danni buried her face in Ronan's chest, shielding her eyes from the illumination. Wasabi stared in awe. Parry and Drew stared up at the ceiling, a mountain of silky pillows cushioning their heads. When the lights began to dim and the power crackled less intensely, Ronan looked up to see the door hanging off its hinges, charred and splintered. He jumped up, accidentally knocking Danni to the floor.

"You did it, guys!" he cheered, helping her up. "Let's go!"

Ronan made for the entrance, but one look at the counterparts and Asterion stopped him dead in his tracks. Each and every one of them looked completely and utterly exhausted. They were physically and mentally depleted.

"This is not a victory," Asterion croaked, holding on to the wall. "Half of us will not be able to fight now. Milo orchestrated it this way. He really is quite clever. I can see how he managed to manipulate everyone on Cassius."

"Bastard!" Castor spat, narrowly missing Drew, who jumped out of the way with a high-pitched squeal.

The Astro A Team, plus Wasabi, helped the exhausted counterparts down the stairs as quickly as they could, no longer afraid of rousing any enemies. As they landed on the ground floor, a swirling heat hit them with full force. The door that Ganymede and Slade had been guarding was wide open. Ronan could see two figures beyond the frame, lying motionless. Danni let out a scream. Slade and his counterpart had been knocked unconscious. A nasty-looking gash adorned Slade's forehead, dripping crimson blood. Ganymede's robe was blackened, and his blond hair frizzed and sparked as though he had stuck his fingers in an electrical socket. Danni and Ronan raced over to Slade, gently lifted him, and sat him against the outside wall. The other counterparts trudged over to Ganymede with less intensity. They struggled to lift him into the same position, energy levels completely drained.

"He smells like burnt rubber." Sirena screwed up her nose in disgust.

"Can you help revive him?" Wasabi placed her hand on the mermaid's shoulder. Sirena jerked up in surprise, clearly unused to being touched in such a gentle manner.

"There is nothing to revive." She eyed the girl warily. "He will come to shortly. He is immortal. Focus on your human boy. He is the fragile one."

"Ganymede can't heal him." Danni frowned. "He's out cold."

"Cerus can!" Parry shrieked. "I remember him telling us that his special ability involved being able to heal all of the zodiac signs, not just his own. We need to find him."

At that moment, Ganymede began to stir. He had been wise to leave his urn on the aircraft. It would have been smashed to smithereens by now. His static hair fizzled and crackled as he slowly stood with the help of the Maiden, who looked more concerned about his new look than his overall wellbeing.

"Milo," he panted, leaning heavily on the Maiden. "He was hiding in his aircraft down the path. He ambushed us once he knew you were safely inside. He's gone back to Graham to end the fight. We need to hurry."

"We are exhausted, darling," the Maiden groaned against her confidant's weight. "We used all of our power to blast open the enchanted door he trapped us behind. I'm afraid we are not going to be of much use in this fight. Nevertheless, we must return. Cerus needs to heal your Aquarian boy. You hardly seem physically able to do it yourself."

Ronan was surprised to see Ganymede stare at Slade with concern and fear.

"Nonsense," Ganymede groaned. "I can do it." Dragging his weary body over to Slade, he placed his hands on the boy's forehead and closed his eyes. After five solid minutes of deep concentration, Ganymede slumped forward, exhausted. The gash was still very prominent and deep.

"You cannot do it," the Maiden scoffed, helping him up. "You, like the rest of us, need to recharge. We must find Cerus."

"Oh, sure, let him take all the credit for my human." Ganymede pouted.

Castor bundled Slade up in his arms, determined to show his strength despite his condition. The group scurried as quickly as they could back towards the battle area. The closer they got, the thicker the atmosphere seemed to grow. Ronan could hear screams in the distance. They never should have left. The first thing he saw as they emerged in the clearing was a large dark figure floating over a chaotic war scene. It was Milo, darting this way and that in order to avoid the beams of power coming from the remaining counterparts. His grotesque scorpion tail jabbed at anybody who got too close. The workers were now battling their brainwashed counterparts, careful not to kill, only render unconscious. The other Astro A Team members weaved in and out of the madness, desperate to reach Graham, but he was well guarded by Issac and some of the more burly workers spinning their pickaxes and shovels.

"Fools!" bellowed Milo, hovering above Ronan's and Danni's heads with a manic glint in his eye. "You are all so predictable. My minion on Corathinia sent word of your plans the moment you left. You walked right into my trap. By the way, how did you like the warehouse? I do have a talent for design, do I not?"

"Milo," Asterion growled, "your reign of power is over. Surrender now whilst you still can." At that, he slumped weakly against Garth, who had rushed over the moment he appeared.

Milo tipped back his head and laughed. "I believe you will be the one surrendering, old man! You may have destroyed my minions, but I can always recruit more. My workers and Graham will obey me to the bitter end. They do not have scruples. They won't hesitate to cut their brothers and friends down. Can you say the same?"

"The Council knows about you, Milo," Garth roared, holding on to Asterion tightly. "They saw what you did at Constellar. Good luck trying to build an empire against a galaxy determined to fight you."

At that, Milo snarled and dipped low, venomous stinger poised to strike. Garth managed to avoid his first jab, but the second pierced the flesh just above his left forearm. Howling, Garth dropped Asterion and cradled his poisoned wound.

"Cerus!" the Maiden screamed.

Within seconds, the bull arrived on the scene, ready to heal both Garth and Slade. Milo attempted to jab him, but at the last moment, Cerus wrapped his tail around the flesh just above Milo's stinger and pulled him down to the ground. Before Milo could get up again, Pollux ran and jumped on top of him, pinning his arms down and calling for backup. Cerus used the moment to perform his healing dance, which had an immediate effect on both the victims. Garth's festering sore disappeared, leaving his skin smooth and supple. Slade's gash vanished. Brodie helped him to his feet. The irony wasn't lost on Ronan that this time, it had been the sister tending to her unconscious brother. The remaining healthy counterparts threw themselves at Milo, giving him zero opportunity to worm away. Aegipan trudged over to Ronan and placed his gnarled hand on the boy's shoulder.

"Son, remember what I told you about the poison in my Coloured Cavern? I think it's time to get your friends together and try to overcome the power of the venom with love. Use your combined forces to break him out of it."

"What about Issac?" Ronan said. "I'm worried he won't allow us to even get close."

"The child," Aegipan groaned. "If anybody can reverse the damage, it will be him."

"Hannah!" Ronan called. A scruffy-looking redhead in tattered clothes appeared, panting but smiling. It was hard to believe this was the same fragile girl he had met only months ago.

"You should have seen me knock out that worker!" She laughed breathlessly. "Don't worry, I didn't do any serious damage. What's up?"

"We need you to go get Karki and Charlie. Bring them here ASAP."

Hannah dropped her shovel, brow furrowing. "Are you serious? Ronan, he could get killed. We need to protect him at all costs."

Aegipan rounded on her with a huff. "Young lady, we will fight to the bitter end to keep him safe, but Issac needs to see his son. It may be the only way to break him out of Milo's spell and reverse the effects of the poison. Please hurry now!"

Hannah scowled at the goat but ran off in the direction of the aircraft. Aegipan nodded brusquely and turned to Ronan.

"Round up all of your friends and go to Graham. Act quickly."

*

Hannah tore through Malvolt at lightning speed. The path to the clearing had been fairly straight, making it easy to locate the aircraft. Upon arriving, she noticed the entrance was wide open and Charlie was playing in a small crater, with Karki watching him. As she neared, he looked up with a huge smile stretching from ear to ear. Her heart melted. She was going to miss that little treasure. Karki also beamed at her. Hannah remembered the first time they had met in the Cavern of White. Karki had told her she loved her after Hannah had sung her a soothing lullaby. It had shocked her to hear such a strong profession so soon, but Karki's feelings were innocent and without guidelines. She had merely expressed what was in her heart at that moment. Hannah had learnt from her counterpart that sensitivity was her greatest strength, not her weakness. The power of love could overcome any obstacle, and she was going to prove it with Charlie's help.

"Hannah!" Karki rushed over and hugged Hannah around the middle. Charlie scrambled out of the crater and joined in. The three of them squeezed each other tightly. "What are you doing here? Did you find Graham?"

Hannah stepped back, releasing them both. "I need you to come with me. Issac and Graham are under a very strong spell thanks to Milo's poison. Aegipan believes that once Issac sees Charlie, he will be able to fight past it and return to normal. I know it's dangerous, but everyone is going to be protecting him. I promise no harm will come to him."

Karki frowned but nodded. She turned to Charlie, who was only a head shorter than her. "Charlie, do you want to see Papa? I know he would love to see *you.*"

"Papa!" whooped the little boy. "Yes! Let's go see Papa!"

"Promise you will stay close to me and Hannah?" Karki patted him on the shoulder.

Charlie bobbed his head eagerly. Karki ran inside the aircraft to inform the pilot of their movements. Once she was done, the three of them tore through the wasteland, all holding hands. Hannah used all of her willpower not to retch by the time they arrived. She was exhausted and terrified that Charlie would be hurt, but she couldn't let them know that. The battle was still in full swing. Milo had broken free of the counterparts and was once again hovering over the masses, jabbing and poisoning at every opportunity. The remaining counterparts were flinging bursts of power at him, careful not to exhaust their supplies, but Milo swerved this way and that, avoiding them at all costs. The workers had nearly overpowered their mind-addled brothers, but Issac and Graham were still well protected by the largest and most vicious men of the pack. Drew, Aegipan, and Ronan raced over to Hannah, Karki, and Charlie, wild-eyed and breathless.

"We need to do this now." Aegipan ushered Charlie over to the rest of the Astro A Team, who looked surprised and concerned at his appearance. "Boys and girls, I am going to need you to form a strong unit and begin advancing towards Graham with Charlie in tow. We will be standing nearby, ready to assist at a moment's notice. I know we are exhausted, but we can handle the workers, just not Milo at this point. The able-bodied counterparts will distract him and ensure he doesn't get wind of our plan. Use all of your combined strength to pull Issac and Graham out of their bamboozled states. I know you can do it."

Aegipan loped off to inform everybody else of the plan. Hannah grabbed Drew's hand on one side and Reilly's on the other. Charlie hid behind both of them, feeling safest at the rear of his two favourite human girls. Danni called down from the far-right end, clutching tightly to Ronan and Parry.

"Guys, this is exactly why we were brought here in the first place. To show the counterparts what unity can do. I love you all, and I believe that the power of friendship and love can overcome any obstacle."

With that, they began slowly marching towards Graham and Issac. In the past, Hannah would have cried and run away, but she was much stronger now. The fate of those she loved depended on their collective bravery. The workers guarding Issac and Graham began spinning their weapons as the Astro A Team approached, but they didn't charge forward. Their tools swung round and round like propeller blades; anyone stupid enough to walk into them would've been slashed to ribbons. They were going to have to do this at a distance. Graham and Issac swayed like charmed snakes, eyes black and unforgiving. Hannah looked over to Danni, who nudged Parry slightly forward. The beautiful Virgo already had tears streaming down her cheeks. Hannah could not imagine what it must have felt like to see her best friend in such a warped state.

"Graham!" she half-shouted, half-croaked.

He continued to sway back and forth, but his head twisted in her direction. It was enough of an acknowledgement for Parry to start speaking.

"Graham!" she repeated. "Do you remember when we were first becoming best friends and you took me out for cocktails at Morrigan's? I drank way too much, but you walked me home, tucked me into bed, and stayed the night so you could make me breakfast in the morning. Do you remember what I said to you over toast and espresso shots?"

Hannah noticed Graham's nostrils flare, but he didn't venture an answer.

"I told you that I would always be there for you like you were for me," Parry continued, voice shaking. "I told you that we had something special and that you were the first man who made me feel truly safe and loved. I'm not giving up on you, do you hear me? I know you're in there. Milo doesn't care about you, Graham. He used you, and now he's taken over your mind, forcing you to obey him against your will. True friends don't do that. I know I wasn't there that night at Constellar when you were abducted, but that doesn't make me any less your best friend. I love you, I love you, I love you, damn it!"

She screeched those last words, forcing a sob to emerge from Hannah's throat. There was no doubt that Parry Mason loved and adored Graham Maltin with all her heart. Soulmates didn't need to be romantic partners; they could be anybody one felt a genuine deep connection with. Parry had found hers. She was lucky. One by one, Danni, Slade, Brodie, Crawford, Hunter, Reilly, Hannah, Drew, Charlotte, Wasabi, Ambrite, and Charlotte screamed the same words of love.

"What a touching sentiment," Milo sneered. He hovered right over Graham, looking more amused than annoyed. "Love is foolish. It will never reverse my power."

Hannah wasn't so sure. Graham was no longer swaying or twitching. He was looking right at Parry with a strange sort of longing in his eyes. Parry kept her gaze level, pouring out her heart with shaky tones. Graham took one tentative step forward, his arm outstretched. Milo's smirk began to transform into a deep frown. At that moment, Charlie tore onto the field.

"Papa!" he squealed. "Papa, it's me! Charlie!"

Like Graham, Issac froze and turned towards his son. "Charlie," he rasped.

"No," Milo whispered, his tail poised to strike.

Issac broke free of his trance faster than Graham; such is a father's love for his child. He raced over to Charlie and swept him up into his arms, crying and laughing. "My son. My darling son!"

Charlie was sobbing against his father's shoulder. Issac patted him on the back, trying to calm him down. "Mama is asleep forever, Papa," he wept. Issac fell to his knees, his child still in his arms. The Astro A Team, counterparts, workers, and others watched father and son grieve on the cracked surface. Hannah felt her heart break multiple times. She went to grab Drew's and Karki's hands, but a cry stopped her in her tracks. Milo was floating towards Issac with murder in his eyes.

"Issac!" Hannah screeched. Before Milo could strike to kill, a whooshing sound travelled through the air as an axe embedded itself in his spine. He crumpled to the floor, groaning in agony. Swift feet ran towards Milo, and a hand pulled out the axe with a sickening squelch.

"Graham," Parry whispered, eyes shining with tears. The Scorpio stood before them, holding the axe with the most clarity he had felt in a long time.

"My darling, you wouldn't hurt me?" Milo looked up at him in terror. "You and I are going to rule. We are so happy together. We could be kings! Don't do this!"

"I absolutely would hurt you. Just like low-rise jeans, your reign is over, Milo," Graham breathed. With that, he brought down the axe over and over into Milo's back, skull, and neck. With one final swing, he took Milo's head clean off. It sailed across the vast landscape. The possessed workers, no longer under Milo's evil spell, stared at the carnage before them, unable to make sense of what was happening.

"Here you go." Graham handed the axe back to one of them. He swivelled to face his friends and broke into a sprint, nearly bowling Parry over. The Astro A Team cheered as Parry and Graham sobbed and hugged and clutched one another in desperation.

"I'm so sorry," Parry choked out.

"No, I'm the one who should be sorry! I was such a damn fool," Graham wept.

"Aegipan, is Milo really dead?" Hannah turned to the goat, who was blinking quite rapidly behind his large spectacles.

"Yes, I can feel it," the goat responded. "It turns out the counterparts didn't need to be the ones to kill him. Graham was fuelled by love, and it turns out that was the most powerful weapon of all. Who would have thought?"

Hannah let out a happy shriek and joined the rest of her friends crowded around Graham. They had their friend back, the enemy had been defeated, and Charlie was reunited with his father. There had been much loss and devastation, but overall, they had triumphed. The workers were hugging one another, the counterparts were clapping, and Asterion and Garth looked like two proud parents watching their children. Hannah felt a tiny hand slip into hers. Charlie was looking up at her with a big smile.

"Hannah, can we go home now?"

Hannah knelt to the brave little boy before her. "Yes, darling. It's time we went home…"

Chapter 21

Goodbyes

After the initial high of having Graham back had slowly begun to die down, the Astro A Team passed out in their beds at the Mission Base and slept soundly. They were tired of talking, crying, and laughing. They were completely and utterly depleted. In the morning, Brodie woke to see all her friends still asleep. She walked into the bathroom, cleaned herself up, and got changed. When she emerged, Issac was standing next to Asterion and Garth, holding Charlie's hand. Brodie walked over to them.

"Issac." She hugged the man. They had all introduced themselves to one another on the aircraft. He had tried to keep it together for his child, but she could see his heart was bleeding from the loss of his wife. "What are you doing here?"

"I'm here to stay, Brodie." He smiled down at her. "Wake the others. We have a special announcement to make."

Nodding, Brodie went and gently woke up her groggy friends, including Wasabi, who had slept in Ambrite's bed. She gave Graham an extra hug before grabbing some breakfast from the buffet. The Astro A Team took care of their basic needs before assembling before the two thrones. The counterparts, except for Equas, were beginning to trickle out of their

Coloured Caverns. Brodie hadn't seen her since before they had left for Malvolt.

"What's going on?" Drew asked. "Please tell me it's all over. I've had enough excitement to last me a lifetime."

Garth clapped his hands. "My friends, it's time to witness something truly special."

"Wait!" Brodie said. "Shouldn't we wait for Equas? She's the only one not here yet."

"She will be along soon, my dear." Asterion winked mischievously.

"As I was saying before I was interrupted" – Garth bristled – "we are about to induct our newest counterpart into the Mission Base." He pointed to Issac, who grinned and took a bow. Charlie let out a loud whoop that made everybody laugh.

"Is that what you really want?" Graham stood. Brodie could tell he would never truly rid himself of the guilt where Issac was concerned. "You don't have to do this if you don't want to. There are plenty of Scorpios who can take your place."

Issac stepped forward and placed his hands on Graham's shoulders. "Son, it would be an honour. I want this. I want to make Ella proud. She would want me to be on Bastion permanently. I won't have to spend weeks at a time on Liria without Charlie anymore. The counterparts have already granted him access to all of the Coloured Caverns. He will never be lonely."

"He will get to spend lots of time on my beach." Karki clapped happily. Charlie grinned shyly at the little girl.

Graham smiled weakly. "Then I am happy for you, my friend. I will never forget what you did for me."

Issac let go of his shoulders and returned to Asterion's side. The Keeper of the Stars rose from his throne. He approached Issac with a golden sceptre that gleamed. Gently, he rested the sceptre on Issac's bent head. Brodie felt like she was witnessing a knighting.

"Issac Venturion, I hereby bestow upon you the title of the Scorpio counterpart. May you live forever, rule amongst the constellations, produce starlight, and exude kindness. You are now one of us. The Cavern of Maroon is your new home. Your child, Charlie Henry Venturion, is welcome to reside here for as long as he wishes. Do us proud."

"I will," Issac breathed.

The moment Asterion removed the sceptre, the air sizzled and warped around the Mission Base. With one great big flash of light, Issac had transformed into a scorpion.

"So cool," Charlie said, gaping. The counterpart strutted around the cave, waving his tail around. The Astro A Team shuffled closer to the centre of the room. They were a little bit over being almost stung. Issac scuttled back to Asterion, did a little hop, and became human again.

"I could get used to this!" He chuckled.

"Papa, you're the best!" Charlie fist-pumped the air.

The counterparts stepped forward and took turns shaking Issac's hand and welcoming him. Brodie couldn't believe how well they were behaving. They were not the same stubborn bunch she had met on arrival. She was about to ask Asterion about Equas again when she heard the sound of high heels clicking along the stone floor. A figure emerged from the Cavern of Blue that took Brodie's breath away. Equas was walking towards her, no longer a stone figure. In fact, her posture was perfectly straight. She had a cute black bob, a blue gown, and stilettos to match.

"Equas, oh my gosh, you're human!" Brodie cried.

"My darling," Equas crooned. Her voice was buttery smooth, nothing like the gravelly tones she was used to. Her counterpart bridged the gap between them and kissed her on both cheeks. "Order has been restored. This is how I look when everything is in perfect balance."

Brodie was overwhelmed by her transformation. She had just assumed that her counterpart would remain statuesque. "I don't know what to say."

"Then say nothing." Equas smiled. "Without you, we would have never found Milo's planet. Don't you ever question your place in the group again."

Brodie held both of her hands and nodded gratefully.

The Astro A Team were set to leave for Earth that evening. Before then, however, they had a lot to do and many goodbyes to make.

*

Their first form of order was to host a mass burial and ceremony for those who had lost their lives at Constellar. The workers who had been on Liria were reunited with various members of their families. Some had lost more than others. It was a difficult morning, watching the town grieve. Beautiful eulogies were given, and Asterion promised his people that a plaque would be erected in the names of those who had fought and died bravely.

Their second form of order was to welcome the civilians from Cassius and the former Unsigned from the valley into their new homes. A town-wide announcement was made, meeting the terms that Wasabi had laid out. To Reilly's surprise, not a single person protested. They were ready for a change, and frankly, it was about time. With death comes new life. It was nice seeing Bastion slowly rebuild itself. Everybody was dressed in whatever colours they wanted. There were just enough people to fill up the homes. They all promised to honour those who had lived there before them. Mr. Arthurton was overjoyed to have proper medical care and a home near all the shops. Reilly saw Wasabi beaming from ear to ear and hugging all of her friends and neighbours from the valley. She was going to transform her father's warehouse into a little pad for her and Ambrite to live in.

It seemed like everything had been wrapped up into a neat little package…except for one big decision. Reilly had to bite the bullet and do what she felt was right in her heart. She snuck away from her friends and made her way to the Mission Base. Her heart pounded with every step she took towards the Cavern of Purple. When she emerged into Chiron's lush pad, she found him reading a book amongst the cushions. Seeing her enter, Chiron put his novel away and gestured for her to sit next to him. She took a deep breath and lowered herself to the floor. He slung an arm around her shoulder and kissed her cheek.

"You're leaving me," he murmured sadly. "I have felt it all day."

Reilly looked up at his beautiful face. She had changed her mind every five minutes, but in reality, there was no other choice. It had to be this one.

"I'm sorry," she whispered. "I am crazy about you, but we've just met, and I have an entire life back home. I have a family that adores me and I them. I have the best friends in the whole world. I have dreams and ambitions that cannot be met here. I hope you understand."

Chiron placed his hands on her face and kissed her deeply. It was full of passion and sadness. Reilly savoured every moment, knowing it was the last one. He broke away with a weak smile. "I do understand. Just know I will miss you, and if you ever change your mind, I will be here."

"When I get tired of crazy planet Earth, I'll hit you up." She grinned.

"That sounds violent." Chiron wrinkled his nose. Reilly laughed in response. A moment later, he joined her. They sat together for the rest of the afternoon, soaking up the feeling of what could have been.

*

It was time to go. The counterparts, Wasabi, Charlie, Asterion, and Garth had gathered by the portal to bid farewell to the Astro A Team. Nobody knew what to say or where to start. They hadn't known one another long, yet they were forever changed by their experiences. The hardest part was saying goodbye to Ambrite. She had burst into tears the second Garth opened the portal. Hunter wrapped her up in his arms and hugged her tightly. Many tears were shed. Karki and Charlie clung to

Hannah. Graham and Parry were wishing Issac well. Crawford and Leonis fist-bumped, Slade was teasing Ganymede good-naturedly, Ronan was ruffling Aegipan's wild hair, and Charlotte was trying to exchange numbers with Castor, which was pointless. Danni couldn't have loved her friends more in that moment. Love made goodbyes hard. She turned to the counterparts standing before her.

"So…are you all going to get along or do we need to come back in a year's time and school your asses again?"

"Not on my watch." Equas winked. "I quite like looking this way. Balance and order will remain. We've been taught a very important lesson."

"Oh yeah, what's that?" Drew tilted his head.

"We are better together than alone," Aegipan bleated. The rest of the counterparts nodded sheepishly.

"Mission accomplished." Garth rubbed his hands together. "I never had any doubt."

Asterion held out his arms and embraced each teenager one at a time. Garth kissed each on the cheek, including the boys, much to their surprise.

"Say, Garth," Slade ventured, "does your dragon pendant allow FaceTime?"

"I don't know what that is." Garth frowned.

"Like can we chat via portal?" Charlotte huffed.

Garth looked up at the ceiling thoughtfully. "I guess? I'm sure you are all itching to return to normal life. Why you would want to bother with our crazy lot baffles me. Let's see what happens."

The portal shimmered impatiently. Now it was really time to go. With one final wave, the Astro A Team linked arms and stepped back to where it had all begun…

Epilogue

One year later…

It was a crisp Friday evening. Danni sat at the edge of the pond in Bouquet Reserve, trailing her fingers in the water. A lot had changed in a year since returning to Earth, but one thing hadn't. The Astro A Team still held meetings every single week at their special place in the park.

Danni was studying astronomy at a university the next town over. She would be looking at a cute rental that weekend with Ronan, who was working as a full-time mechanic. Reilly was taking an event planning course and seeing a cute cater-waiter named Mark. Hannah and Drew were engaged. Their families weren't too pleased because of their age, but they didn't care. When it was right, one just knew.

Hunter and Parry had tried dating, but it had felt a little bit too forced. They swore they were just good friends, but Danni had caught them making out a few times behind the trees after meetings. She was just waiting for them to make it official already. They weren't fooling anybody. Graham and Charlotte had both enrolled in the same design school. Out of all her friends, Danni was the happiest for Graham. He had finally found true love with a guy named Jed. They had met at Maltin's Tanning Salon when Jed had come in asking for a seaweed scrub.

Graham had begun seeing Dr. Yates to discuss his trauma with Milo. It had been extremely healing. Of course, he had left out the parts about it all taking place on another planet. Danni was proud of his progress. Brodie and Crawford had announced six months earlier that they were a couple. It had surprised everybody in the beginning, but now they just made sense. Brodie grounded Crawford, and they made one another laugh. He was a completely different guy since leaving Bastion. Slade was working in graphic design. He had a bright future ahead of him. They had all come such a long way.

Danni glanced at her watch. It was almost time to begin their meeting. She was just waiting. Right on cue, the pond began to glow and bubble. Everybody leaned forward eagerly. The water rippled, revealing the rest of the members. Crowded together sat all of the counterparts, Ambrite, Wasabi, Charlie, Asterion, and Garth.

"Is this thing on?" Aegipan grunted. He adjusted his spectacles and sniffed.

"You say that every single week," Ares groaned.

"Hi, Astro A Team!" Danni waved.

"Hello, Danni, dear." Asterion waved back.

The rest of the group chattered happily. As per usual, Chiron focused all of his attention on Reilly. She flushed and wiggled her fingers at him.

"Coward," Danni whispered to her best friend.

"Shh," Reilly snapped. "I'll tell him about Mark next week."

"That's what you said last week." Drew rolled his eyes.

Hunter and Ambrite launched into their own discussion about their week. Parry and Wasabi grinned at one another. Distance didn't matter in a friendship.

Issac was bouncing Charlie on his lap and chatting to Graham about Jed. Karki was oohing and aahing at Hannah's engagement ring, much to Calypsee and Sirena's distaste. The Maiden was genuinely interested in Charlotte's studies at design school. Equas and Cerus were laughing with

Brodie and Crawford.

"Silence!" Danni yelled. Everybody stopped and focused on the Gemini among them. "We can catch up later. For now, let the meeting begin!"

Acknowledgements

I meant to publish *Aligning the Signs* in 2017. I had a set plan. Then I fell pregnant, and four years later, I picked up right where I had left off and finished what I started. Even though so much time had passed, it felt completely natural returning to the world and characters I had created. When I began *Astrology Pond*, my mentor told me to make things easier for myself. She told me I was doing too much. Not only was I writing from the perspective of twelve different teenagers, I was writing them in third person. It was challenging, to say the least, but I honestly wouldn't have had it any other way. I became a better writer by pushing myself.

I also became a better writer through the encouragement, support, and love from my own Astro A Team. To my family, friends, and readers, I appreciate every kind word and gentle nudge to complete the trilogy. It would take too long to individually name you all, but you know who you are. To MMH Press, thank you for publishing my trilogy and making my dreams come true. To Stephanie Parcus, thank you for designing the incredible cover and bringing the characters to life with your artwork. To Lia, thank you for reading over my story and being an amazing sister-in-law. To my wonderful husband, thank you for being my biggest cheerleader. You are the Ronan to my Danni. The Capricorn to my Gemini. Finally, a gigantic thank-you to my daughter, Abigail, for just existing. I write so you can be proud of me. I hope you are…